MARGARET
RONALD

WILD HUNT

An Imprint of HarperCollinsPublishers

This is a work of fiction. Names, characters, places, and incidens are products of the author's imagination or are used fictitiously and are not to be construed as real. Any resemblance to actual events, locales, organizations, or persons, living or dead, is entirely coincidental.

EOS
An Imprint of HarperCollins*Publishers*
10 East 53rd Street
New York, New York 10022–5299

Copyright © 2010 by Margaret Ronald
Cover art by Don Sipley
ISBN 978–0–06–166242–3
www.eosbooks.com

First Eos paperback printing: January 2010

HarperCollins® and Eos® are registered trademarks of HarperCollins Publishers.

Printed in the U. S. A.

10 9 8 7 6 5 4 3 2 1

This book is for all the teachers who,
in between all their other lessons,
taught me never
to give up on myself.
There aren't enough words
in the world to thank you.

WILD HUNT

One

Yuen died twenty minutes after I arrived, and I was there to make sure of it.

His daughter hadn't said anything about dying when she called with his request, and I was too startled by the call itself to question it. There weren't many constants in Boston's undercurrent, but one of them was this: people called Yuen, not the other way around.

What he'd asked for, translated of course, was this: *Come here, come alone, and do not tell anyone where you are going.* Nothing more, not even a mention of our usual arrangement, and certainly no explanation.

Not many people can ask that kind of blank-check favor from me, and of those who can, even fewer have anything to do with the undercurrent. I may not have been in the business long, compared to those adepts who've spent their entire lives soaking in the kind of magic that doesn't just steal your soul but also goes out and gnaws on other people's. But you don't need to know your own ass from a summoning circle to know that not everyone with a talent for magic has your best interests at heart.

Unfortunately for me, Yuen was one of those few who could ask a favor: I owed him, and I trusted him, to whatever extent the practicalities of the undercurrent let people trust each other.

I ditched the last of my courier runs—my day job, for when I needed regular money that didn't depend on clients who conveniently went out of town or cranks who only paid their bills in the dark of the moon. The last few weeks had been hell on my schedule no matter which job I chose, and I wasn't about to let Tania or the rest of Mercury Courier forget it. I coasted into Chinatown half an hour after Yuen called, weaving my bike through the afternoon congestion with ease.

Yuen ran the Three Cranes Grocery and Medicinal and, more significantly in financial terms, owned the three apartments above it. He lived on the first-floor apartment, just above the basement grocery itself. When I needed to talk to him, though, we met in his shop, either up front or in the back room that was crammed from floor to ceiling with spices and strange dried things, half of which I was sure were for show. (The other half, well, I tried not to turn my back on them.) Yuen knew not to let magic too deep into his normal life.

But this time, when I pulled up (veering around a pack of pedestrians and a shopping cart that had been left in the middle of the street), Yuen's daughter was standing on the stairs that led down over the basement entrance to the Three Cranes. She waited with clasped hands as I shucked my helmet and locked my bike to the closest fence. I slung my courier bag over one arm. "Is—er—is Mr. Yuen in?"

Yuen's daughter nodded. She'd tied back her hair with a broad white ribbon, matching the brilliant white jacket and trousers that seemed somehow out of place on the grubby steps of the Three Cranes. The back of my own head prickled; I'd chopped off most of my hair recently, and sometimes still felt the phantom weight of it, though mine had never been as straight or sleek as hers. "My father is in, Miss Scelan," she said, her tone as carefully neutral as always. "Come in, please." To my surprise, instead of opening up the grocery she ascended the stairs and stood by the front door.

I cast a glance over my shoulder as I followed her, unable to shake the feeling that I was entering by the wrong door. She led me into a bright and glowing atrium much more in line with the high-rises several blocks away than with the rest of the neighborhood. My cleats clacked against the polished tile, and I tugged at my sweat-wrinkled courier gear. Yuen hadn't said anything about looking presentable, but I didn't usually have class insecurity when dealing with my undercurrent clients. And it wasn't just money here, it was taste. Some people had it; I most definitely did not.

Besides, I had enough trouble with the room's scent. Instead of the casual sterility that its appearance would indicate, the air smelled of ozone and curry, thick with a cool, clammy dampness, behind which lurked a persistent scent of ammonia filtered through jasmine. Not a physical smell, but an undercurrent one, the kind that my brain translated as scent. Which was why Yuen called me what he did.

I shook my head, trying to rid myself of the heaviness of the scent. It wasn't that I didn't appreciate the warning—I'd be an idiot not to appreciate anything my nose told me, given that that sense had saved my life more than once—but it was disconcerting, like having someone always whispering into your ear.

Yuen's daughter led me down a hall, past a kitchen that gleamed with unused stainless steel. Through a doorway I caught a glimpse of a small, gray-haired woman dressed all in white, kneeling before a tiny altar. A faint incense scent hung over the room; sticks of it had been piled up on either side of her, as had little paper figures and stacks of something that looked like money but had a fiery scent all its own, one strong enough for me to catch it even from this distance—

I jerked my attention away, exhaling sharply. Yuen's daughter turned to look at me, and even though her expression didn't change, my face went hot with embarrassment. When she looked away from me again, I rubbed at my eyes and risked a glance at her. It wasn't her lack of response that bothered me; Yuen's daughter rarely showed emotion when I was around. But I'd always put that down to her role in her father's business. This was something else.

She'd brought me this way for a reason, I thought. Only I couldn't yet guess what that was.

We finally reached a set of steps down to the back entrance I recognized. To our left was the storeroom for the Three Cranes, to the right, the back alley through which most of Yuen's undercurrent contacts entered the shop. I prided myself, or I had, on how I'd never needed to use that entrance. Yuen had always met me at the front, even if we did end up in the back room to talk.

A man spoke up ahead, and another voice answered, too soft to understand. Yuen's daughter paused, and I stumbled over my own feet to keep from running into her. "He's got a visitor."

"You are a visitor too." She said it without bothering to look at me.

I nodded. Fair enough.

Neither of the voices were ones I knew, but the scent at least told me Yuen was in. After a moment I realized the lower of the two voices was Yuen's. He was speaking English. I glanced at his daughter. She pressed her lips tight together, but didn't otherwise respond. "I am sorry," Yuen said. "But other arrangements have been made."

"It's not like you're even going to use them," the other man said, and while I couldn't see him, from his voice and scent I could get a good idea of what he must look like. Whining, just a little weasely, and with a greasy sheen to him, like motor oil and Brylcreem. "Think about it. Why let it go to waste? There are people who'll pay good money for something like that, and that's just the tip of the iceberg—"

"There are people," Yuen said, and this time I knew it was him—that understated scorn was a tone

I couldn't help but recognize—"who will pay good money for anything, including dog turds. That is no reason why I should be handing out free dog turds. Goodbye."

I expected a protest, a last plea even, but the other man just sighed and muttered a goodbye. He stepped out into the hall, and I was professionally pleased to see that I'd guessed right. Take away the fireworks-and-rain stink of magic, the prematurely graying hair, and the defunct hermetic-symbol necklace, and you'd have a grade-B slimeball, the low-level scum that clots bars all over this and every city. He saw Yuen's daughter and smiled, showing lots of very white teeth. "Nice dad you got, sweetie."

She didn't answer, but I saw her hand close into a tight, white-knuckled fist. I cleared my throat and stepped forward, trying to think of the best way to get rid of him.

The guy's eyes flickered to me, and he went ashen. "Shit," he breathed, "shit, sorry, I didn't know—look, I'll go away now, okay?" He folded into a crouch that in other circumstances might have been a bow, then made a little gesture in front of his chest that probably indicated deference—or maybe protection—in whatever tradition he ran.

Two months ago, this man wouldn't have wasted the energy it took to sneer at me. Now all of a sudden guys like him were noticing me and, more, making sure I noticed them. I wasn't sure which I disliked more. I eyed Yuen's daughter, who hadn't moved. "Out," I told him, deciding on expediency.

"Yes ma'am, miss, Hound, sorry." He crouched again and scuttled past us, banging the door shut behind him.

"Sorry about that," I said.

Yuen's daughter looked me up and down. Her fist hadn't unclenched. "This way," she said, and led me into the room.

This was the one room I knew in Yuen's house. Ten

or so years back, I'd presented my credentials to him, explaining what I could do and how I did it, not yet aware of how little I knew but very aware of how little money I was making. Yuen hadn't done anything as blatant as sponsor me, but he'd taken me in and served me tea, and he'd recommended me to a few of his customers, both those who dealt with the undercurrent's standard weird shit and the normal people who'd never bothered with magic. It wasn't as dramatic as hanging out a nameplate, but it was a start, and it was as good an official welcome as one got without running into the large scary aspects of the undercurrent. And back then—hell, until recently—there had been a lot of large scariness to go around.

Back then, this room had been a strange cross of an office and a living room: chairs that were more comfortable than tasteful, a pot of tea that didn't ever seem to be empty, and filing cabinets draped with bright cloth and misaligned slightly for some feng shui reason I couldn't fathom. Yuen had kept a single altar to Guanyin in the corner, the significance of which he refused to discuss, and she'd watched over all of our dealings with a benevolent stone gaze. Most of all, I remembered the persistent, warm scent of tea, comforting to my nose even though I hated the taste of it.

That scent was long gone, and the rest of the room had changed to match. The TV in the corner had been replaced with a flatscreen monitor and fashionably tiny computer. The altar to Guanyin in the corner was as I remembered, but all traces of incense had been swept away from the little bowl before her, and a white cloth had been tied over the bodhisattva's face like a blindfold. That gave me the cold shivers, but I tried not to show it.

Most of all, though, the chairs in which Yuen and I had sat together had been replaced with a cheap daybed. Yuen lay on it, propped up with pillows, and he looked terrible. His skin was the color of very old paper, brittle and discolored, and his fingernails were so dark they might have been painted. The room smelled not of medicine, but of the burgeoning unpleasantness of overripe vegetable matter.

Yuen's daughter went to her father's side and said something apologetic in Chinese. Yuen took her hand and patted it, murmuring in return.

I set my pack down beside the bed. "I got your call," I said.

Yuen answered in Chinese, and his daughter took her place on a stool at his side, her face now set in a more familiar stoicism. "Hound," she translated. "You were very nearly late."

"I had my phone switched off," I said, and Yuen's daughter murmured a translation. I looked around for a chair, saw none that were convenient, and stayed where I was. "I've been working for the Armenian brothers. They've got this thing about cell phones. I can't even have mine on in their presence."

Yuen chuckled. "That's nothing new from them," he said through his daughter. "You wait until each one discovers the other's sleeping with his wife."

"I think I'll stay out of that," I said. "There's only so much drama I can take." Yuen grinned.

I glanced at his daughter as she related my words to him. She didn't react to them at all; the words passed through her without leaving a mark. She kept her eyes fixed on a spot just beyond my left shoulder.

Everyone who has to deal with the undercurrent and yet remain part of society has a way to keep it at arm's length. I had my own codes, even if they'd fallen apart a bit lately. Yuen refused to speak English to deal with undercurrent matters, or even to anyone touched by the undercurrent. Instead his daughter translated for me, acting as a filter between one world and the next. I'd always wondered how he reconciled himself to putting his daughter in danger that way, or whether he even saw it in those terms. Until now, I'd never thought of how she viewed the situation.

Now that I'd heard him speak English, I could

tell how halting his Chinese was. Yuen was second-generation at least, and though he'd taught his daughter what he knew, it was clear that the language was only for these situations.

Yuen's daughter murmured again, not translating this time, and Yuen's grin faded. "You saw my wife on the way in. Had she burned anything yet?"

"Not that I saw." I couldn't smell any smoke, and if I couldn't sense it, a smoke detector sure as hell wouldn't. "Is there . . . Is she likely to set anything on fire?"

"She won't. Not for a while yet. She disapproves of what I am doing." He said something more, then, when his daughter hesitated to translate it, drummed impatiently on the side of the bed until she did so. "She is in mourning," his daughter finally said.

"For whom?" The words slipped out, but I'd had a guess. I just didn't like it.

"For me." Yuen smiled as his daughter translated his words.

I stared at him. The first thing that came to mind—*You don't look dead*—didn't seem to be the right thing to say. Yuen turned to his daughter and motioned toward the wall behind me, whispering something clearly not meant to be translated. She nodded and walked past me, reaching for a framed photo on the wall. "It is not entirely unexpected," she translated as she followed his directions. "That is, the event itself is not. The timing of it is. I thought I would have another few weeks with which to settle matters."

I tried to speak, made an embarrassingly squeaky noise, and cleared my throat. "I'm sorry," I managed at last.

Yuen smiled again, though this time it was a more controlled, less happy smile, born of wisdom rather than mirth. "So am I. I am, though, fortunate that you were on hand. I would like you to verify something for me."

"I—" I shook my head. "Wouldn't it be better to

have a doctor instead? Come to think of it, wouldn't a doctor—"

Yuen waved one hand. "The time for doctors has come and gone. And none of them would be able to understand what I am asking." He sighed. "My wife agrees with me on this at least.

"Listen to me, Hound. I have had my sixth heart attack this year. My body will take no more strain. It is only through luck and will that I am alive this long, and it is your bad luck that I could not stay longer. I had planned for a friend to be here, but in his absence, I must ask you to do something for me. It will not . . . compromise . . . you in any way." He hesitated over the choice of words, and his daughter imitated the hesitation, though I suspected she knew the appropriate translation immediately.

I nodded, first to Yuen and then to his daughter. She ignored me and unhooked the photo from the wall. A faint scraping noise followed—not the click of a safe opening that I'd expected—and a thin, putrid scent crept into the room. I flinched at the scent and started to look behind me, then thought better of it. Yuen, noting my reaction, nodded.

His daughter carried a small ceramic jar about the size of a large coffee mug to her father and set it in his waiting hands. Unconsciously, she wiped her hands on her slacks.

I motioned to the jar. "What *is* that?"

Yuen turned it around in his hands. It was unadorned, plain unglazed stoneware sealed with wax, and it made me ill. There was something both pitiful and disgusting about it, like a baby rat. "It's a jar," his daughter translated. "You tell me what's inside."

Yuen said something further—either *Have a look* or *Catch* or whatever the Chinese equivalent was—and tossed the jar at me. His daughter cried out, a second too late. I jumped backward to catch it, fumbled as the skin of the jar seemed to warp under my fingers, and caught it a second time, bracing it between my forearms and stomach. The touch shivered across my skin like ripples from a stone. When I looked up, Yuen's daughter's head was bent, and she glared at her father's hands.

I let out a slow breath. "Yuen, you pick the weirdest times for tests like this."

He smiled, but it didn't touch his eyes. "You tell me," he repeated.

I turned the jar over in my hands, rolling it between my palms. It was lighter than I'd assumed, light enough that it had to be either empty or packed with something like feathers. I held it to my nose and sniffed, then scratched at the rope seal with one ragged fingernail.

"Don't open it," Yuen and his daughter said together, each in a different language. Some things don't need translation to be clear.

"I don't need to," I said. "It's not an antique, and not Chinese. Local clay, I'd say from New Hampshire. There's something mixed in the clay, ivy maybe. Hard to say, since it was fired quite a while ago . . ." I shook it, gently, and watched their reactions out of the corner of my eye. Yuen's daughter winced, but Yuen himself didn't let a flicker cross his face. "It used to be in your shop, but it hasn't been for some years. Five at least. You moved it . . . you'd had it on the shelf behind the counter, next to the stone turtle."

At that Yuen raised his eyebrows, impressed. I smiled, but honestly I was a little weirded out. Not by the jar—well, not so much—but by how much I could tell about it. This time last year, I wouldn't have been able to discern so much about a static object without a good hour's concentration.

The trouble with having a blood-magic like mine is that sometimes it gets a little stronger than you'd like.

"As for what's inside it . . ." Nothing. I wasn't getting anything from the rest of the jar; it was just blank, like static or white noise. I turned it over again, trying to find meaning in its gritty, unmarked surface.

There. Like a spider scuttling out and over my fingers, the scent of it shivered across my senses. The smell of something not just rotted but frozen in that state of rot, with a horrible awareness about it, a gelid sentience like the idiot response of an anemone. I gagged and wanted to spit, but some things you don't do in a nice house.

Yuen nodded. "So you do sense what's in it. Good. Please give it back."

His daughter came forward. I set the jar in her hands, noting the careful stillness that came over her the moment her fingers touched it. She didn't like it any more than I did. "What's in there?" I asked softly, speaking to her rather than Yuen.

But it was Yuen who answered, and his words she translated. "A mistake. A failure. An act of hubris." He took the jar from his daughter and cradled it on his chest like a reliquary. "My father."

I glanced from father to daughter, confused by the generational switch. "Your—"

"Please listen carefully, Hound. You can sense the . . . ghost . . . of my father—" *ghost* was in English, the word out of place and somehow incorrect in either language, "—within this jar. When I am dead, I will want you to confirm that it is gone. Do you understand?"

"I do," I said. Never mind that I didn't understand why; asking why in the undercurrent often leads to more answers than you'd ever want. And, when it came down to it, I did trust Yuen not to deliberately harm me. "And if it's not gone?"

"Then my daughter will know what to do." She didn't even blink as she translated. "You will not have to wait long."

I stepped back a pace. "That's okay. Really. I can come back—"

"Please. Have a seat." He spread his hands and smiled, then turned to speak to his daughter. She handed him the jar and listened, ignoring me entirely. I backed up to give Yuen's daughter room to move, then tried to stay out of her way.

I'd been in the same position as Yuen's daughter once before, waiting for my own mother to die. But I'd never been a witness to the same event from outside the family. Remembering how badly I'd taken it—for a number of reasons—I wanted to do what I could for Yuen's daughter, even if all I could do right now was to give her space.

Space didn't seem to be what she needed, though. She affixed several carved wands, each as long as my forearm, to the bed, then joined her father in repeating several phrases. They didn't sound Chinese, but they also didn't sound like any language I knew. This was a small-scale ritual, I realized, the last step of some magic already almost complete. That was what I'd scented on my way in; they'd gotten the big stuff taken care of first and left the last step until I could get there. The moment of that magic had drawn out tight on the brink of completion, and it occurred to me that Yuen's wife was right to be mourning her husband already.

I glanced behind me, at the place from which Yuen's daughter had taken the jar. It hadn't been in a safe, only a niche in the plaster, lined with thin gold foil. That meant Yuen wasn't too worried about keeping it safe, at least from mundane burglars. The photo that had hidden it lay on a nearby table. It was an old sepia-toned photograph, one I'd seen on previous visits and remembered only because it didn't seem to match the aesthetic of the rest of the room. In fact, I had my doubts about whether it was real; it looked more like one of those photos you could get at an amusement park of you and your friends in cowboy costumes: six men in front of a building that could have been a saloon flat in any Sergio Leone film set. Their faces were all a little too serious for fake old-time fun: to a man, they squinted into the sun as if assessing its weaknesses. Every one of them wore a belt with a six-gun, even the weedy greenhorn guy in the middle, who looked like he belonged in a sanatorium rather than a saloon. I know, technically you could say the same

WILD HUNT   13

thing about Doc Holliday, but for my money Doc Holliday could have killed this guy by breathing on him. The photo had faded over the years, obscuring many of the other faces, though the man on the far left had a handlebar mustache big enough to lose a cat in.

"There are some things," Yuen said behind me, "that you hold on to. Even when you know you shouldn't. Even when holding on costs you everything."

I nodded, then realized Yuen had spoken in English, without the protective formality of a translator. "Yuen?" I said, turning.

"Papa?" his daughter said with me, her voice barely above a whisper.

He clasped her hand. "Bring me the photograph. Not you, Elizabeth," he added as she started to move. "Hound. You bring it."

I did. He took it by the frame and, with a grunt, turned it around so it faced him. "Not that I've held on," he continued, seemingly oblivious to our shock. "But we don't like to think that our parents were fallible. It reflects badly on us. So if we cannot ignore those mistakes, and the worst of them we can never ignore, then sometimes the best thing to do is clean up after them."

He regarded the photo a moment longer, and I noticed that there were two pages stuck to its back, tacked there with rusting staples. They looked handwritten, but carefully so, as if they'd been copied out by someone not entirely familiar with English letters. A faint scent of rot clung to them, maybe one that had seeped out from the jar, but with a heavier touch to it, like spoiled meat.

As if in rebuke for my scrutiny, Yuen flipped the frame around. "We clean up after them," he repeated. "Because only the dead can kill the dead." He handed the frame to his daughter—Elizabeth, though I'd never heard her name till now—then put his arm around her shoulders, pressing her forehead to his. "Take care of those," he said, and more, too soft for me to hear. I looked away and thought of my mother, and a woman not my mother, gone for not so long but in too similar a way. When I looked back, Yuen had that limp stillness that nothing alive can replicate. Even though I'd known it was coming, the shock of it still hit me like ice water to the chest.

Elizabeth, though, moved quickly, cracking a vial of what smelled like blood against the jar and using the broken ends to pry away the wax seal. She pressed the opened jar against her father's throat as if applying a salve and muttered a phrase that I couldn't quite hear. A gunpowder stink billowed through the room. My ears popped, and through that pressure came a faint gibbering, a babble that not only didn't make sense but had been far away from sense for a long time. Then Yuen and his daughter together—don't ask me how, since at this point Yuen was definitely dead—spoke the last word, and, like the stilling of a bell, the magic was complete and ended.

Elizabeth caught her breath in something not quite a sob, then let it out slowly. Without looking at me, she held out the jar. I couldn't see her face, but I had a guess as to what it had cost her to spend that last moment carrying out that ritual instead of saying goodbye.

I took the jar from her and sniffed. There was a remnant of the putrid, corrupt smell, but no more than that, like a footprint that the tide has washed. No ghost, though what had been in there had not technically been a ghost, at least not as I understood it. The only trace of rot now in the room came from the pages on the back of the photo. "It's clean," I said. "Empty. Uninhabited."

She drew a ragged breath, then turned away from me and took the blindfold from the statue of Guanyin. "You'll be compensated for your time," she said briskly, her tone high with suppressed shock but still somehow different now that she was speaking for herself. "I'll send a deposit to your account." She wadded up the white silk and placed it in the offering bowl.

I looked around for a place to set down the jar. "There's no need—"

"There is. I intend to discharge my father's debts, and this is one of them. You're also overdue to come in for some of your armaments work—" so that was how Yuen referred to the bullets he cast for me, "—so I'll put you in touch with someone who can handle that aspect of our business." She took the jar from my hands and placed it on top of a cabinet, among the receipts to be filed. Her movements were brisk and efficient, and I thought of Yuen's words about cleaning up after one's parents.

Taking a long kitchen match from the stand by Guanyin's feet, she struck it and touched flame to silk. "Don't get me wrong, Miss Scelan. This wasn't charity on your part, and it isn't on ours." She was still a moment longer, gazing at the flames. Then, moving like a spring uncoiling, she tore the hidden pages from the back of the photograph and chucked them into the fire. The flames blazed up brilliant green, turning Guanyin's serene expression into a scowl.

"Wait!" I took a step forward, then stopped as she turned to look at me. "Er—didn't he just tell you to keep those?"

"Yes." She poked at the fire with the wooden end of a match, then dropped the match into the flames as well. It didn't smoke, and the fire itself smelled like the residue under a slaughterhouse. "But it's my house now, and I won't have things like that in it."

I glanced from her to the flames. Already the papers were gone, though the silk was taking more time to burn. "What were they?"

"All you need to know about them, my father already told you." She glanced sidelong at me. " 'Only the dead can kill the dead.' I'm sorry you had to be the one to see this."

It wasn't an apology. I understood her well enough. "Thank you," I said, and picked up my courier bag, wincing from its drag on my muscles.

At the door I turned back. "What will you do? I mean, the Three Cranes is kind of a fixture here. I could help, maybe—" Yuen's daughter shook her head. "Elizabeth," I said, then stopped. "I—I don't think I even knew what your name was."

"You never cared before. What difference would it make now?" She turned her back on me, one hand on the jar that had held her grandfather's corroded ghost. I nodded and let myself out, burning with shame at my own ignorance.

Two

An ambulance drove by as I left Chinatown—no sirens, no flashing lights. Maybe they knew not to hurry. I pulled over anyway and stood watching it disappear down the street.

I used to be able to deal with these things better. I used to not care what happened in the undercurrent, so long as it left me unscathed. Life's a lot simpler when you don't pay attention. But lately the strict division I'd put in place between work and life had started to crumble. Maybe, despite my insistence to the contrary, it had never been all that strong to begin with, and the events of six weeks ago just cast that into stark relief.

A hulking SUV lumbered by, kids yelling from the backseat. I shook my head and moved back out into the street, flipping off the guy behind me as I did so. Six weeks ago the Fiana, the organization of magicians who had once ruled Boston's undercurrent, had come looking for me, and all my boundaries between work and life had evaporated. I'd found out what had happened to my first lover, been betrayed by a man I'd come to trust, discovered more about my talent than I'd ever wanted to know, and become the pawn of a goddess seeking freedom. Along the way, I'd destroyed the Fiana's top men and their power base.

The repercussions couldn't just be written off lightly.

Too many people got that spooked, closed-down look when they saw me these days, too many of my old contacts got really quiet when I was around, and I still had nightmares about a golden chain wrapped around my throat.

But more important, two of my friends had been yanked headfirst into the deeps of the undercurrent. One, Sarah, had gotten involved knowing some of what she was doing, but that hadn't kept her from getting hurt. And that made things more awkward between us, these days.

The other . . . Nate had as much natural connection to magic as a seagull does to rugby. But because of me, his little sister had been kidnapped, and he himself had been enspelled, dragged under Fenway Park, and mauled in a magically, physically, and emotionally nasty fight. And after the whole thing was over, when I was a basket case, he'd helped me come back up to the world.

And then he'd taken me to a Sox game. Damn.

There were obligations, and then there were things that you couldn't ever pay back, not fully. I hung a left on Charles Street and headed over the river, toward MIT. Another truck had gotten stuck under a bridge on Storrow Drive, and the drivers in the long stream of stopped traffic watched me zip past with envy. I envied them only a little; at least they had air-conditioning for August days like this.

Not counting business trips, I'd been on the MIT campus only once before. (Counting business trips, it came to something over a dozen, but those were a different matter entirely.) It wasn't my favorite place. It wasn't that I disliked MIT; hell, aside from Nate's psycho-control-freak advisor, most of the people I met seemed decent enough, and I shared the same attitude of bemused incuriosity that most Boston residents had toward this place. After all, most of their big defense work took place outside the city, and aside from the occasional police car that ended up on top of a building, the university rarely made headlines.

But I'd dropped out of Boston University after a semester and a half, and I hadn't had the best record there even before family matters intervened. I wasn't a college girl, and I had never been. It wasn't just class issues—my mother might have worked two jobs just to scrape up rent every month, but she had all the dignity of a duchess—but there was a sort of intellectual pressure to which I was a little too sensitive. It made me itchy.

Nate was about a year away from completing his doctoral work, which to an outsider like me meant that he ought to have an office all his own. But he didn't; the last time I'd been here, all he had was a cubicle tucked away in one of the libraries. I locked up my bike and spent twenty minutes staring at a campus map trying to remember where I'd found Nate that last time—what was a cyclotron, anyway?—then said the hell with it and went with what I did know.

The scent trails crossing the green were as vibrant as any on Boston Common, with if anything a greater taste of the bizarre to them simply because of the different blend of people here. I didn't even need to close my eyes before I'd locked on to Nate's scent, a fact that I noted with more than a flicker of discomfort.

Nate had crossed the river on foot, probably after dropping off his little sister at day camp, then followed the river instead of taking the direct route. If I knew Nate, this was probably the only luxury of time he allowed himself. I followed his trail past the weird little brick thing that looked like a missile silo, past another building that looked like the rest of the buildings had been beating up on it, then into another, smaller hall. There wasn't any security at the front door, but a desk stood on the landing of the third floor, manned by a sharp-nosed woman working on a crossword puzzle. "ID, please," she said as I started to walk past.

"I'm meeting someone."

"I still need to see your ID." She held out her hand, and while she was still smiling, it had gone from the pleased-to-meet-you smile to the make-this-quick smile.

I tried to look innocent, or, failing that, honest. I knew what she saw—grubby bike messenger with black hair sticking out from under her helmet in all directions and the kind of sunburn you only get if you're naturally pasty white but insist on staying out in the sun. "I'm not with the university. I just need—"

Down the hall, one of the chairs I'd thought was empty rustled, and a serious face—as serious as an eight-year-old could get, anyway—surrounded by flyaway brown hair peered out at me. "Evie!" Katie Hunter said, and slid out of the chair, lugging a book that was about as long as my forearm. "Are you here to see Nate? I brought my backpack!"

She hefted a bag that looked heavier than she was. "What are you doing here?" I asked as she dragged it around the security desk.

"I got out of day camp early. And Nate had to check some records." She gave me a hug, whacking her book against the back of my legs.

I winced and patted her head, a little awkwardly. I wasn't good with kids, but Katie seemed determined to forget that. "I'm with her," I said to the guard.

Her eyes crinkled up at the corners. "Cute. But I still need ID." She shrugged in response to my exasperated look. "Dean's request. It's just for the rest of the summer."

"Evie." Katie tugged on my shirt until I looked down at her. "We went to the Fens today for day camp, and we got to go into the Gardner Museum, only you weren't there—"

A door down the hall slammed open, followed by a yell of "*Fuck* you!" I stepped in front of Katie—for whatever good that would do—just as the speaker reeled out into the hallway: a teenager in a polo shirt and shorts. His face was the color of roast beef, and it only got redder as he yanked a textbook from his bag and threw it overhand into the office he'd come out of.

The security guard glanced over her shoulder and sighed. "What's going on?" I asked, dropping to a whisper.

"Probably needed something for pre-med," she said wearily. "Happens all the time."

By now the angry student had moved on to throwing papers, none of which had the same dramatic impact as the textbook, and screaming about the professor's limited mental capacity, tiny genitalia, and propensity for self-abuse. The security guard yawned, and Katie shrank behind me a little further. "Cover your ears, kid," I said. That got me a scornful look, but at least I had deniability if Nate wanted to know where she'd learned that kind of language.

The kid concluded by yelling something about the professor's mother and her predilection for livestock, then stood there panting. I started to relax, then tensed again as the door creaked and opened further, and Nate stepped out into the hall, thrown textbook in hand.

For a moment I didn't recognize him, and that wasn't good: I'd been following his scent, and scent is one of those things that, while it may shade one way or another, remains fundamentally the same. Nate's scent had gone icy. It wasn't just a matter of keeping his temper; this was a complete shutdown, the emotional equivalent of those big scary blast doors they have in second-rate action movies.

This wasn't the Nate I knew. *But then*, I thought, *you saw another side of him, under the streets, at the same time as he saw another side of you . . .*

The student seemed to recognize that he'd stepped onto dangerous ground, even if he was too mad to have any common sense. He went from red to dead white, and while Nate didn't move any closer to him, he backed up until he ran into the wall. The contact seemed to wake him up, and he muttered one last "fucking asshole" before taking off down the hall.

"Nate—" I stopped as Katie squeezed my hand hard: telling me to stop, or comforting me?

Nate darted a glance over his shoulder like a soldier expecting a new attack, then saw me. The lines of his shoulders slowly relaxed, and the man I knew came back into focus. "Evie? What are you doing here?"

"She's with me!" Katie announced with more enthusiasm than accuracy.

He crossed the hall in a few long strides, caught me by the hands, and pulled me to him for a hug. "God, it's good to see you."

I stiffened and returned the hug about as smoothly as I'd returned Katie's. It wasn't that I didn't enjoy it—the opposite, in fact. But I didn't often get this close to someone. And Nate was attractive, in a stretched-on-the-rack, all-elbows sort of way. And this was a very brotherly hug. Dammit.

"Thought I'd come see you," I said, and pushed myself away at last. "What was all that about?"

"Summer classes," he said. "It's easy to slack off on them, but it's not a good idea if you're already taking a remedial course. He wanted a grade change, and I told him to go to the professor for it." He smiled a tired smile at me, one that told me that yes, he'd been through this before, right down to the profanity. "It'll be okay. Katie, you've got everything?" She nodded and took his hand.

We headed out onto the green, then along the Charles River, me walking my bike along the side of the road to keep out of the way of the militant joggers. Katie, following some obscure little-kid logic, ranged ahead of us like a dog on a long leash, coming back every now and then to point out something new. "Does that sort of stuff happen often?" I asked, once I was sure she was out of earshot.

Nate shrugged. "Not in that way, usually. Though

that's actually easier to deal with than the truly con-
trite ones. It's not a bad setup," he added. "He'll probably get the grade changed, but my advisor thinks it's
better to have someone turn down all requests first. I
get to be the ogre at the gate."

"That sucks," I said.

"Sometimes," he said, and I knew that was all the
acknowledgment I was going to get of this particular
situation. "So what brings you out here? I haven't seen
you in ages."

"Ages" in this case meant two weeks, and it was
probably a bad sign that it had started to feel like
ages to me as well. "Had a bad day," I said. "Undercurrent bad."

"Ah." He waited till we'd passed a woman with a
stroller three times the size of the baby in it. "You all
right?"

"Yeah. A little freaked out, but okay." I hesitated,
then gave him the bowdlerized version of what had
happened: called in to witness a death, then to witness
what that death had done on a magical level. No mention of Yuen's name, no Wild West photo, nothing of
the weird guilt I had felt around Elizabeth, or the in-
tense creepiness of the jar.

"Can you do that?" Nate asked after I'd finished.
"Preserve someone's soul after they die?"

"*I* can't. Wouldn't. But it's possible to trap a fragment of someone as a locus, yes." I didn't have to explain loci to Nate; he'd been around me when I was
complaining enough to know that a locus was a magician's link to power, and that it was usually a scrap
of someone else's soul. "But not after death—well,
it's hard to keep anything going after death. You get
remnants, imprints of emotions, but actual sentience is
damn near impossible, and especially not if you want
it to keep any trace of the person it had been. It'd . . . I
don't know, rot or something." Which was pretty close
to what I'd smelled in the jar. But even with the rot
taken into account, nothing should have lasted more

than a few months. Not years—and Yuen's father had been dead when I got to Boston, so we were talking about decades.

I thought of the spoiled-meat scent of the pages Elizabeth had burned. That was closer to the kind of necromancy needed for something like this. Maybe she was right not to want them in her home.

"What really got to me was that I had to be there with him and his daughter at the end. I mean, I'm not good at this sort of stuff to begin with, and now I feel like I wasn't just intruding, I was . . ." I kicked a flattened coffee cup off the sidewalk. "I don't know. I shouldn't have been there, that's all."

"I get it." He would. Nate and I had both been children of single moms, though they'd been single for different reasons. After high school, we'd both lost our moms at about the same time, mine to a nasty form of cancer, his to a stupid car accident. Neither of us had been around our fathers much, either before or since. Even so, it was a hard thing to imagine, and harder still because we both knew the loss of one parent.

"If I'd been in her place," I said, partly to forestall that line of thought, "I wouldn't have wanted anyone there, 'verification' or not. And I don't even really like my dad."

Nate nodded absently. Katie came ranging back to us, this time holding half of a pair of sunglasses. "Look," she said, holding them up to her face. "Pink! And they've got rainbows on the inside."

"I'll take your word for it," I said.

She turned the glasses over and looked down at them, frowning with an expression very like her brother's. "Do you ever go to the Gardner Museum, Evie?"

Nate blinked, caught out of his momentary funk. "Whoa. Where'd that question come from?"

She glared at him. "We went there today for day camp. Remember? I *told* you. I was telling Evie."

I scratched the back of my neck. Last week's sunburn had mostly faded, just in time to be replaced by this week's. "Is that the place with the glass flowers?"

"That's at Harvard," Nate murmured.

"Then no." I hitched my bike up onto the curb to get out of the way of a honking SUV. "Never been."

"Oh." Katie gave me a thoughtful look, then ran off to the next trash can to deposit the broken frames. Beyond her, where the green along the river gave way to scrub trees and a semblance of a park, a small group of young men loitered. One of them turned up the radio as we approached, and another stuffed a beer bottle into a sack. *Too slow*, I thought. *Any cop coming by would notice that.*

"You ought to visit the Gardner sometime," Nate said, still with that distant look in his eyes. "It's beautiful in winter . . ." He trailed off, then sighed. "Can I pick your brain for a moment?"

I shrugged. "Fire away."

"Do you know anything about the name Sigmund? Not Freud; that was my first thought." He paused. "At least I hope it's not Freud."

I blinked. "Wagner, right? That's a character in one of his operas." Now that was a buried memory, and not even buried for any good reason, just time and disuse.

Nate raised his eyebrows. "You know Wagner?"

"My mom did. Listened to opera all the time." I didn't share her appreciation, but those records had been my background music growing up, and there were still several Romantic-era operas whose plots I could thread my way through. "I think it's *The Valkyries*, unless it's the other one." I watched Nate's face, waiting for some response and getting none. "What's this about?"

Nate slowed to a stop, gazing ahead. For a moment he looked as if he was actually in pain, as if what he wanted to ask was a question wrapped in thorns. Then his eyes focused, and his expression turned to a more immediate dismay. "Damn," he muttered. "Should have known he'd come down this way."

I turned to look. One of the young men had stood up, and I recognized with a sinking stomach the guy who'd been in the hall just now screaming about his grade. "Shit. You want to turn around?"

Nate shook his head. "You know, most of them aren't like this, but there's one in every class, just that one . . ." He shook himself, and an expression of forced calm settled over his face as the guy got closer.

The scent of cheap beer—whatever crappy kind was currently in vogue among the asshole demographic—reached my nose, and I shifted my feet, trying to suppress my impulse to move in front of Nate. He didn't need my defense, I told myself, even if this guy did need a good shaking.

"Listen up, dickhole," the crappy student hollered, even though we weren't more than a few feet away. "I talked to my dad, and he's going to have your fucking nuts on a platter for this—"

"Nate! Nate, look, I found the rest—" Katie ran up to her brother, holding the other half of the sunglasses.

What happened next happened very fast. Katie skidded on the gravelly pavement, collided with the student, and he knocked her out of the way—straight off the curb and into the traffic of Memorial Drive. I yelled and jumped forward, but before I could even touch her, Nate was there, grabbing her by the arm and swinging her around and into me. A bright blue sedan veered around us with a scream of horns and brakes, coming within an inch of Nate, but even as I wrapped one arm around Katie, he was back on the sidewalk. Across the street, a woman dragging an empty cart screamed belatedly.

Nate caught the guy by the collar of his polo shirt and swung him against the railing so hard the cast iron clanged. "You do not ever do that to a little kid," Nate snarled. "Ever. Do you understand?"

The student went white. He hadn't meant for it to happen, but that wouldn't have helped Katie. She had gone still as stone against me, frozen like a rabbit in a field, and though I could feel the panicky gasps running through her, she hadn't yet made a sound. "She's okay," I said. "Nate, she's okay."

Nate didn't move. I couldn't quite see his face from where I was, but I could see how his hands gripped the guy's shirt almost to the point of ripping it. What was worse was that his scent had gone cold and scary again, but this time I had a glimpse of what was behind it. Blast doors? Yeah, that had been an appropriate metaphor.

The woman across the street was yelling something about child endangerment, but none of us paid any attention to her. Except for maybe the crappy student. He looked from Katie to Nate and for whatever reason, booze or arrogance or sheer panic, made the wrong decision. "You fuck—"

Nate backhanded him, not even bothering to wind up, just a casual whack so quick that I only saw it from the guy's head snapping back. "Do you understand me?" he repeated.

"Nate!" I caught his shoulder. It was like grabbing hold of an oak door.

Nate glanced at me, his lip curling back. For a second, he saw me and recognized me, and the faint shiver that ran through him had nothing to do with the student or Katie or any momentary anger. I caught my breath, unsure of what I was seeing but very aware of its effect on me. Then his gaze shifted, focusing on Katie, and though his expression didn't change, his grip on the kid's shirt slackened.

The loudmouthed student sidled away from Nate. I could see a thought forming behind his eyes, and I dragged my bike forward, then cursed. "Katie, hold this just a second, okay?" I said, and she nodded, watching her brother. Nate didn't even seem to remember that we were there.

I caught up to the kid in a few paces. "Listen," I

said, glancing first at his cohorts (who even hadn't noticed the incident) and then at Nate. "You could have killed that little girl."

"Fuck off," he mumbled, but his hands were shaking, and while his shorts looked dry, my nose could tell that they weren't.

"You could have killed her. You understand that? So you gonna tell me you didn't deserve that just now?" I stepped in front of him, but he wouldn't look at me. "Now maybe you can tell your dad about this too, and maybe he might raise a fuss. But it looks to me like we've got at least three witnesses who'll say you just pushed an eight-year-old into traffic. Somehow I don't think that'll help you get into med school."

He flinched at that. I waited for him to look up. "Bitch," he finally muttered in tones of defeat.

"Oh yes," I said.

When I turned back to Nate and Katie, Nate had knelt and was talking to her in a soft voice. "I'm okay," Katie said and said again, but she was still pale, and when he stood up, she tried to hold on to his hand and my bike.

He turned to look at me as I reached them. "You okay, kid?" I said to Katie, taking back the bike before she lost her grip on it.

She nodded. "Thanks."

"Thank your brother."

Katie shook her head. "I did. This is different."

"Just so long as you're all right." I touched her shoulder, then glanced at her brother. Nate reddened and wouldn't quite meet my eyes. "Are *you* okay?"

"Fine," he said, and it almost sounded true. If I hadn't just seen what I had, I might have even believed it. "Look, Katie and I ought to get on home, and I know you've got work—"

"I can walk with you," I tried, even though I knew a dismissal when I heard one. "I'm not meeting Rena for another couple of hours."

He shook his head, still not quite looking at me. "I

don't think that'd be a good idea. Maybe some other time, though."

Some other time. What kind of time did the two of us have, these days? But I said okay, and gave Katie another long hug, and waved to them as they crossed the bridge.

The broken sunglasses still lay where Katie had dropped them, at the edge of the curb. I nudged them with my foot, then picked them up and tucked them into one of the pockets of my courier bag.

"Jackass," I muttered, and I wasn't sure whether I meant the kid, Nate, or me for getting my damn hopes up.

 Three

I haven't bothered dressing up to go out ever since Sarah tactfully pointed out that I wear all my clothes as if they were disposable. There's no point in owning something nice if you're just going to wear holes in it. So these days, if I'm going clubbing with Rena, for example, I just wear something out of the back of my closet, usually jeans and a shirt without too many stains on it. It'll pass, and it's not like I'm out there to pick up guys.

It's still a little too informal for a police station. I kept feeling like someone was going to accost me for loitering with intent as I waited in the office for Rena. "Could you page her again?" I asked the officer on desk duty. "Rena Santesteban. She should be just getting off duty—her shift ends this time of day, and she knows I'm here to meet her."

"She might not be in," he said, not looking up.

"She's in." We'd set this up weeks ago—well, we'd originally planned for a girls' night out three weeks back, but first I had an unexpected double shift and then she'd had food poisoning and then I'd gotten behind . . . Anyway. Fourth time was the charm, and after the day I'd had I could really use the chance to forget everything for a couple of hours. "Could you just page her, please?"

He shrugged. "Give her time."

Well, what kind of hurry was I in anyway? I kept pacing, then stopped and sniffed the air. "Is that coffee? God, I'd kill for a cup of coffee—" I stopped, remembering where I was. "Not really. Um."

The officer gave me a long, bored look. "You don't want this coffee," he said finally. "Trust me."

"Why not? Coffee's coffee."

He shook his head, then turned and muttered into the phone again, either paging Rena or asking for patience.

The door opened, and Rena emerged in the blue shirt and jeans that were about as close to a uniform as you could get without the actual tags. It was for her what passed for informal. It was also not what she usually wore for our nights out. "Evie, I'm so sorry," she began.

"Oh no. No, don't apologize straight off, it sets the wrong tone for the whole evening—" I stopped. Rena usually looked tired and angry—it was part of her whole aesthetic—but just now she looked both worn down and energized, like a catcher one inning away from a playoff win. "What's up?"

She glanced over her shoulder. "Can we have a moment?" she asked the officer.

"You can out in the hall," he said, again without looking up.

Rena sighed, then shepherded me out into the hall. "You don't happen to have a cigarette on you, do you?" she asked as the door closed behind us.

I shook my head. "I don't smoke. You know that."

"Yeah. I was just hoping you might have brought one as a kindness. God, I need a smoke . . ." She closed her eyes and leaned back against the wall. "I can't go tonight, Evie."

"What? Oh, come on, Rena—"

"I can't. I've got too much going on." She glanced back at the door, as if it might open at any moment. "This is one hell of a case, Evie. It could be big."

"Bigger than Napoleon Night at the Paradise?"

"Bigger." She paused. "Hang on. Are they the guys with the ruffles or the guys in the loincloths?"

Trust Rena to remember a band by their clothing, not by their music. "Ruffles. You're thinking of The Lamentations of Their Women. They played last week." And we'd missed that show too. "Well, hell. We're putting this off another week, then?"

"Make it two." She grinned, her dark eyes sparkling with a kind of manic glee. "Evie, if I could tell you about this, I would. It's just that awesome. It's big enough that I could get in trouble just for telling you it exists."

"Then you'd better shut up about it." I grinned back. I couldn't help it, postponed evening out or no. I'd never seen Rena this excited about a case—worried, angry, frustrated, yes, but never actually excited. "Tell me about it after it hits the papers."

"You got it." She thumped my shoulder, and I punched her in the arm. "You'll be okay?"

I shrugged. "I'll just have to hit the books instead."

"You're kidding me. Since when are you studying for anything?"

Since my lack of knowledge kicked my ass, I thought, but she didn't need to know that. "Gotta get into *Haavaad*," I said, and got the door for her. "See you around."

The little fountain in the corner of my office had gone wonky again, this time spattering the ceiling as well as leaving a puddle all around its base. It started up again as I unlocked the door, tinkling merrily away, like a puppy sitting in the middle of a damp patch and wagging its tail. I sighed and went to get the paper towels.

The fountain and the giant desk that took up most of my office-cum-apartment were the only holdovers from the previous occupant, a psychiatrist who'd had to leave town in a hurry (nothing to do with his practice, everything to do with his losses on the horses at Suffolk Downs). Though the desk was useful, the fountain had broken a long time back and its habits were as irregular as my own. Even so, after a day of dealing with unexpected crap, I found its unpredictability comforting. At least it could be depended on to act funny.

There were four messages on the aging answering machine: two old clients saying they'd have my payment ready any day now (different phrasing, same sentiment), one robocall from the bike shop advertising a new sale that still wouldn't bring most of their stuff into my price range, and Sarah asking if I'd borrowed her copy of something called *Dawlayres*.

Probably not, though I'd borrowed pretty much everything else from her. I glanced at the stack of books on the far side of my desk, then picked up the volume on top. *Celtic Mythology*, by B. Austin, with a folded receipt from the BPL stuck two thirds of the way through. Below it was *A Survey of Deities*, which despite its "survey" title had been tougher than any book I could remember reading in my brief time at BU, and which had stymied me by chapter five. *Bulfinch's* below that, Lady Gregory below that, *D'Aulaire's*— aha, that's what she meant—and the big book that really shouldn't have been at the bottom of the stack but had to be for simple reasons of size, *Dictionary of Myth*.

This was not my evening reading of choice. I'd much rather stretch out listening to the Sox game, reconstructing it in my head like a little mirror of Fenway Park, maybe taking care of some much-needed repairs to my courier gear. Hell, I had a book of William Trevor short stories tucked under the futon that served the office as a couch, and even if I only managed a few pages a night, I preferred that to dusty gods and even dustier religion professors.

But half the reason the Fiana had had a hold on me was because of my connection to a figure out of myth—Sceolang, one of the hounds of Finn Mac Cool.

Sceolang had become human after the stories ended and had gone on to sire an awful lot of descendants, self included. Because I hadn't known my way around the mythology, I had left myself vulnerable. I couldn't afford to miss cues like that. And since Boston was a mishmash of cultures, even more so now that the faux-Irish shadow on the undercurrent was gone, I couldn't confine myself to just one set of myths.

I'd fallen asleep at my desk five times in the last two weeks just because of these stupid books, and it wasn't even as if I had far to go between desk and sleeping place (the futon folded out to make a passable bed). Making a face at *A Survey of Deities*, I leaned back in my chair to reach the radio. The Sox were up two-one already, and it wasn't even the second inning. I turned it up and sat back, book in hand.

By the third, it was four-two against the Sox, and I hadn't managed to read four full pages. "Serves me right for listening to Sarah's book recommendations," I muttered, and dragged the dictionary out from the bottom of the stack. If I had to do research, I might as well at least look up what I liked. I thumbed through to the entry on "Sigmund," just so I could pretend I was helping Nate.

Maybe it was the style of the dictionary, maybe it was the still-resonating emotional charge, but I sank much more easily into this. The legend wasn't at all like what I remembered from Mom's operas, which was kind of a relief, since I'd wanted to smack pretty much all those characters. (Mom had said that was the point. I'll never understand opera.)

Between the book and the Sox game, I was just about dead to the rest of the world. When I noticed the knock at my door I was pretty sure I'd heard it twice already. "Just a second," I called, then set down the book and checked the score (still not good for the Sox).

The peephole showed two men standing in the hall, the taller one in a shabby gray suit, the shorter in a brown bomber jacket and jeans that looked like they could stand on their own. Neither was familiar—but the woman's voice that came with them was. "For crying out loud, Evie, are you home or not?"

Sarah. I looked again and yes, there was a hint of her dark brown curls at the bottom of the lens. Sarah's not a tiny woman, but she's short enough that she can lurk under the range of the peephole—or, if she's close to the door and whacking on it, she can pretty much disappear. "Goddammit," I muttered, but smiled anyway, shaking my head. Weird company or no, it was good to see Sarah.

I opened the door, and Sarah glared up at me. "You had the baseball turned up again, didn't you?"

"Guilty," I agreed. "Who are your friends?"

A little of the merry gleam in her eyes faded. "Not my friends. Both of them were hanging around outside." She nodded to them. "I figured you'd rather have them inside where you could see them, and we could at least get that part out in the open." She gave them both an admonitory glare.

Yeah, I could see that. Sarah's reaction to prowlers is to yell at them—she once shamed a mugger into giving her his wallet—and I could easily see her marching these two to the door just out of pique. And the somewhat shamefaced expressions on these two backed her up.

The shorter man cleared his throat. "I can't speak for my colleague," he said, shrugging his jacket as if it might provide a little extra protection, "but I came here to seek audience."

"Audience?" I glanced at Sarah, who raised her eyebrows: *who knows how adepts think?* The taller man looked me up and down disapprovingly, as if I were applying for a job and had arrived at the interview in pajama pants. "All right. Come on in, all of you."

Sarah flashed me a quick smile and slid past. I caught the glance between the two men and nodded. *Yes, I've just invited you in. I know, that's not what adepts do.* And these were adepts: the shorter one was a gray-haired professor type with a persistent facial tic and spectacles that kept sliding down his nose. He absolutely stank of the fireworks-and-rain scent of magic. The other, though he lacked the most obvious scent, had the wasted, tired look of a man who'd used too many loci, cut off too many pieces of his own soul. He smelled like a shadow, like a depression in low grass, and—this much I could tell from his lack of expression alone—he didn't much like me.

That was fine. I didn't much like adepts. I smiled at both of them, showing my teeth. *I'm not one of you. I'm not even like you.* I turned my back on them and followed Sarah in.

Sarah settled into one of the chairs on either side of the futon. She was more conservatively dressed than usual, I finally noticed, which for her meant that her skirts only had one layer of ruffles and her hair had been pulled back into a less-than-effective bun. She frowned and nodded to the radio. "Any chance you can turn that down while we talk?"

"No," I said, leaning against the corner of my desk. The taller man's lips twitched as he closed the door behind him, though in amusement or contempt I couldn't tell. "What did you want to talk to me about?"

"Well—" Sarah took a deep breath and let it out through her teeth.

The shorter man, who seemed to be unhappy with all of the available chairs and had settled for pacing by the door, spoke up. "Audience," he repeated. "One falls, another rises. Horizons open."

Goddamn adepts. "In English this time?"

"What my . . . colleague . . . is saying," the taller man continued with a half nod, "is that we both wanted to see you."

"Really." I crossed my arms and leaned back.

The two men looked at each other, and it suddenly struck me that they weren't here together. Whatever reasons had brought them both here, it wasn't a common cause—and now they didn't want to talk in front of each other. The taller man with the shadowy scent seemed to win their stare-off; he leaned back in his chair and closed his eyes.

The shorter man seemed to have gotten his facial tic under control, but he paced, as if stilling one part of him meant that another had to be in motion. "Boston is well known. You don't go to Boston unless you want to be part of something. The Bright Brotherhood were known, and now they're gone. Because of you." The fountain spat water at him, and he started, then craned his neck to study it as if it were a new species.

While each sentence he'd spoken had been technically correct, I couldn't quite figure out the whole gist of them. "It wasn't my doing," I said, and it was only half a lie. "There were a lot of factors involved . . . Let's just say I helped the Fiana trip over their own feet. What's that got to do with you?"

He blinked at me, as if I'd completely managed to miss his point. Maybe I had, but the way he stared at me through his coke-bottle glasses suddenly seemed idiotic, as if he were no more sentient than a cow. I started to shake my head, think up some way to get him out of here, then stopped as something else caught my attention.

A thin scent of gunpowder wound its way through the room. Not much, no more than a breath, but enough to tell me that someone here was working magic. I pushed away from the corner of the desk and stood in front of the taller man. "Stop that."

He shivered back to full wakefulness. One hand was in his jacket pocket: probably holding a locus. It wasn't big magic, but for a petty aversion spell, it didn't have to be. "Stop what?"

I leaned down, grabbed his shirt, and dragged him to his feet. "Stop working magic. Not in my house." I gave him a quick shake, then pushed him toward the door. "Both of you, out. I don't care what you want to ask me; if you're going to work magic on me you lose all right of audience."

"I protest," the shorter one said, the words coming out in a bleat. "I have worked no magic in your presence."

"But it'll be a while till that ward wears off," I pointed out. "Maybe some other time."

Mollified, the shorter one went, with one last glance at the fountain. The taller, to his credit, didn't try for one last stare-off, but bowed his head and murmured a meaningless courtesy as he passed me. I closed the door behind them and waited till I heard the outer door latch, then turned to face Sarah. "What the hell is wrong with those guys? I can't turn around without running into half-baked adepts these days."

She let out a long breath. "Boston's changing, Evie." She folded her hands in her lap and didn't smile when I looked at her. "You have to have noticed it."

I'd noticed a few things, but in all honesty I'd hoped to stay out of the worst of it. I was still, as most of these guys perceived matters, relatively powerless. Blood-magic could only get you so far, and since I limited any excursions into ritual or spirit magic to the minor invocations—well, these days I did, and involuntary possession doesn't count—I thought I'd stayed a minor player in this game.

The trouble was that it wasn't quite as true as I'd have liked. I couldn't turn off my talent anymore—couldn't keep from noticing the scents that everything carried, in a way that was more distracting than a busload of kindergartners in a chamber-music concert. And, it now seemed, my own opinion of my status didn't matter nearly as much as other people's opinions. "You heard them. They were sizing me up. They think *I*—" I shook my head, almost nauseated by the thought. "They think I'm the reason the Fiana fell."

"Well? Aren't you?"

"No! Not alone, anyway!" Sarah raised an eyebrow, and I glared at her. "You know what I mean."

"Maybe. I never did get the whole story out of you."

"Yeah. Well." I glanced down at her hands. It hadn't

been more than a couple of weeks since the bandages
had come off, and though all her fingers and tendons
were where they ought to be, it could easily have gone
the other way.

Sarah and I had both been part of the whole cata-
clysm that pulled down the last remnants of the Fiana.
Granted, we'd been working at cross purposes for a lot
of that, due to several miscommunications, but when
it came down to it we were allies, and more important, still friends. But while I'd walked away with no
ill effects (physically, at least; the jury was still out on
emotional and magical matters), Sarah had gotten the
equivalent of a heap of broken glass in her hands. She'd
made it out like it was no big deal, claiming that it just
gave her an excuse to stick her assistant on counter
duty more often, but it didn't take any great degree of
empathy to see that she'd been rattled pretty badly.

"That's not the point," I said finally. "They were
here to check me out. To see what brought down the
Fiana. Sarah, that's beyond creepy. That's bordering
on perilously fucked up."

"Exactly." She got to her feet. "Evie, they're not the
only ones. We have a serious power vacuum in the city,
and just because there aren't many other magical organizations out there—"

"Or magicians who can organize worth a damn,"
I muttered. Most magicians were what Sarah calls
"entropogenic," the kind of people who automatically
destabilize any situation they come into contact with.
And on top of that, the undercurrent is a paranoid
place, one that almost completely precludes coopera-
tion. You don't see jackals working together for much
the same reason.

"It doesn't make us any safer." She reached back
and fiddled with her bun, dislodging more of the curls
that had never wanted to be there in the first place.
"I've been in touch with some of the coven members,
and the others. Like Deke, and the Roxbury families.
We're trying to start a, a neighborhood watch."

"In the undercurrent? Good fucking luck. Magicians don't work together, Sarah. You taught me that, and Fiana aside, it's still true." The only reason the Fiana had held together for as long as they had was the unnatural amount of power they had been able to draw on, a locus as bright as the sun and as dangerous. But that locus—that goddess—was dead or free, depending on how you looked at it, and there was no way the Fiana could pull together again. As for enlightened self-interest, I'd look for that in a cat before I'd look for it in magicians. "What are you going to promise them? Join the watch and get a free toaster?"

"We've got you."

I choked on my next retort. Sarah watched me intently. She was serious, I realized.

"You brought down—or appeared to bring down—the Fiana. You're known, like it or not. People will listen to you, at least for a little while. And if we get everyone in one place, we might have a chance of putting something together. It'd be very low key, like a code of conduct—no poaching loci, no more screwing each other over."

"You might as well ask them to stop breathing."

"Evie, it's not just possible, it's necessary. Those two, they were the nicest of the guys coming in from out of town. We're going to have newcomers, and not all of them are going to be good additions to our fair city." She smiled as she said the last bit, and I tried to smile back. "Will you at least give it a try?"

I shook my head. "Sarah . . ."

"Just invite some of the locals. I'm having an organizational meeting tomorrow evening at Summit Hill, in Brookline. It's neutral ground; the seer enclave's vouched for it. If you just ask a few people, spread the word, then they'll come. I know it."

I rubbed my hand over my face. It was true that people had gotten dragged into the undercurrent and hurt just because there wasn't any fellow-feeling among magicians. Even a half-assed honor code might be better than nothing. I looked down at Sarah's hands again, at the network of scars. "Okay. Fine. But you're going to be out a lot of punch and cookies if this doesn't work."

She grinned at me. "Thanks for the support. Can I ask you to do something more for me?" She fumbled around in her purse—I'd never seen the point of carrying anything smaller than a messenger bag, but Sarah seemed to cram everything into a reticule the size of a biscuit—and produced a stack of flyers, the kind that wouldn't last more than ten minutes if they were stuck up on a telephone pole. "Just pass this around, if you can, and I'll spread the word through my own channels . . . How's the research going?"

"Oh, hell." I nudged *A Survey of Deities* with my foot. "I'm not cut out for studying. And there's a crapload of hounds out there. Seems like every single European nation has its own batch."

"Well, they were an important animal to primitive people," she said, writing on the back of the flyers. "And you still are."

"Arf." I took the flyers and set them on top of the books. "I hope you know what you're doing."

She smiled. "This time, I think I do."

I let her out, then stood by the window for a while, only barely registering the flow of the game in the background. I didn't want to admit it to myself, and I sure as hell wasn't going to admit it to Sarah, but I could feel a flicker of hope. Maybe we could put something together. Maybe being in the undercurrent didn't have to mean that you were on your own.

It was a scary kind of hope.

I sighed, then cursed as I finally heard what the radio was telling me. The Red Sox had gone even further into the hole, twelve-two. Goddammit.

 Four

The next morning Tania demanded to know why I'd missed the last deliveries from the day before, then stuck me with an extra shift to make up for it. Not even that could dent my mood; I'd woken up smiling, full of hope for both Sarah's plan and the Sox's post-season outlook. I rode out on my rounds with Sarah's flyers tucked into the front flap of my courier bag.

One of the advantages this job had over waitressing (which was what I'd done to fill in the cracks before the finder work had really taken off) was that I could use the scraps of time I had to make contacts all over the city. My first run was down to the Longwood area, so it made sense to stop by the drain under the River-way where I knew Deke was living these days. Deke wasn't technically homeless, but he didn't like sleeping at home more than two nights in a row. For a more attractive guy this might not be a problem; for Deke it meant the drains.

He was practicing the T. E. Lawrence trick with a Zippo as I scrambled down into the culvert. "Heya, Deke. Things better than they were?"

"You know not to ask me that," he said serenely, not taking his eyes from the flame. Deke always smelled slightly burnt, although I knew he was careful with his fires, or at least when they got out of control they didn't hurt anyone else. I didn't mind the smoky scent, partly because it mitigated his natural damp-woodchuck smell.

I didn't "know not to ask him," but you don't argue with crazies and adepts. "Sarah asked me to drop this off for you." I put the flyer on top of his sleeping bag, getting just enough dew on it so that he wouldn't immediately use it for kindling. "She's holding a meeting tonight."

"I know," he said. "So she's serious about it."

"Serious as Sarah ever gets."

Deke grunted in reply. I hitched my bag back into place and started up the hill, thinking our conversation was over. "Hound?" he called after me.

I turned. "Yeah?"

Deke had found a pencil from somewhere and had used it to drag the flyer closer. "Will you be there?"

"Yeah. Sure."

"Huh." He gave me a long look, first one eye then the other, then closed up the Zippo and nodded. "All right."

Well, that was encouraging. So I followed the same pattern for the rest of my day. I dropped off packets for lawyers on the waterfront and handed a flyer to Tessie, who hadn't stepped off her boat in twenty years but whose contacts ranged all over the docks. I took copies into the North End and dropped in at the court at Tomato Gianni's (and mooched a piece of their garlic bread while I was at it). I weighed a flyer down with a brick so that Maryam would see it when she crawled off her bed of gravel, and I gave three identically creased copies to the Triplets down in Dorchester.

And the more I did this, the more I got the sense that Sarah was right: Boston had changed. It wasn't anything you could point to on a map or note down in a survey, but it was there, even if only a few people were positioned to notice it. If I'd been inclined toward poetry, I'd have called it a sense of absence; if I were more practical, I'd have called it too many presences. As it was, I called it a damn nuisance.

I'd gotten through my first sixteen years in this city without noticing the big magical presence that pulled most of the undercurrent's strings in Boston, like a cyclist paying attention only to the road right in front of her and not the tractor-trailer coming up on her left. But just as there were some doors that opened only one way, there were some things that stayed noticed once you learned to notice them. And acknowledging the Fiana meant that I couldn't ignore the way things had changed after their fall.

There was a lot of new talent in town, for starters. It wasn't just a matter of shadowcatchers on street corners, though I still found a few and did my damnedest to send them off somewhere they could recover. No, the recent arrivals included low-class wardwatchers and fire-eaters, people with just enough talent to stand out but not enough to defend themselves against more savvy adepts. Who had also moved into town, drawn partly by the influx of prey and partly by the new territory up for grabs. And then there were the homegrown adepts, the ones who'd had the sense to get out when the Fiana were in power and now discovered they could actually come home again.

And pretty much everyone who came into town had heard something about me. The reverse was not necessarily true.

By the end of the second shift, I was starting to get that boneless feeling that twelve hours of Boston potholes will do to you (if they don't dislocate your goddamn shoulder first). But my last stop was in Chinatown, and so as much as I dreaded it, I stopped in at the Three Cranes.

I don't know what I'd expected, but the huge moving truck blocking half the street was not it. Yuen's wife directed a small army of movers, screaming like a drill sergeant at any who got out of line. I locked up my bike and edged past the truck, scraping my butt against the wall, and headed down the steps to the Three Cranes.

A couple of movers who'd escaped from above worked on strapping what looked like Saran Wrap around a rack of boxes, and a third tested the weight of a crate before setting it down and shaking his head. Most of the assorted jars and tanks on the racks had been boxed up, and the ceiling looked a lot higher now that it didn't have bundles of unnamable plants strung up to dry. I realized I was crouching, not out of habit but as a reaction to the weird openness above me; the unexpected space made me feel unnaturally vulnerable. It smelled of dust in here, dust kicked up after many years, and that was enough to hide most other scents from me.

At the far end of the shop, where Yuen had held his informal court, a woman in a pin-striped suit and an older man in black bent together over a glass case. He pointed at something inside, and she nodded, speaking too quietly for me to hear.

"Hi," I said, then stopped, recognizing Elizabeth Yuen's muted scent before I made the connection between her and this sharp young woman. She'd cut her long black hair into a bob, and the suit, while it looked good on her, was a far cry from her earlier traditional white clothes. She didn't look like anyone's daughter now. "Miss—" I tried, uncertain how to address her.

The old man stood up, laying his hands on the case as if protecting it from a blow. Elizabeth turned to see me and nodded. "Hound." She gestured to me. "This is the one I was telling you about. When you didn't show, we had to make other arrangements, and she had to take your place."

"You couldn't even wait a day?" the old man asked. He was shorter than me, with that stooped look some people get as they grow older. What was left of his hair was a white-gray fuzz from one ear to the other, and liver spots dotted his already-dark skin. I could catch a little of his scent through the dust: oil of some kind, not unpleasant, and a furry undertone to it that for some reason reminded me of weak coffee in paper cups.

"No, we couldn't," Elizabeth said, searching through the papers on the desk.

"Hm," said the old man. He produced a pair of glasses from his breast pocket and put them on. "How'd she do?"

"Um," I said, and took a flyer from my bag, hoping that it would draw some attention. Well, how *do* you interrupt people who seem determined to talk about you like you're not there?

"Well enough, on short notice." *High praise*, I thought, then kicked myself for it. This woman's father had died the other day; I had no cause to be getting snotty with her.

The man looked me up and down, eyes narrowed, as if either committing my features to memory or checking them against a list. "What's her name?"

"Scelan," I said. "Genevieve Scelan. And yours?"

"This is Reverend James Woodfin," Yuen's daughter said. Woodfin's expression softened a little, and he smiled at her. "You brought your weapon?"

"I—what?" I glanced back at the movers. "No, that's not why I'm here. It's this—there's a meeting, and I thought you might be interested in it."

Elizabeth took the flyer out of my hand, gave it a glance, and shook her head. "Idiots."

"It's all right," Woodfin said. "I can work with the specs you gave me."

Specs? I caught the flyer as Elizabeth was about to toss it away. "Mind telling me what's going on?"

Elizabeth glanced at me as if surprised to find me still there. "He'll be handling the last of the obligations my father incurred. I'm discharging my debts, Hound," she added as she tugged the flyer from my hand and folded it in half. "I did say I would."

"But my weapon—" This was an iffy subject for me these days. While the gun I had on hand for the difficult cases no longer felt like it would burn my fingers, it still felt like what it was: a murder weapon. I'd never been comfortable carrying it, never mind the legal trouble I could get into for the modifications I'd had made (concealed weapons permits were very picky about things like unconventional ammunition). But somehow knowing how *not* to use it had made a difference. Now, though, I couldn't make that distinction. I'd used that gun to kill a man, and that would always be part of the weapon.

"The reverend is a gunsmith," Elizabeth explained. She nodded to the case, and I took a step closer to see that it was a display case, fronted with glass. Six niches each held an old-fashioned revolver, although one of them was melted down to a lump with charred grips and another looked like it had been dipped in ink. I craned my neck to see past the glare off the glass, but could only make out the writing below one of the intact guns: *Skelling.* "I promised you I'd find someone to fill in for my father," Elizabeth added. "For the armaments, at least."

"Don't throw that away," Woodfin said, catching the flyer before it could hit the trash. "If this lady's going to be there, then I can meet her there. I can get a look at the in-practice marks on her weapon then."

"Sorry? You want me to carry a gun into a meeting of magicians?"

Woodfin shrugged and settled into one of the chairs behind the counter with a grunt, then nodded to Elizabeth. "Will that work for you?"

"I suppose so. Bring the gun with you tonight, Hound. The reverend will meet you there." She glanced at the flyer again, and her lip curled. Woodfin muttered something to her in what sounded like Chinese, and she responded in kind. I felt a flare of monolingual jealousy and quickly stifled it. All this weird shit lately had gotten to me: who was I to expect every person in the undercurrent to acknowledge me?

Granted, I thought, that might make it easier to keep track of who was about to do something monumentally stupid.

I pulled up in front of my office and gazed at it blankly. I had maybe two hours before Sarah's meeting, and originally I'd planned to use the time to take care of the last household tasks for the week (I had a jar of pickles and half a gallon of lumpy milk in the fridge, and the hamper was so full of dirty clothes that they sprang out onto the floor when I opened it). But just now I felt a little too drained—and, somehow, insulted—to put that time to any good use.

"Excuse me?" said a woman's voice, just over my shoulder.

I jumped—for a moment I'd mistaken her for Mrs. Heppelwhite, the neighborhood scold. Mrs. Heppelwhite's notice would have been all I needed to turn this day lousy. But the speaker wasn't her: instead, a dainty, pale woman in her sixties smiled at me from the end of the walk.

Her face was wide and young-looking, but with worry lines at her temples and mouth, and her hair looked as if it had once been an indiscriminate shade between brown and blonde and was now an indiscriminate shade between brown and gray. It was cut short, shorter than mine was these days, and had a simple sweep to it that made me think of pictures from the 1940s. She smiled at me, a little awkwardly. "I'd like to get through, please."

"Oh . . . sorry." I got off my bike and pulled it out of her way.

"Thank you. Oh—one other thing." She reached into her purse—she was even wearing gloves, I noticed, which just added to her general air of anachronism—and took out a slip of paper. "Could you tell me whether Number Ninety-three is on this side of the street?"

"This is Number Ninety-three." I was Number Ninety-three, apartment 1B. "Who are you looking for?"

"Someone by the name of G. Scelan. Do you know him?"

I smiled. A client, I thought, and not just that, but a client who despite her old-fashioned dress seemed pretty much normal. Which meant I might have a chance at a simple hunt to recharge me. "I'm her. Genevieve Scelan." I shook her hand. Her fingers were as slender as reeds and probably about as strong. "Come on in; I'll need a moment to get settled."

I showed her in and pulled a jacket over my sweaty courier gear. She took a seat, purse propped in front of her, legs crossed at the ankles, and waited for me to settle into the chair on the far side of the desk. "Right," I said. "What's your name, and how can I help you?"

"Abigail Huston. Pleased to meet you." She smiled again, and despite the lack of laugh lines in her face, there was a twinkly quality to it.

"And how do you like Boston, Abigail?"

She blinked, startled, then laughed. "No, I suppose I don't look like a native."

"Not really."

"My brother always claims I can blend in anywhere." She smiled. "He's a flatterer. No, this is my first time here; the closest I ever got before now was out in Central Massachusetts." Her smile thinned a little, as if it wasn't a good memory, but the moment passed.

"Ah. How long are you here for?" Smile or no, there was something I couldn't quite catch . . . I shifted a little in the chair. Was it the light in here?

"Well, that rather depends. You see, it's somewhat of a long story—my mother passed away some years ago, and her executor finally transferred some of her possessions to me . . ."

Not the light. Not her voice either. I sniffed, and Abigail paused. I shook my head. "Go on. Please."

She hesitated, then fidgeted, pulling off her gloves one finger at a time. "Well, one of the things that was deeded to me was a set of chests belonging to my great-great-grandmother. I've only just started cataloguing the contents, and unfortunately, I think some of the items within might be stolen property."

It couldn't be her scent. That was flat normal . . . no, not normal, but colorless, bloodless. I'd never known anyone to have a scent that made less of an impression on me. If it hadn't been for the continued sparking scent from the fountain and the assorted trails of the office itself, I'd have thought I was catching a cold.

"What I'd like is to return the property to its rightful owner. But there's an awful lot of different things in those chests, and I don't know who the owner might be, or if they're—if he's even still reachable." She laid her gloves over her purse, smoothed them flat, then clasped her hands over them. "I'd been told you had some . . . some amazing successes in finding items, and I wondered if you could turn that around and find an owner."

It wasn't her body language either. This wasn't a learned approach, the way that some people who'd gone through nasty situations learned to hide themselves. This was something else. "What makes you think that some of your inheritance is stolen property?"

Abigail was silent a moment, staring at the edge of the desk. Even her eyes seemed washed out, and that shouldn't have been possible with brown eyes. Finally she looked up at me. "Nightmares," she said, clipping off the word.

And that was it. With that word her scent changed, a flash of real emotion as bright and fleeting as the glare off a blade. She was scared, scared enough that her fear could break through what I realized was a highly controlled mask, one that went deeper than just composure.

She was an adept.

I should know better to rely on sight rather than scent. But scent is such a nonverbal trigger that it's hard to translate into words, and so if I have an idea, it comes through as hunches or unconscious aversions long before I can say what it is or why. I exhaled slowly, and this time I noticed how Abigail tensed when I did so. She knew what I was looking for and how I was looking for it, which meant she knew about me. Which meant she wasn't just a nice little old lady.

"Well," I said, leaning back, "I can see why that would be a problem. Didn't your wards keep them at bay?"

Abigail started, then straightened up, the twinkle gone. "No," she said. "I don't bother with wards against dreams. They're impractical, and a waste of time and energy."

I grinned. This was the real woman now, not the milquetoast of a moment ago. She still had the same bloodless scent, the same delicate care in how she moved, but now there was a center of stone to her mien. "I could say the same thing about wards in general. But then again, I'm no magician."

"And I am, I suppose, by your lights." Abigail sighed, a very grade-school-teacher sigh. In fact, she would not have looked out of place in a teachers' lounge, right down to the cardigan and the little floral pin over her left breast. But while there were bags under her eyes, they didn't have the ground-in look that most teachers' had. These were more recent. "Fine. I should have come clean about that to begin with."

I shrugged. "I can understand why you didn't. People can react strangely, especially if they're not aware of the undercurrent to begin with."

Abigail mouthed the word *undercurrent*, as if testing it. Now that I was seeing her as a magician, a whole new set of implications slid into place. The excessive care she took with her clothes was a marked contrast to most adepts, who usually ended up so steeped in their magic that they couldn't remember which end the pants went on. The exceptions tended to be both very fastidious and very powerful—but I didn't get that sense from Abigail. She wasn't small-time, but she didn't have the arrogant power that I associated with that kind of adept. (And let's face it, most of them were male.)

"Even magicians have grandmothers," Abigail said, folding her gloves one over the other. "My story still stands. And yes, the nightmares are even more of a problem for someone in my position. If you don't do this sort of work, I'll take my business elsewhere."

"I never said I wouldn't do it." I opened my desk drawer and rummaged around for a contract. "Here. Take a look. There's a list of work I won't do on the second page."

She took the contract and flipped the first page over. "Photography?"

"People wanting to catch their spouses cheating on them. There are enough PIs in the city who'll do that for less." Granted, I'd had to do a little of that sordid work when I was starting out, but then the undercurrent stuff had come in, and I'd swapped one flavor of sordid for another. "But yes, photography, intimidation, papers served, or bodyguard work. And I reserve the right to step away from the case if something starts going—"

I stopped. Just for a second, that sudden shift in Abigail's scent had come and gone: the rank scent of adrenaline and terror, like a spatter of blood over her pale scent.

"Do you usually back out of cases?" she asked. Her voice—again calm and controlled as a teacher's—broke into my thoughts. She was good, I thought; she might be scared, but she was used to hiding it.

"I haven't much, lately." It was part of why I was careful about what I took on; obligations wore on me, and I found it very hard to walk away from them.

"Good." She took a fountain pen from her purse and uncapped it. Her nails were bitten to the quick, I saw, and beyond; at the tips of her fingers were little half-moons that barely deserved the term fingernails. It was the only thing out of place on her. "I'll take care of finding out which of the items is the problematic one, and I'll have it to you in a couple of days."

I reached out and slid the contract out from under her hand. "Whoa. I haven't yet said yes, or set terms—"

"Two thousand per day," she said without looking up. "Five thousand more on completion, and a down payment towards that before you begin work in earnest."

Well. That was nice—that was several times my usual rate, and the work itself seemed simple enough that it could have been worthwhile in any case. I wasn't hurting for money at the moment, but I'd been living paycheck to paycheck for so long that having any kind of cushion had its own appeal. "Hang on. How are you going to find out which thing's been stolen?"

Abigail hesitated, then gave me a narrow look. I had to restrain my impulse to sit up straight and present my homework. "Since you're acquainted with this sort of matter," she said, using the same tone of voice as my mother did to describe toilet humor, "I suppose I can tell you. I'll be calling up my great-great-grandmother and asking her directly."

"Whoa." I held up my hands. "Wait a minute."

"Do let me finish. My great-great-grandmother is buried in Mount Auburn Cemetery, at the feet of Isabella Stewart Gardner. She owned the boxes, she knows what's in them, and she should know where they came from. She'll tell me what was stolen, and how to return it."

"But you're a blood relative," I said. "And we're talking necromancy now."

Abigail shook her head. "That's a very New Age term for it. Besides, my belief system precludes meaningful existence after death in the physical world." I tilted my head to the side, and she sighed again. "You might as well describe talking to a portrait as holding a conversation."

"Portraits can't answer back. The dead can."

"Don't split hairs. Like talking to an answering machine, then, or the recorded response on an automatic call. Necromancy would mean actually contacting the spirit, while this is just . . ." She waved one hand dismissively. "Research among old effects."

"Research or not, it's still dangerous for a blood relative to do that kind of work." Magic didn't have many constants—it depended too much on the magician in question, the ritual or heredity or favors involved, and so on—but the one thing that affected pretty much every kind of magic was blood, in both the literal and metaphorical sense. Actual spilled blood would do strange things to a spell, and family ties could enable certain actions, which, since family members were aligned on that level of blood, could be good for some rituals but made possession or other complications a much more likely danger. "Can't someone else do it for you?"

Abigail gave me an affronted look. "I'd rather not bring in anyone else. I'm not happy about this whole situation to begin with, and I'd rather not announce to the world that my great-great-grandmother owned stolen property."

I drummed my fingers on my desk. "I could do it."

She glanced up from the contract. "What?"

"I could do it. I know the basics of a graveyard ceremony, and I'm not a blood relative. It'll be safer for me." *And whatever it is that's scaring you about it, you'll have some breathing room.*

"You're not—" Abigail stared at me, one of her hands twisting against itself as if scrubbing something from the fingers. "You would do that?"

"I—" *Oh, crap.* I could tell this was a bad idea, but I was going to go ahead with it anyway. "Maybe. Or at least I might be able to find a way around it." She gave me a skeptical look. "Boston's undercurrent has been isolated for a while. There might be problems here that you wouldn't run into elsewhere, and maybe some alternate avenues. Ones that wouldn't endanger you. At least let me look into some things first, before you do anything drastic." Looking things up was easy enough. Maybe I could find some way to do this that didn't involve either putting Abigail in certain danger or—as my first instinct had been—putting myself in her place.

Her mouth quirked into a sad smile, but she nodded. "I'll write down what I was planning to do. You can tell me what elements should be cut out." She flipped the contract over and began writing in a careful hand.

"Just give me a day or two. I'm sure we can find something that doesn't involve the dead." I waited till she was done, then countersigned the contract and ran it through the little machine that served as fax and printer and photocopier all in one. As an afterthought, I tucked one of Sarah's flyers at the back of Abigail's copy. What the hell; a slightly sane adept might be a good thing to have at this gathering.

"You don't have to do this," Abigail said again as I handed flyer and contract back to her. "I'm perfectly willing to begin on my own."

"I don't doubt it. But give me one day anyway, all right? You wouldn't have gotten me to start work any earlier either way." I paused. "What was your great-great-grandmother's name?"

"Abigail Huston." Abigail smiled tightly. "Like me."

 Five

I had just enough time to get to Sarah's "community watch" gathering if I hurried. Trouble was, I didn't want to hurry. I didn't particularly want to be there at all. Abigail's plans had left a bad taste in my mouth, even if I could find a way to work around them. I didn't like the idea of jumping in to take the risk on my shoulders, but it was still preferable to letting her do it. And the whole situation, magic and guilt and all, made me that much less enthusiastic about spending my evening with another gaggle of magicians.

But I'd promised Sarah. And I'd as much as promised the same to Woodfin, so that he could get a look at my gun. Even if it meant I had to wear the crappy-ass batik jacket that was the only thing that hid my shoulder holster. I slid gun into holster (unloaded—I was not about to tempt fate that way), holster onto my back (where it sat nicely against the sweaty spot from today's work), and jacket on top of that. I shouldn't have felt like I was wearing a costume, but I did. Everything but the mask.

The office fan thrummed, and the fountain gurgled away at me, happily oblivious. "Fuck it," I said finally, and turned over the stack of books, searching till I'd found the right one. "Sarah can wait," I added, and stuffed a slim volume into my bag. If a side trip could save my sanity, then a side trip it would be.

I can't stand coffee shops. Don't get me wrong: I love coffee, to the point where "love" is probably the wrong word. It's more of a co-dependent relationship; if I leave, I regret it real fast. But I was raised to drink plain coffee, not the stuff with milk and sugar and whipped cream and jimmies on top. If I look at it objectively, I can almost see the point of it, but I'll stick to my road tar, thank you very much.

Sarah says this explains a lot about my aesthetics. I'm pretty sure the last time she said it I told her to cram her aesthetics up her filter.

All this is a lengthy way of saying that it takes a lot to get me through the door of your basic coffee shop. Or at least it used to. These days, it seems like all it takes is Nate.

He was finishing up a tutoring session as I walked in. His student was a young black girl with her hair up in multiple pigtails and an expression of deep concentration, about as different from Chuckles the Angry Undergrad as possible. I waited until she'd closed her brick-thick textbook and left, then went over to Nate's table. "You all set?"

"I'm almost done here," he said without looking up. I waited a minute, and his pen stilled on the page before him as he connected voice and place. He blinked up at me, as if washing away a moment of sleep. "Evie?"

"If you're almost done, then come on." I picked up his bag and headed for the door.

He followed, scrambling for the last of his papers. "Everything all right?"

"Just come on." I took him by the wrist and led him out the door, glaring at the barista just on principle.

Nate didn't protest, and after a moment he caught up to me. I realized a little too late that I was no longer dragging him along and probably should let go of his arm, but by that point I'd been holding on long enough that releasing him would have been obvious and silly.

I led him around a corner and into one of the little half-block parks that don't show up on most Boston maps, that thrive or wither depending on who the neighbors are. I'd locked up my bike here, and I let go of Nate's hand to dig a book out of my saddlebag. "Okay," I said, flourishing the book at him. "Sigmund. Volsung saga, loads of other sagas, gets picked up by Wagner later on. Boinks his sister, sneaks off with their son, runs around with him in the forest for a while, gets turned into a wolf for a bit, then does something stupid and ends up killing the kid. In Wagner's version he doesn't even make it through the second opera before Siegfried the Idiot takes over. There's a few other Sigmunds, but Sarah's the go-to person for those kinds of myths. You want to talk to her."

I handed him the book—not *Dictionary of Myth*, but one of the little ones that Sarah had foisted on me. Nate reached out and took it, looking from me to the book and back. "That's what you wanted me for?"

No, I thought. *I wanted you to remind me that I'm human and capable of making good decisions. I wanted to make sure you're all right. I wanted to see you.* But if I said, "I needed to talk to you," it would sound as if there was something life-threatening at stake instead of just my own mental state. Or at the very least I'd sound desperate.

"Mostly," I said.

"Huh." He gave me a sharp look, then opened the book and flipped through it. An old man with five pugs on their leashes, all snorting and panting, shuffled past, and Nate stepped out of their way, just a bit closer to me. He hadn't shaved that morning, I noticed, and the last August sun picked out the gleam in the scruff along the line of his jaw. Absently, he licked his finger to turn the page.

I looked away, silently blessing my summer's worth of sunburn. "So," I said, and cleared my throat.

"Hm?" Red and blue ink streaked the middle finger of his hand. *He's left-handed*, I thought, trying to concentrate on that irrelevancy in the face of the full-scale revolt my body was trying to pull on me. My cell rang, and I slapped at it, switching it off.

The book, I told myself. *I just came out here to give him the book.* "So. Sigmund. Why did you want to know?"

A cloud descended over his expression, and he closed the book. For a moment he gazed at the cover, not really seeing anything, then shook his head. "Hell," he said. "I got a letter—well, a lot of letters, over the past couple of weeks. From my father."

I nodded, still gazing at his hands, then blinked. "Wait. What?"

Nate laughed without smiling. "That's what *I* thought."

I didn't know much about Nate's father, other than he got Nate's mom pregnant when she was seventeen and promptly skipped town. Nate didn't talk about him, hadn't ever since I knew him. Because I'd also had an estranged dad, I knew how easy it was to create an imaginary father, one who was sympathetic and smart and very cool regardless of what you remembered of him in reality, who would always take your side in whatever argument you and your mom were having at the moment, and so on.

But those ideas fall away early, and from Nate's expression, his illusions had dissolved a long time ago. "Jesus." I shook myself, forcing away the disturbing awareness of his body. "What happened?"

Nate shrugged. "I don't know. Nothing. He just started writing me letters. Not really harassing me, just writing, a lot. After what happened the . . . the first time I met him, I figured he wouldn't want to cross paths again, but in the last few weeks I've been getting a lot of mail from him. And he keeps referring to something about 'Sigmund,' like I'm supposed to know what it means." He rubbed at the corners of his eyes, then glanced at me, trying to smile. "Somehow I don't think the Volsungs play into it."

I drew a deep breath and let it out. There were a lot of things I could say to him, and so many of them were the wrong thing to say. And none of this was made any easier by the sudden reminder that I hadn't gotten further than second base in, oh, at least a year. Romance is for people with clear calendars.

"So does this make you Siegfried?" I finally asked. "Because I always thought he was a colossal prick, and you don't seem the type."

Nate smiled, and I knew I'd said the right thing, or at least not a horribly wrong one. "I hope not."

"Yeah, well, if the Rhinemaidens start coming up out of the Charles, I'm blaming you first." That won me another smile. "I'm not in touch with my father," I said after a moment. "I mean, we know where we stand, and I figure if something big happened he'd contact me. But we haven't really spoken since he called to apologize, a few years after Mom's death." Nate glanced at me, and I managed a smile. "Yeah. Shitty timing. But it still mattered that he got in touch that one time. Maybe it might be worth it for you to talk to your father. Even if it's just this once."

Nate didn't answer. I thought about Abigail, about what she'd planned to do just to escape her own nightmares, about what I had offered to do in her place. And briefly, why I'd come out here, or the reason I'd told myself I had to see Nate. "Is that why you asked me?" I said after a moment. "Because I'm estranged from my father too?"

He shook his head. "I'm telling you because I can't tell anyone else."

Blame it on the hormones. Blame it on the way he'd looked at the Red Sox game, getting rained on and still yelling his heart out in perfect unison with me, blame it on my own issues. Whatever the reason, I reached out and touched him on the shoulder—nothing much,

I told myself, just the sort of thing one friend would do for another.

His body stilled under my touch, and he reached up to cover my hand with his own, relaxing for just a second. Then a shudder passed through him, and as quickly as he'd moved to yank Katie out of traffic, he stepped closer, close enough that even in the warm air I could feel the heat of his skin. I caught my breath, momentarily unable to hear anything over the blood rushing in my ears. For a moment I forgot this was Nate, forgot that we were friends, that it had always and only been friendship between us.

And then whatever damnable self-preservation instinct or Catholic guilt or whatever you wanted to call it spoke up in the back of my head: *the last man that made you feel like this tried to turn you into a thrall of the Fiana.*

The thought dropped like a seed crystal into my mind, and I froze up. Nate sensed it, and with all the finality of a lock snapping shut, his scent changed, shutting him off behind that wall of iron. He let go of me and stepped back like a cat springing away from a firecracker. "Sorry. Um. I should go," he said, not looking at me. "My advisor wanted a revised chapter by the end of the week—"

"Yeah." I cleared my throat, trying to shake the buzzing from my ears. "Yeah, I have, um, a meeting to get to."

He moved so that he stood with his back to the sun, and even in the low raking light, his face was hidden in shadow. So I couldn't see the look in his gray eyes, only imagine it, only remember that weird shift in him that I'd seen on the banks of the Charles, that I had seen under Fenway when he lost control before. I hadn't seen it this time, but I'd felt it—and I didn't yet know what I thought of it. "I'll. I'll see you."

Without another word, he turned and headed back the way we'd come. I sank onto the closest bench, my legs feeling like they had turned to rubber. *Not now,* I told myself, *not now, not you, not Nate. He doesn't deserve the kind of crap you could give him.*

If I'd wanted an example of what the undercurrent can do to ostensibly sane people, I wouldn't have to look much further than the cluster of people down at the far end of Outlook Park. I'd taken the T down—no point in biking, not if I was going to have to hold my jacket shut the whole way—and climbed up one of the footpaths to the top of the hill, winding my way between the Brookline townhouses. Someone was having a cookout; charcoal and hamburger scent wafted past on the evening air. I was the only one who seemed to notice.

"It's like watching an elementary-school play implode," Sarah muttered to me. She nodded to the magician currently in the center of the circle, who, in his attempt to explain the need for a unity of purpose among Boston adepts, had invoked the Templars and the Anasazi burial rites, and was now on the verge of a full-blown tangent about fluoridation. "You keep expecting the teacher to come out and nudge him off the stage."

"So why the hell did you let him talk?" I glanced at the gathering of maybe thirty people, more than I had expected but less than Sarah had hoped for. A few of the scattered adepts (and charlatans, and practitioners, and even one or two really low-tier shadowcatchers) looked away as soon as I turned. I tugged at my jacket, trying to hide the telltale bulge of my gun.

"Because this is a communal effort, and we can't just shunt aside the part of our community that doesn't follow the same Western logic as the dominant culture." Sarah nodded toward the far end of the circle. "And he's got influence among a few of the Oak Square neo-chiromancers."

"Sarah, just because there's a significant wacko contingent in the undercurrent doesn't mean you need to have wacko representation."

She didn't hear me. "Goddess wept, he's starting in on the Grail crap . . . That's it. I gotta go be the grown-up." She hopped off the rock she'd been sitting on, dusted off her butt, and swept to the center of the circle. I glanced at the other adepts as she put a hand on the poor man's shoulder and kindly steered him out of the way. Some of them were still listening; most of them had moved into the perpetual cat game of watch-me-watch-you that came so naturally to magicians of any stripe.

So far, Sarah had made her point in a number of different ways, most of which would have at least made a dent or provoked some kind of debate among normal people. But there hadn't been any debate. There hadn't been any argument. There had just been a group of magicians eyeing each other, listening politely, and ignoring what was said. Both of the men who'd come to see me the night before were there, and both looked a bit repentant when they saw me. I'd looked for Abigail, but she'd found something else to do, and frankly, I was glad she wasn't here.

Sarah, for her part, could handle any amount of embarrassment without even blinking. Better, she wasn't a magician, and under her cynical shell she was a squishy optimist. That was part of why I wasn't too worried about her: if this crashed and burned, she'd find something else to renew her hope in humanity.

As for me . . . every time I turned my head, I caught a glimpse of someone else looking away. Too many people were watching me, and I was starting to sweat. I didn't like being the focus of attention, especially not when I was carrying a weapon—I cursed Woodfin again for asking me to meet him here, and cursed myself for not protesting more. And as for the meeting itself, even though getting these adepts together at all was an accomplishment, I was starting to lose hope in Sarah's vision.

By now, Sarah was in the midst of a very cogent plea for some sort of internal policing within Boston's undercurrent. I hunched over a little, gazing out across the slope of the park. Headlights limned the trees far to my left, and the sound of a car motor valiantly chugging up the hill followed them. I stretched a little, fumbled my jacket back into place, then froze as the headlights paused and someone played a merry staccato on the horn.

Far from scattering as I expected—hell, as I'd done in the past when someone drove up to a party that wasn't exactly legal—the adepts merely glanced over their shoulders, if that, and kept talking. Sarah nodded to me, and I muttered a curse under my breath. *Sure, send the sane person to deal with the cops.*

Only it wasn't the cops. It wasn't even a curious local. As I reached the sidewalk, a man emerged from a tiny car and waved. "Glad I caught you!" Reverend Woodfin called, his voice carrying probably all the way to Worcester. "Sorry I'm late—I tried to drive up here on my own, but the old boat wouldn't take the hill, and I had to go back to borrow Elizabeth's car. You brought it?"

"Quiet. Yes, I brought it." I slid the jacket off, wincing from the stickiness of it, and loosed my gun from its holster. "Can we make this quick? I'm not exactly comfortable with doing this out in public."

"Oh, very nice." Woodfin took up the gun and sighted down its barrel. "Yes, this is Yuen's work."

"Jesus," I said, then stopped as he glared at me. "You could maybe be a little more careful about waving it around."

"No one's looking." Woodfin laid the gun on a picnic table.

It gave me the cold shivers to see it there, not twenty feet from the playground. "Yeah, well, that's not the point—"

"Pewter," Woodfin announced. His hands moved over the gun with practiced ease, disassembling it as quickly as if it were made of Legos, despite the dim light. "With just a flake of gold leaf . . . witch hazel? No, ginseng . . ." He stopped, peering into the innards of the gun, then regarded me a moment. I did my best to return his gaze without flinching. "You haven't been taking care of this," he said finally.

"Not really," I admitted. The gun itself was perfectly legal, and I had the permits to prove it, but the ammunition was something else: Yuen's own design, of the kind that might not kill everything I'd run into in the undercurrent but would at the very least slow it down. The gun itself didn't work so well with normal bullets anymore, but then, I had no plans to use it in normal situations.

I glanced over my shoulder just in time to see one of the weedier adepts—the kind who could only aspire to Deke's level—wander over to the water fountain and fill a plastic bottle. His eyes widened as he took in the gun and my shoulder holster, and he practically skipped back across the street in his desire to get away. I sighed and tried to block any more inadvertent glimpses of Woodfin's work.

Woodfin finally snapped the gun back together and handed it to me by the barrel. "Put that away, and if it's in bad condition in a year, you'll have only yourself to blame."

I slid the damn thing back into its holster and secured it. "Thanks."

Woodfin waved over his shoulder as he walked back to Elizabeth's little car. "Give me a couple of days, and I'll have a clip to you."

I watched him drive off, then stood by the tree at the top of the hill for a little while. A matron walking her puppy—no, it was a cat, and it practically dragged her across the road to get away from me—passed by, followed by a tired young man in Orthodox black. I shifted in place, trying to find a way that the gun didn't hang heavily on me, then remembered my cell. Hadn't someone called, earlier?

I pulled it out and checked it. Yes, and whoever had called had left a message. Still gazing down the hill, I dialed voice mail and waited.

Rena's voice came over the line, scratchy and distracted by the office noise behind her. "Evie, it's Rena. I'm still working—yes, hang on a moment, I'll be there—" She paused, muffling the phone and talking to someone else. I smiled. "Yeah, still working on the case. But I wanted to tell you that Sun City Grill is doing their Kamikaze Karaoke night in a couple weeks. If I'm not done with this case by then, I'll eat my badge—Shut up, Foster! I will too!—So what do you say? I know you can't get enough of me embarrassing myself."

"In a manner of speaking," I murmured. Of the two of us, Rena was the one who really loved karaoke, but she'd only admit it after a couple beers. If I could just keep her from the Bonnie Tyler section of the song list, we'd be fine.

"So yeah, two weeks, Sun City." She was almost laughing as she said it, and I could hear the relief in her voice at the thought of this light at the end of the tunnel. "We are on, girl!"

"We are on," I repeated, and saved the message. I'd call her back later and confirm it. That would be something to look forward to after all this. I gazed down the hill at the gathered magicians and shook my head at what they were missing.

Sarah's voice, raised in argument, drifted up from the hill. "—doesn't matter if no one else—"

Christ. I tugged my jacket shut again, then leaned against the tree.

"That's a bit pathetic."

I opened my eyes to see a blond young man in a double-breasted gray suit standing next to me with his hands clasped behind his back. He looked—well, there was only one word for it, and that was out of date: he looked dapper. Aware of my scrutiny, he tilted his head to the side, as if I were a particularly difficult work of art that needed studying. "Is there a problem?" I said.

He smiled briefly, as if I'd made an appropriate but not particularly funny joke. "Not really. Not for me." He nodded to the circle—no longer a circle, I noted, not now that it was starting to break up into hushed and vicious conversations. "Maybe for them."

"You're here for the meeting?" He shouldn't have been able to sneak up on me like that, I thought; usually I have some vague idea of scent, even if I can't quite verbalize it. But his scent seemed almost blank. Not in quite the same way Abigail's had been; instead of effacing itself it just receded, lightly touched with fireworks, as if magic was something he'd given up a long time ago. Only he looked no more than eighteen, so he'd have had to give it up at ten . . .

"Oh yes, I heard about it." He smiled. "Not my sort of thing."

Well, I didn't see that it was anybody's thing, the way it was going. But that was another matter.

"What's your name?" he asked.

Direct, for a magician. "Scelan," I said. "Genevieve Scelan. Hound. You?"

A flicker ran over his face, shivering over his scent. There *was* a trace of real scent to him, I realized; it just faded into the background. "My mother named me Patrick."

That wasn't quite as evasive as I was used to. I nodded, a little mollified.

He turned and, with a somewhat mechanical grace, imitated my posture against the tree, so that we were now standing side by side. "Do you mind the company?" At my shrug, he smiled again, almost regretfully. "It's not going to work."

"Sorry?"

"This . . . the magic, the group. It's not going to work." He tipped his head back, eyes half lidded, serene as a Zen master. "You know that too, don't you."

It wasn't a question. I shrugged again, a little needled that he'd put my own thoughts into words. "It might."

"No. The thing is . . . magic ought to be respected. Not some debased thing, something that can be bartered and squandered and . . . stolen." The last word seemed to catch in his teeth, momentarily spoiling his calm. "It's a matter of respect."

I thought of how the Fiana had taken a goddess and turned her into a decrepit old woman, how they had treated beings that ought to have inspired loyalty as if they were no more than servants. "If you say so," I finally said, since he seemed to expect a response.

"I do." He closed his eyes. He had very long eyelashes, just a few shades darker than his yellow hair. "Could you respect that down there? Any one of those chattering idiots?"

"A few." Sarah, yes. Maybe Deke, in some circumstances. But the rest . . . hell, the sanest adept I knew spent most of the day facedown in gravel, convinced that she was all that held together the New Madrid fault line.

Patrick didn't acknowledge the lie, though it sounded pretty transparent. "I think, perhaps, it might have been better back then."

"Back when?"

"Back when people were scared. When they knew that there were things in this world no one could understand, and as a result, things that had to be respected." He opened his eyes and met my expression with a confident smile. "Do you see what I mean?"

Yes. "No," I said. "Not really. I don't think it was ever like that, good old days notwithstanding."

Patrick tilted his head to the side, that white-noise scent of him fading a little, as if he no longer cared enough to keep his presence here. "If you say so." He stood upright, nodded to me, and strode off down the hill.

I watched him leave. He was attractive, he seemed

sane, if a bit arrogant. Why couldn't I be attracted to men like him instead of Nate? Even if that made me a cradle robber. At least I'd have some idea of what kind of crap a magician might pull on me. Or, if that didn't work, why couldn't I just swear off the whole matter entirely?

Maybe I was just picking up on the general air of frustration on the hill tonight. The magicians' circle was finally breaking up, this time with epithets tossed back and forth despite Sarah's attempts to smooth things over. I headed down the hill and met her by the rocks as the last few adepts wandered off. "Well," she said as I reached her. "I think we're making progress."

"You're kidding me, right?"

Sarah gave me one of her I-am-in-touch-with-my-inner-serenity-and-yet-you-still-persist-in-being-stupid looks. "That was a lot more than I expected. They're talking at least, and no one accused anyone else of stealing loci or using the meeting for nefarious ends." She sat down, then lay back to look at the sky and its ropes of cloud drifting across the stars. "I call that progress."

I shook my head and joined her. The rock was warmer than it should have been; perhaps it'd kept the sun's heat longer than the dirt. Or perhaps Deke had been fiddling with pyromancy again. "I suppose it helps to set the bar that low."

"I'm just being realistic, Evie. Like you."

For a moment we were silent. I thought about Nate, and about the cold weight of the gun against my shoulder, and about the dead. "Sarah," I said finally. "Remember when we started to get caught up with—with what ended up being the Fiana?"

She raised a hand and flexed the fingers, one by one. "I'm not likely to forget."

"When that started, I thought I was helping someone . . . Sarah, what if I want to help someone, but it's likely to put me in danger?"

She rolled over so that she lay on her side. "Evie, I

know you. You'll do it anyway, and you'll do it even if I tell you not to."

"I might not." Right now, I wanted to stay out of it, maybe tell Abigail that I'd find a way around it that didn't involve the dead.

Sarah made a *pfft* noise. "And I might say I'll swear off sex, but that's not gonna happen either." She lay back. "Just promise me you won't do something dumb without letting me tell you how to do it."

Well, that was probably the biggest endorsement I was going to get. "I need to know how to call up the dead," I said.

Sarah sat bolt upright. "You *what*?"

I grinned at her. "Told you."

 Six

a draining, heavy heat lay over Boston the next day, and my schedule only got worse. Tania sent me out to Mission Hill twice, the second time because some idiot had forgotten a document for the first packet. I nearly got hit by a van on my way down the hill the second time, I'd only had time for half a sandwich at lunch, and I still had to deal with the whole Abigail problem. Jumping into this sort of ritual cold was one of the most dangerous things I could do, and I wouldn't even have considered it if not for the fact that it was even more dangerous for someone else.

At last I decided to bother the one person I knew who'd had dealings with the dead lately. I coasted into Chinatown, past the great red gate, and locked up my bike on the sidewalk. The heat had intensified the scents of frying food and spices, and I lost myself in the haze of it for a moment before shaking myself out of the trance. If I wasn't careful, I'd end up drooling.

Technically, I was still on shift, but I'd managed to switch out with one of the other couriers. I'd done him a favor a little while back (advice: if you're carrying packets of confidential documents across town, don't stop for a drink). As long as Tania didn't ask "me" to come in to the office, no one would know the difference.

Unfortunately, the Three Cranes was closed up tight, and the windows of the apartment above were dark. I muttered a curse as I reached the basement door and confirmed that yes, there was a CLOSED sign taped over it. I started to turn away, then stopped, hearing the faint thump of music through the wall.

I'd never heard music here before, but that wasn't any indication that it was forbidden, and, after all, Elizabeth ran the place now, so she could play anything she liked, right? Only she didn't strike me as the kind of person to listen to continuous soft rock. Or to have it cranked up to ear-bleeding levels.

I glanced over my shoulder. The only thing unusual in the street was a black Jeep Cherokee parked with its nose up against a fire hydrant. Unusual, but . . . I was rationalizing. I sidled up against the door to the shop.

Even through the wall, I could get some sense of what was inside just by scent, the same way that I'd been able to tell what was inside Yuen's father's jar. Spices and old silk, a strong medicinal reek—

I caught my breath and had to stifle a coughing fit. Yes, that was a smell native to the Three Cranes; it was the preserving solution for some of the weird stuff on the back shelves. But I'd only smelled it before when the jars had been opened, and never in this quantity.

The CLOSED sign had covered the top part of the lock, but it slid aside as I touched it, revealing the remnants of a padlock still hanging in place. The lock itself had been kicked to the side, into a pile of detritus where it looked so at home that I hadn't noticed it before. Right. I eased my way inside, dragging the door back into place behind me.

The stink of preservation fluids intensified, followed by the high crunch of breaking glass. Something from a rack by the door brushed against my hand, and I picked it up—one of those bamboo parasols, the kind that lasts maybe a day. It wasn't much, I thought as I took out my cell phone and switched the parasol to my other hand, but it'd do. And it was a lot better than having my gun out. I didn't want to bring that into an unknown situation.

No smell of magic. That at least was something.

I flattened myself along the wall. The back entrance to Yuen's condo was shut and locked, and to my surprise someone had jammed a chair under the doorknob as if to barricade it, so that no one could wander from the apartment into the store. Whoever had done it had used a folding chair, so they weren't as good at this as it seemed. Down the hall was the Three Cranes proper, and that's where the scent came from.

I sidled along the wall until I was close enough to the entrance to see the first rack of boxes. Not everything had been packed up; a few jars of mushrooms, crammed in so they looked like grisly trophies, lined the top rack. I closed my eyes and inhaled, but there was too much scent here, and no sense to it. More than one person, probably, and while there wasn't any of the acrid adrenaline of fear, the grubby, old corn-chip smell of the intruders made me grimace.

Another jar crunched to the floor, this one releasing a stink of preserved ginger. "Fuck it," a man's voice said. "Let's go."

"Quit worrying," said another. "The place is closed, right? I say we get the pages too. That's an extra two hundred apiece, in case you're forgetting."

"Fuck two hundred," the first muttered, but not heatedly. I crouched and peered out.

Two young men—kids, really, barely out of their teens—stood on either side of the counter, one carrying a bulging bag, the other fidgeting with a utility knife. Both were in black T-shirts turned inside out; neither looked particularly bright, even for thugs. A third had his back to them, standing at the furthest rack, and he was meticulously opening jar after jar, setting each one aside after he looked inside. It would almost have been funny if not for the fourth person in the room: Elizabeth, masking tape over her mouth, tied to a chair with clothesline. She didn't look scared;

she looked angry—no, not even that. Irritated. Annoyed that these three cretins had interrupted her day.

The third thug opened another jar, then sneezed. Black pepper; I pressed my arm against my face to stave off a similar reaction. "What the fuck are you doing?" asked the first guy, the one in a hurry.

"Could be anywhere," the third guy said. "Rolled up in one of these things, maybe."

"God, we're gonna be here for-fucking-ever," moaned the first guy.

Elizabeth rolled her eyes. I agreed.

"Then we'll speed it up." The second guy, who if beard scruff was anything to go by was the oldest, nodded to Elizabeth. "She's gotta know where it is."

The first guy's expression went from frustration to shamed glee. I rose to my feet and shifted my grip on the parasol, just as the third guy opened another jar—not a spice this time, but preserved fish of some kind. I gagged, not quietly enough.

The second thug—I could just see him between the boxes, so long as he didn't move too much—glanced over his shoulder. "Go check that out," he said.

"I didn't hear anything," whined the first guy, but he slid out his knife and headed my way.

There had been a time not too long ago when I'd had the advantage in a hand-to-hand fight. Of course, then I'd had a battle goddess riding me, a goddess whose skill and ruthlessness had coursed through me like molten lead. Not only was she no longer with me, but now if I tried to remember how I'd fought then, the memory of what had happened after sickened me. Now all I had was the skill that I'd learned from having a lousy temper, just bar-brawl tactics.

Well, that and a parasol. I slid my grip back, loosening it just a bit, and waited for the thug to get closer.

He wasn't nearly as observant as his buddies. "I told you I didn't hear—" he whined as he reached my aisle, and I whacked him in the throat. He reeled back, breath wheezing through his mangled larynx, and

I struck him on the wrist, knocking the knife down among the boxes.

A faint frisson ran down my back, a memory perhaps of the Morrigan's possession or perhaps just my own canine nature rising up. I bared my teeth in a grin and hit him a third time, this time in the crotch. He went down with a whimper, and I stepped to one side, careful not to turn my back on him.

The two remaining thugs stared at me, and I raised my phone. "I've got nine-one-one dialed and ready to go," I said. "Move and I'll have the cops here on you before you can think. I got your license number—" *yeah, license plate, that would have been a smart thing to notice back there,* "—and now I want your names." The guy on the floor whimpered again, and I edged further away from him. "Drop your weapons and put your hands behind your heads."

The bearded guy, the halfway competent one, eyed me with an air of calculation, and I noticed a little too late that his own knife was out and close to Elizabeth's throat. (Elizabeth, for her part, looked even more annoyed with me. I could almost hear her thinking, *One more damn thing to worry about.*)

Things might have gone all to hell if the third thug, the methodical one, hadn't been in such a hurry to comply with my orders that he dropped the jar he was holding. Camphor spilled out from the broken jar in a glutinous wave, and the scent of it hit me like a pickax between the eyes. I bent double, gagging. "Run!" yelled the thug I'd hit. I tried to stand up and shake off the sensory overload, but the second guy whacked me on the back of my head with his bag as he ran past, and I lurched forward, banging my knees on the concrete floor. Gray sparked across my sight. To top it off, the last guy out knocked over one more jar as he ran— pickled cabbage—throwing another sucker punch at my already vulnerable nose.

I staggered to my feet and ran after them, but didn't make it halfway down the hall before I heard the Jeep start up and drive off. Bastards. As I paused, fuming, Elizabeth yelled at me through her tape.

She had it nearly off by the time I stumbled back into the room. "Give me a hand here, Hound," she said through the last of the tape, pushing it off with her tongue. "Get the ropes."

I tried to respond, gagged on the camphor scent again, and stumbled around to the back of the chair. Crappy knot tiers, all of them; the Boy Scouts would have thrown them out for this (well, after throwing them out for all the other reasons first). "Sorry," I said as I tugged the last knot free. "That turned out to be a pretty lousy rescue."

Elizabeth shook her head, dislodging the last bit of tape. "I can't believe you threatened them with the police. Do you know how laughable that is?" She rubbed the red spots at the corners of her mouth. "My father said you were something of an innocent, but he didn't say you were an idiot."

My head throbbed. "Maybe because I'm not," I snapped. "Look, what was I supposed to do? Walk away from a break-in? I thought I could help, and yeah, they got away, but we both saw them. You can give a description to the police—"

Elizabeth got up from the chair, dusting off her skirt. "They broke in," she said as if explaining to a child, "on the orders of someone who, I would guess, doesn't answer to the police. How many magicians do you know who'd even bother to provide an alibi instead of just warding off their work?"

I was silent a moment. *Shit.* "You're sure?"

"Don't question me on this, Hound. Okay?" She picked up the tape and wadded it up, sighing as she scanned the mess the thugs had made. "I know what they were looking for, and only magicians would bother with it. God, I just packed up half of this stuff; I can't believe I've got to go through that again . . ." She turned and saw my expression, and her own softened a little. "I'm all right, Hound. This is just the sort of thing that's been going on lately."

"Lately?" The word stuck in my throat.

"Yes. Lately." She bent to pick up the clothesline, wound it into a loose coil, and dropped it on the counter. "I know you think you did a good thing. I'd even agree with my father that, on balance, getting rid of the Bright Brotherhood was probably good for everyone in the long run. But we knew where we stood with them, even if that meant we were at the bottom of the heap."

"But that can't—You can't possibly prefer that."

"Did I say we did? But now there's no solid ground. New talent comes in, they don't know or care what the deal is or who's got arrangements with whom, and they figure the best thing to do is jump in feetfirst." She circled the counter and pulled open a drawer, then snapped her fingers and brought out a box instead. "I'm surprised no one's tried to take you out yet," she added as she stowed away the rope that had been used to bind her. "Maybe they think it's better to stay on your good side for now."

I was silent a long moment. The clamoring scents in my head didn't do much for my clarity of thought, but overall the main thing that came through was that I'd fucked up again. "I didn't know."

"I kind of thought you didn't." She wiped dust off her hands, wrinkling her nose at the camphor scent. It wasn't pleasant for her, but she at least could ignore it. "But that doesn't change it. I'm sorry, Hound. And for what it's worth, thanks. Those lumps weren't magicians, but that could have gotten unpleasant."

"You're welcome." I leaned against the counter and pressed my hands against my head.

Elizabeth watched me a moment in cold sympathy, then shook her head and began rummaging behind the counter. "Now. What did you come here for? I'm assuming you weren't with them, and I very much doubt you'd orchestrate such a clumsy scene just to win my friendship."

I snorted, then giggled weakly. I couldn't help it; the idea of stage-managing a debacle like that poked the raw spot over my funny bone. "Oh, God help me if I did . . . No, I wanted to ask about . . . it doesn't matter." I paused, thinking back over the conversation. "Hang on. How did you know what they wanted?"

She smiled. "They wouldn't shut up. Didn't say who'd hired them, but I do know such wonderful things as how the tall one got herpes from his girl-friend." She bent down and hoisted a picture over the counter: the Wild West photo that had been in her fa-ther's office. "I moved this down here because the rev-erend wanted a look. Those idiots never knew that the pages from the Unbound Book had been so close to them."

I glanced at her, then down at the picture. "They wanted the pages from the back of this. The ones you burned."

She nodded. "More reason not to regret what I did."

Something about the casual way she said it made me think it wasn't simple as that. I thought of Abigail and the nightmares that had told her she now owned stolen property, and touched the glass gently.

Elizabeth glanced at me again, then tapped the photo. "Notice anything?"

I followed her gesture. On a second glance, the photo wasn't an average Wild West group: two of the men wore bowler hats and clothing more suited to New York City, completely out of place, and the youngest man on the end had Asian features. Yuen had spoken of his father while looking at the picture. "A relative?"

"Great-uncle. My grandfather's elder by ten years." The picture showed a very young man, stuck in among men in their thirties, with the exception of one very polished man with white hair. "He had the sense not to do what my grandfather did."

She was silent again. I glanced at the other men—
and one woman, I finally noticed, though she had
faded into the background so much that there might
have been an aversion ward on the photograph. She
stood behind the man with the impressive mustache,
possessively close to him, and her dark features and
the feather knotted into her hair marked her as more
of a native than any of the men. There was something
vaguely familiar about not just her, an element of her
stillness maybe, but also about the man she was with.
Maybe without the mustache . . .

Elizabeth turned the photo over to show the blank,
unfaded spots on the back and the rusting staples that
had held the two sought-after pages. "They couldn't
get the pages, and they taped my mouth before I could
tell them I'd burned the foul things. But they were
partly successful." She turned the photo around again,
this time so that she could examine it, and a sad smile
flickered around her lips. "They stole the jar that once
held my grandfather."

Seven

I got maybe ten paces out of the Three Cranes before noticing the guy on the corner. He wasn't one of the three idiots who'd robbed the place; he was older, maybe in his fifties, and lacking the rough-edged incompetence that had been their greatest strength. He wore a black suit, more than a little at odds with his sunburned skin, and the lazy carelessness in how he leaned against a bus sign seemed to imply that he'd be much more at home in a smoky room with a drink to hand.

It's an easy trick to tell when you're being watched; anyone can do it, and we do, regularly. The trouble is telling who's watching you. I had something of an advantage in that regard, but even so, I couldn't quite tell where this guy's heavily hooded eyes were looking. All I had was that prickle on the back of my neck.

After a day like today, though, that was enough. I tracked the man back to his aging sports car, then followed him out of Chinatown and into the vast wasteland of parking lots on the far side of Fort Point Channel, and that's where I lost him. It wasn't entirely my fault; traffic had thinned out to the point where I couldn't keep up by weaving through the jams, and every third car in these lots was too similar to the one I'd followed. I slowed as I passed the courthouse, angling between rows of parked cars.

Which was when someone entirely new came out from behind an SUV with a baseball bat. I yelled and twisted out of the way, but there are some maneuvers that aren't safe on gravel-choked pavement, and that's one of them. The bike went down and I went with it, scraping my left leg all to hell. My cleats caught in the pedal again, and I dragged my other foot out of the way, digging a divot out of my shin.

"Shit!" I rolled away from the bike, then rolled again, this time away from the guy with the bat, who didn't seem to hold to the principle of helping up a fallen opponent. His stained shirt read YANKEES SUCK in flaking letters, a sentiment that I'd normally agree with if the owner weren't trying to bash my head in. The bat hit the ground between me and the bike, splintering a little, and at the back of my brain the uninvolved, gibbering part of me got pissed off that he was ruining a good baseball bat.

I finally found my footing and managed to block the next hit by catching the bat with both hands as he raised it, before he could put any weight behind the swing. "What the fuck are you doing?" I snarled, some stupid instinct telling me to keep my voice down.

Yankees Suck managed a shrug—I'm not sure how he managed it while trying to wrest the bat back from me, but the meaning came across. "Just a job."

"Just a—"

The perky chime of a cell phone interrupted me. Yankees Suck immediately reached back with one hand. "Yeah," he answered, paying no attention to my utter bewilderment. "Yeah, she's here. It's for you." He held out the phone to me.

There was only so much bizarro-world I could take in a day, and this was rapidly approaching my limit. I yanked the bat away from him, then took the phone, backing away as I did so. "Yeah?"

"Sorry, Hound," said a man's voice. "Wanted to see how you react in a crisis."

My mom always said that if I left my mouth open,

flies would get in, and it's a wonder I didn't get a mouthful right then. Plus, my leg was starting to throb from the skinning I'd given it. "What the hell are you talking about?"

"Over to the left. Sorry, my left, your right." I glanced off to the right (Yankees Suck didn't move; in fact, he seemed·to have lost interest completely) and saw the man in black standing on the other side of the chain fence that separated parking lot from sidewalk. He waved, and I started to wave back before realizing that I still held the bat. "Can we talk?"

"Can I have my phone back now?" Yankees Suck said.

"Jesus Christ on a three-legged mule," I muttered, and clicked the phone shut. Yankees Suck took it out of my hand, but when I—out of whatever shock-induced courtesy—held up the bat, just shook his head. Yeah, I didn't want it either. I dragged my bike upright, checking to make sure it hadn't suffered any damage (it hadn't; I'd taken the worst of it), and glanced at the man in black.

What the fuck. Why not? If I didn't, he'd pull something like this again. At least this way I could tell him to go away. I took a deep breath to shake the worst of the adrenaline away (it didn't work; I'd still have the shakes pretty soon), and nodded.

The man waited till we'd reached a gap in the fence, then handed Yankees Suck a wad of bills, and Yankees Suck walked off counting them. I eyed him as he passed, but he paid me no attention. The new guy, though . . . despite his Johnny Cash aesthetic, the clothes didn't look quite right for him. He wasn't bad-looking, though, in that older-man kind of way, and the smile he turned on me was pure charm. "I've got something for your leg, if you need it. Sorry about that; I asked him to scare you, not outright attack."

I shook my head. Faced with this blasé response, I didn't think shouting would do much good. "However much you paid him, it's not enough." I pointed over my shoulder. "You see that big brick building? That's a federal courthouse. You want to know what assault on federal property works out to?"

He grinned and pushed away from the fence. Something about the movement seemed familiar; I'd seen that simple grace before, in someone else. "I don't see anyone riding to your rescue."

Okay, so he had a point.

He waited until I crossed the gate to the sidewalk, then ambled over to me. He had white-blond hair and a nasty sunburn, or else he was just so pale that blood showed up too easily; I felt a faint twinge of sympathy and rubbed at the dark spots on my hands—tan now, but reminders of the burn I'd had at the beginning of the summer. "You're a hard woman to get hold of," he said. "Got a few minutes?"

"You could have just left a message."

"Okay, okay, you're a busy woman, I understand that." He raised both hands. "Ten minutes. That's all."

After a stunt like that, I'd normally have been inclined to say fuck off, but at that moment I realized why he seemed so out of place in the city. It was his smell. It wasn't that he smelled wrong—few people do, when you get down to it—but something about it just . . . got to me. There was an element of musk to it, and sweat, and hair, and combined with the aftershave he was wearing (one of the cheap brands that passed for expensive) it gave me the feeling that he was wearing a mask of some kind, hiding something a bit more animal than the smiling face before me.

Nothing against animals—by some standards, I was one, and my scent had its own mark of wet dog on certain days—but somehow this one went straight to my hindbrain and twaddled everything there, mixing up flight responses with confusion and an odd fascination. *Just till I figure this out*, I told myself. *Just for ten minutes.*

"Karl Janssen," he said, holding out one red and callused hand.

I didn't shake it just yet. Instead I looked him up and down, then unclipped my helmet and shook my hair out. Ever since my involuntary haircut, I'd had to get used to the lack of a braid down my back, and for some reason it made me feel naked. "Not here," I said. "If we're going to talk, let's not do it right out here on the street."

Janssen grinned. The man was like a damn jack-in-the-box. "Anywhere's fine. Dinner, maybe, or I can buy you a drink."

It should have come off as sleazier than it did; this man was old enough to be my father. But there was an edge of charisma to it, long blunted, that weird kind of allure that makes you feel like you're the center of the universe. "This way," I said finally, and turned toward the channel.

I led him down under the bridge to the boardwalk that runs between the Children's Museum and the Barking Crab. Our feet thudded over the boards, echoing off the low bridge above. Someone had stashed a blanket in one of the niches, and a seagull had found it, jabbing at it in case there was food. It flew away as we approached, crying an idiot lament.

I paused halfway under the bridge, the flow of traffic above me, the flow of tides before me. It wasn't truly protected, but the currents were enough to disrupt anyone trying to watch, and on the more mundane level, there were people to either side. And if something went wrong—which, after all, was a possibility—I could attract attention easily.

Janssen sniffed at the culinary scents from the Barking Crab. "Here?"

"Here's fine."

He chuckled. "I never did understand all the weird conditions you guys had for meetings. Bridges, islands—would you believe one of your lot had me meet him in a subway tunnel?"

"I'd believe it." *One of your lot*? The hell?

I must have let something show on my face, because he stepped back, raising his hands as if to push me away. "Sorry, sorry. Didn't mean to associate you with them. You're different, yeah, I understand that." He did a weird sort of head tilt too, lifting his chin as if to point with it, exposing the shadow of an Adam's apple in his throat.

I set my helmet at my feet, then straightened up, aware on some visceral level of how he looked at the gap where my shirt fell open. It wasn't even a come-on, just an acknowledgment of my femininity, what little of it there was. It said a lot about my state of mind that I was grateful for even that. "Do you mean the community-watch thing? They haven't had any meetings beyond the first one, as far as I know. And yeah, you can associate me with them if you like." Not that it made much of a difference.

Janssen smiled. "No, no . . . cute, but no. I'm talking about the big guys. You know them?"

Even if this wasn't undercurrent cryptic, it was still cryptic, and I didn't much care for it. "Not really. Look, what do you want from me?"

"Well, you're the Hound, right? Wanted to be sure I got that right." He waited, and after a moment, I nodded. Not like I could hide that, these days. "Okay. Well, first of all, I gotta say I like how the city is now. I've been in and out of this town coming on four decades, and this whole shakeup is, way I see it, good for everyone involved."

"Get to the point." A seagull dove under the bridge and veered around us, squalling.

Janssen shook his head. "Not much for small talk, are you? Or what was it you folks call it? Blarney?"

Any Irish I had in me was outnumbered by generic pasty mongrel, but I knew that wasn't what he meant. The part of me that drove my talent was Irish, and old-blood Irish at that. Very old.

Janssen didn't seem to care that I hadn't agreed or

disagreed. "What I'm saying is this: I understand that there's a new setup in the city. I'm fine with that—I'm flexible."

New setup? *He doesn't mean Sarah's group*, I thought, and the back of my neck went cold.

"But you're going to need contacts," he went on. "Go-betweens. Especially if you're planning the sort of action that I've heard about—and by the way, I will forgive you for not cutting me in on that, but I don't mind telling you that you lost out on a lot by not contacting me first. I mean, you could get a much better deal through me than on your own. I'm hurt, really I am." He waited to see if I'd elaborate; not knowing a thing about it, I stayed mute. "Besides, I am the best of the best when it comes to easing the way for dealings with the big guys. You'll want help."

I swallowed, hoping still that I'd misinterpreted what he'd said. "And what makes you think I'm the person to go to?"

Janssen shrugged. "Stands to reason, doesn't it? I mean, I know the bright boys have gone under, and you're the one who gets credited as the cause of it. Now, I'm not sure I buy everything they're saying—I mean, no offense to you, you look pretty capable, but anything on that scale isn't a one-man setup. So you must have had some good backers."

I didn't answer. Yeah, I'd had good backers. Divine intervention, even, depending on how narrowly you wanted to define *divine*.

Janssen seemed relieved that I didn't argue the point. "So I know the traditions you guys had. The one who brings down the old boss becomes the new boss." He glanced at the children running up and down the boardwalk, then sidled closer. "You didn't really bite his head off, did you? Because damn, that's hardcore."

"I didn't." Not technically. My mouth was full of the remembered taste of blood. "And that's why you figure I'm in charge now?"

"That's how it's done here." He said it as one might

state any other fact: the sky is clear, the ocean is salty, Genevieve Scelan is the Hound. "I mean, that's how it's done everywhere. Even if it's not technically the guy who held the gun stepping into the boss's shoes, it's still the same chain, the same pattern."

I turned red under my sunburn and had to swallow before answering, forcing down my gut reaction—which was mostly profanity, and there were kids nearby. *String him along*, the rational part of me thought, *keep him talking, get what you can out of him and then go home and wash off the slime.*

But the slime itself was becoming almost irrelevant to the keening at the back of my mind. The Fiana were gone, their power broken, the last stragglers leaving one by one. I hadn't killed Boru just to take his place. Had I?

Did it even matter *why* I'd done it?

A truck rumbled overhead, drowning out thought and speech both. "And so you want to be part of the new situation," I said thickly once it was gone. "That's a little crass, isn't it?"

"That's business," he said, again simple as truth. "I'm not a partisan—I can't afford to be, in my work. I don't make alliances, I make connections, and if one connection goes dead there's a dozen others. I can't afford to get a name as someone who gets tied to one faction." A boat coasted down the channel behind him, trailing gas rainbows in its wake, and he waved. No one on the boat acknowledged him. "Besides, you need me," he added in an undertone.

Now the spotlight charm seemed something else, like I was caught in a greasy flame rather than the center of the universe. The man had all the oiliness of a cheese left out in the sun. *Time to end this*, I thought. "I think we're done here," I said, and started back toward the street.

He stepped in front of me. "Uh-uh. Hear me out. For precedent's sake, if nothing else—I handled the first one, you know? That's precedent, and I did a good job, there's no one can say I didn't. I got buyers all over the goddamn planet just for a job like this. Ten in Japan alone who'd sell all four islands just for the scraps from the table. You *need* me, Hound."

He was sweating—we were both sweating, it was a hot day and even the breeze from the channel couldn't cut the impending heaviness of the air. But his grin was harder now, his teeth parted as if he were panting through them, and I suspected that his sweat had nothing to do with the temperature. And then there was the way he kept tipping his head back as he talked. It felt like an artificial gesture, one without a point, and yet there was something familiar about it. Something that I ought to know, instinctually if nothing else, even if I'd never seen it before.

"You need me," he repeated. "I'm the goddamn best in the business."

I took a deep breath, focusing on the scent of dying marine creatures to keep from getting nauseated. "If you're the best," I replied, "how come you're doing the hard sell? The best shouldn't need to boast. I think one of us is desperate here, and it isn't me."

Janssen's face fell. "I have contacts," he mumbled.

"I don't *want* your contacts. And that's another thing. The best would have done some goddamn research first." I kicked my bike free and steered it past him. "The Fiana is done," I said over my shoulder. "Finished. Ended. Their leaders are dead and their power is broken. I didn't go through all that just to set myself up in their place."

I'd said it as much for my own benefit as for his, so I don't know what kind of response I'd expected. Whatever it was, I didn't get it. Janssen gaped at me a moment, then threw his head back and laughed. I turned to stare at him. "I get it," he said. "I see—oh, I just got here too early! Jumping the gun again, I guess."

"What are you talking about?" Had we even been having the same conversation?

"You're so *cute*!" He reached out to pat me on the cheek. I jerked away, and he grinned. "You sound so dramatic, real Academy Award stuff. Or at least a Tony. I can't even begin to count the number of times I've heard the same speech from some noble kid, all holy and righteous, and then six months later I'm working for him, same as I always was. San Francisco, Mumbai, Lisbon, it's all the same. It's like you kids get a crack at the script for the naive hero part before you move on to the grown-up way of looking at things. Especially . . ." He lowered his chin, looking down his nose at me, and his eyes went hooded and dark. "Especially you occult types, with your loci and your *geisa* and your silly little restrictions."

I stepped back, but there wasn't anywhere to go— just the channel behind me and the bridge before me. Even his scent had changed: suddenly, even though we were outside with open air on three sides of us, I had the sense of space closing in, heavy cave walls and the smell of carrion.

"Of course I know about it," he said, almost growling now, if a sound that gravelly could be considered animal rather than mineral. "Just because I stay on the surface doesn't mean I'm ignorant about what's underneath." He grinned, showing all of his teeth. In the light under the bridge, they seemed yellower than they had up top, yellower and longer. "Even the words you use—good Lord, 'their power is broken'? Power doesn't break, little girl, it just changes hands. If not your hands, then someone else's."

I made an inarticulate noise, and Janssen straightened up, stepping away from me. The heavy, claustrophobic air began to clear. "You know, I know someone who thinks the same way you do. Thinks if he ignores something he doesn't like, it'll go away. Doesn't work that way. You can ignore the facts all you like, but they'll still be there. They'll still get into your blood."

"I don't need your services," I said, trying not to snarl.

"Oh, I know. And you mean it too. You probably don't even know anything about what's going on under the pretty little savior-of-the-city façade you've got up. Community watch? Don't make me laugh." He bowed, a mocking, archaic gesture. "And I'll let you be—and in six, eight months, I'll stop by here again. And then you'll need me, because while I may not be the best, I sure as hell am the most humane in the business. I'll be a goddamned relief."

He clasped his hands and smiled at me over them. "You've got my number."

"Get out of my city," I growled, and only a second later realized what I'd said.

Janssen laughed. "See you in the spring."

Eight

The phone number Abigail had left connected to a Newton hotel on the Charles, out at the furthest extent of my range as a courier. She hadn't ventured far inside the Hub. I kicked gravel out of the way as I walked my bike back up to street level, phone crammed up against my ear.

She finally picked up just as it was about to go back to the front desk. "Hello?"

"Miss Huston?" I shifted the phone so I could speak into it. "This is Genevieve Scelan."

"Genevieve." She said the name slowly, as if it were a password. "Of course. What is it?"

I took a deep breath, still trying to convince myself that I couldn't get out of this. "I've thought about it, and I'll take care of that preliminary matter we were discussing."

There. Done. Everyone has things they can't walk away from, obligations they take on simply because that's how they see themselves and it's easier to change the world than change that image. The geisa we lay on ourselves, a woman of my acquaintance had said, and even if my status as Hound meant that no external bindings could hold me, the ones I put on myself stuck. And even if I couldn't protect a whole goddamned city—as the break-in at the Three Cranes had shown in no uncertain terms—I could at least keep someone else from putting herself at risk. "I'll go tonight," I added before cowardice could stop me.

She was silent a moment. "I do wish you'd told me before now."

Damn. "You haven't gone and—you didn't go yourself, did you?"

"Oh, no," she replied, and I sighed. "Not at all. But you took so long I made some other—well. It doesn't matter now, and they're easily remedied. Thank you."

I didn't like the sound of that "other," but I wasn't going to argue just now, not if she was safe. "Is there anything I ought to ask your—ask about besides the stolen property?"

The phone creaked, and it took me a moment to recognize the sound of someone sitting down on a creaky hotel bed. "I don't believe so. Just where to find the original owner. And what was stolen, of course. If you know that, you should be able to track the rest down."

I nodded. Damn right I could. "You think she'll know?" Would there even be enough left of the ghost to answer?

Abigail chuckled, a dry sound like twigs crackling underfoot. "If she's there, she'll know. Tonight, you said? That'll work well for me. You will be careful, right?"

"I will." I couldn't help smiling. Adept or no, she had the social cues that most adepts lost in the haze of loci and magic. There aren't many sane ones out there, and of those, even fewer who are pleasant to be around for any length of time.

Another reason why I was doing this for her. It wasn't much—even compared with Sarah's frail community watch, it didn't have much of an effect. But it was something. And it was one in the eye to Janssen's perception of me.

The buses out to Mount Auburn Cemetery are the weird electric kind, the ones that stagger and jerk in their courses slightly more than your basic MBTA diesel beast. My head bounced gently against the window as the driver veered around another pothole, and I tried not to think about what I'd agreed to do. Ahead of me, a young mother held her child up to the window to watch as we passed a bend of the Charles River. The kid made sounds of infant glee; the two commuters across from her looked much less impressed.

I got off at the stop closest to the cemetery itself, glanced back at the gates, and decided to give it another half hour. The park rangers or whatever you called people who took care of cemeteries had probably made a sweep right after closing, but I didn't want to risk running into them. Instead I found a little tree-lined avenue and settled onto a bench, grateful for the chance to rest. It seemed as if I'd been in motion for the better part of three days now—hell, three months if you wanted to look at it that way.

My phone trilled: the one damn noise that would bring me out of just about anything. I spent a moment trying to remember where I'd put it when I changed out of my courier gear, then finally fished it out of the paper bag I'd brought. The number was one I recognized, and I gazed at it a moment, a heavy uncertainty tightening my throat. At last, just before it swapped over to voice mail, I picked up. "Hi, Nate."

"Evie, I—ah, damn."

"Nice to hear from you too. What's up?"

He muttered another curse under his breath. "Well, I originally wanted to invite you to another Sox game, but I just got an e-mail from the guy who had tickets. He's not selling."

I shook my head, both disappointed and relieved. A Sox game would have been great . . . and with Nate . . . but right now, I wasn't so sure whether that was a good idea. Simpler just to forego another chance to go out with him; simpler to push everything down. "Bastard."

"Yeah. Hell." Nate took a deep breath. "So. How

are you?" he said, the good mood as fake as a purple Christmas tree.

I smiled. "Working." A brown-and-white dog, one of those herding ones that probably have pedigrees but just look like patchwork animals to me, wandered over, tail waving. I leaned down and scratched its ears; it grinned and flopped down next to me as if it belonged there.

"I'll call back."

"It's okay. I have to wait for another half hour or so anyway." When was moonrise? It didn't matter in magical terms, but I didn't like the idea of blundering around a cemetery in the dark. "So how's things?"

"Not as good as when I thought I had Sox tickets."

"Hey. I'll take whatever I can get." Which was true, and kind of sad. "Sorry. It's been kind of a long week."

He didn't say anything for a moment. Funny how this silence was better than the silence yesterday, how it wasn't the lack of things being said but rather the consideration of things to say. Not that it kept me from remembering some of the inconvenient sensations of the time. "Want to talk about it?"

"I don't know." In theory, I didn't have to pussyfoot around this with Nate; he'd seen the worst of it and the worst of me at the same time. But there were too many other topics to avoid. I sighed. "You remember the Fiana?" The dog sighed too and stretched out, exposing its belly in hope of a scratching. I reached down and obliged. "I'm wondering if it was the right thing to do. To take them down."

Nate whistled. "It must have been a bad week, if you're wondering that."

"Yeah, well." I sketched out a broad outline of what had happened, mixed with Janssen's assessment of the situation and the break-in at the Three Cranes. It ended up getting a lot more garbled than I'd meant, and I kept waiting for Nate to interrupt me, tell me that I was making too much out of it, tell me that I was being an idiot.

But he waited until I ran out of steam, and when I finally came to the end of it ("and all this shit was right under my nose, Nate, right under my goddamn nose and what good is my nose if I'm not noticing anything?"), he didn't immediately speak. For a moment I wondered if he'd hung up on me.

"You're worried that by fixing one thing, you broke something else," he said at last.

"Broadly. Yes."

"It still needed fixing. And, frankly, I'm glad that you did fix it, because Katie and I wouldn't be here if you hadn't."

Yes. There was that. "So am I," I said. The dog pawed at my hand, and I resumed rubbing its tummy. At least that much was simple.

"You're okay with talking about all this over the phone? I mean, the first time I ever talked about this stuff seriously with you, you made me turn on every tap in the bathroom."

"Yeah, and my landlord hasn't let me forget about that. Apparently the water bill skyrocketed that month." I'd wanted running water at the time, anything that might dull any magic around us. But then I'd had reason to believe we were being watched, and even if I didn't quite trust Abigail, I didn't think she'd be scrying me. Mostly because that took a huge amount of power and tended to be about as reliable as a junior meteorologist. "I'm all right here, Nate. And I trust you." The words were out before I knew it, and I hastened to cover them up. "I mean, you'd find some way to let me know if some crazed adept were listening in on your end."

A teenage girl came out of a house down the street and began calling for Calico. The dog immediately rolled over and bounced to its feet, then trotted to the curb and waited, grinning, for the girl to come to it. "I'd like to think so," Nate said. "You want to work out a code just in case?"

"Ha. That could get ridiculous very quickly."

"What, more than it already is?"

I smiled. God, I could imagine him sitting and talking, could almost see him . . . why was it so much easier to talk to him like this on the phone, without the distraction of his physical presence?

"Evie? You still there?"

"Yeah." *Rein in your imagination, girl.* "Yeah, I'm here. Thanks."

"I think you're doing the right thing. I mean, I don't know how much one person can do in this . . . this undercurrent, but what you've done should be considered enough."

"*Enough* smacks of slacking, my mom used to say."

"Remind me to tell you sometime about the Aunts. They had the same approach, and my mom hated it."

"Tell me sometime, then." I got to my feet, then rechecked the contents of my bag. Salt, water, resin . . . and Mount Auburn looked quiet, even for a cemetery. "Well, wish me luck."

"Luck? Evie, what are you planning?"

Could I tell him? *Oh, nothing, just planning to contact the dead in a ritual that's less risky for me than for anyone who's got relatives in the cemetery but is still fairly risky.* No, probably not. "Nothing you ought to worry about."

"Dammit, Evie—"

"Look, I'll tell you about it. I will. But not now. Let me keep my composure for now, okay? I'll find you later and tell you. It's what I do, right?"

Nate hesitated, and I took the opportunity to say goodbye and click the phone off before I could change my mind.

I walked up toward the main gates of the cemetery. Because of some Egyptian fad at the time of their construction, they'd been built to resemble the sandstone pillars that warded the halls of dead kings—although the resemblance was about as strong as mine was to Queen Elizabeth. Still, it unnerved me to see a sun disk carved into gray marble when I looked up at the entrance. Had they known how much history, how much of the undercurrent, they were invoking here, and whether it would follow them? Or had it just been part of the fad, like the pseudo-academic theories that had left their marks on the crazier members of the undercurrent?

It didn't matter, I told myself. I dug a disk of carved bone the size of my palm out of the bottom of my bag, touched it to my forehead, and slid it into my bra. The faint puff of fireworks scent from it made me grimace. Aversion wards weren't pleasant things, even linked to an item rather than free-floating, but they were useful. I'd gotten this one from a Russian émigré who'd needed information in a hurry, and I'd only used it once before now.

The main gates had been closed and padlocked, but the padlock had been designed to be more ornamental than useful. I hitched my bag over one shoulder, glanced down the street, and scrambled over the low iron gate.

The beam of a flashlight passed over where I'd been, but the aversion ward had taken hold, and for a little while at least it'd help me elude a casual glance. I wasn't entirely happy about the skin contact needed for it to work—you try keeping something the size and texture of a sand dollar in your bra for an hour and tell me it's no big deal—but right now I needed it.

The cemetery wasn't as dark as I'd expected; even without a cloud cover, the haze over the city reflected some of the sodium glow. My eyes adjusted after a moment, so long as I didn't look back at the street. Still, I kept glancing over my shoulder as I made my way along the paved paths, one too many horror movies coming back to haunt me. Whoever had decided that this place needed more trees had obviously given no consideration to the needs of nocturnal visitors; every other flutter of a leaf had my heart thumping.

In theory, I could do the ritual anywhere in the cemetery; all I needed was space to draw a circle and patience to wait in it. But I didn't have the mental barriers that most mediums used to keep ghosts from latching on to them, nor did I have any particular skill at this. I sure as hell was going to take all the precautions Sarah recommended.

If a ghost was of a mind to move—and most of the ones outside graveyards weren't; they were attached to that place by the effusion of emotion that left their imprint to begin with—it would catch on to a person through one of several ways. Shed blood was the easiest. Blood was one of those all-purpose things in the undercurrent; just as a magician could work sympathetic magic on a victim using her blood, so could a ghost get the identity of a medium. And then there were the magical implications of heredity and its different blood link, the way it made some actions easier and therefore more dangerous . . . I didn't understand all of them, and didn't care to.

I touched the side of my bag, then flexed my leg, feeling the bandages over the afternoon's scrape tighten. I was probably all right on that score, at least.

But there were other ways for a ghost to catch hold of a person. Names, obviously, since so many magicians worked power into their names. Shadows, less important now at night. And, for some reason, footprints. Failing the obvious safety of being surrounded by running water, a site off the ground offering even minimal topological discontinuity would be enough to break the trail. (*Amateurs*, I thought with a mental sniff.) So I could do the ritual on top of one of these mausoleums . . .

The horror-movie images came back with a rush, and I shuddered. No.

If I remembered right, there was a tower somewhere in the cemetery. I looked up, trying to get my bearings, and there it was, a shadow on the highest hill. It'd do. I started hiking.

Trees creaked in the breeze up here, and the winding trails led me wrong twice. They'd obviously been designed for meditation and reflection, not summoning the dead . . . I smiled at the thought, then choked as something white and flapping loomed out from behind the next tree. It didn't move as I approached, and I realized a second later that it was a statue, shrouded against the weather for restoration. Fine. Fine. Tell that to the way my heart was racing.

I was going to double Abigail's damn rate for this.

I finally reached the top of the hill, cursing all nineteenth-century landscapers in those last few gasping minutes. A last set of stairs led up to the base of the round two-story tower, and two giant obelisks—no compensation issues *there*—stood just below the crest of the hill. Even from down here, I could see the skyline of Boston, glittering like spilled glass. Someone was having a party on the other side of the Charles; every now and then the heavy thump of a bass beat echoed across the river. I stretched my legs in a futile attempt to work out the soreness and climbed up the last few steps.

A steel-mesh door blocked the entrance to the tower—locked, padlocked, and bearing a sign saying that the tower was closed daily at dusk. I'd gotten through locks before using Deke's breaker charm, but right now I didn't want to use more magic than I had to. The aversion ward on its own was throwing off my sense of what to look out for, as the wrapped statue had proved. What I did have was a pair of wire cutters. Ten minutes' work was enough to cut the mesh around the lock itself. Unsubtle, but no one's ever accused me of subtlety. I squinted into the blackness beyond, then fumbled for the light on my keys.

I could start to put something together in the Fiana's wake, I thought as I climbed the tight spiral stair, thin red light held before me as if to warn the tower's inhabitants of my approach. Something to protect people like Elizabeth and the shadowcatchers and the magicians who didn't have enough power or sense to protect themselves. Something that wasn't just winner-take-all, big-guy-gets-little-guy's-stuff. Something more than Sarah's ineffective community watch, but less than the gang that slugs like Janssen expected. If I could ever do it, now was the time.

I passed the exit opening onto the first floor, the balcony that girdled the tower—still high up, but not enough room for a circle—and kept climbing. The walls began to arch in around me, as if clasping me in hands of stone. My breath sawed in and out of my lungs, and it wasn't because of the climb.

The air opened up above me at last, giving way to stars and an endless whistle of wind. I ran the last few steps despite the seizing up of my muscles, then stood for a moment, clasping the iron rail, unable to move back into that claustrophobic space. The lights of Boston and Cambridge spread out before me, glowing softly in the heavy air. A breeze tugged at my hair, then subsided, as if it wasn't worth the effort.

This was my city. I'd said as much to Janssen, and I didn't regret it. Here, in this high place, I could see it all—and further, the heavy green of trees in Cambridge and Newton, the Blue Hills through their haze, Summit Hill and its park, the great coliseum of Harvard's stadium across the river. A gust of wind carried a shout of music past me, like an acclamation.

For a moment I forgot the task ahead of me, forgot Nate, forgot even that I was standing in a graveyard. *I could make it work*, I thought. *I could protect this city against people like Janssen and the thugs and the slimeballs. I could prove him wrong.*

I gazed down at the lights, then saw the one thing that was a constant for me: the neon Citgo sign, flashing on and off in its usual pattern. And beyond that, the brilliant lights of Fenway.

I was missing the Sox game for this. Shaking my head, I got to work.

The bag I'd brought yielded several small bottles, as well as a zipped plastic bag of what looked to the casual glance like the kind of pot even a burned-out hippie would turn down. First the holy water, in a wide circle around the top of the tower, then a ring of salt just inside that. I'd have to hope that the wind and rain would carry any remnants away before the park rangers noticed them. Then the aversion ward, taken out of my bra (where it had burned a nice brown circle into the fabric, like an iron forgotten against silk) and put two steps down on the staircase, out of the way. I didn't want attention averted from me just now. And then, finally, brandy splashed onto the parapet, with the bottle set next to it, and a smear of maple syrup beside that.

You could do this with rum and sugar cane, with Kahlúa and chocolate, or vodka and beet sugar, and it'd still work. The basic tenets of the ritual were the same no matter which culture passed it down. You presented the dead with a gift, something that reminded them of life, got them to take it, and then asked for what you wanted in return. Exchange for exchange, the undercurrent balance sheet kept clean. The syrup was a sentimental touch on my part; the sugar didn't have to be palatable to the ghosts to draw them, but I liked the thought of having something familiar. But the one thing the ritual always needed, no substitutions allowed, was blood.

The pig's blood I'd procured had clotted the sage and stuck to the inside of the bag, but it still made a decent paste. I turned the bag inside out to smear it in a line across the railing of the tower, careful not to get any on my fingers. I wouldn't have dared to do this if I were menstruating—the blood scent from me might not be strong enough for a ghost to detect, but I'd sure as hell notice it, and that would be enough to put me off my stride. Among the many other things blood can do in the undercurrent, the one thing I can absolutely count on is for its scent to distract me. Hence the sage.

I retreated to the center of the tower, then closed my eyes and spoke aloud the words that Abigail had taught me.

For a long moment there was nothing, only the rumble of traffic to either side and the almost subliminal beat of music from across the river. I glanced down at the salt and the gaping hole of the stairs leading down, and when I looked back the darkness over Boston had a new opacity to it, as if a filter had come down. This wasn't night anymore; this was an *inhabited* darkness.

My lips went dry, and a whispering, crackling sound like a distant fire swept around me. It smelled arid, the cool drought of winter, even though the air kept its August heat. A second later I heard the clink of the bottle tipping over, and tasted the momentary tang of alcohol on the air.

I cleared my throat. "That's mine."

The air seemed to flex in front of me, like a tapped soap bubble, and for a moment I caught a glimpse of the two obelisks partway down the hill, framing a pillar of mist as tall as the tower. "It's not yours now," said a voice—no, voices, a chorus of them. It was as if four different people had responded, and some amateur audio technician had spliced the tracks so that each word came from a different speaker. And behind each voice came a dull susurrus of answering voices, a concord of souls answering as one.

I hadn't planned for this. I'd expected a crowd, not an amalgam—the remnants, fragments left behind with the body when the spirit went elsewhere, without even the impetus of strong emotion. Over time the remnants had melded, becoming one entity, and that was what had responded. Not an individual ghost at all.

I shifted, turning my head back and forth. The voices were so tightly focused that I could hear them in my left ear but not the right. I was the only one who had their attention, for what that was worth.

I cleared my throat. "Am I speaking to Mount Auburn?"

There was a soft laugh, edged with affronted cries

and one or two mutters. That was an advantage I had: it's hard to get an amalgam really angry. Kind of like getting a committee to agree on anything. "Maybe. Your drink?"

Technically, what I ought to do now was extract information in exchange for the sugar and alcohol. But that was what magicians did. "Consider it a gift," I said. "Can I ask you a few questions?"

The weird opacity to the darkness shifted, like a flock of bats between me and the light. "Ask?" the chorus said, some of the voices trailing out of sync behind the others.

"Ask," I confirmed. Not demand. Not cajole, or trade. Just ask. These dead might not be quite sentient any more, but that wasn't any reason not to treat them with respect.

Another laugh, quickly swallowed up in the babble of voices, none coming close to saying anything real. "Ask," it said again, and I couldn't tell if it was an order, an invitation, or simply an idiot repetition.

I'd take even that, though. "All right," I said. "I need to talk to Abigail Huston."

"Huston," said a chorus of voices, and for a moment I thought I heard an echo on the far side of the hill. "Husss . . ."

Abruptly a woman's voice spoke about two feet behind me. "I won't say I don't appreciate the gift, but it's a little thoughtless to offer that. *Some* of us keep teetotal."

I glanced over my shoulder. The air behind me was as still and heavy as the more palpable darkness before me. I couldn't even see the tower railing, let alone the landscape beyond it. They were *all around me*, I realized, and the fluttery feeling in my chest increased to outright pounding, as if my heart wanted to flee but the rest of me was too stupid to follow.

Okay, I told myself. *This is what you wanted. Ask about the stolen property and you're done.* "Am I speaking to Abigail Huston?"

The woman's ghost laughed, changing to a child's mid-chortle. "Hardly," it said, and the chorus echoed it. "We don't care for her kind here. Little schemer."

I still couldn't smell anything—ghosts don't have a scent, not unless they've been around the living long enough to accrete one. Without my talent I was lost, and the safeguards I'd gotten from Sarah suddenly seemed too flimsy.

"Hardly," the amalgam repeated, amused now. "A woman like that? Really now."

"Thief," another element of the amalgam tolled, the susurrus of its voices coming together like spotlights on a stage. "Huston is a thief."

"She is?" I caught myself. "She *was*?" Well, that explained how she'd acquired stolen property. Though I didn't know what these fragments of Boston Brahmins would consider thievery. Bad manners? Blackmail?

"Poor little idiot, so scared of what she did that she fled here seeking sanctuary." The amalgam rumbled with satisfied scorn.

"She's not the one you should worry about," a child's voice said by my elbow, unexpectedly clear.

I glanced down—again, nothing, but an echo to it that didn't quite register as scent seemed familiar. Maybe I'd met someone related to this particular remnant, and now he felt the need to warn me. Or was this a veiled threat? "I don't understand."

There was a watery, gulping chuckle. "Be glad you don't. Be glad this is the first time you have called up the dead." A wind curled down the side of the hill, tossing my hair in front of my eyes and stroking the darkness as one would soothe a pet.

I had patience for only so many cryptic warnings. "Please. I need to speak to Abigail. I need to know what she stole."

The mottled darkness paused, a moiré filter between me and Boston. "She hid herself too well," it said at last. "Dug down deep at her patron's feet . . . she is hidden from everything, including herself." There was a moment's silence, and it seemed the physical presence was receding—until I realized that my perspective had been warped, and what looked like shrinking shadows on either side were only shrinking in relation to the looming mist curling closer to me. "It would take a lot more than you, little puppy, to dig her out of that hole."

My hair felt as if someone had dragged a fur coat over it. "Okay. Then maybe you can help me." Silence, not yet hostile but not far from it. "There was something she owned. Something she passed down to her descendant."

"Thief," one of them whispered.

"Wretch," said another.

"Whisht." I caught a third hiss that didn't even sound like a real word, but the amalgam caught it up in a whispering chorus. "Whisht."

"I don't care if she was a thief," I snapped. "What did she steal?"

There came another laugh, but this one was gentler and somehow clearer, as if the radio station of the ghosts had hit a signal. "Everything. Everything that didn't exist."

Oh, great. Now we were on to philosophy.

"Gabble," muttered the ghosts. "Gabble, gabble, gabble."

"Gabriel," another said, almost singing.

"Gabriel?" I said. "Is that who she stole it from?"

Nothing. Back to the endless "gabble" chorus. But now under their nonsense came the unwelcome sound of boots crunching on gravel. *Shit*, I thought. *One of the park rangers came up here, and either he's a sensitive or he's noticed the wreck I made of the door.* "Look," I said, taking a step closer to the line of blood and brandy and sugar, "I need to know what it was she had. I don't care if she stole it or not. She had something that caused nightmares, an artifact of some kind. Maybe even a ghost."

The protrusion of mist flinched, and somewhere

within it I could hear a voice yelling, though whether that was in response to what I had said or a natural side effect of an amalgam, I didn't know (after all, if our subconscious could speak, how many of us would be surrounded by shouting angry voices all day?). The yelling ceased abruptly, as if switched off. "Why?" it whispered, its voice dry and soft as a lizard's skin.

Hell. This wasn't good—I knew little about inter-rogation, but I did know that it wasn't good if the bal-ance shifted, if the questioner became the questioned. "I need to return it to its rightful owner," I said.

The darkness turned in on itself, considering. I edged closer to the stairwell, but just then I heard the *clack* of a boot heel below me. Someone was on the stairs, someone close . . . *clack*, and a jingle, like keys or spurs, *clack* . . .

With a shock like ice against the base of my neck, I realized that I'd made one big error in drawing my circle: I'd drawn it around the edge of the tower, in the largest circle I could reach. Which meant that the en-trance to the tower was included in it. I backed away from the gaping stairwell, up against the chill of the circle itself.

Then, "No," one voice said, and though the mist roiled ever faster, this new voice remained singular and unblurred. "I lived long enough in the old country to re-member them. I lost cattle to that host, I lost sleep—"

The babble merged around that one voice. "—lost anything left outside to their jaws—"

"—daughter saw them in their courses, never right again—"

"—whistlers, all seven of them, always for death—"

"—hurled—"

"—*wretch*—"

The voices swelled to deafening, and the shadows spun themselves into a pillar as high as the tower. I turned in place, trying to see a way out, groping for the words of a dismissal, even though by now that would be about as useful as a paper shield.

All sound ceased, and when the dead spoke again, it was no longer as an amalgam, but with a single united purpose. "*You can't have it.*"

"I don't want it," I shouted back, and the wind carried my words away. "I don't even know what it is!"

"*Liar!*" At the back of its scream, I could hear the grinding whine of granite wearing down. These stones would be eroded the next time I saw them. If I saw them again. "You want it, you need it like a lion needs a pride, like a bitch needs a pack. You're just like Skelling. He wanted it, you'll want it too."

"Skelling?" The name slipped out before I could stop myself.

The mottled darkness halted, and that sudden stillness was more frightening than anything before. Somewhere on the far side of the hill, back where buses ran and people lived without the dead intruding, a dog began barking hysterically. "Skelling," the voices said, savoring the name, and the pillar began to revolve again, slowly and with a dreadful purpose.

Shit. Saltwater and hope weren't going to be any good against this.

"We know you now," it whispered. "Skelling. Hound. Bitch." The air around me went bone dry, so dry my eyes almost crackled, and I choked. "Bitch!" the amalgam screamed. "You'll steal it, you'll take it as Huston did, as her son did, as Huston did! *Bitch!*"

I staggered and dropped to one knee. How far could I get? Even if they had the wrong name, they had a link to me—how long till I left a footprint, till the ghosts grabbed hold of my shadow?

The aversion ward. That might help, even for only a second. I dragged myself to the edge of the stairs, but someone was there before me. A shape rose up from the gaping blackness of the stairwell, a man in a robe or a long coat, no more than a shadow against shadows. A snarl cut through the amalgam's screaming like a sword through a snake. I scrambled back on all fours, but the shadow turned away from me, toward the amalgam. "Go," said a man's voice by my ear. "If you have any pity, bring it back safe and return it."

"Who—" I said, though I was already moving, edging through the thin envelope of breathable air that clung to the dark shape. "Abigail?"

"She's buried far too deep, girl. Some sins may not be forgiven." The shadow turned, just enough that the light of the half-moon above limned features that weren't there. I caught a glimpse of blue eyes and a red mustache . . . "Don't let it happen again," he said, and pointed west.

Where he pointed a path gleamed, silver and unreal above the treetops. The amalgam roared again, screaming *Skelling* and *Gabriel* and *Wretch* in a chorus of the damned. I lurched to my feet and reached out. My left arm broke the circle first, and pain shot up it with a sizzle. I clamped my teeth over a howl, vaulted the railing, and ran—

—and *ran*.

Nine

I stumbled to a stop, and the world slammed back into place around me. Too much, too fast; I tried another step and missed my footing, landing with one knee on gravel and the other in gooseshit.

The faint thump of music I'd heard from the tower was now a steady thrum, and I could hear voices over it, the chatter and call of a party in full swing. I drew a few gasping breaths, choking on the dampness in the air. My left hand throbbed, and I held it up, hissing as the glow of streetlights hit it. The skin looked red and chapped, cracked open in places, and though the damage didn't seem to be more than skin deep, skin deep still hurt a hell of a lot. I tucked my hand under my other arm, gritting my teeth, and rocked to my feet, then stared at the ground. Gravel? Gooseshit?

Where the hell was I?

The obvious answer was not the one I wanted to believe first. But there it was: the bright lights that were no part of Mount Auburn, the kiosk emblazoned BOSTON KAYAKS to my left, the glow of a party beyond and, faintly, the flare of police lights as they made their way toward that same party. I wasn't in the cemetery any more, unless they'd radically changed their policies. At last I turned to see the slow current of water, the Charles River murmuring to itself, and beyond that—well beyond that—the hills of Mount Auburn Cemetery. The sky overhead had turned opaque, mist dissipating into cloud cover.

I had the river at my back, and I wasn't on the Cambridge side of it. I'd crossed the Charles, putting running water between me and the dead.

Had I just blacked out? In a rational universe, I ought to have run out of the tower (or, if I really had jumped over the railing like that, broken all my bones on the hill below). In a rational universe, I could assume that I'd just erased the journey in my head. But I couldn't assume that in the undercurrent.

What I did remember was the path, unrolling before me like a shadow. No—more slippery than a shadow, the sense of a road that wasn't mine but that I could use, a toll road perhaps, and someone who'd set my feet on it—

For a moment I thought I saw the flap of a duster in the corner of my eye, a long coat drifting in no breeze. Of course there was nothing when I turned to look— only a lingering absence at the edge of my vision, a persistent blind spot at the limits of perception. "Shit," I whispered, and as if in response, a burst of laughter echoed across the park.

I tried opening and closing my left hand. It still worked, at least, even if it stung like blazes. With the pain came the realization that the only reason the amalgam hadn't hurt me more was because the interval between when I left the circle and when I stepped onto the road (the road that I was very determinedly not thinking about) had only been a split second. In the circle, I'd been safe. I could have waited it out, huddled down while the amalgam screamed itself into forgetfulness, even dismissed the second ghost that had found its way up into the tower. But I'd panicked, and I'd been shown a way out. And I'd taken it.

I'd gone long enough claiming to myself that I wasn't a magician, that because I didn't have the neuroses or the loci or the desperate need to be fucking with the laws of the universe, I could stand apart from them. But when it came to taking magic's easy path, I was as much a part of it as any gibbering adept in his mother's attic.

Maybe Janssen had a point. I recoiled from the thought as if it were venom coated, but it wouldn't go away.

I turned my back on the river, on the implications of what I'd done consciously and unconsciously, and pulled out my phone. I didn't even need to look as I dialed. "Hey," I said as soon as Nate picked up. "It's Evie."

"Evie? Are you all right?"

Okay, so I wasn't so good at hiding the quaver in my voice. "Yeah, yes, I'm fine." My left hand twinged, and I pressed it tighter under my right arm. "Can I—look, can I come see you?"

"What? Of course."

"I'm just—" I stopped myself before my voice broke.

"That bad, huh?" Nate started to say something more, then yawned, a real jaw-cracker that I could hear even over the line. "Sorry. Yes, come on over. Katie's asleep, and I'll be up grading papers for a while. We're not getting the Sox games over here, though."

I managed a shaky laugh. "Doesn't matter."

He whistled. "It really *is* that bad, then. Take care on the way over, Evie."

"I will." I clicked my phone shut, then glanced back at the hill. The blind spot followed me, a gap in my senses.

It started to rain just as I reached their apartment, a sticky unpleasant rain that didn't cool anything down and tasted faintly of gasoline. Nate and Katie lived on the top floor of an aging triple-decker, the kind that you find all over Allston, and a light was on as I approached. The main door had been propped open with a copy of *Omega Numerology*. Nate's, of course; skewering really dumb math was a hobby he'd picked up over the last few months. He probably hadn't wanted me to wake Katie with the buzzer. I tucked the book under my arm and closed the door behind me.

The stairwell leading up was cramped and crooked, and when I knocked on their door I got no response. The door was open, though, and I slipped inside. "Nate?"

No answer. The light I'd seen from the street was from a desk lamp by the sofa, both of which faced a big window. Nate's apartment was the kind meant for college students, two bedrooms plus a common room plus a closet-sized kitchen. But Nate had turned what would usually be a place for two futons and a papasan into a pair of informal studies, one desk piled high with papers, the other half-height and with one of Katie's schoolbooks propped open on it. They didn't have a TV, but there was a stack of Disney DVDs, half of them with library stickers, beside an aging laptop.

The empty door to the kitchen showed only darkness, and the doors to both bedrooms were closed. For a moment I wondered whether Nate had just gone off to bed, or if he'd stepped out to get something, but then I heard a long, slow sigh.

I peered over the edge of the sofa. Nate lay on his side, one arm crooked around to make a pillow for his head. A pencil lay in his other hand, and the stack of papers in front of his chest now bore a long scrawl over the top as a result. He shifted a little in his sleep, mouth twisting as if he were trying out different smiles, and sighed again.

I edged around the side of the couch and moved the stack of papers to the floor. He didn't even wake up when I sat down next to him.

He deserved better than this. He deserved better than a lot of what he'd gotten—a cramped apartment with roaches in the bathroom sink, three tutoring jobs for rich kids who'd grow up to be good stockbrokers like their daddies, an advisor from hell, and a job that from what I'd seen consisted of getting yelled at. It wasn't that he'd given up on himself, but he'd made a decision to be a parent to his little sister first, and it was slowly killing him.

I'd hoped to have some time to talk, maybe ask for reassurance that I wasn't what Janssen said. But the man didn't get enough sleep, and right now I couldn't grudge him the rest.

I touched his shoulder, then, not quite believing what I was doing, shifted until I had curled up on the couch next to him, my left hand stretched out in front of me so it dangled off the edge. *Just for a moment*, I told myself. *You don't deserve anything more than that. Just for a moment.*

Nate's body radiated heat almost to the point of being uncomfortable. His right hand crept around my waist and stayed there, still holding the pencil, and he murmured unintelligibly into my ear before sighing a third time and bumping the back of my head with his nose.

It was enough. I gazed across the room to the dark window reflecting Nate's worklight, across Katie's toys and books scattered over the floor, then closed my eyes. It was enough. Just for a moment longer.

I should have known better than to think anything like that.

I count it a good night when I can't remember my dreams; usually, anything bad enough to break through to my conscious mind isn't something I want to have in my head. But tonight, when the day should have receded into exhaustion and dreamless sleep, I couldn't escape this one fragment, pulling me from dream into something else.

I dreamed a sound, a long, ringing sound like a bell struck far away, like a train coming over the mountains, and that sound caught the dreaming me by the scruff of the neck and dropped me in another direction. *Time*, it called, *time to run, time to do what you've always wanted to do, time for the culmination of all your desires.*

In the dream I made the connection between this call and the tower: this was what Skelling (whoever he was) had wanted and yes, I wanted it too, hungered for it with teeth and claws and sinews. My lips twitched back from my teeth in a canine grin, and I tasted the call as well as heard it, tasted it like fresh coffee or spilled blood. I *needed* to follow, to the point where it was no longer need but truth.

I rolled off the sofa, dropped to a crouch, and ran to the door. If I could just get outside, I knew, I knew I could get to them and then it would be all right. But for some reason I couldn't make my hands remember how to undo the locks. I whimpered—it was like hearing a party in the next room, the best party of your life, and knowing that everyone there would welcome you with raised glasses and applause if you could just get there—and clawed at the door.

It was the clawing that did it. Not the locks—I still didn't have enough motor control to figure those out—but Nate's door was paneled with a couple of cheap blocks of wood, screwed into place so the landlord would have something to fix the deadbolts onto. Splinters dug into my abused left hand, tiny spikes of pain like caltrops.

I swore and jerked back—and the dream fell away like a cut curtain. *What the hell?* I thought, blinking myself awake. I was standing in front of Nate's door, splinters stuck in my hand, but there wasn't any sound beyond the drone of late-night traffic outside. "Sleepwalking?" I muttered aloud. "That's a new one."

Something clattered and crashed to the floor behind me. I turned to see the sofa empty and papers scattered, one of the chairs knocked askew, still rocking from the blow. "Nate?" I said, my voice coming out as a squeak.

Another crash came from the kitchen, and this time I recognized the timbre of it: a pan falling to the floor. I paused at the doorless entry to the kitchen, squinting into the darkness. "Nate, it's me. It's Evie."

"Go away!" he snarled, and my eyes finally adjusted. He was crouched against the far door, the one that led down the back stair. His eyes gleamed in the faint light from the living room, and his scent—

For a very brief moment, no more than half a second, I thought Janssen had gotten in and was standing somewhere I couldn't see, pulling the same looming trick he'd done under the bridge. I caught my breath and put a hand to my throat, suddenly very aware of how vulnerable it was. "Nate, it's okay," I said, but there was so little conviction in my voice that I wouldn't have believed me either.

"What the hell are you doing here?"

Okay, that's never the response you want when you're trying to be reassuring. "I called you. Don't you remember? You even propped the front door open for me."

The shadow that was Nate didn't move. Something seemed off about his eyes—the gleam had gone when he shifted position, out of the light—but that wasn't the only thing wrong, and that I couldn't put a name to it didn't help matters. "I don't need your help with this," he growled, setting the hairs at the back of my neck pinging to alertness. "Go away. I can handle this without you."

"For fuck's sake, Nate, this isn't about you! I came over not because I thought you needed help, but because *I* needed *you*!"

There was a long silence, and I replayed my words in my head. *Crap.*

"Oh," Nate said, and it was recognizably him now, sheepish and a little surprised. He unfolded from his crouch, his shadow slowly becoming something I could identify as human. One hand reached out, fumbling along the wall as if unsure what it was, then found the light switch and snapped it on. Both of us winced away from the glare. "I'm sorry," he said.

"It's okay." I squinted at him. The lights were bright, but they threw heavy shadows, and right now he looked haggard, as if he'd spent the intervening hours—three o'clock by the microwave—actually grading papers rather than succumbing to sleep.

He managed a smile. "I meant to stay awake."

I shrugged. "I should have gone when I saw you were asleep."

He frowned, scratching the back of his head. "It wasn't that. I had this dream, and I guess . . . I reacted badly to it. It happens sometimes."

His demeanor said that this was no big deal, that I shouldn't bother with it. But he'd been scared—yes, scared, that was one part of the change in his scent, though it wasn't the one that had triggered that momentary dread in me. And then there had been my dream . . . "What kind of dream?" I asked. "Maybe there was an ambulance, maybe the same siren woke us both."

Nate shook his head. "No. It wasn't a siren. I remember hearing this noise, and I just . . . It was like those nightmares where something nameless is chasing you." He exhaled slowly, picked up a fallen pan, and set it back down where it had fallen before looking over at me, suddenly hopeful. "What about you—do you ever have dreams like that?"

I hesitated. I knew that hope—the hope of having someone to connect with, on one point if nothing else— and I wanted to let Nate know that he wasn't crazy, that it was all right. But I couldn't lie to him. "Not quite," I admitted, taking a step into the kitchen. "I dreamed I was going to . . . to chase something down." And I'd gone to the front door, hungering to join that chase, while Nate had tried to get away from it.

Nate stared at me for a moment, and his eyes went wide. "*Katie*," he said, and pushed past me to the living room.

I half expected him to fling open Katie's door and run into her room, but instead he carefully pushed it open a crack, just enough to peer inside. He was still for a moment, then sighed, his shoulders slumping. "She's asleep," he said, closing the door.

"You're sure?"

"If she were awake, she'd be fake-snoring. Katie's a champion sleeper. It takes a lot to wake her up once she's finally down." He exhaled, running both hands through his hair. "Evie, I'm sorry. I'm not usually . . . I usually have that under control."

"Well," I said, carefully setting aside for now what "that" might be, "I'm not usually clawing at the front door and forgetting how locks work, so I suspect we've both had a bad evening." I started to lean against the door frame, then hissed as my hand, splinters and all, scraped against it.

Nate reached for my hand. "Jesus, Evie, what did you do?"

Hell. One more undercurrent matter I'd be dragging him into. "Would you believe me if I told you?" I snapped, moving out of his reach.

He was silent a moment. "I seem to remember," he said finally, "telling you that I'd believe anything you ask me to. It's still true."

I couldn't look at him. *I can't do this to him*, I thought, *can't keep dragging him back into the undercurrent, not when it harms everything it touches*.

But he was right. He'd believe what I asked, and I needed that.

"Ghosts," I said at last. "Angry ones. I was trying to ask them something on behalf of a client, and it kind of got out of control." I glanced up at him. He'd gone pale, but not horrified or scared or repulsed—all reactions I'd gotten from people who'd learned about my undercurrent links in the past. "I'm here, though, and I think I'm all right."

"And that's why you're here," he said slowly, gesturing to the apartment, including it (and the couch) in that *here*. "I'm glad. Here, let me do something for your hand."

I followed him to the bathroom and watched as he took down several bottles from the medicine cabinet. "I won't need all of that."

"Can't hurt to have it." He turned on the light over the mirror, then took my hand and turned it over, palm up.

A little electric shiver ran through me, and I caught my breath without meaning to. His fingers were warm on my skin, and somehow their pressure didn't hurt as much as it should have. I couldn't help remembering that just a little while ago I'd been curled up close to him, his breath in my hair. Even if it had been innocent—and I knew myself too well to assume such a motive—with just such a simple touch, it no longer was.

A sudden, quick pulse fluttered in the hollow of his throat, where the lines of sinew and bone met in a curve just barely touched with sweat. I curled my other hand against my side to keep from reaching up and following that curve with my fingers.

It took me a moment to realize that one, my hand still hurt, and two, Nate hadn't moved. He stood with his head bowed, looking at my hand instead of my face, still as deep water save for that quickening pulse. For just a flash, I remembered the look in his eyes when he'd struck the idiot undergrad, when we'd touched before—and the glint of eyes in darkness just a moment ago—and the air seemed to leave the room.

The tweezers dropped into the sink, and he let go of my hand so suddenly that it grazed the porcelain. I hissed in pain. "I'll, uh, I'll let you do this," he said in a low voice, and edged past, careful not to touch me.

I stood there for a moment, chilly for reasons that

had nothing to do with either the undercurrent or the weather. "Goddammit," I said finally, and fished the tweezers out of the sink.

When I emerged, Nate was as collected as I imagined he must be when teaching. "It's about four o'clock," he said. "I can call you a taxi, if you want, or you can stay here." When I looked up at him, that same iron control was down over his features. "If you give me a moment, I can make up the couch for you. It's not too uncomfortable; I end up sleeping here half the time anyway." His smile was a little too strained, and I refrained from pointing out that he—we—had been doing just that before whatever psycho wake-up call had jolted both of us out of bed.

"Don't worry about the couch. I'm fine with just a place to lie down." I stopped, then sighed. "Nate," I said, "do you want me to go?"

"No," he said automatically, but he looked away as he said it. Slowly, as if without his volition, his hand reached out and snapped off the desk light. It didn't leave us in darkness—the streetlight was directly outside, and a greasy orange glow lit up everything in the room—but it was enough of a shock to my eyes that I couldn't quite see his face. "No, I don't want you to go," he said, so softly I almost couldn't hear him.

"Then why are you shutting me out like this?"

"It's nothing," he said, and again it was a growl, a sound that shouldn't have come from the man I knew. "It's—look, don't worry about me."

I shook my head. "You're not making sense."

"I have to make sense for ninety percent of my day, Evie. Forgive me if I can't explain everything clearly just now."

"Goddammit, Nate—" I stopped, biting back my words. *I need you to be normal,* I wanted to say. But my eyes had adjusted, and I could finally see his face again, even if most of it was in shadow. "Okay. All right."

For a moment I felt that same prickle, that same sense of something not quite right. But he nodded, and when I settled onto the couch in the same hollow that our bodies had made, he looked away from me. "Sleep well, then," I said.

He winced as if I'd cut him. "Sleep well," he said, and didn't look at me as he went to his own empty bed.

 Ten

I woke the next morning to sunlight flooding in from the wrong direction, a pillow that wasn't lumpy enough to be one of mine, and knots in both legs. The door to Katie's bedroom creaked open as I sat up, and I was still too out of it to do more than blink sleepily as Katie emerged in a nightshirt that, judging by the nigh-illegible Celtics logo, had probably started life as one of Nate's tees. "Hey, kid," I said, and managed a smile.

"Evie?" she said, then, before I could croak a response, ran over and hugged me. My ribs creaked. "I thought you weren't supposed to be here yet."

"Change of plans," I said, then paused. Katie had a little touch of Sight on her—nothing big, nothing that had messed up her life yet, but enough that she could sometimes unnerve people who weren't used to her. And enough that it sometimes became difficult to parse her words, especially when she got her grammar confused. I had to get this kid to visit the seer enclave sometime soon. "What, was I supposed to be here later on?"

She shook her head against my shoulder, but that could have meant either *no* or *I don't want to talk about it.* "Are you okay?" she said, pulling back a little so she could look up at me.

"Sure," I said automatically, then stopped. I raised

my left hand and flexed it. "A little sunburned." A thin network of red lines remained, but the skin wasn't in that scary flash-fried state anymore. I'd have to put something on my hand to make sure my biking glove didn't chafe against it. "How about you?"

Katie took my hand in hers, scrutinized it, and gave me a long look that was far too serious for her years. Goddamn Hunters; they both had the same eyes. "*I'm* okay," she said, and let go. "Are you staying for breakfast?"

I cleared my throat. "I don't think—" An alarm chimed behind Nate's door, and I sprang up from the couch as if it'd been my own. It was the second time I'd heard it, I realized; that was the sound that had woken me up. "I'd better go." Shoes, where had I put my shoes? And my helmet—no, I hadn't brought my bike over, I'd walked. What was I missing, and what could I afford to leave behind?

Katie followed me like a diminutive shadow, so close behind me I almost tripped over her when I turned to scan the room for anything else of mine. "We're going to Revere Beach today for day camp," she said. "You could come."

"Thanks, but no." Too late. Nate stepped out of his room, still fastening his belt over jeans a size too large for his narrow hips. Damn. He looked straight at me, and my language centers shut down in self-defense. "Good morning," I said, although it came out more like *gmurn*.

"Morning," he echoed. Goddammit, I was already blushing. And it wasn't like I'd had any cause for it. Nate swallowed, then seemed to shake himself. "Katie, get dressed. We're on an early schedule today."

Katie sighed, the momentary strangeness of her Sight falling away to reveal the ordinary kid underneath. "I can't find my clothes," she whined.

"Top of the dresser, right where you put them last night." He was moving as he spoke, heading for the kitchen and picking up the pans that had fallen as if it was totally normal to find them on the floor first thing in the morning.

Katie thumped into her room. I briefly felt sorry for their downstairs neighbors; no one thumps quite like a sullen eight-year-old. "Nate," I began.

Katie stomped back as if the door had bounced her out. "They've got Little Ponies on them. Only babies wear Little Ponies."

"Then you've got two minutes to find something else. Move."

Katie got a mulish look on her face, but she looked at me and ran into her room. I glanced after her, then at Nate, who had unearthed a pair of lunchboxes from the pile of cookware. "Is it like this every morning?"

"Sometimes." He shook his head and took a jar of peanut butter from the cupboard. "I don't know, last night she was fine with the Ponies shirt."

"I was *not*!" Katie yelled.

"Okay, sorry, Katie, you weren't." He made a pair of sandwiches and cut one into triangles. "Usually we've got a little more time. I wasn't kidding about an early start." He hesitated and glanced over his shoulder at me. "We don't have much of a selection for breakfast, but you're welcome to join us."

And it was easier to talk to me in daylight with a pint-sized chaperone, I thought sourly. But after last night—all of last night—I could use the reconnection with the real world. The undercurrent has a nasty habit of dragging you in as soon as you set foot in it, and I had enough trouble keeping myself balanced.

Maybe Janssen was right that pretending something didn't exist didn't make it go away. But that didn't mean you had to drag it to the top. "I probably shouldn't—"

Katie burst out of her room wearing a red tank top turned inside out and jeans with faded pink ribbons sewn onto the pockets. It didn't quite match, but it looked okay. Nate glanced at her, then at me, his lips quivering in a suppressed smile.

"What?" I said, then realized that I was still wearing the clothes I'd changed into after work yesterday: jean shorts and a sleeveless top a few shades darker than Katie's. I sighed. "Okay. Maybe coffee."

I watched Nate as he packed an apple and celery into each box (one showed a peeling corporate logo, the other several Disney Princesses with their dresses colored over in black marker), cajoled Katie into finishing her cereal even though it was the last "fuzzy" stuff from the bottom of the box, and remembered in time that I took my coffee black. It wasn't just that he seemed like a different person, I thought. That would have implied an act of some sort. But Nate seemed normal, natural, and his scent was as I'd always known it. I could see a trace of the man I'd seen last night, but it was quiet, turning its attention elsewhere.

Just then Nate looked up from his coffee and met my eyes. I went scarlet—well, redder than usual—and he froze like a rabbit under a hawk's shadow. No, I thought, more like a dog when someone moves to take its food away . . . Coffee slopped over his hand, and Nate cursed, coming back to himself.

I looked away, anywhere but at him, and just then the phone rang. Nate frowned and glanced over his shoulder. "Katie, get your books together."

"I don't need books for day camp!"

Nate was already at the phone. Katie shrugged and dragged her chair a little closer to mine. "Why aren't you eating?"

"Not hungry."

She tipped up her cereal bowl to finish it. "Sarah thinks it's gross that I drink the milk when I'm done."

"She does, huh?"

I watched as Nate straightened up, still holding the phone. His back was turned, but something about the lines of his shoulders made me think this wasn't a good call. " . . . get this number?" I heard faintly.

"Do you drink the milk when you're done?" Katie held up her bowl to demonstrate.

"I don't know. I hated cereal as a kid." Or maybe I was just finding an excuse to ogle Nate's back. *Mind out of the gutter, Evie.*

Katie made a thoughtful noise, then got up and set her bowl on the thin strip of counter next to the sink. "So what did you have instead?"

"Toast. Or oatmeal." I'd hated oatmeal too, but my mom had had limited patience in the mornings. Nate was speaking again, but the sound of something dragging over the floor drowned out his words. I turned to see Katie pushing a stepstool into place next to the sink. "What's that for?"

"You wash your own dishes." And she did, fumbling a little with the faucet, since it wasn't designed for the reach of shorter arms. "I'll wash yours, though, since you didn't know."

"I'm not done with it yet." I finished the last of my coffee as Nate hung up. "Who was that?"

Nate didn't look at me. Instead he picked up his coffee mug and drained it. "Katie, go get your books."

"I told you, I don't need books for today—"

"Then get your backpack. And make sure you bring sunscreen this time." She climbed off the stepstool and retreated to her room. Nate ran a hand through his hair, disheveling it even further. Was it possible to have permanent bed-hair? "That was my father," he said finally, still looking into his mug.

"Ah." *Shit.*

Nate shook his head. "I don't know how he got my number, but . . . he wants me to meet him. Says if I just meet him once, he'll stay out of my life."

It sounded like emotional blackmail to me, but then again, I didn't have the best relationship with my father either. Distance was something I knew better. "You'd like to talk to him one last time."

He smiled thinly. "First is more like it. I wasn't in a mood to actually talk the last time we met."

"Why? What happened?"

"I'd rather not talk about it." He finally glanced

over at me. There were lines starting at the corners of
his eyes—nothing new there; I was starting to get a
couple as well—but somehow on him it just made him
look more ground down. "I've arranged to meet him
tonight. Get it over with quickly."

I thought about reaching out for him, but couldn't
make myself do it. "Are you sure about this?"

"No." Nate poured the last of the coffee into his
mug, dumped another three spoonfuls of sugar in,
and took a sip. I winced at the thought of how it must
taste. "But I think I owe him this much. This much,
and no more." He stared into his mug, then drank
down the rest of it in a few quick swallows, grimacing.
"Last night—"

"Don't."

"No, Evie, that's not—" He ran a hand over his
face. "What you were talking about last night. The
ghosts, your hand . . . Will you be all right?"

"You're asking *me* that?" I grinned at him.

Nate blinked, then grinned back. "Yeah. I guess I
know the answer."

"You know I will, Nate. I'm used to dealing with
this sort of thing." Maybe not ghosts specifically, but
the undercurrent for one, and the elements of Boston
life that turned nasty fast. I handed him my coffee
mug, and my fingers grazed his palm. Goddammit.
"Good luck."

First thing I did when I got home was put on a fresh
pot of coffee, then shower. My clothes still smelled like
salt and desiccation—the result of the amalgam's ire—
and there were spots on my jeans where the cloth had
dried out so thoroughly that the threads had frayed.
Still, the shower helped, and my hand had almost
started to feel normal, enough that I didn't bother to
get out when the phone rang. The machine picked up,
and I ducked my head under the water again, trying to
keep the world at arm's length a little longer.

As it turned out, it wasn't yet another call asking

for something from me, but a cancellation: Rena, sounding like she hadn't slept in a week. "Evie, it's me. Forget what I said about the Kamikaze Karaoke night. It's not going to work. Don't ask why, just—God, this case is either going to put my name in lights or pull me over the rack, I swear to God. Why the hell did I agree to quit smoking?" She sighed. "Anyway. Maybe a week after that we might be able to do something. I don't know. I'll call."

Damn. I didn't know what this case could be, but Rena was seriously going to need some club therapy when it was done, regardless of the outcome.

I argued with the radio while I got dressed. The Sox hadn't been doing so well of late—enough that the pessimists were starting to say that this was just like every other year: now that the All-Star game was over they'd crash and burn, moan moan moan. Two of them had managed to clog up the radio's comment lines, and it was only a stroke of luck that the host was in no mood to take their crap either.

Unfortunately, the persistent blind spot was still there, right over my shoulder. I'd forgotten about it in the confusion of last night, but it remained like a gap in my perceptions. "Fuck it," I muttered, switching off the radio. "At least it won't stop me from working."

Once showered and dressed and ready for the day, I took down my bike helmet from its place above the little waterfall. Today could be a good day. And the Sox were playing tonight. My stomach gurgled, and I snapped my fingers. Breakfast. And maybe more coffee. Feed the addiction, Evie.

I took two steps into the kitchen, then stopped dead. Abigail Huston sat at the table, hands clasped around an empty mug. "You don't have any tea."

I'd like to say that I had a witty retort ready, that I was so used to unusual appearances that I could take one more in stride. Instead I just gaped at her. "What?"

"I said, You don't have any tea. I expected a little better of you."

I stared a moment longer, trying to understand what my nose was telling me. Yes, she was real. No, there wasn't any trace of her on the threshold or in the office, and there weren't any windows in the kitchen itself. No, she hadn't materialized, because magic of that sort takes five years to set up and is a lot less efficient than taking a taxi. Yes, she was actually present.

I hated impossibilities. Just once, I'd like for what I knew of the undercurrent to not be yanked out from under me. "How long have you been there?"

Abigail shrugged. "Since you came home. A little before, really." She sniffed, which I gathered was going to be the only comment on my scandalous absence. "You just didn't happen to see me before."

"How the hell did you get in?"

She smiled, her lips pressing together thinly rather than curving. "I won't insult you by saying the door was open." She ran a finger along the rim of the mug as if searching for dust. "You don't have wards up."

I took a deep breath, set my helmet down, and leaned against the door frame. "Would they have mattered?"

Abigail shrugged.

"Christ." I shook my head. "This is just too much. Where do you get off—"

I stopped. Abigail raised her chin. "Do go on."

But I couldn't, not now that I understood what my nose was telling me. While Abigail's scent hadn't changed much since I'd seen her, there was a thin edge to it, like the whine of an off-kilter ball bearing in the sound of an otherwise smoothly running engine. Beneath the ice of her demeanor, she was terrified, and while she wasn't so gauche as to show it, the fact that I could scent it at all meant that things had gotten worse.

One of these days this was going to get me killed.

I grabbed the second chair from the other side of the table and spun it so I could sit straddling it. "No," I said. "No, I don't have any tea. I can't stand the stuff."

"That's too bad. I'm partial to a cup of Lady Grey in the mornings. Even Lipton would do."

She hadn't slept, I realized. "I can give you coffee," the wretched hostess inside me offered.

Abigail shuddered daintily. "No, thank you." She nodded to a little leather scrap lying in front of her, like the suede bits Sarah used to wrap some of her wares in—the items that are a little too likely to draw attention, that need the distraction that organic material provides. This leather was black with age, huddled and lumpy like a long-dead mouse. "I brought your down payment. Did all go well last night?"

I stared at her a moment—she was so damned serene, even as her scent was screaming panic at me. I'd once heard that the best quality in an adept wasn't intellect or determination or even plain talent; it was the ability to hold two contradictory lives in one's head at the same time, living in one world while working magic in another. I had my disagreements with that theory, but Abigail was a walking demonstration of it.

"No, it did not." I said, trying very hard to keep my voice under control. "I got jumped by an amalgam of the remnant ghosts in the cemetery, and none of them had anything good to say about your great-great-grandmother. Whatever it was that got stolen, it's a sore point for them."

Abigail frowned. "I didn't think they would have such a violent reaction."

"No. Really?" I didn't mention the figure who'd distracted them long enough for me to run—and I sure as hell was not going to mention the path I'd run onto. "I didn't get in touch with your great-great-grandmother at all. They called her a thief," I added, watching for her reaction.

She folded her hands, twisting them over each other as if applying invisible lotion, and one nasty-looking hangnail cracked open. "She was. A very good one." The blood welled up slowly, a little blot of red against her washed-out hands.

Okay, that was slightly less than reassuring. "Well. The upshot of all this is that I've only got a name—Gabriel—and a lot of gabbling."

"Gabriel?" Abigail gazed at me in perfect incomprehension. "Are you sure? And—gabbling?"

I hesitated. "Okay. Not quite gabbling, but they kept saying that word, so it kind of stuck."

Abigail's brows drew together. "Gabble . . . Gabble Retchets, by any chance?" I shook my head. "You're sure?"

"No. I'm not sure. Mind telling me what the hell's going on?"

"If I knew, I would." She got to her feet, straightening her dress.

"No." I stood up and blocked her way. "You know a lot more about this than you're telling me, and if you don't let me in on some of it, I'm going to consider our contract terminated. You can take your down payment and go home." It was a bluff, yes, but she didn't need to know that.

Abigail went very still, one hand on the little leather-wrapped lump, lying dark and forgotten on the table. "Please," she said finally. She twisted her hands, as if trying to scrub them clean of something. The spot of blood on her thumb smudged and broke. "Can you give me one day?" she pleaded. "Tomorrow—no, tonight, I can bring it to you tonight. Please, if I tell you now, then—" She hesitated, and the scent of her seemed to fade, receding further into the background.

One of these days . . . "One day," I said. "But keep the down payment."

"I won't. You keep it. Please." She managed a shaky smile. "Let me keep to my standards in this respect at least."

I scooped up the lump and unrolled a long strip of dark leather. Four green rocks lay within, bright against the dull brown skin, and while I wouldn't know a gemstone if it yanked on both earlobes and yelled its monetary worth in my face, these did have some of that potentially valuable look. They smelled like dirt, like clay and river water, with a brittle crystalline quality that I could only assume was the natural scent of gemstones. There was a wild hint about these, something like what greenness would taste like if it were freed from artificial mint and sour apple and left to endless fields, but a moment's perusal showed that this was from the leather alone. It was probably deerskin, or something else that carried a trace of its former home.

What wasn't on the stones was any trace of magic whatsoever. No hint of fireworks and rain, nothing even to show that they were supposed to be somewhere else. If anything, they seemed incomplete, truncated.

"Emeralds," Abigail said helpfully. "Uncut, but two of them have no flaws, and they're certainly worth whatever you'd charge me for this work."

"I'd be happier with a check," I said. Abigail breathed a laugh through her nose. "I'll keep these," I said, "but not as a down payment. When I finish this job, you'll get them back, and you'll pay me in full. And in dollars, not favors."

"Done," she said. She extended her hand for me to shake, and I shifted the emeralds to the other hand to do so. The blood spot from her hangnail had hardened into a small dark blot. "I'll see myself out."

"Wait." I jumped to my feet. "I know there's something wrong. But I can't do anything about it unless you let me. What can I do?"

She smiled. "You're doing it."

"I'm serious. If not me, then someone—" I snapped my fingers. "Your brother."

The smile dropped away. "What?"

"You said you had a brother. The one who said you could blend in anywhere. The flatterer. Wouldn't he—"

"He won't help me," Abigail interrupted. She pulled her gloves on, finger by finger. "I'm not worthy of respect, by his standards. Not at the moment."

The bitterness—and a pain deeper than that—in her voice stole any response I might have made. "I'm sorry," I said finally.

"So am I." Abigail looked down, took a deep breath, then smiled brightly. "May I use your bathroom?"

What? "Go ahead." I folded the leather back around the emeralds and looked for some safe place to stash them as she closed the door behind her. Normally I'd put them under my bed or at the back of the freezer, but Abigail's appearance had made me feel a little less secure in my own home. Finally I tucked them into the bottom of my bag, wrapped in a spare shirt.

I closed up the bag and looked up, frowning. The door had been closed for a while, and I hadn't heard a sound even through the cellophane-thin walls. I tapped on the door. "Abigail?"

No answer. And, when I opened the door, no Abigail. No trace of her, and no scent, and no sign that she'd even been here. Save for the emeralds in their scrap of leather, and the empty mug on my table.

Eleven

After that, the morning just didn't fit together. A quick check of the name "Skelling" on my dinosaur of a computer got me about fifty *Nightmare Before Christmas* fan pages and nothing else. I could have taken a little more time for research, even asked the staff at Mount Auburn (if I wanted to go back there). But Tania was going to kick my ass across the Charles if I didn't sign in on time today, and sometimes the mundane matters make the best excuses.

I called Rena on my way out the door. No answer, of course, but I left a message to tell her that I didn't mind the karaoke cancellation and could she do a quick informal check on Abigail Huston? I hung up without much hope of a reply. Whatever was eating Rena these days, it would keep her busy.

The courier work for the day took its toll on me. No Mission Hill this time, but the same damn shuttle back and forth between Cambridge and the Seaport, ferrying pages for law offices whose elder partners were still superstitious about electronic communication. By three o'clock my legs felt like Jell-O and my head not much better.

I'd just dropped off the same dratted package for the sixth time at the Cambridge office when a funny shiver ran over me from crown to soles, like the quiver of lightning just before the bolt comes down to earth. I stumbled and dropped my helmet, catching myself against the bike rack.

There. A soft cry, like the note of a bell, present more in its echoes than in its actual nature. But the echoes were bad enough: for a moment I had the urge to run, to follow that call, to go where it led and do what it said and find the pack—

It was the same sound I'd heard the night before, the one that had grabbed me by the neck and set me clawing at the door. And now I didn't have the veil of sleep to distance me from it; only the sunlight and the knowledge that I was expected at Mercury Courier in another half hour.

Don't, whispered an echo behind me. I glanced back to see a shape like negative space: a man in a long coat, his face only visible in flashes of reflections, a broad mustache and sad, drooping brows. I shook my head, ignoring him in favor of the sound and the call.

Somewhere close by . . . not a scent, but a path, almost . . . I could almost feel the pressure of it next to me, like a road running parallel to my own.

I might have lost the chance last night, but right now I sure as hell wasn't going to lose it again. I turned, and there it was, the silver road just a half step away.

Yes, I said, and stepped onto it.

I didn't get the blackout sensation this time, the loss of time between one step and the next. Instead my entire body shuddered, as if I'd relinquished control of it to some other entity that didn't quite know how human bodies worked. I didn't exactly stumble, but I lurched forward, doubling over as I ran. And though I could still see the Cambridge streets, the trees and brick and startled pedestrians, they didn't quite matter here. I didn't quite matter.

Only I couldn't fully step onto the road. Something was still holding me back, and I glanced over my shoulder to see the man from the tower, clinging to me

as if I were his one link to meaning, a terrible expression of longing and dread on his face—or perhaps I
still couldn't see it, perhaps his reaction communicated
itself on the link that he still had with me. I snapped
at him over my shoulder, no longer able to remember
how to curse.

Ahead of me, detectable only by the ripple in this
place's geography, something else ran, and it was in
those footsteps I followed. I wanted to cry out to them
to wait, let me catch up, but there wasn't quite enough
air in my lungs. And each time I tried to run faster, the
shadow clasping my heels held on that much tighter.
Bastard.

To the river and across it, onto the Esplanade and
beyond. I blended in here, to whatever degree it was
possible for a bike courier to blend in without her bike.
Here were joggers, people out with their dogs—all of
whom ducked out of my path as I approached, some
cowering. If I'd had any brain left to wonder, it would
have wondered at that. But the only part of my brain
not consumed with the urge to follow the call had now
become distracted by the fact that running in bike
cleats *hurt*.

Further, further on . . . something cried out ahead
of me, a *halloo* like the note of a dying sousaphone,
and a cry formed in my throat to answer. In the back
of my head, in a part of me that didn't have anything
to do with perception or canine instincts, the treacherous thought came forth: *This is what that man meant
by power you could respect. Power to be scared of.
Power like the Morrigan's, like the Fiana's, the unlim-
ited wildness of it. This is what kept people scared;
this is the power that encircles the world.*

And, like snow down the back of my shirt, *He was
right.*

The taste of dead leaves and frost filled my throat,
and with one last desperate shudder I pulled free of
the ghost's hold. The world went silver, and I nearly
howled with the joy of it. *Wait for me*, I cried—

—and stepped off the path just as quickly, stumbling into an ornamental shrub. Prickles shredded the bandage over my calf, and I yelped, lurching to the side into another hedge, this one no less prickly.

I was in a park, still close to the river but nowhere I'd been before. The smell of traffic was still strong, but muted by trees and river scent, and the scene didn't look anything like what I knew of Boston. Ahead of me, brilliant white in the sunlight, stood a gazebo.

I wanted nothing more than to ask, "What the hell was that?" and choke down the terror with a good dose of self-delusion. But I knew. I was a hound, descendant of hounds, and if one trait of my ancestry was this talent of scent, then the other talent of Finn's pack should run in my blood as well. One of his hounds had run three times around Ireland; maybe I had the same endurance. Only that didn't feel quite right. I'd run on the wrong path, using someone else's shortcut, the path that the ghost had been scared to use a second time.

I looked around. There was no sign of whatever I'd followed here—whoever had called me.

"Who's there?" A woman's voice, sharp and scared, came from the gazebo, and a figure within stood up. Beside her, a second figure rose, then slid away as if it were restricted to the shadows. I shaded my eyes and squinted at the woman: gray hair under a white sun hat, gloved hands, a blue dress with white piping—

Abigail. She stared at me, her face crumpling with more emotions than I could read—pain, and loss of something great, and an unreadable anger. I opened my mouth to call out to her, but before I could do more than draw breath, the shadows exploded.

From every stark shadow, from every seam of darkness at the edges of things, came a flickering, a yelping, like the call of a thousand wild geese. I lurched forward as something snapped at my ankles, in and out of the shadows in less time than it took to think it. Heavy and rank, their reek curled around me, flickering in and out of existence as they slid from shadow to shadow, thick with the musty scent of oak leaves and unclean blood.

Was this what I had followed? I cupped my hands over my mouth. *"Run!"*

Too late. They had her, snapping at her ankles and bringing her down onto the steps of the gazebo, where the roof cast a heavy shadow. Abigail started to cry out, but stifled the sound, jamming her forearm against her mouth as if she too wanted to bite down on it. Blood spattered across white gravel.

Not as much blood as I would have thought, I realized, as I vaulted the hedge—even in shadow, the hounds couldn't fully seize her. And now I could see that they were hounds, though no more than hound-shaped holes in the shadows, like a water lens making the shadow momentarily deeper. On that thread of alignment, the link that had brought me here, I sensed a trace of frustration that they were so crippled, and even a hint of irritation: *how does he expect us to work in these conditions*?

The thought wasn't theirs. It was mine. I shook my head to rid myself of it as I reached the edge of the gazebo. "Abigail!"

She turned, too quickly, and her wounded ankle gave way. "Keep away from me!" she screamed, holding up her hands as if to fend me off. Shadow blurred across them, and she choked as punctures opened up first in her arms and then, blossoming red, across her throat.

I hesitated—to my shame, I hesitated—then jumped forward, sweeping my arm through the shadow as if to clear out cobwebs. I felt nothing, but for just a moment I caught a glimpse of something receding, eyes like pits turning to watch me, and a strange echo of puzzlement. Hot breath steamed over my wrists, and I shuddered, praying for sunlight. Whatever alignment I'd shared with these things, it was receding, fading as they recognized that I was not, in fact, one of them.

A second low note sounded, closer but less compelling: *Home, home, time to come home.* The breath on my skin receded, and though for a moment I had to fight down the urge to follow, I held my ground.

Abigail lay still as a sodden kerchief. I knelt next to her, trying to close my nose to the heavy, rich smell of blood, and started fumbling in my bag for something to stop the bleeding. Paper, no, spare shirt, yes —

"Oh my God!" A teenage girl with startlingly blue hair emerged from the far side of the gazebo. "Oh my God, is she okay?"

"No," I said, and tugged my cell phone out of the bag. "Call an ambulance, and then call the cops." I tossed the phone at her, and she fumbled with it for a moment before flipping it open. Abigail's breathing creaked and bubbled.

A dull clatter caught my attention, and I looked up to see the broken end of a jar roll slowly off the end of the gazebo, trailing dirt. It smelled of incense and emptiness, of the absence of its inhabitant—the jar I'd tested to see if Yuen's father had left it. It bounced as it hit the earth and came to rest at Abigail's feet as if offering itself as a poor vessel for her soul.

Twelve

Someone had given me a blanket, possibly out of the mistaken idea that mental shock required the same treatment as physical shock. The blanket itched and hung heavy over me like a wool tent, but I couldn't make myself shrug it off.

The ambulance had come, and gone, and judging from the EMTs' expressions, they weren't optimistic about Abigail's chances. She'd lasted long enough for the ambulance, I told myself; that had to mean something, right? But that self-consolation was a weak shield against the memory of that wound in her throat—hell, of all the wounds. And of the jar, the damn empty jar from the Three Cranes. Had her attacker used it to call down a death on Abigail, in some weird inversion of sympathetic magic? Or had they just left it behind, now that it was used up . . .

A police car had followed the ambulance, and the younger of the two officers had listened to a trimmed-down version of my story, then told me to stay put. That had been maybe half an hour ago. Since then I'd watched one long procession of police, panicked witnesses, Animal Control officers, and staff from the hotel that was the closest building to the park. I thought I recognized the name of the hotel, then realized I'd called it the other day: it was where Abigail had been staying. Of course.

Tania had called twice. I didn't have the guts to call her back.

Right now the officer who'd taken my first frazzled statement was talking to a determined young woman with a notebook, explaining that no, there was no dog problem in the park but yes, they would be conducting a full investigation. I huddled a little further into the musty heat of the blanket.

A shadow fell over me. "I told you everything already," I muttered, pulling the blanket back down, then stopped. A small, dark-haired woman holding a Boston Police Department badge loosely in one hand gazed down at me with an expression of mixed shock and dismay. "Jesus," I breathed. "Rena, my God, it's good to see you."

I got to my feet and almost hugged her. Almost. I noticed two things in time: one, a tall black man standing a few paces behind her, watching me. Two, Rena may be a hugging person, but only when she's off duty. And now she wore her duty like a coat of armor.

I didn't often see Rena in her official capacity, mostly because when I saw her she didn't want to remember that it existed. When she put on that badge, it was like her entire skeleton was rearranged, making her stand a little taller, a little broader, radiating a sort of quiet immobility that I usually associated with bedrock. Whatever she'd been so excited about a few days ago, none of it showed now.

I didn't know the guy with her, though he looked more at ease. He was younger than Rena, though they seemed to be on equal footing. I wondered if they'd partnered him with her to make up for her lack of height, and decided they'd have to be idiots to do so. "Excuse me," he said, with that peculiar cadence that cops have when they don't mean excuse me at all. "Do you know each other?"

I hesitated—the last thing I wanted was to get Rena

into any trouble—but she answered for me. "We do. Evie—Ms. Scelan, this is Assistant Detective Foster. May we ask you a few questions?"

"I don't think I can stop you—" I caught Rena's sidelong glance toward the officer who'd been first on the scene, and I finally registered what had been bothering me. The side of the first officer's car didn't show the BPD logo; it was a Newton Police Department car. *Newton? How the hell did I get to Newton?*

Well, I knew the answer to that question. It just wasn't one I liked.

So Rena and her partner were outside their jurisdiction, and she wanted to quiz me anyway. Any other cop and I'd have said no. But Rena had called me in to deal with tattooed bodies and dismembered cats and other cases that no one else would look at, and she'd seen things that would have driven strict rationalists batshit insane. And she sang a mean karaoke. Inasmuch as I could trust a cop, I trusted her.

"Go ahead," I said. "I'll tell you what I can."

Rena pressed her lips together, but she nodded. If her partner had only been with her for a little while, then there was only so much I could say about undercurrent matters. *Bruja* shit, as Rena called it.

"I was out for a run," I began. Foster glanced at my biking cleats. My feet still hurt like anything, and I tried not to shuffle them. "I came around that way," I continued, pointing to the mauled hedges, "and heard a snarling sound. That's when I heard the old woman yell something, and so I ran toward her."

Rena raised her chin a little—not much, but enough of a tell that I knew she was trying to suppress her usual tics. She'd caught on that I was leaving a lot out. Whether she'd ascribe that to bruja shit or guilt on my part was another matter. "I didn't see the dogs," I went on. Best not to lie about something when I could tell a half-truth. "I saw her lying on the steps, and I started trying to bandage the gash."

My hand went to my throat, and for a split second

I had a flash of Janssen tipping his head back. He'd been showing throat, consciously or no. Realizing that should have made me feel better, but it just gave me the chills. "And that's when the young woman came over. I gave her my cell phone and told her to call nine-one-one." She'd handed it back to me as the ambulance arrived.

Foster wasn't buying any of this. "You went for a run in those shoes?"

"I didn't have a chance to change."

"Let it be, Foster," Rena said. "Did you know the victim?"

For a moment I thought about lying. But I owed Rena the truth, or at least as much of it as I could give. "She was a client of mine," I said.

"And when did you see her last?"

I shrugged the blanket off my shoulders, then took a moment to fumble it back into place, thinking furiously. What could I afford to tell them without screwing things up for Abigail? Or, for that matter, getting tossed in the looney bin? "This morning."

Foster and Rena exchanged glances. They had to be new partners, I figured; otherwise they wouldn't be giving this much away. "I met her a few days back," I went on. "She stopped by this morning to talk about a job she had for me." Rena took a notebook from her front pocket and started writing in it. That I didn't like.

"What kind of job?" Foster asked.

"I can't tell you that." I met Rena's gaze. "I'm sorry, but I do have a confidentiality agreement with my clients. As most of my work goes, it was pretty innocuous." I paused a moment, thinking over the rest of our conversation. "She seemed . . . spooked, this morning. Like something had gone wrong for her. But she wouldn't tell me what." Instead she'd asked to use my bathroom and left. Goddammit.

"I see," Foster said, with that cop inflection that clearly means *and I don't believe it*. Rena had the same look on her face, and her pencil had stilled on the page.

"Look, if I'd known—I would have done something—" I remembered and snapped my fingers, dislodging the blanket again. This time I didn't bother to retrieve it. "She left a down payment with me for the work she wanted me to do." I dug into my much-abused courier bag. Tucked at the very bottom was the leather-wrapped bundle that Abigail had left with me.

Rena leaned closer, and I unwrapped the emeralds for her to see. "Foster," she said.

His eyes narrowed. "Hard to say," he said.

I started to speak, then paused. Foster prodded at the emeralds with a pen. "They're not stolen, if that's what you're thinking," I said.

"As a matter of fact, that is what I was thinking, Miss Scelan," he said without looking up. "Mind telling me what makes you so sure they're not?"

The same thing that had told me Abigail was scared to death, but I couldn't tell him that. "I'd probably have heard about it."

"I'm inclined to agree with her," Rena said. I did my best not to look grateful; Rena didn't need me bollixing this up for her.

"Look," I said, "how about you take them in and have your lab rats do whatever tests they need to. Hell, you can keep them as long as you want, so long as you give me a receipt."

I'd thought that was a decent concession, all things considered, but if anything, Foster's demeanor only became chillier. Rena, for her part, had that weary look she sometimes got when I started talking Sox games or when one of us had done something really stupid the night before. "I see," Foster muttered, the blankness of his expression saying volumes. He pulled a pair of latex gloves from his shirt pocket. "We'll give you a receipt, as requested. In the meantime, I'd like to take them in and do our 'lab rat' stuff, as you put it."

"Oh, be my guest," I said. Rena gave me a warning glance behind Foster's back: *Watch it.*

"We'll be in touch," she said, scribbling on a form and handing it to me.

"You know my number." I stuck the receipt in my wallet. Foster held up two plastic bags, one with the emeralds, the other with the leather strip that had held them, then packed both away. I suppressed a sigh as he did so; that was a couple of months' rent right there. "Rena, can I talk to you for a moment?"

Foster gave her a glance, but retreated a few car lengths into the parking lot. "Your new partner's kind of a dick," I said.

"He's new. And you got under his skin." Rena gazed past me, toward the gazebo and the fluttering crime-scene tape. "He's just up from forensics, and I don't think he liked being called a lab rat."

"Whoops." Well, there went my hope for a playing-nicely-with-cops merit badge. "Tell him I'm sorry."

"Won't help."

I picked up the blanket and started trying to fold it up. "Seriously, Rena, what are you doing out here in Newton? You couldn't have come out here just for me."

She snorted. "Don't flatter yourself."

"Then what the hell was it? You've complained about the local PDs before; it's not like they're going to volunteer information just to be neighborly. And hell, dog attacks aren't your beat, are they?"

"No, they're not. More yours, from what I hear." She held up a hand as I started to sputter. "Not what I meant. Evie, I can't tell you what I'm doing here."

"What do you mean, you can't?"

"I mean, this isn't any of your goddamn business." She glanced over at Foster, reached for the pack of cigarettes that I knew no longer lived in her pocket, and shook her head. "Shit. Evie, you just had to get involved in this, didn't you? I swear, this *bruja* shit better not mess with my case."

"It might. I don't know. I could tell you if I knew what your case was—"

"No. You can't. And I can't tell you, okay? I'm not any more happy about it than you are. Less, even." She drew a long breath, the kind that ought to be drawn with a mouthful of smoke, and let it out slowly. "I wish to God you hadn't been the one to find this woman."

"You and me both." Even though I'd shaken off the urge to join the pack, the memory of it revolted me. "Rena, if I learn anything more, anything that isn't weird shit, I will tell you. Okay?"

She didn't look convinced. But she didn't look disappointed either, and that was enough from Rena. "We're on for a week from Saturday, right?"

"Last I heard."

"Maybe I can tell you about it then."

My bike was still there when I made my way back, footsore and out thirty bucks for the cab ride. Tania had called a third time, and I'd finally answered to say that I'd been in an accident. Well, it was close enough to the truth. She asked how I was, how my bike was, and whether I could pull another shift tomorrow, at which point I pleaded PTSD and told her to fuck off. Not in so many words.

A shiver passed over me as I unlocked my bike, and I looked up to see—well, nothing. Again. That damn blank spot, the ghost who had latched on to me at the tower and now seemed to unwilling to let go. "Skelling," I murmured, and must have imagined the flicker of absence at the back of my perceptions.

Skelling. That was it. I hadn't heard the name before; I'd seen it, seen it written on a card in a display case. I swung my bike lock over the frame and gritted my teeth at the pain in my soles. Elizabeth Yuen. She'd know what Skelling did, or at the very least her father had. And if I could find out, I might have some idea why Abigail had been attacked.

Unfortunately, Elizabeth had finally had enough of Boston. I made my way through the clutter of traffic in Chinatown (some idiot had parked an RV on a one-way street and refused to pull over further so that traffic could go around him) and pulled up in front of the Three Cranes to see the windows of her apartment dark and shuttered. My heart sank, but I locked my bike to the closest rack and hurried down the stairs.

Boards had been nailed over the door, and the original sign had an addendum tacked to it: PLEASE DIRECT INQUIRIES ELSEWHERE. Hell. How else to find this Skelling? Mount Auburn probably had records, but I got the shivers about going back there, even in daylight. Maybe the library—and where would I even begin, once there? The vast repository of information and porn that was the Internet? I turned away from the door, intending to head on home, then stopped as someone clomped down the stairs toward me. I caught the scent a moment before I saw him, and my lips curled back from my teeth.

Janssen saw me too, but a moment too late. He backed up a step, the shit-eating grin dropping off his face. "What the fuck are you doing here?"

"None of your business." I tried to move past him.

He moved into my path, hands out in a placating gesture. "Hang on, hang on, I didn't come here to fight. They're closed up? For real?"

"Yes, for real." I paused. "You didn't know that?"

Janssen grinned. From this angle he looked different, off, some aspect of how he held his head, how his body language had changed from the cravenness of the day before. I didn't like it. "I don't usually bother with the small-fry stuff. But there's only so many places you can get certain things . . . What about you? Fair's fair."

"I ran out of Tiger Balm." If Janssen hadn't known about the Three Cranes being closed, he wouldn't have been the one to hire those three bozos from yesterday.

They'd counted on the "closed" sign keeping away witnesses. Just because he didn't have anything to do with it didn't mean I liked him any better, though. "I thought you were getting out of town. Mind telling me what made you stay?"

The grin widened and turned oily. "Oh, I'm not telling you anything. Wouldn't want to hurt your virgin ears." With that, he deliberately turned his back on me and climbed the steps to the street. The same cherry-red sports car stood at the curb; up close like this, I could now see the rust spots all along the side.

"It hasn't gone your way, though, has it?" I called after him. He stopped at the edge of the sidewalk. "Otherwise you'd be out of town already. You wouldn't be coming by here to hassle the—what did you call them?—small fry?"

His smile thinned out. "Why do you care? Now you've learned the score, you finally want in on the game?"

Game? "Maybe." That's right, Janssen had mentioned something big going down . . . but aside from the attack on Abigail, I hadn't noticed anything big. And somehow Janssen didn't seem the kind of guy who'd be drawn to that pack at all. The opposite, in fact.

Janssen didn't notice my pause. "Oh, how soon we lose our innocence!" He glanced down the street, then moved closer. "But you're right. It's less than ideal for me right now. In fact, I could have used your help a little while back, if you'd been quicker on the uptake. The guy who pulled it off doesn't like my kind."

"What, assholes? Can't say I blame him."

"Oh, you're funny." He reached out to pat my cheek, and I jerked away. Janssen laughed, the sound like nails dropping into a jar. "But you're a little late. There's a way around everything." He jerked his head toward the boarded-up door of the Three Cranes. "As soon as I find another place that sells—well, sells what

I need for negotiation—then I'll be all set. So go on home, Hound, and maybe when I come back in six months you might be relevant—"

He paused, staring behind me. I glanced over my shoulder, but couldn't see anything. "What?"

"Shit," he whispered, the color draining from his face. "Shit, I'm not ready for this . . ."

"What the hell are you talking about?" Aside from us, the street was deserted, though the cross street was full of people (and finally moving traffic, now that the RV was out of the way). "Janssen—"

Janssen leaped to the side of his car, fumbling with his keys. "Fuck off, Hound," he spat over his shoulder. "I got work to do."

"Go to hell," I snapped, but . . . but wasn't there a change in the air, like a cloud coming over the sun, only the sky was as hazy as it had been all damn day? A dimming of the light, somehow, as if my eyes were starting to give out . . .

I turned to face it fully as a hot wind blew across the street. Dust spun up from between the cracks in the pavement, hot and dry in my throat. My long coat rippled around my ankles—

Janssen's car started up with a scream of abused engine, and I blinked and shook my head. There wasn't dust, or wind, or cracks in the pavement, and I sure as hell wasn't wearing a long coat. I caught my breath, then jerked to one side as Janssen's car careened up onto the sidewalk and past me. "Out of the way!" he yelled out the window, following it with a blistering curse as something went *crunch* under the front of the car.

"Son of a bitch!" That crunch had been my bike. Janssen didn't even slow down. He leaned on the horn as he drove off, scattering pedestrians in his wake. I crouched by the mangled remains of my bike, too furious to even draw breath. One wheel was intact, but the other looked like a Möbius strip, and the frame was bent, completely useless. "Shit, shit, shit," I muttered, running my hands over it as if I could magically bring it back to wholeness. There went my bike, my transport, my fucking paycheck—

The shadows of my hands on the frame suddenly faded, as if the sun's light had waned. I paused, then looked over my shoulder, unable to shake the feeling that I'd done this already.

Past the intersection, on the far side of the street, stood something in the shape of a man, his hands clasped in front of him as if he were posing for a picture. He was in silhouette, shadowed by the lights beyond him, but the stillness he radiated implied that he was an adult, without either the restlessness or the vitality of a younger man.

For just a fraction of a second I caught a whiff of death-stink, not the sweetish scent of a corpse but something fouler, like the thing in Yuen's jar. Only where that had had the unformed feel of a grub, this was the full cockroach.

I stood, one hand pressed against my nose in an instinctive, inadequate attempt to block that reek—then had a flash of something I'd never sensed before. Olfactory double vision: two scents in the same place at the same time. The second one was frail, almost a negative against the crippling rot of the other. I shook my head, and they canceled out, becoming not one scent but a palpable absence, the way a radio station playing dead air has a sound.

And yet I took a step forward, leaving my poor, mangled bike behind, drawn by a sense I couldn't quite name. It wasn't the lure of scent or of the hunt, or even simple curiosity—I knew all of those, and could step away from them even if it hurt to do so. This was new, and I didn't know how to defend against it. It was like the call of the hounds this afternoon, the call that had pulled me to Abigail's side too late.

This was the man who'd summoned those hounds. I bared my teeth, unsure whether I was acknowledging my place as one of them or denying it. Either way, I couldn't keep from walking closer.

The silhouette leaned to one side, as if regarding my progress. For a moment I had the sense that someone was walking beside me, copying my movements, long coat flapping in a nonexistent wind.

I'd reached the intersection. Soon I'd see his face . . . I should have been able to see it by now, shouldn't I? I curled my hands into fists, balking at the call that pulled me forward. I wanted to know who he was, but on my own terms, not this strange compulsion.

A car horn blared, so loud my skull seemed to shrink, and a brown-and-white blur shot in front of me, between me and the silhouette. I jumped back, tripping over the curb to land on my butt. The blur resolved into the side of a van—no, an RV, squatting there like a train car dropped onto the street.

A door in the RV opened up two feet down from me. "Get in!" yelled Reverend Woodfin.

Thirteen

I pulled myself in, expecting a passenger seat or something that would at least pass for it, but a giant folding sign advertising *Woodfin Ministries* took up most of the space. "What the hell?"

"Close the door!" Woodfin wrenched the gearshift into place, and the RV's engine groaned in response. Through the driver's side window, I caught a glimpse of the silhouetted man receding, walking away as if this no longer interested him. I fumbled the sign out of the way and yanked the door closed. "Have you no sense at all? It's damned lucky for you that I came back."

"What are you talking about? Who was that?" I tried to manage some kind of sitting position next to the sign, and succeeded only in whacking my head on the sunshade. The inside of the reverend's RV smelled like a dorm room, with the additional edge of what I slowly recognized as real gunpowder, not the scent-analogue of magic.

Woodfin glanced at me. "You saw a person?"

"I—" *No*, I wanted to respond, because that scent hadn't been a person's scent. But I had seen a shape. "Sort of."

"Interesting." He pointed ahead, to where the snarl of traffic signs gave way to large, red DO NOT ENTER signs. "Does that mean this turns into a one-way street?" A car honked at him, and he sped up.

"Jesus!" I huddled down further, trying not to imagine what I'd look like after going through the windshield. "Yes, yes, turn left here!"

"You don't have to shout." Woodfin shook his head and jerked the wheel to the left, careening around a corner far too tight for this whale of a vehicle. "Myself, I didn't see any person, just got the sensation of the unclean. You get to recognize that, after the kind of work I've been doing. Yes, yes, I see the red light; don't worry, it'll be green by the time we reach it."

I whimpered and clutched the sign, very aware of how inadequate a safety measure it was. I wasn't used to being either this high up or this unsteady in a car, and Woodfin drove as if major road signs were only guidelines. A chorus of horns followed us as we wove through traffic like a guinea pig through a doll-house, and the reverend's only response to them was—again—to speed up. He fit right in among Boston drivers, I acknowledged grimly.

"It so happens," he said, as we rounded another too-tight turn, "that I was in town to pick up one last thing Elizabeth left behind, so that I could give it to you. Fortunately, I can now do both at once." He gestured to the back of the RV. "Your clip is in the back, on the table. Go on back, I'm a safe driver. You'll be fine."

I doubted that. "My clip?" I tried to stand and clutched at the closest handhold, which turned out to be a bit of paneling that, on closer inspection, looked like it hadn't been securely attached to the wall in years. "This is about *ammunition*?"

"No, it's about debts." Woodfin pulled into a new stream of traffic and trundled over into the left lane. I lost my footing and slammed against the wall. "You did my job," he continued as if nothing had happened, "you ministered to Yuen at the transition from one life to the next. I was supposed to be on hand to do that, to make sure that his passing ended his father's unfortunate—hm—extension. So I'm paying off my debt to you. Believe me, I don't want to write those debts off just because you haven't got the common sense God gave a possum."

"Point taken," I said, deciding not to antagonize the crazy man anymore. I made my careful way into the swaying, thumping back end of the RV. The walls were covered with pictures—posters for gun shows dating back twenty years, Civil War-era photographs of stoic men before their amputations, advertisements for reenactments and historical replicas. Most of the pictures had notes written on them in a careful, round hand: *Chippewa Motor Lodge, 3/13* or *Contact Terence Bradlee* or *See Waldrop brothers about DeWitt-Horowitz connection.* "Where are we going?" I called over my shoulder.

"We? I don't know about *we.* *I* have to get to a quarry out in—" He paused, and I saw with a kind of fascinated horror that he was checking a notebook from the glove compartment. "Assawompset. What kind of a name is that?"

"Got me." I caught the side of what probably had once been a kitchen table. It had been turned into a work surface: a mess, but a carefully ordered one. Most of it had been covered with webbing to strap everything down: fine cloths of varying thickness, a pile of small green-bound books, a stack of small tools like jeweler's calipers. The tools lay on top of a barricade made of what I had assumed at first were steel bars. A second look revealed them to be silver ingots with scrapes all up one side that suggested they'd been grated.

A single clip of ammunition, like the kind that Yuen used to supply for my gun, lay in a webbing of its own. I picked it up and slid it into the outer pocket of my courier bag. "Any chance you can take me back to where you found me? My bike—"

"No." We jounced over another pothole, and I clutched

at the edge of the table. "I may not be as experienced in the particulars of this trade as Yuen was, but I do know not to drop someone back in the midst of that. In fact—" He pulled the RV to the right, blocking two lanes at once. "In fact, I don't think you ought to go back there for a while. You'd make it too easy for that thing to find you again."

If he wanted to find me, I didn't think I could stop him. And if I didn't get back there soon, my bike would be sold for scrap metal . . . but it hadn't been reparable. I'd seen enough to know that. The most you could do with it was to take it apart and use the unhurt pieces—if there were any—in other bikes.

I put my head down a moment to mourn the loss of that poor, beaten-up thing. It'd put up with a lot from me, and if I ever saw Janssen again, I'd return the favor. "You can just let me off here, then," I said finally.

"In the middle of traffic? I don't think so. Ah," he added, and cranked the wheel to the right. "This ought to take me where I want to go. What were you doing at Yuen's, anyway?"

"I needed to ask Elizabeth—" I failed to move with the RV, and was slammed up against one of Woodfin's posters. "Ow. I needed to ask her about a name I saw at her place. Skelling."

Woodfin made a pleased sound. "Look at the picture next to you. Should be on your right."

I craned my neck around to look at the poster and then realized it wasn't a poster at all. It was a copy of Yuen's photo—the six men in the Old West. Notes in illegible script had been scrawled on the frame and on the picture itself, arrows and circles running from one man to another. Woodfin had blown up several sections, each of the men's faces in particular, and tacked them around the periphery. "Who are they?"

"My life's work," Woodfin said, beaming as he cut off another SUV. "I'm a gunsmith, a restorer of old weapons, and I'd assembled the full collection from this expedition. It's how I met Yuen, originally." He leaned on the horn, and I peered out the curtained window to see the Public Garden across from us. Two skateboarders flipped us off as Woodfin honked again. "Six men got hired by a consortium of buyers on the East Coast to transport a few, hmmm, potent talismans across the country. Couldn't take them over the iron road, couldn't drive, not that there were many motorcars back then, in nineteen-oh-eight. They had to ride or walk, from San Francisco to New York, carrying some of the nastiest stuff you're likely to find in this life or the next." He grinned. "Their backers had commissioned a set of pistols for the expedition, all made specially. Kind of like your ammunition, come to think of it. Took me ages to track down all those guns, and longer still to track down their stories. Not how my daughter thought I'd spend my retirement, but I gotta say I like it better than playing endless games of checkers on the porch."

I remembered the case on Elizabeth's counter: the six guns, each in its own niche, and the name beneath one: *Skelling*. Two of the guns, I remembered, had been damaged to the point of no repair. Somehow I didn't think they'd had an easy journey. "Which one is Skelling?"

"Rory Skelling. Far left." Woodfin wrenched the wheel around again, and the Public Garden gave way to brownstone houses, still rocketing by at a distressing speed.

"What, the one with the mustache?" I found the blowup of his face and squinted at it.

"Yes, him. He's the only one who didn't have any extant correspondence—you wouldn't believe how long it took me to track down his history."

The sepia tones washed out any elements of color, but the silhouette was right: long coat, broad-brimmed hat, bright eyes shaded by heavy brows. I'd found my ghost . . . and now that I was looking at a larger picture, I could see something else. Take away the mustache, turn Irish red hair to Irish black, smooth out some of the planes of the face, make it a little more feminine and a bit uglier, and you'd have the face I saw in the mirror each morning.

What had Finn said about the descendants of his hound Sceolang? Once or twice a generation, someone will have his talent . . . "I think," I said slowly, "I think we might be family."

Woodfin's answer was drowned out by a metallic clatter on the roof, and he grunted in annoyance. "Maybe. But Skelling didn't have any descendants," he said. "He died before the expedition ended."

And I'd bet anything that his remains ended up in Mount Auburn Cemetery. I shook my head, then paused. "What the hell was that noise just now?"

"Traffic strip. Nothing big." Woodfin turned a little in his seat. Beyond him I caught a glimpse of the Charles, gleaming in the sticky afternoon sunlight—only it was on our right, and so was the Esplanade . . . "Now, Skelling's an odd one, because he didn't get killed on the job. That woman behind him in the photo, that was his wife, an outcast Lakota girl, and she—"

Esplanade on the *right*? Esplanade even this close? "Jesus Christ, you're on Storrow Drive! What were you thinking?" I pushed the sign out of the way and leaned over the dashboard, trying to see whether there was any way out of it before we hit one of the bridges. "Turn around! Take an exit!"

"We're perfectly fine," Woodfin asserted. "I'm making good time for the first time today. Now, the Lakota girl didn't leave a record of her own, but halfway across Massachusetts she and Skelling killed—"

"We are not fine!" Christ, couldn't this man read the height limit signs? "Take an exit now!"

Too late. We rounded a corner and came up on one of the bridges that made Storrow Drive such a pain for anyone in a vehicle larger than a minivan. Woodfin hesitated, then hit the accelerator, just as I yelled and ducked.

The low brick arch scraped along the top of the RV with a screech, followed by an almighty bang. In the rearview mirror, I saw a chunk of aluminum-wrapped machinery fall off the back of the RV and roll to the side of the road.

There was a moment of dead silence, loud enough to drown out the chorus of horns behind us. "Air conditioner," Woodfin said finally. "I always forget to add that into my height allowance. Well, it needed replacing anyway."

I stared at him. "You're insane. Completely insane."

"Then you're in good company."

Woodfin turned onto an exit without further comment, heading toward Boston University. "What happened to the rest of them?" I asked after a moment.

"Oh . . . Kolya, he's the mean one in the middle, he settled in Atlanta until someone got sick of him. DeWitt started up a saloon in San Francisco, once he got back West. Georges didn't even make it to the Mississippi. Ants." He gave an involuntary shudder. "Prescott—I was about to tell you what happened to him. He ran off with some of the packages they were transporting, about the same time that Skelling and his wife killed each other. The others caught up to him out by—" he checked the notebook again, this time keeping an eye on the road, "—Assawompset. Yuen's uncle seemed to come out the best of them, and he had his own problems. His idiot brother was fool enough to misuse what he'd brought home." He smiled grimly. "Which gets us back to you, again."

"That's why Yuen's father was imprisoned in the jar?"

Woodfin shook his head. "Poor bastard tried to use some of the learning in the Unbound Book. Normally, I'm not one to say that greater knowledge is a bad thing, serpent and Eden aside, but that book's a poisoned well. I know for a fact Yuen wished that his uncle had just let Prescott run off with the whole thing."

"'Only the dead can kill the dead,'" I murmured, thinking of Elizabeth, and the pages she burned. I hesitated, just long enough for the blind spot at the back of my perceptions to wake up again. *Stolen property*, I thought, *and Skelling wanted it, and whoever attacked Abigail was connected somehow* . . . "What were they carrying?"

"Hm?" Woodfin pulled across three lanes of traffic into a BU parking lot and wrenched the gearshift back down into park.

"The expedition. The six men and their guns. What were they transporting?"

"Oh, a lot of things." He tipped his head back and closed his eyes, then recited as if reading from a list. "A harmonium built by John Dee—that's now in the Cloisters, though they're smart enough not to put it on display—the pages from the Unbound Book, a necklace made of fulgurites, half of a harlequin costume, two ampullae of Christ's blood from a Papist church, no offense, and at least three spearheads that were claimed to be the Lance of Longinus." He opened his eyes and shrugged. "Jack shit, really, but they wouldn't put the important things on the official list, so it's hard to say what else they carried over."

Of course. "Thanks," I said. "And thanks for the rescue."

"Don't be dumb enough to need a second one." He leaned over and opened the far door, as he had when he'd pulled up in Chinatown. "I don't particularly want to be owing any more debts in this town."

I walked the rest of the way home and arrived sore and dusty, and not even the warble of the fountain could cheer me up. A drift of mail, mostly bills, lay on the floor in front of the mail slot, and I kicked it out of the way.

I pulled off my shoes and sank onto the futon. Bike

gone, leads gone, a ghost latched on to me, and something weirder following me. And worse, there was Abigail, now in the hospital. At least I hoped she still was; that would mean she was still alive. I sighed in guilty frustration. I'd known she was worried, I knew she'd been scared of something, and yet I'd let her walk out. I hadn't wanted to deal with her problems, not in the midst of my own, not when she was the cause of some of mine.

The downside of doing something big enough to change a city is that people expect it again. And the downside of *that* is that when you turn them down, what comes after is pretty irrevocably your fault.

I put my head in my hands. My cell phone burred against my hip, and I didn't answer it till I'd locked Woodfin's clip in my desk drawer. "This is Scelan."

"Evie?" Katie, speaking faster than she usually did and with a high, nervous edge to her voice. "Can you come over? Like, right now?"

Fourteen

It took took me far too long to get over to Nate's apartment on foot, long enough that the stars had already come out and the street was quiet. I couldn't tell if the lights in their apartment were on; hell, had she even been calling from home?

I rang at the main door to their apartment, but either the speaker was broken or Nate didn't bother to ask who I was before buzzing me in. The hallway was darker than it had been the night before; a bulb on the second floor had burned out and no one had replaced it yet. I knocked at Nate's door, then tried the knob and found it unlocked.

The apartment was dark, save for a light in the kitchen. I closed the door behind me and edged around the dining table, trying not to knock anything over.

The scene in the kitchen was one I knew well, although from a different perspective. For a moment the remembered greasy smell of our old oven rose up in my mind, along with the taste of the dinners Mom had left for me on the nights that she'd worked late. But I'd been at least ten when that had started, and a lot bigger than Katie.

She'd pulled the stepstool up to the stove and was using it to stand on as she worked. Bubbling away on the front burner was a full pasta pot that must have weighed ten pounds. A smaller saucepan lying empty by the sink explained how she'd managed to fill it, and the starchy smell of cooking pasta thickened the air to the point of stifling. Katie turned and smiled brightly at me. "Hi."

I leaned against the door frame. "Hi." Nate's kitchen was about half the size of mine, even though his was, technically, a larger apartment. But while mine served as the only real private room I had—since the office was my bedroom and aside from one notable incident, I hadn't had many conversations in the bathroom—his was clearly only a place where cooking got done. "Katie, why'd you call me over?"

"For dinner," she said, but there was a calculated innocence in her voice. "I'm making mac and cheese."

"Where's Nate?"

"At work." She caught a piece of macaroni on the end of the spoon and blew on it before popping it in her mouth. It crunched audibly.

I sighed. "Katie . . ."

The phone rang. Katie glanced over her shoulder at it, then at me. "Could you answer that? Please?"

A suspicion started working its way to the front of my mind, but I went and picked up the phone anyway. "Hunter residence."

" . . . Good God. *Evie*? Is that you?"

Nate. Crap, how was I going to explain this? "Yeah, it's me. Katie invited me over for dinner." I leaned back to see into the kitchen, and Katie gave me a thumbs-up. I glared at her. "We're making mac and cheese."

"Um. Thanks! I didn't know she'd . . . er." He sounded about as awkward as I felt. "I was calling to let Katie know that I'd be home in an hour. My advisor's asked me to sit in on another meeting, and I can't really get out of it. There's sandwich makings in the fridge—but I guess that's moot now."

"Apparently. I'll stay here with her. See you soon." I hung up before he could ask any more questions. "Katie?"

She kept stirring the pot. "Yes?"

I went to stand next to her at the stove. She'd used far too much water for the amount of macaroni, I noted; probably wanted to make sure she didn't get it wrong. "You called me in to cover for you, didn't you?"

Katie gave me a smile that was equal parts shame and glee. "He doesn't like it when I use the stove. And I didn't want a sandwich."

"I see." In his place, I wouldn't be too happy about Katie using the stove either. "Okay, kid. I'll join you for dinner. But if you ever," I leaned down until we were on the same level, practically cheek to cheek, "*ever* do this again, I will make sure every single article of clothing you own has a My Little Pony on it somewhere."

She giggled, then stopped as she saw my face. "You wouldn't do that. There's no way you could."

"Can't I? Ask Sarah sometime about the twinkle incident." I stood up, ran my hands through my hair, and sighed. "So. Do you want a hand with that stuff?"

She shook her head. "Only I'm not so good at draining it, so you could do that if you wanted."

Did she honestly thing I'd stand by while she did the rest? Christ, the kid was just like her brother, infuriatingly self-sufficient. "When's your bedtime?"

"Eleven," she said, but the sidelong glance she gave me betrayed the lie. She saw my raised eyebrow and corrected herself. "Ten thirty."

Sure it was.

We lasted till nine thirty, Katie talking most of the time about day camp and the books Sarah had loaned her. (I didn't even know there was a book of *The Black Cauldron.* When I asked about what I remembered from the movie, Katie got a pitying look on her face, and I changed the subject fast.) I put the last of the mac and cheese in the fridge, cleaned up with Katie pointing out where everything went, and nodded in all the right places until Katie wound down. When she did, it was like a current shutting off: one minute she was bouncing up and down, talking about when she got kicked out of the local Brownie troop (telling the troop leader's future was apparently a big problem if you were scary accurate), the next she was slumped against the back of the couch, mouth open in a silent snore.

I picked up a few of the stuffed animals she'd brought out to show me, looked around for a clue as to where they belonged, and settled for stacking them next to Nate's laptop. For a moment I considered letting Katie sleep where she was, but my neck hurt just looking at her, and so I finally slipped an arm under her shoulders. "Come on. Bed."

"'m not tired," she muttered.

"*I* am. So, bed." I picked her up—she had bones like a bird's, and about as much body mass—and nudged her door open with my hip. Her room looked out on the street, and for a moment the weird red light coming in startled me until I realized it was from the stained-glass decals she had pasted all over her window.

"Evie," she mumbled, clinging to my shirt. "Nate won't be mad, right? That I used the stove." She blinked at me; each time her eyes closed, they began to roll back.

"Maybe. But he'll get over it." Her head lolled back as I set her down on the bed. This morning's outburst notwithstanding, there was a stuffed pony in first place next to her pillow, complete with a fraying yarn bridle. I pushed her hair back from her forehead, then leaned over and turned the fan on. She could sleep in her clothes tonight; I didn't have the patience to find her nightshirt. "Don't worry about it now," I said. "Go to sleep."

Even before I'd said it, she was out. I got up and closed the door behind me, then turned out the lights in the kitchen. Just as I did so, the light in the hall came on again, a flicker under the door.

Nate didn't seem to remember I was there. He unlocked the door and dropped his bag, then slumped against the door, moving like a man who'd already run a marathon today and had twenty more miles ahead of him. "She's in bed," I said, and he started. "You okay?"

"Yes. Yes, I'm fine." He went to Katie's door and opened it a crack, the same way he'd done the night before. "She called you over?"

I nodded. I'd keep her secret for now.

"Thanks. Christ, I don't know why . . . I'm sorry, Evie. I didn't expect to be gone this long." He rubbed at his eyes. "I make a lousy dad."

"Good thing you're just her brother."

He smiled, but it was gone in an instant. "And this was after you had a rotten night too."

Not that rotten, I thought, remembering those few moments of sleep with Nate's arm around me. "It wasn't, wasn't anything big. Well, aside from the ghost latching on to me, and I think I have some idea how to get rid of him . . ." I stopped. Nate was staring at me, one hand over his mouth in a poor attempt to hide a disbelieving smile. "What?"

He laughed, the sound coming out of him startled and happier than I'd heard in a while. "And just like that, all my problems are put into perspective. You had a *ghost* on you?"

I shook my head ruefully. "Something like that. It's nothing I can't handle."

"Uh-huh. And do I get to say that to you when you tell me my schedule's too full?"

"I —" I caught a laugh, then stepped back, hands on my hips. "Okay. Fine. You want to compare crappy days, let's go."

Nate nodded slowly, his smile widening. "Okay. Advisor meeting."

"Double shift, two days running."

"Chapter three of my dissertation due next week." He leaned against the little table that passed for his desk.

"Crazy preacher practically kidnapped me," I countered, making my way around the end of the sofa.

"Tutored the guy we ran into on Memorial Drive."

I stopped. "You're kidding."

"I'm not." He grimaced. "Henderson said that would be the best way to get him through the course."

"Jesus. Um. Okay. Ghost summoning went wonky on me."

"Last-minute committee meeting that turned into creating three new committees." Nate paused. "Hang on. You mentioned that last night. Did it get worse?"

"Well, I'm not dead. And I'm not on a committee, so I call that a toss-up." I thought about including Abigail, but that wasn't my misfortune, and to claim it as such would be disrespectful. "Jackass ran over my bike."

He winced. "Ouch. Bad?"

"Totaled."

"In that case, I think you win."

I put my hand over my heart and bowed. He laughed, and for just a second the air felt clear again, in spite of the lingering scent of mac and cheese. For a moment we just stood there grinning at each other like a pair of loons.

Then something in his bag chimed, and Nate's brow furrowed into its usual lines. His face fell as he dug out his phone and read the glowing screen. "Damn. I'm supposed to be meeting my father in half an hour. Maybe I should just call it off."

"I can stay here," I offered. Hell, it wasn't any less comfortable than my office, and I'd already slept on this couch once before. "If you need someone to keep an eye on Katie."

He shook his head. "It's not that. I've—well, I know I can leave her here for an hour on her own, as long as Greta downstairs knows. But you ought to get on home—"

"No." We both turned at the same time. Katie stood with one hand on the door to her room, swaying a little, eyes wide from sleep held at bay. "She has to go with you," she said. "You have to take her with you, Nate. Or you'll get mad at him."

Nate crouched by his sister and smoothed his hand over her tangled brown hair. "Go back to bed, Katie."

"You *have* to," she repeated, the creepy prophetical aspect of it fading away into a child's whine. "Promise."

"I promise. Okay? Now go on back to bed." He gave her a quick kiss on the forehead, and she received it with somnambulant dignity before walking back into her room.

Nate stood and glanced at me. "Well."

"I think," I said slowly, "I'd better do as she says." Had I ever told Nate about the flicker of Sight on his little sister? It had been one of those things that I'd meant to do, but between the Red Sox and the lost time and the damn idiot ghosts it had fallen out of my mind.

"If it were anyone else telling me this . . ." He exhaled slowly, then nodded. "All right. I'll let Greta know."

I waited outside while he negotiated with his downstairs neighbor—not, as I'd expected, one of a gaggle of BU students, but their summer sublet, a Danish woman in her late fifties. "She'll check on Katie every hour or so," he told me as he descended the porch steps.

"Are you sure you want to do this?" I asked.

"No. Not really." We walked in silence for a moment, threading our way closer to the more vibrant parts of Allston. An MBTA bus roared past in a cloud of dust and diesel fuel. "But I do think I owe it to him. After the last time we met, and I lost my temper . . . Katie's probably got a point about that, at least. But if it'll keep him out of our lives from here on out, yes, I'm happy to meet him." He glanced back at me, the light catching the early gray in his hair. "That's the most important thing."

We arrived at the agreed meeting place: a microbrewery bar, the kind that had about twelve thousand kinds of beer on tap, where the waitresses would chuck you out for ordering anything that could be found in a can. Or at least so I remembered from my days before I went on the wagon, and honestly, those memories weren't exactly crystal clear. Nate scanned the room as we entered. "He's not here yet."

"Then sit down. I'll get you a drink."

"Anything with caffeine." He managed a smile that turned a little more real as he met my eyes.

I smiled back and went off to mightily disappoint the bartender. She insisted on giving me some kind of weird microbrew version of ginger ale, and sniffed as she poured a Coke for Nate.

The bells at the door jingled as I moved away with our drinks in hand, and I automatically looked to see who'd come in. "Shit," I muttered, and hurried over to Nate. "Excuse me a moment," I said, setting the glasses down. "The asshole who crushed my bike just came in—I didn't realize he'd been following me. I'll make this quick."

"Who?" Nate asked as I turned back around. Janssen saw me and paused in the middle of focusing the dregs of his charm on the bartender. For a very brief moment he looked scared—no, not just scared but shocked, as if he'd spent hours constructing an elaborate structure only to have a stray breeze threaten to knock it all down. "Evie—" Nate said.

"Just a moment." I walked up to Janssen, and he retreated a step. "I don't know what you're doing here," I told him, "but you crushed my goddamn bike, and so help me if you're still following me—"

"What are you talking about?" Janssen spread his hands. A battered shopping bag dangled from his wrist, its gold logo flaking off. It made him look like someone who'd gotten stuck carrying his society wife's shopping, and it stank like old shoes. "I'm not here for you at all."

"Then what—" I should have seen it before. I turned, moving a little out of the way, to see Nate standing at the far side of the bar, watching Janssen with wary recognition.

I looked from one to the other, my eyes filling in the details that my brain hadn't wanted to synthesize. The line of the forehead, the curve of cheekbone and jaw . . . the deeply set eyes that were watery blue in this man and Hunter gray in Nate . . . Even their builds were similar, Nate's frame a leaner version of Janssen's bulk.

I'd known there was something familiar in Janssen's scent. But that very familiarity made it horrible now.

"Oh, you're with him?" Janssen's grin widened. "That's just perfect. And he never had a word to say about his old dad? He must not trust you very much."

The bartender set down a narrow glass of some thick golden drink, and Janssen swept it up, his hand dwarfing the glass. "If you'll excuse me," he said, carefully stepping around me. He settled into the chair across from Nate and lifted his glass in a salute. "Good to see you again."

Nate darted a glance at me, then slowly sank into his chair.

"You bring her here to meet me? That's sweet. Didn't think you needed a nanny, though." Janssen chuckled, the simple sound of it unclean.

"Don't," Nate said tightly. His scent had changed almost as soon as Janssen appeared, becoming that controlled, closed-down iron. He glanced at me a second time, then shifted just a little, drawing attention to the third chair at the table.

I took a seat. My face still felt as if I'd been splashed with boiling water, burning with shame and suppressed rage and an awful lot of other confused feelings. Janssen gave me a sour look, then snapped his fingers. "Bike. Right." He took a roll of money from his pocket and peeled off several bills, tossing them in front of me. "That ought to cover it. Now let me talk to my son."

It'd cover it all right; it'd cover a better bike than

my old one had been when I first got it. I swallowed—
now that Abigail was in the hospital, any chance of the
money she'd offered was gone. The prospect of that
much cash was tempting, but I left the money where
it lay.

"Anything you want to say, you can say in front of
Evie," Nate said.

Janssen made a face and muttered something that
sounded suspiciously like "pussy-whipped." But he
turned that smile back on again, and took a long sip of
his drink. "Has my boy been talking to you, Hound?
He tell you what he did the first time we met?"

Lost his temper . . . I shrugged.

"Broke my fuckin' nose. Wouldn't think it to look
at him, would you?" Janssen's smile widened, revealing
even more of his teeth. "Starved little cub that he is."

"Good for him," I said, then remembered to look at
Nate. A muscle twitched at the corner of his jaw, but
he didn't say anything.

Janssen chuckled. "That's what I thought. Good to
let those impulses out now and then, mm?" He deliberately turned so that he was no longer facing me. "All
right. You got my letters, right? With the story of Sigmund and Sinfjotli, right?"

Nate glanced over at me; I shrugged. "I didn't understand them," he said carefully. "I don't know much
Wagner."

Janssen choked on his drink. "Wagner? The man
wouldn't know a Volsung if one tore his head off.
Fuck." He turned and spat on the floor. "'Scuse me.
No. What I wanted to tell you was the story of Sigmund and his son. This is important, boy. This is the
sort of thing you need to know about."

Nate curled his hands around his drink, his expression a combination of embarrassment and utter confusion. I shrugged; I was as lost as he was, and I was
used to dealing with crazy on a regular basis. "I guess
I didn't follow that part of it."

"Hell. You really are an idiot." Janssen shook his

head, then turned to face me. "I don't suppose we could have a little privacy?"

"Not really," I said.

"Then be a good little doggy—" he paused to drain the last of his drink in a few quick swallows, "—and go fetch me a new one of these. Keep the change," he added, slipping another bill under the glass.

I was about to tell him to fuck off, but something about Nate's expression made me stop. Honorable intentions aside, I didn't have a place here, and it wouldn't do Nate any favors for his last meeting with his father to turn into a snipe fest between me and Janssen. "This once," I said.

Janssen smirked. "So. Sigmund, the Volsungs, the Ylfings. Damn, I feel like a nursery-school teacher, having to spout this to you. Sigmund and his son found a hut in the woods, with two wolfskins hanging from the door. Are you listening to me, boy?"

I took the glass up to the bar and watched over my shoulder as Janssen went on, waving his hands to illustrate parts of the narrative. Nate's expression didn't change; if anything, it just became more lost. The bartender finally handed me a cool glass, damp with condensation, full of something that smelled like flowers gone to rot. "It's pretty potent stuff," she warned me. "You shouldn't chug it down like it was beer."

"I don't think he'll notice," I said, nodding to Janssen.

He didn't seem to care if Nate was following him, just so long as he could keep talking. "—called Ylfings, you understand? Because of the skins—oh, are you back already?"

I set the glass down just far enough away that he'd have to stretch for it. "If that's all you have to tell me," Nate said, "then I think we're done here."

"You'll be missing the best part." Janssen glared at me. "Go away, why don't you?"

I ignored him, concentrating on Nate instead. He no longer seemed as closed down, but there was something else in how he looked at Janssen: a desire to understand, a hope that there was something *to* understand rather than just plain crazy talk. I had no right to take that from him. "I'll be back in a moment," I said. "We can go then."

"Okay," Nate said without looking at me.

I left them talking and headed to the ladies' room, always the best place for a third wheel to escape to. "She's got a nice ass, but a face like a startled horse," I heard Janssen say as I walked off. I shrugged; he wasn't wrong, about the face at least. And it hadn't stopped him from hitting on me earlier, although the thought of that was enough to give me the shudders again.

I washed my hands and waited a moment inside, listening to the perky pop that passed for Muzak here. I thought about my own father, who despite his prior history of being a jerk was at least sane. In Nate's place I'd be just as confused, and probably angry about being fed this saga crap instead of something real. I shook my head and stepped back out—

—just in time to see Janssen pull something rank and ugly from his shopping bag and hit Nate across the face with it.

Nate staggered back, one hand going to the sodden gray thing that had hit him. I shoved my way past a pair of shrieking girls and yanked Janssen to his feet. "What the hell was that for?"

"Family business," he said with a grin.

"Family business my ass! What did you do—" I glanced over my shoulder to where Nate stood, his hands braced on the table, shaking his head as if trying to dislodge something. The gray lump lay over his shoulder as if it were part of a sling, staining his shirt gray and bile-yellow. Somewhere, the bartender was ringing a large bell and calling for a little help here, please. "What the hell did you hit him with?"

Janssen's grin narrowed, became feral and triumphant. "You've got no place in this, Hound, not even if you were what you claim to be to this city. This is personal business between me and my son, and you—"

I heard a growl behind me, and turned in time to see Nate reach for me. Without even looking at me, he grabbed me by the shoulder and pulled me off Janssen. I let go without thinking, and Nate took my place, hands locked around his father's throat. His scent shifted even as I tried to understand it; this wasn't the cold, locked-down rage I recognized from before, but something else, something more akin to Janssen's stink.

Two large men in band T-shirts pushed their way through the crowd and grabbed Nate and his father. One of the girls shrieked again, tentatively, as if testing her range, as they dragged them past her. I fought my way through the crowd behind them.

The bouncers tossed the two men out into the street, and in the time it took for me to get past the crowd at the door, Nate had grabbed Janssen by the front of his shirt and swung him up against the wall. "You rotten shit," he grated. "You even come *near* her, and I'll—"

I caught his arm, or at least got my hands on it. It felt like iron. "Nate," I said. "Nate, stop it. They'll be calling the cops any minute now."

Nate didn't answer. Janssen raised a hand, or at least a few fingers. "This isn't any of your business, Hound. You just go on home. Besides," he added, long teeth flashing in a grin, "I want to know what he was going to say. What'll you do to me if I ever come near your little sister?"

Nate's hand went from Janssen's shirt to his throat, digging in so hard the skin around his fingers went white. "You can go to hell."

One of Janssen's hands clutched at Nate's in a feeble attempt to pry it away, but his grin never wavered. "Better to let it out now," he choked, the lack of air giving his words an unintended sibilance. "It'll always get out eventually."

"Nate." I reached across his arm and took him by the shoulder, tying the three of us in a bonny knot. My fingers grazed the lump still stuck to his shoulder— leather, soaked in something like paint thinner and urine. "Nate, let go. We can deal with this guy, both of us, just let him go."

"Let go," Janssen echoed, still grinning.

"Shut up," I said over my shoulder. "I don't know what you did, but if I ever catch you in my city again—" Janssen gurgled a laugh, and I kicked him in the shin, hard. "If I ever catch you near here again, I'll show you exactly how the Fiana went down."

That shut him up. It didn't reach Nate at all, though, and for a moment I thought he'd tossed me out of the way just so he could tear out his father's throat. But he drew a deep breath, and the lines of his face smoothed out almost as if the bones had shifted under the skin. "Get the hell away from me," he said, clipping off each word. His hand dropped away from Janssen's throat, where the lines left by his fingers remained for a pulse or two before fading.

"Told you it was family business, Hound," Janssen croaked.

"Fuck off." Nate rubbed at his mouth, then pulled the lump of foul leather from his shoulder. "Evie, let's go." He turned his back on Janssen and started walking, but blindly, stumbling over the cracked pavement.

"It doesn't go away!" Janssen yelled after us. "Just because you don't like it doesn't make it go away!"

"Keep walking," I said to Nate.

"He's wrong," Nate said, but he kept walking. "He's wrong."

Fifteen

I didn't want to leave him. "At least let me check on you tomorrow," I pleaded at the steps of his apartment. "I wouldn't trust him not to keep harassing you."

"He got what he wanted. He'll stay away." Nate rubbed at his mouth again, then turned and spat on the ground. "Christ, I can still taste that thing he hit me with."

"What is it, anyway?" I reached to take the mess from him, grimacing a little at its smell.

Nate jerked away from my touch. "No." He looked at the gray lump, and a bitter smile cracked his lips. "I'm going to take this thing home, and first thing tomorrow I'm going to burn it. No more trace of him." Still holding the vile thing, he stretched slowly. I looked away. "Evie, I will be fine. Go home."

"Are you sure—"

"Positive." He glanced at me, then, as if dragged on a leash, turned and lurched up the stairs.

So I went home. And remembered, as I passed more and more streetlights that seemed to cast the wrong number of shadows, that I had an unwelcome passenger.

Fine. I had a ghost on me, and I had questions. Time to set a trap.

There aren't many times when I can sympathize with the priorities of those who've gone further into the undercurrent. Most of the time I'm fine with not knowing the secret name of Lilith just so long as I do know to put my pants on before my shoes. But staying out of the depths doesn't mean they'll stay away from you, and sometimes that ignorance works against me.

To take a particularly salient example, most adepts don't worry about being haunted—mainly because they're not stupid enough to let a blood relative get a grip on their soul, but also because they know the tricks to drive off a ghost. Me, I have a talent that lets me find things and a few hedge-magic tricks, none of which would last beyond a full adept's sneeze. Which meant that even though I had an idea of how to construct a ghost trap, I didn't really know what I was doing.

I'd never let that stop me before, though.

I stopped by the all-night corner store, avoiding a few concertgoers who'd managed to get very lost and very drunk, and picked up a few essentials for the night: bread, milk, and a big container of salt. The clerk gave me a weird look—I'd been in here twice in the last couple of weeks, buying salt each time, but the stuff had enough use in general house magic that I kept running out. Besides, he had to have seen stranger purchases.

The fountain in my office had gotten something stuck in it so that it now sounded like a naiad with asthma. It choked and sputtered when I thumped it, then went back to its usual arrhythmic flow. I scattered salt on the threshold and windowsills, bound a silver chain (well, mostly silver) at the foot of my bed, and, after a long search in the backs of my cabinets, found half a jar of crystallized honey that I could leave out. No liquor, not in my house for the last ten years, though this was one of those times I felt the lack. Then I turned the lights off, lay down, and hoped that the party two doors down blasting "Destroyed Eighties Hits II" on repeat wouldn't affect my trap.

At some point I must have slept, but the dreams I

had were so damn dull that I kept waking up just to get away from them—walking down a long path in a land flat as a sanded-down board, traveling alongside a wagon stacked high with boxes, following the progression of a locomotive across the plain ahead and envying its swift passage. Then back to more walking. Even the dim interior of my apartment was more interesting than that. In those brief flashes of wakefulness, I sensed the gap in my perceptions coming closer, the emptiness of a ghost scent moving in toward the gift.

Empty scent, I thought, half out of dream. *I should remember that. There's something important about it.* But dream dragged me down again, this time into a slightly shifted landscape: cornfields, rolling hills, the tang in the air of a New England August turning toward September.

"It's a simple matter," a voice said, and I flinched before realizing that I was back in the dream, now following that wagon through a small town, past one of those ubiquitous Civil War statues. "You've wanted to walk off with it too. I've been watching."

In the dream, I turned to see the speaker, but there was none, only a sense of . . . something, some emotion attenuated by time and events. Betrayal? Regret? Longing? Could have been anything, from the echo I felt. Skelling may have had enough strength to grab hold of me, but there wasn't much of him left.

"Do you know how debased these things are? And the people we're bringing them to? Thieves and whores, every one . . . You understand this." The same voice, a man's, mature but not cracked. I turned in place again, searching for the voice, but the landscape folded in around him. "It's about respect. How can we respect our own employers when they're the kind of people who'd . . . who'd turn magic into a crass commercial trade? Why *should* we treat them fairly?"

"I don't trust you," I said, and it was a man's voice that I spoke with, creaky and dry. "Sorry to say it, but I don't."

The speaker sighed, and I turned again. A Native-American woman gazed back at me, and though she gave no sign, I knew somehow I'd fallen short in her estimation. "That's really too bad," the unseen speaker said.

I raised my hand, noting absently that it held an antique six-shooter, and pointed it at the woman—or where she had been, because now there was nothing but a blur of red and gray, of tooth and bone. Behind that thing stood another shadow, not the woman's but another's, a man in silhouette—

The gun went off, and I shuddered awake, staring up at the ceiling. Hazy sunlight filtered through the blinds, thick and golden like Janssen's drink last night. The air felt like soup, and I'd kicked off not only the covers but the silver at my feet.

And that persistent blind spot still hovered at the edge of my senses. Skelling hadn't gone anywhere.

I managed to catch an early-morning Green Line train out to Sarah's shop. It wasn't open yet, but I'd called ahead and threatened Sarah with an impromptu Axl Rose imitation outside her bedroom window unless she came downstairs.

She met me at the back entrance, still in her bathrobe. (There are advantages to living above one's workplace.) "You are an evil woman," she informed me, "and you look like crap. What the hell happened that you have to wake me up this early?" She yawned, then handed me a folded-over manila envelope. "Never thought I'd be selling incense to you."

"How much?"

"Ten bucks even. Why do you even need it? You hate that stuff."

If I hated it, so might another Hound, even if he no longer had a corporeal nose. "Long story," I said, not wanting to admit that I'd messed up the summoning ritual after all her help. "If it doesn't work, I'll let you know."

"Hmph." She eyed me narrowly. "I'm thinking of holding another organizational meeting in a couple of weeks. Are you available?"

"Don't know." I rubbed at my eyes. "Oh, yeah. Have you heard of something called Gabble Retchets?"

Sarah laughed. "Funny, I figured you'd already know, being the Hound and all. Gabble Retchets, Gabriel Hounds, Seven Whistlers . . ." She arched her eyebrows, surprised by my lack of response. "You've never heard of them? It's a term for the hounds of the Wild Hunt."

I paused in the act of tucking the incense away somewhere it wouldn't break and incapacitate my nose at a bad moment. "The Wild Hunt."

"Yeah." She grinned. "You do know that term, right?"

"Sort of." You couldn't go twenty pages in the folklore books she'd loaned me without stumbling over it. There were Wild Hunts in every part of Europe, and none of them could agree on what they were. They were the souls of sinners, condemned to wander the earth (probably waving to the captain of the Flying Dutchman whenever they crossed paths); they were the host of Faerie-however-you-spelled it, loosed once a season in a sacramental hunt; they were unbaptized children haunting their parents; they were Odin and his riders, chasing down anyone unlucky enough to get in their way. And half a dozen more. "Is there a . . . a definitive Hunt? One that has some basis in something beyond local legend?"

Sarah snorted. "Let me check with my consensus of pagan experts and we'll get back to you."

"Goddammit, Sarah—"

"Oh, look who's cranky today. It's not my fault you're dating a goddamn Vulcan." She paused, waiting for me to either rise to the bait or deny everything, then sighed. "Evie, there isn't one Wild Hunt that all the others spring from. It's a legend that's dispersed all over—hell, often it's a local landowner, like Red Edric or Black Matilda, who leads the hunt, instead of Odin or Gwyn or even Hecate. It's just a face to tack on to the idea of a spectral host. You can't reduce them to just one ur-myth."

"I thought you were all for syncretism."

Sarah winced. "Yeah, well." Her enthusiasm to believe that one aspect of the Triple Goddess was the same as another had been part of what got us into trouble with the Fiana, and while she didn't regret it, I thought the brush with divinity in that particular form might have soured her on theory. For a little while at least. "This is folklore. Folklore doesn't have to have a unifying myth; in this case, the Wild Hunt is a spontaneous reaction to the nights drawing in and the concept of mortality." Theory or no, clearly she hadn't soured on lectures just yet. "Look, if you need me to look something up for you—"

"I don't. Probably not." No point in having her chase down the wrong Hunt. Not when I wasn't yet sure what I was dealing with.

"Good. Because I was about to say that I can't. I've got too much on my plate, what with the organizing and all. I really think we're making progress."

Progress for this lot, I thought, would be not throwing chairs at each other. *Could you respect them?* The memory made me redden. "Sorry."

"What for?" She seemed to soften a little. "Look, how about you come in for coffee? Alison's sleeping, but I've got to wake her up in ten minutes for her deposition work anyway, and we can talk."

"Can't. Got work."

"Work? It's a Saturday, Evie, there's no way you can be doing work on—" She stopped. "You're hunting, aren't you?"

"Got it in one."

Sarah drew away, shaking her head. "Oh no. Look, Evie, if you . . . If there's a reason you're asking about the Wild Hunt . . ." She hesitated, and a flicker of actual fear, something suppressed for too long, slid under her voice. "Evie, they're dangerous. Old-blood

dangerous. Chaos-and-inexorable-winter dangerous.
You don't mess with them, in any form."

"I know." Which was why I really, really hoped that
I was wrong about this particular hunch.

The best plan under the circumstances was for me to
go back out to the park where Abigail had been attacked, find the scent of her attacker, and follow it
from there. (Well, not quite. The plan that made the
most logical sense would have been to show up at
Mercury Courier, beg forgiveness, offer proof that my
bike had been totaled, and ask for an extra day off to
procure a new one. But I didn't really consider that a
viable option.) That way, I'd have the whole panoply of
scents: the shadow-scent of the hounds, Abigail's faded
lilac, and, if I hadn't just been imagining it, the scent
of her attacker.

It was a good plan, and if I'd still had my bike, I'd
have gone with it in a heartbeat. However, I was at the
mercy of the MBTA, and while that was fine for some
parts of Boston, the T didn't stretch out to the suburbs.
It certainly didn't stretch out to that part of Newton,
unless I wanted to take the commuter rail followed by
a series of buses. I might be able to get there later, but
I wanted to check out closer places first.

Instead I went against Woodfin's advice and headed
back to Chinatown. After I verified that, yes, my
poor wrecked bike had been carted away long since,
I walked down to the cross street. I switched off my
cell—the damn thing could bring me out of even the
deepest trances, and I wasn't in the mood to deal with
interruptions today—and sniffed for remnants of a
trail. There wasn't any trace of the silhouette I'd seen,
but if I sank in, if I gave myself over to searching . . .

It occurred to me, not for the first time, that—although the patterns of scent in Boston were chaotic
tangles overlaid only with what order humans chose
to give them—each separate neighborhood had its
own distinctive pattern. Whether it was the spices-

and-fried-tasty-goodness element that separated Chinatown from the dry-paper scent that permeated so much of Beacon Hill, or the brilliant interweaving of Dorchester as opposed to the quiet intensity of Longwood, or whether it was actual scent or just the interactions of each neighborhood's people, the result was fascinating. I was starting to be able to find my way through Boston solely by scent.

I smiled and knelt on the sidewalk where I'd seen the silhouette. *My city.* I liked how that sounded.

Enough people had passed over this spot in the last fourteen hours that the pattern of scent was dizzying, but only a few had stopped in this very spot for more than a couple of seconds. A woman with a dandruffy Pekingese—no, three people smelling of new raincoats and suntan lotion, probably tourists—no, a homeless man with a touch to his scent that probably marked him as a seer who hadn't made it to the enclave—no, though I ought to try to find him at some point.

There: the blank, doubled scent that I'd noticed before. It wasn't much. In fact, the weird, duplicated quality to it made it seem as if it wasn't even there. I could, I supposed, follow it by that absence (Skelling's presence over my shoulder stirred, but I ignored it), but that'd take a lot more patience than I had to spare. Besides, in that state I'd very likely be concentrating so hard that I'd walk out into traffic.

But there was an edge to the scent, like a distortion, like the lump in the sheets when you make the bed over something. I could only catch the barest hint of it: dry leaves, frost, a chill like December in the back of my throat. It wove in and out of the scent like a child hiding behind a sapling: never quite out of sight, never quite clear.

It wouldn't have been enough two months ago. It was barely enough now. But it was more than the empty scent of the silhouette, and present enough that I could keep hold of it. I could track it.

I smiled and rose to my feet, sensing the world

around me both as sight and scent together. The hunt was on.

Through the streets, left and right, then a straight shot down Tremont. It wasn't quite leading to Newton, though I had the sense there were several directions it could go, depending on the timing of the path— whether I was following him from this place or the route he took to get here. If I wanted, I could probably follow one of the offshoots back to the park . . . I shook my head. Maybe later. This trace of the scent was strong enough now.

The streets began to fill with early Saturday-morning shoppers and tour groups. I frowned as, ahead of me, a bus full of seniors disembarked at the Symphony, probably for a noon concert. This was all getting a little too close to the way I'd come. He hadn't come straight from my house, had he? Or had he gone there afterward . . . the scent was too fragmented for me to even figure out his direction.

I thought of how Abigail had just shown up out of nowhere, and decided that wards or no, I probably needed a burglar alarm.

But the trail missed the first turn toward my apartment, and I breathed a sigh of relief, only to find the trail attenuating even further. What traces I could pick up of the cloaking scent—and there weren't many, not even a fragment of the rotten scent that had preceded it—were becoming more and more unreachable, as if they were receding behind a mirror. I paused as I reached the Fenway and swore; almost gone. *Not yet, please not yet.*

No use. I got two blocks past the Museum of Fine Arts, only to find that wild, dry-leaved scent dying in one last burst, as if it had only seen the light for a brief moment before being hidden again. I turned in place, searching for any last hint—only to come up against a wall, both literally and figuratively.

The building to my left rose up in a forbidding mass of brick and tile. Two stone lions stared up at me from

shin-level, and above the door an inscription pro-
claimed *C'est Mon Plaisir.*

This Is My Pleasure, I translated with the little
French I remembered from high school. And despite
the medley of scents of the Fenway, the museums and
colleges and informal dorms leaking scent like Berklee
leaked music, this building had no scent. It stood like a
safe-deposit vault, forbidding and enigmatic.

Why had this trail led me here, of all places? To the
Isabella Stewart Gardner Museum?

Sixteen

The Gardner Museum was built to resemble a Venetian palazzo. Think for a moment about the differences between Venice and Boston and you'll see part of the problem. This is not to say that it was totally impractical; in fact, from the outside the Gardner looks more like an institutional building, maybe a college rec hall, than anything else. In some ways it's a good symbol of Old Boston: gray and bleak on the outside, full of marvels once you get in. Or so I'd been told; I'd never ventured inside.

I couldn't tell you why; I'd just never really noticed the place, and since getting involved in the undercurrent, I'd had even more of a blind spot. It didn't really show up on my radar. For one thing, based on what I'd heard of Isabella Stewart Gardner, she sounded far too sane to be an adept. Boston had its own history of eccentrics, and she didn't even come close to the top of the list there. For another, magic in Boston had been very carefully controlled for nigh on a century, and the people who controlled it were not ones who ran in her social circle. Let the spiritualists do as they liked; when it came to control, Boston's undercurrent was well in the hands of the lower classes.

Although, now that I was here and looking at the building—and noting that it didn't really have much of a scent, at least not one it allowed to escape its walls—I wondered about that. If she'd known about the undercurrent, she might have built her stronghold here as a way of making a statement, like putting a statue in the middle of enemy territory. You didn't need to be an adept to do that; you just needed guts. And from everything I'd heard about Gardner, she had that.

Maybe the Fiana hadn't liked that assertion. Maybe that was why, when there had been a theft from the Gardner some years back, none of the paintings had ever been found. The Fiana might not have pulled strings there, but they'd had their hands on enough to do so easily. That was a stretch . . . but right now, I was willing to entertain the idea that Gardner hadn't been as ignorant about the undercurrent as I'd thought.

I'd never been inside. I'd never even come close to it before, and its aggressive I'm-not-here stance on the magical level had sunk it further below my notice. But now, with that fragmentary scent dissolving just steps from its door, I found my interest sharpening.

A friendly volunteer took my money at the front desk and handed me a little clip to fasten onto my clothes. There was something off about the scent in the little anteroom—enough that it could give me a headache if I stayed there too long. Something about being neither one place nor another . . . I shook my head, trying to shake the feeling that I'd just stepped out of Boston, and walked into the museum proper.

Scent hit me like the floor hits a drunk. I stumbled at the threshold and caught myself against the wall, barely seeing anything before me. The security guard jumped to attention. "Miss? Miss, are you all right?"

I didn't answer. I couldn't. There was too much to deal with—sensory overload on every level, not just through my talent, had swamped any responses. I slumped against the cool stone, staring.

The building that was such a drab block on the

outside held a garden within. An atrium four stories high looked down onto green grass and running water, fountains and sculpture and tiles side by side as if strewn by some titanic hand. Sunlight filtered down in a cool glow, free of the painful heat of the outside air. Arched windows looked down from every story, and tiles and stones of a dozen different kinds notched the walls between them, a winged bull next to Moorish peacocks, Roman dolphins below.

I had thought it silly to try to make an Italian palazzo in Boston. Gardner hadn't done that. She'd brought Europe, a square of it, and surrounded it with a palazzo to remind it of what it was. Beyond these walls, the world changed and corroded; here, Isabella Stewart Gardner had preserved four stories' worth of beauty from time, drawing her line in the sand and saying this far and no farther, this was what she protected.

And the scent—even though I couldn't stop staring, the majority of the input screaming through my skull was scent. There were thousands of scents, thousands upon thousands, all clamoring for attention. Normally I disliked museums because of the way all the scents were muffled, stuffed behind glass, and here, yes, the physical scents were quiet. But the rest—incense, silk, oil of a hundred kinds, oil *paints* of a hundred kinds, stone competing with stone—I hadn't realized stone could have so many different scents, but now it was obvious how the sandstone of a carved lion differed from the marble of a sarcophagus . . . My head spun, trying to make sense of everything that my nose caught.

But beyond that, because so many of the items had been left out and not sealed away, because the museum itself was a sealed entity, the scents had all blended together into one great confection. I fumbled for a metaphor to encompass it and could only come up with inadequate, pedestrian ones: a stew pot, a pressure cooker, locking in all the different things Gardner had found and merging them into a greater whole. Magic, yes, there were loci here and more than loci, but that trace of fireworks scent was only a single note in the symphony.

The security guard was still talking, still asking if I was all right, reaching for his radio. Sight seemed like such a pale sense in the wake of everything else. I could go mad here, I realized dimly. I could spend days without moving, just reveling in the scents, and no one would ever be able to coax me out of it.

Something flickered out of the corner of my eye: a shadow, a long robe or coat. *And what good would it do if you got lost here?* a man's voice asked in the back of my head, and I smiled, acknowledging his point. If I did that, I'd never get to hunt again. I closed my eyes against the beauty, closed my mind against the scent, and exhaled slowly. "Sorry," I said aloud. "Just a little dizzy."

When I opened my eyes, the guard was watching me—not with pity or confusion, as I'd thought, but a sort of amused sympathy. "This is your first time in here, isn't it?"

I nodded.

"It takes some of us like that." He smiled proudly, gazing out at the atrium.

"Yes. Yes, I can see that. Thank you." I managed a smile, and if he didn't quite believe I was harmless, he at least wasn't going to throw me out just yet.

How was I going to find the scent of the silhouette—never mind that I seemed to have lost what trail it had—in this place? Needle in a haystack didn't even come close; needle in a sewing shop, maybe. I walked down the long stone hall that led to an arch and a painting of a dancer in mid-flourish, lit so that she seemed about to step off the canvas. In this place, she very well might. I pinched the bridge of my nose and tried to ignore the insistent scent of a nearby stone

basin that still carried chrism in its aura, like a priest
who'd long since left his pulpit. Too many distractions,
too many small, incidental scents.

Maybe it was because of the chaos, but when Skelling stirred beside me, I noticed it immediately. He
wasn't quite leaving me, but he seemed to be drawn
somewhere, pulled as if by an invisible leash. *Appropriate metaphor*, I thought, and followed him past the
atrium and its perpetual fall of water. Up the stairs,
past a tapestry that smelled of old silk and songs half-
remembered, over tiled steps smoothed by age and
travelers' feet. Past several of those travelers as well: a
school group listening dutifully as their guide spoke in
French, several older couples, a young man sketching
the delicate structure of a silver ostrich. Skelling moved
through them as if they weren't there—to him, they
weren't—and I followed, weaving my way through the
people.

Up another set of stairs and through a door flanked
by pillars, into a room where a rose window shed
warm light across a red tiled floor. Cabinets and cas-
kets lined the walls, offering a collection of icons and
miniatures to the air with only a rope to separate them
from any onlookers, and a long table held a number of
aging books and reliquaries. Gilded angels gazed down
on ghost and woman alike, and a tall blonde woman
in a security uniform straightened up at the far end of
the room.

I tried to look inconsequential as I began a circuit
around the room. The guard's gaze unfocused, becoming that I'm-not-looking-at-you-but-you-better-believe-
I-see-you expression I knew well from Rena. I drifted
over to the arched windows that surrounded that inner
courtyard. Skelling faded, becoming less of the autono-
mous blankness and more an echo.

The blur of scent began to separate out in the back
of my mind, becoming less of a monolithic entity and
more of a choir. I circled the table, examining but not
touching each book: Eighteenth century, but kept in a

wine cellar for ages; fifteenth century, and with a lock that someone had wisely left broken; a silver bull's head on a staff, from who knew when; nineteenth century, but as elaborate as any on the table and with some nasty gunpowder scent wreathing it . . . I'd hate to be the one to catalogue that, you'd have headaches and nightmares for months . . .

Unraveling scents is, for me, like putting together a monumental puzzle—although I suppose taking one apart would be a more apt metaphor. This was a tangle, a snarl of trails against the rioting background of the Gardner itself, the olfactory equivalent of a Jackson Pollock painting projected over a screaming paisley pattern. If I'd had to just look at it, it would have given me a headache in no time flat.

But I didn't have to look. All I had to do was find the one important thread. I smiled and raised my head, trying to separate the scents. Past the fresh trails of yesterday, still luminous in the quiet air, through to the ones of days before. Here the traces I followed stopped bearing any relation to real scent and became the metaphorical elements that my talent treated as scent. The strangeness of the different objects in this room began to emerge at this level: I wasn't used to scenting objects that were more than a few hundred years old. And Mrs. Gardner had brought over enough of Europe that I was in way, way over my head.

I loved it. I turned slowly in place, on some level aware that I was swiftly losing all credibility with the security guard. But compared to the wealth of scent that surrounded me, that was a minimal distraction.

It wasn't like paisley and Jackson Pollock, I realized. The pattern of scent here was closer to a pointillist painting than the usual tangled Book of Kells knotwork I visualized. Instead of the endless weave of minute detail making up a greater whole, this was a pattern made of self-contained spots, all the separate bits of the museum coming together in a great choral shout.

I tried to pull my mind back to my work. Was that something? Not an actual trail, because I'd have latched on to that in a heartbeat, but a . . . flicker. Like a layer of glass positioned in just the right way, or a heat ripple in the air without the heat—a distortion, somehow, throwing off the patterns but not a pattern in itself. A *Mad* magazine fold-in, I thought, and stifled a giggle.

The guard cleared her throat meaningfully, and I had just enough self-preservation instinct left to snap out of it and open my eyes. I'd crossed the room— well, yes, I could dimly remember that—and stopped in front of a low glass-fronted cabinet, one hand raised as if to open it. No, I realized, lowering that hand and glancing guiltily over my shoulder at the guard—not to open it, but to reach on top of it. I stepped back a pace and squinted into the cabinet.

Several silver teapots, each on its own etched tray, a shallow Chinese dish next to a framed watercolor of a pair of dancers in masks . . . and a slightly discolored square on the shelf, about as wide as the length of my forearm. Something had been removed, something that had been here for a while. It didn't have the exact mark of that dry-leaf scent that I'd followed here, but it was close.

"*Skelling*," a low, refined contralto murmured in my ear. "*I expected you ages ago. What on earth kept you?*"

I jumped back and spun around. There was no one behind me, only the icons and sculptures and a full-length painting of a woman in black, a pattern behind her head like a medieval halo. She didn't move—of course not, she was only paint—but for a moment I had the distinct sense that she'd only just jumped back into place.

"Excuse me," another woman's voice said, this one crisp and controlled. I turned to see two people standing a little ahead of the security guard: a slender Indian man in a suit jacket a size too large and a woman not much older than me with her hair up in a bun tight enough to use as the core of a baseball. She lifted her nose slightly as I met her eyes. "May I ask what you are doing?"

"I'm not—I was only—" I stopped. Abigail had been savaged, I thought, and whatever had done that to her had come from here. From this very room. I was not about to be intimidated by propriety.

I glanced at the door with the pillars. No one coming in, no one else in the room. The security guard tensed as I walked closer to the two curators. "What's been stolen from this room?" I asked.

Even though I'd kept my voice down, the question seemed to bounce off the tiles and window to settle into the center of the room, large and uncomfortable. The Indian man went gray, and the severe woman's eyes flashed. "Nothing's been stolen! Where on earth did you get the idea—"

"Please. I don't have time to talk this out of you. Something's missing from this room, and I need to know what it is."

"There is *nothing*—" Her voice rose, and she pressed her lips together as if hearing it for the first time. "I'm going to have to ask you to leave."

"Are you her boss?" I turned to the man. A fraction of a smile—this woman has a boss?—touched his lips, but he shook his head. "May I speak to the person in charge?"

He shook his head. "Sylvia and I are the people to talk to today."

"Today?" I thought about the call I'd first heard while sleeping on Nate's couch, the first inkling I'd had that someone had loosed a hunt on Boston. "I take it someone's out?"

"He's sick," Sylvia snapped.

"Dog attack?" They exchanged a glance. "Look. Something was—is missing from here. I'll bet you anything it was taken two nights ago." The same night I summoned the dead . . . *no, don't think about that.* "And someone was badly hurt in the process."

"It's—" Sylvia's response was almost a sob, and she caught herself before her voice could break. Her arms were tightly crossed, and even though she had assured me twice over that nothing had been stolen, her eyes kept darting to either side of the room, as if searching out one item after another. Not because of guilt—at least I didn't think so, not yet—but because theft meant something horrible here. "It's none of your business. Now, please go or I'll have you escorted out."

"What was stolen?" I repeated, this time trying to draw on whatever uncanniness Skelling's presence lent. It wasn't much.

"A costume piece," the man answered.

Sylvia shook her head. "Ravi—"

"What's the harm in it?" He didn't take his eyes from me. "She knows it's gone. She even knows about Theo."

"That just means she had something to do with it!" Sylvia switched to a panicked whisper, glancing out the windows to the atrium as if an eavesdropper might be clinging to the inner wall.

Something—not the blank spot that was Skelling, but a similar shape—shifted the pattern of scents behind me. "*My apologies,*" the contralto voice said in my ear. "*I'm afraid I mistook you for your relative.*"

I turned to look—again, nothing but that portrait, the woman presiding over this room like the image of a saint—and when I looked back, Sylvia's expression had changed. Ravi still looked glumly determined, but Sylvia had lost that edge of panic. "Very well," she said. "Ravi, get the box and meet me in the gardens. I'll take her out by way of the Dutch Room."

She stalked to the pillared entrance, her heels snapping on the tiles like rifle shots. "And," she added as I reached her, "I'll show you just why nothing's been stolen."

I followed her down. "I should tell you that I'm not with the police," I admitted. "But if something has gone missing you should call them in. I know a few of the detectives, they're good people—"

"They weren't any help before, were they?" She paused at the edge of a door and gestured for me to go inside.

I did so. There were more glass cases here, furniture too baroque for me to even think of using, sculptures smiling blandly. I raised my eyes to the far wall, where more art that I didn't have the brains to understand hung, and that's when I saw it.

They hadn't changed the room. They'd left it all just as it was—though it can't have been that way when they found it after the theft; no thieves were that courteous. They could have rearranged the other paintings to cover the gap, could have put up a discreet REMOVED or EXHIBIT TEMPORARILY CLOSED sign, gray with time and optimism, could even have put up curtains or a little explanatory plaque. Instead they'd left the frames, the empty frames, hanging on the wall. Through them only the green silk of the wall showed, like windows onto nothing, like open wounds.

The entire room mourned their absence, mourned without hope of surcease. Even the smell in here was different, bitter, like swallowed tears.

"Three Rembrandts." Sylvia came to stand beside me. "One Vermeer, and a masterpiece it was. A Manet, a Flinck, sketches by Degas, a gilded eagle, and a Shang dynasty beaker." She sighed. "This is a loss. A theft. Not that gimcrackery you're asking about."

I didn't say anything. Couldn't say anything.

"You feel it too, I can tell. Mrs. Gardner—well, she watches over this place." She drew a shaky breath. "None of the security cameras show anything happening two nights ago. But I checked on Theo before I left, and I know he was here. And then he turns up across the river with his face half bitten off, and it takes us forever to discover that one box is empty when it shouldn't be. That's not a heist, that's a vicious practical joke."

"I'm sorry," I said, knowing it wasn't enough.

"I imagine you are."

Even the gardens bore a trace of Mrs. Gardner's painstaking genius. But there was enough air out here that I wasn't overwhelmed. I stepped out into the sunlight and inhaled, trying to ignore the heavy dampness in the air.

Ravi had gotten there before us, and he'd pulled a screen around one of the flagstone patios. "Please, sit," he said. "Will you need to dust for fingerprints?"

I refrained from telling him that if I did, most of the latent prints would be gone by now. "Different methods," I said. "May I?"

He held out the box, straining a little from its weight, and when I took it from him, I understood why; it was a lot heavier than it looked. It resembled a lavish jewelry box, the kind that ladies of good taste keep on their dressers, or that traveling divas place in their safe-deposit boxes. My callused hands caught and dragged on the silky-smooth wood. A pattern of oak leaves had been carved into the sides. "This is what was stolen?"

"No," Sylvia said. She remained standing, casting a wary eye over the rest of the garden. "That's just the box."

"We've actually been able to find records for the box itself," Ravi said, happily moving into antiquary mode. "Mrs. Gardner had it made on the advice of one of her buyers."

Sylvia sniffed. "Hangers-on, in this case. Poor woman practically begged to be buried at Mrs. Gardner's feet."

I turned the box around. The hinges were gold, and imprinted with that same oak-leaf pattern—but instead of being polished to a mirror shine, they'd been varnished over.

Ravi produced a folded paper from his jacket. I unfolded it to reveal a sketch of a masked character in a black-and-white costume, caught in mid-prance. "It's a costume piece, from Harlequin. He's a *commedia dell'arte* character, usually wearing that diamond pattern you see—I've got a paper Theo wrote up somewhere on the provenance of the name . . ."

"For heaven's sake," Sylvia snapped. "It was a little horn on a strap with a black-and-white checkerboard pattern. It was barely worth five dollars."

I nodded absently, flicked the latch, and opened the box.

The garden seemed to shudder a moment, or else I did, and for just a second I had the sensation of imprisonment, of the home of something trapped for a very long time and now flown, like the inside of a cage after the lion has departed. I made an inarticulate noise and curled my hands over the end of the box to keep it from falling.

Ravi craned his neck around to get a glimpse of the inside. "Oh yes, I should have warned you about that. That's what makes the box so heavy, you see."

"It's lead." I hesitated a moment, trying to remember what my mother had taught me about lead poisoning (other than "stop eating paint"), then said the hell with it and touched the lining. It was cool, colder than it ought to have been, and dented in the middle, as if someone had carelessly crammed something into it.

"Lead, silver, and a very thin layer of steel under that, according to the sketches. You can see the tacks holding it together at the corners—see? Like a quilt, almost."

No quilt had ever been made with this purpose in mind. Lead was a grounding factor, a metal that molded itself easily to human whims and so would shape itself to the desires of its maker. Silver and steel too each had their own properties against different magics. I'd bet my left hand that there were words incised under that metal, words that neither I nor anyone would ever read, but that had acted as a Möbius loop for whatever lay inside. If Mrs. Gardner had ordered the box made to her specifications, she'd either known a lot about magic herself or had connections with someone who did. I rather suspected the latter, based on the lingering echo of her spirit in the museum. Adepts didn't become loci; they devoured them.

All this work, this protection, for a little horn on a strap. Would it even be functional? From Ravi's description, probably not, especially if it was part of a costume.

Costume. There was something to that. Perhaps the horn hadn't been part of a costume, so much as a costume itself—no, that didn't make any sense. But I couldn't shake the idea of costume, masks, something hiding under another name.

There was no scent inside. Nothing. The horn had rested here for a long time, official records or no, but it hadn't left a trace. Which meant . . .

Which meant that whatever had been here, Mrs. Gardner hadn't wanted it tainting the rest of her museum. And too, that it was either self-contained enough that it wouldn't leave any kind of trail, or it was ephemeral enough that it hadn't had a trail to leave.

Neither was a good option.

"Call me crazy," I said, "but I wouldn't order a box if I didn't have something to put in it."

"That's just what Theo said," Ravi exclaimed, then paused. "Says. Theo *says*. But while there are records for the box, there's nothing official for the contents. The horn's not even part of the collection, at least going by the lists."

Sylvia cleared her throat. "That's not quite the case." Ravi gave her a surprised look. "Well, you hadn't been examining all of her correspondence, had you? No." She turned a little toward me, somehow managing to indicate that she had her back to him even though we were roughly in a circle. "Mrs. Gardner made a few purchases that are off the official rolls, notably around the time this box was made. She backed a—hmm, I suppose you would call it a consortium—to bring back several items from the West Coast. Even went so far as to have pistols made for the escorts—I suppose she got a kick out of the Wild West idea of it."

I blinked. *Skelling, you're late.* "This wouldn't have been in nineteen oh eight, would it?" Sylvia's eyes narrowed. "Don't ask me how I know."

"Wouldn't dream of it," she said tartly.

Nineteen hundred and eight. The expedition that Skelling was part of—and the things that Prescott stole . . .

Prescott couldn't possibly still be alive, could he? No, Woodfin had named Prescott the oldest member of the group, and there was no way he'd have lasted this long, even if you pickled him . . .

. . . or if you put him in a *jar* . . .

I didn't like where this thought was going. Yuen's father had managed to seal off his spirit, but he'd done so poorly, leaving himself stuck. But couldn't someone else have done the same thing, and done it right?

Goddammit, I'd have noticed if there was something that long dead walking around Boston. Wouldn't I?

I shivered, and then, disregarding how these good people would react, bent over the box, curling over it as if it were a private pain. Scent, there had to be a scent, there had to be something—

A distortion, a blankness like the emptiness under your foot when you miss a step on the stairs. I shuddered, digging my fingers into the sides of the box so hard they hurt. At the very edge of my senses, a trace of wildness, sharp as frost in midwinter, like an ecstatic scream into the stars . . .

I sat up so abruptly I nearly smacked into Sylvia's head as she leaned over me. "Are you all right?" she demanded, plainly expecting a *no*.

"*Urng*," I said, or close to it. God, what kind of horn was that? No painted clown ever carried anything like that, no costume ever had something that powerful. What would a horn like that call up? What could it summon?

In my memory, the sound of a low, hollow note rang through my head: the note that had called me to witness Abigail's mauling, that had called the hounds that attacked her. I doubled over again, teeth clamped shut as my stomach tried to evict the morning's breakfast.

"Oh, that's it," Sylvia snapped as the box slid off my lap. Ravi caught it, grunting from the weight. "Ravi, I'm an idiot for ever listening to you." She straightened up and marched off, and through my haze I heard her call for security.

I leaned back, panting, to see Ravi staring at me with an expression of shock and bafflement—and, painfully, hope. Well, even if they thought I was crazy, maybe I could still help. "Don't put it back in the museum," I managed through what felt like cotton in my throat. "It was—it shouldn't be there."

He nodded, slowly, then fumbled in his coat pocket and pressed a business card into my hand. "Call me. If you find anything, call me."

Small chance of that, and I almost told him so, but just then Sylvia returned with the two guards I'd seen earlier. The guard who'd helped me at the entrance. One of them put his hand on my shoulder. "Don't make this difficult, please," Sylvia said.

As they hustled me out of the gardens, I heard the voice again. "*Don't bring it back,*" Mrs. Gardner murmured. "*Not to me.*"

"I won't," I said.

"Yeah, you just bet you won't," the other guard muttered.

Seventeen

I switched on my phone as I walked away from the Gardner, doing my best to ignore the guards watching my back. *Rena*, I thought. *I need to get in touch with Rena. Prescott might try to attack Abigail again. If he's the one who did it.*

I misdialed her number, cursed, and tried again. It didn't make any sense. Nothing about this—the Gardner, Skelling, Abigail—made sense, especially the ghosts. For someone's imprint to linger after death in a recognizably human fashion, you'd need either a major spark—like ghosts that remain where they were murdered, for example—or artificial power. A ghost with a locus, for example, though loci could make up for the lack of vitality for only so long.

A truck blared at me, and I jumped out of the intersection. I knew this corner, it was my neighborhood; I knew it so well that I hadn't thought about looking before stepping into the street. But I'd corrected my mistake in time. And that was a reason why the entity that had spoken to me in the Gardner couldn't be a ghost, not by the usual standard. She'd mistaken me for someone—clear ghost pattern there—but then she'd realized her mistake and changed it. Ghosts don't do that. Ghosts are dead, and one thing the dead have real trouble with is adapting to new information. That's why some of them walk through walls in the houses they haunt: when they were there, the walls weren't, and why should they change?

If a ghost could fit events into a pattern it knew, then it would do so, and damn any rough edges that didn't quite match. A ghost couldn't correct itself, or apologize for getting something wrong.

A ghost couldn't plan a robbery. Not in such a way that it would come off with any degree of success, anyway.

The line connected and went to voice mail almost immediately. "Rena, it's Evie." I switched my cell phone to my other ear, mentally cursing Rena for not picking up. What was the point of having a cell phone if you never bothered to switch it on? "I've just run into some very serious *bruja* shit, and I need you to call me. Abigail Huston, the woman who was mauled— look, if you can spare anyone to keep a guard on her, I think she may need it. You would not believe the hornet's nest I've just stepped into. I'll explain when I see you—I'm on my way to see you now."

I didn't like being so cryptic, but Rena had told me once that she wasn't the only one who listened to her messages, and I didn't want to give her a name for getting crazy weird shit. Assuming she didn't have it already . . . I glanced over my shoulder at the receding stone bulk of the Gardner, then jumped as my phone buzzed in my hand. Not a call, but messages on my voice mail. Guess I wasn't in a position to complain about people not picking up.

First: "Evie, it's Nate. I know you're busy, but could you . . . shit, I shouldn't have told you to go away last night. I need to talk to you. Something's wrong, and I can't say exactly what it is other than it's like, well, like that Fenway stuff."

That gave me pause—Nate hadn't ever referred to what happened in the tunnels under Fenway. What was he talking about, though? Fiana? Magic in general? Or . . . without wanting to, I remembered the taste of blood in my mouth and the Morrigan's quiet approval of Nate's purely mortal rage.

I shook my head. Second message: "Evie, it's me. Don't come over. Just stay away. Okay? My father's been calling, and—Jesus, something's wrong, and I think it's me—"

The message cut off there. I stopped at the corner. The T station was this way, and ten minutes' ride would take me to Rena. But Nate was the other direction . . .

My phone service didn't care about private dilemmas. It switched to the next message with a merry chirp. This one began with a clunk, then a moment of silence. No, not quite silence; something chirped far in the background, like a pen of ducks in another room, or a one-sided conversation heard through a wall. I turned away from the traffic, curling around my phone as if to hold in the sound.

"*Ah.*" It wasn't a voice, not quite, because "voice" would have implied some kind of consciousness behind it. Instead it was a degree removed from that, as if the speaker had heard of words but didn't quite understand the concept. "*Ahh,*" again, only this time there was a note in it I knew well—the sense of relief one gets when beginning a hunt, when all the difficult things drop away and it's only one task, one mission ahead of me. The letting go that is so seductive about hunting.

It didn't sound like Nate at all. I hadn't thought Nate even *could* let go.

For a moment the message was empty, only the soft percussion of breath disrupting the static. I pressed my free hand to the ear not against the phone, trying to block out everything but that breath, forgetting for the moment that it was recorded, recorded hours ago, and that I couldn't respond.

The message went from silence to a splintering screech. Nate—or someone—had broken his phone in mid-message. I turned away from the T station and started to run.

* * *

A smell hung over the porch of Nate's apartment like a body from a noose, rank with adrenaline and sweat and something more acrid, something that made me draw my lips back from my teeth. I don't have much in the way of instinct—most of it took off with my common sense when I started getting involved in magic—but instinct told me that this was not a good place for me to be.

I ran up the porch steps two at a time and stopped, panting, in the doorway. The stairs creaked as someone descended—a man's shadow, huge on the wall, diminishing as it came closer. "Nate?" My voice cracked, and even the sunlight flooding in couldn't keep me from shivering as I made my way up the stairs.

But the man coming down from the third floor wasn't him. Janssen turned the corner and stared at me, then scrambled back a step like a recently declawed cat dropped into a dog kennel.

"No you don't," I snarled, and leaped at him, grabbing him by the shirt. "What the hell are you doing here?"

Like mold growing over a clean spot, his natural charm reasserted itself. "I'm not the one you're looking for," he said, raising both hands and smiling.

"No shit. I don't know what you did here—"

"*I* didn't do anything—"

"Shut up." I jerked my head toward the door to the apartment, which stood partway open. "What do you call that? And where's Nate?"

His eyes widened. "Oh, this gets better and better. Were you screwing him? Because that'd—"

I swung him around, into the wall on the other side of the stairs. Something on the other side of that wall crashed to the floor.

Janssen's grin didn't falter. "That'd just be the icing on the cake, wouldn't it?" He spread his hands. A thin, dry strip of leather was wrapped around his left hand—the thing he'd hit Nate with last night, now sapped of whatever foulness it'd held. "As for me, I'm just visiting family."

"Fuck you." No blood, I realized. I couldn't sense any blood, but the scent that was there was Nate, Nate and adrenaline and a horrible burnt stink that made me want to run like hell, didn't matter which way. Janssen's smell was there as well, and that was almost worse—

No. It wasn't just Janssen's smell. It was familiar, horribly familiar, and too much like Nate's own—

"You rotten shit," I hissed through my teeth. "What the hell did you do to him?"

"Him, nothing. No more than what I gave him when I fucked his mother." Janssen's grin turned into a smug, secret smile. "Heredity's a wonderful thing." I tightened my grip, pressing my fingers into the soft spaces just behind his jaw. Janssen's eyes watered, and he choked on a laugh. "I told you my business contacts didn't like my kind."

"Your kind? What the hell are you talking about?"

He shook his head, as if I were an idiot child who persisted in not getting the joke. "You don't expect me to let an opportunity like this go away, just because I've got a few embarrassing personal problems? So I handed those over to my son, let little Nathan take the brunt of it. All he's good for, really, out of all my bastards. Call it a hand-me-down curse."

"What do you mean, curse?"

His eyes gleamed. "What do you think?"

Snarling, I swung him around and shoved him down the stairs. Janssen caught himself with a neat two-step. "If you've hurt him," I spat, "if you've even touched him or Katie, I will tear your fucking throat out."

"I'm insulted." Nevertheless, Janssen's hand crept up to his neck, as if not quite sure that he could keep me from it. "Hell, I even fixed his door for him. I've got some decency, right? Don't want to leave his apartment open to any two-bit thief."

I stared at him. He honestly thought that this half-assed kindness on his part made him a good guy. Probably also considered his babbling about Sigmund to be fair warning as well. "Get out of here. If I even catch a whiff of you again, I swear to God—"

"Swear me no swears, little girl. I've got business to do, and between you and the well-meaning officer who thinks he can follow me, I've already had a full day." He glanced up the stairs. "I always told him the wild part would get out and, well, not my fault if he tried to stuff it away. Now it's his problem." He made a little bow, then turned his back on me. "See you later, Hound."

I turned tail as soon as he was down the stairs. The door to Nate's apartment was a mess, even with Janssen's "repairs": splinters everywhere, one of the hinges twisted almost off. In a dizzying flash I remembered how I'd scraped at these same locks, unable to fathom how they worked. I dragged the door open.

The room had been torn apart. If I'd been looking with just my eyes, I'd have thought Janssen had done it—but his scent stopped at the door. The table was on its side, a broken chair next to it, and a long slash knifed across the cushions where I'd slept not two nights ago. One of the bookcases lay on its side, across the door to Katie's room, textbooks and papers spilled everywhere. Nate's desk had been overturned onto Katie's, as if sheltering it against the wall.

And the only scent in the room was Nate's.

"Jesus," I breathed, and took a step inside.

Something crunched underfoot, and I looked down to see the remnants of Nate's cell phone. "Nate! Katie!"

I hadn't expected anything—Nate's scent was strong in the air, but cold; he was long gone—but an inarticulate, muffled cry came through the wall.

"Katie!" I clambered over the wreck of furniture and grabbed the bookcase, dragging it aside. I tried to open her door, but something blocked it. "Katie, are you okay? Where's Nate?"

Her reply was too garbled to understand, but the hysterical tone of it said more than I wanted to know. I put my shoulder against the door and pushed. The room was dark inside, but not so dark that I couldn't see the dresser and chairs that had been dragged in front of the door. Katie climbed over them and practically fell onto me, sobbing. "I'm sorry, Evie. I'm sorry, I couldn't, I'm sorry—"

"Sorry?" She flinched at that, and I hugged her tighter, her barrettes digging into my collarbone. "Katie, what happened?"

"I didn't see it!" she wailed against my chest. "I thought I was good at seeing things, but I couldn't see this happening at all, and I couldn't do anything—"

"Katie, stop. Stop." I set her down on the floor and took both her hands in mine. "I can't understand you. Just tell me what happened."

She gulped for air, then sniffled. "That guy kept calling," she said. "The one Nate doesn't like to talk to."

"Janssen?"

"I don't know his name. He just kept calling, and—and after a while Nate just—he got mad."

My spine went cold.

"Real mad. He—" She swallowed and glanced around the living room, her eyes widening as if she were seeing it for the first time. I realized that was exactly it—she hadn't seen it in this state before—and hugged her closer. "He told me to get in my room and not make a sound. And then he, he yelled and—" She gestured to the table and the couch, her hands shaking. "And he left."

Left. Oh God. "Katie, when was this?"

Her lips pressed together, as if holding in a great cry. "This morning," she whispered. "Early."

"And you've been in there the whole—"

She nodded.

"Jesus. Jesus, Katie—" I touched her hair gently, and she burst into a fresh bout of tears. "It'll be okay. It will, I promise." I dug out my cell phone and tried to think of who to call as Katie sniffled against me. Police? Exorcist? Locksmith for the damned door?

Hell with it. You went with what you had. I rocked Katie back and forth and waited for Sarah to pick up.

Whatever wise-ass comment Sarah had prepared died as she reached the apartment twenty minutes later. "It looks like a tornado hit this place," she managed, finally. "Bad breakup?"

"Don't start, Sarah." I scrabbled in the wreckage of Nate's desk, trying to see if he'd left any clue to where he might have gone. His computer didn't look hurt, but it wouldn't turn on either, and I couldn't make heads or tails of the sticky notes on it. "Don't fucking start."

"Okay. Right." She stared around her, shaking her head. "I had no idea . . ."

"Neither did I." That was a lie. *I should have stayed with him last night. I should have stayed.*

There were so many things that I should do. Call Rena, put out an APB, make sure Katie was all right . . . All the logic I had told me I ought to stay behind and take care of things here, trusting that Nate would be all right until I could find him.

Logic could go fuck itself. "Sarah, I need you to take care of Katie. If you can, call Rena Santesteban at this number." I scribbled her number on a scrap of paper and pressed it into her hand. "Tell her I'll call when I can, and to make sure Abigail is safe. I'll be back with Nate."

Katie emerged from Nate's room, dragging a backpack twice the size of hers. "You'll need this," she said, panting.

Sarah glanced from her to me. "For what?"

"For the hunt." I hefted the pack and slung it over my shoulders. "I'm going to hunt Nate down."

Eighteen

Nate had kept to the back alleys, but he'd been moving out toward the edge of the city. That much I could tell just from a cursory touch on his scent. He hadn't cared too much about traffic either, judging by how his trail weaved across the roads. *That would be a pisser, wouldn't it?* I thought I heard Janssen say. *You reach him, and he's roadkill on Route 128.*

That wouldn't happen. I wouldn't let that happen. I focused, zeroing in on Nate's trail . . . there. Over the Market Street bridge, over the Massachusetts Turnpike (and oh, Nate knew his tricks; that constant flow could disrupt a scent as easily as a stream of running water), then west—west past the markers the Fiana had once set to track anyone who left the city . . .

My feet hurt with every jolt on the pavement, and yet I was grinning. I've never been a marathon runner—one of my friends from high school was into it these days, and what she'd described sounded like nothing I ever wanted to try—but there was something about this ceaseless motion that felt right.

On the heels of that thought came a memory: the path from Mount Auburn, the road that had taken me halfway across the city in a flash. It wasn't a safe path, I knew, and something about its presence here felt wrong. It wasn't supposed to be this accessible . . . but I could still use it.

Don't, Skelling's voice whispered behind me. *That's not your path.*

I bared my teeth, scaring a jogger. "I don't have to own it to use it," I snapped, and took that half step sideways, into the unreality that was far too close to the physical world.

The world shrank and flattened, becoming only me and the hunt, me and the scent, me and the fact of running. I moved in long, easy steps now, the silver ground passing unregarded under my feet as if its only duty were to be where I needed it to be. Buildings and streets and hills faded, unimportant to the point of insubstantiality. Like the space behind mirrors, the unreality of a reflection cast on water, where I ran did not exist and yet was no less useful for all that.

This way.

Nate's scent was so bright it should have been written in red letters three feet high. He hadn't bothered to hide it, as any animal would have done; he'd just fled. I could taste the adrenaline in his system, even if I didn't know where it came from or why it was written on his scent so plainly.

This way.

In the back of my mind, as if obscured by layers and layers of gauze, the visceral memory of pain lingered, a throb in the skin of my hand, along the abraded flesh of my calf, in my knotted muscles. But here there was no pain.

I exhaled, dismissing it all, including the lack of air passing over my lips. There was no such thing as running too far.

This way . . .

But the memory wouldn't quite go away, even if the pain was long since past. And Skelling too, in the dream and on the tower. He'd known this path, had understood it well enough to open a way for me. But he hadn't used it, though he'd wanted to.

Skelling wanted it. You'll want it too. The ghosts of Mount Auburn hadn't been so wrong after all.

This way, called the hunt. But I turned aside, just a moment, just long enough to see the world around me.

A world in shadow.

I gasped, choked on the emptiness that served as air here, and stumbled over my own feet as I tried to stop. *Nate, I was trying to find Nate. I wasn't just following the hunt.* Abruptly the world slid back into focus as that other space spat me out like a drop of water from melted wax.

I doubled over, panting and staring at the ground under my feet. Bare ground, thick with tufts of grass and pine needles, soft enough to squish under the toe of my left sneaker. *At least I'm not in the middle of a highway,* I thought, and the laugh that followed it wasn't quite a sob.

I straightened up, one hand on my neck, and exhaled slowly. A high stand of pine trees stood on my left, source of the needles now underfoot, and to my right stretched a silvery lake, shimmering in the day's heat. At the water's edge was a thin strip of sand and gravel, the kind of beach that didn't deserve the name anywhere outside New England. In the middle stood a white sign with peeling letters: FOR YOUR SAFETY, DIVING IN THE QUARRY IS PROHIBITED.

Quarry. Ha. Weren't hounds supposed to find a different kind of quarry? I shook my head, grimacing, then froze as someone gasped and whispered behind me.

I turned to see two girls a few years older than Katie staring at me. One wore a T-shirt proclaiming PROPERTY OF CAMP WATHAWACKET; the other's shirt bore an imbecilically cute cartoon cat. Both of them shut up and took a step back. "Hi," I said.

"Hi," said Cartoon Cat.

"You came out of *nowhere*!" said Wathawacket.

Well, that told me something about what had happened. "Yeah," I said, glancing out at the quarry. The sun was low in the sky—about six o'clock? Seven?

I'd been running for *eight hours*? Oh, that couldn't be.

Not my path, I remembered. Hell. I should probably make sure that it was still the right century. "I got lost hiking. What's the closest town?"

"Assawompset," Wathawacket volunteered. "Only we're not by the lake, it's that way and the town's further—"

Cartoon Cat yanked on her shirt. "Shh!"

"Is that in Massachusetts?" Crap. Eight hours, assume a speed of four miles per hour, only I couldn't really assume that . . . Was it outside Interstate 495? I didn't know what was outside the Hub. Moose, probably. And Worcester.

Wathawacket nodded. "This is private property," Cartoon Cat said, trying for as much authority as she could in a shirt like that. "The whole camp's private."

Summer camp. Well, that explained the kids. At least I was still in Massachusetts. And with any luck, I hadn't outrun Nate.

Yes. There was his scent, still as fresh and as brilliant as when I'd stepped out of his apartment. Would he know I was looking for him? "Either of you see a man with brown hair, a little taller than me, looks like a scarecrow who's missed a few meals?"

"I could ask the counselors," said Wathawacket.

Cartoon Cat glared at her. "Don't *talk* to her!" she stage-whispered.

I looked away from them, two fingers pressed to the spot between my brows. Now that I had an idea of where I was, the scents were slowly beginning to come together. On one side of me were smells of cooking and kids, probably the camp itself. Nate's scent was on the other side. He'd be staying away from people.

A chill settled over me as the thought formed. I still couldn't quite analyze everything my nose told me, but that didn't mean I didn't trust it. For whatever reason, Nate would not want to be around people.

"Forget it," I said, and started walking. All the exhaustion and pain of my earlier run had returned, and my legs felt slow and heavy. I paused about ten yards down the shore. "Stay in the camp," I called over my shoulder. "It might not be safe out here."

That'd probably scare them more than was strictly necessary, but if it kept them out of harm's way, all the better. And I wasn't yet sure what I would find.

I walked along the side of the quarry, picking my way over outcroppings too regular to be natural. Nate was here—I could scent him, but there was still something off about what I was sensing. Why had he come here anyway? For the view?

That was ridiculous. But as I clambered over boulders and edged along banks, the thought kept coming back to me. The quarry was a beautiful place, after all, not the kind of thing you'd expect from an abandoned pit left to fill up with water . . . lucky campers, they probably had it all to themselves for part of the year . . . You'd think there'd be more lakeside homes, given how fast waterfront property usually gets bought up . . .

Maybe there was a reason Nate had come here, one that didn't have anything to do with rational thought. Maybe this place had its own magic. The thought jostled something loose—something about Skelling? Woodfin, he'd mentioned a quarry, hadn't he, or had he been talking about his own work . . .

I swung under a leaning birch onto a ledge of white stone, then dropped to the sand beside it. There was only a scrap of a beach here, maybe enough for one picnic blanket and a cooler, but it was the sort of place I could imagine spending a quiet afternoon, just lying in the sun, doing nothing, listening to the slow lap of waves. No one would ever find me, here in this little sheltered inlet.

My mouth was suddenly dry—how long had it been since I'd had a drink? I rummaged in the backpack, coming up with only a half-empty plastic bottle. The water in it was flat and tasteless, without any of the crisp clarity of the quarry, and I bent to refill the bottle at the water's edge. Some remnant of wilderness lore—or maybe just my mother's voice saying *Don't drink that, you don't know where it's been*—kept me from drinking right away. Instead I stashed the bottle in the pack and shook the water off my hands, savoring the coolness of it. The clothes on my back seemed to crawl with sweat and grime, and for a moment it seemed like the most natural thing to strip and wade into the quarry, wash off what I could, duck my head under the water . . .

If I hadn't just stepped out of one unnatural space, I might not have noticed the spell. There hadn't been any scent, no crackle as something latched on to me, no echo of a border crossed. But I was familiar with aversion wards, the persistent way that one's mind would slide off something. This was similar to an attraction ward, on such a subliminal level that it snuck into one's brain without even having to touch conscious thought.

Well, I might not be a magician, but there were a few things I did know. I took out my utility knife, unfolded the dullest blade, and jammed it between the stones at my feet. "Turn, and turn about," I said, and made a sign in the air that Deke had taught me a long time ago. "Show yourself."

It wasn't even a spell, just a simple thing that minor adepts do on a regular basis—like throwing salt over your left shoulder or touching wood or repeating whatever it was you'd been doing when the Sox pitcher struck out that last guy. I'd done it partly to distract myself, remind myself that I was being enspelled. So I didn't expect the response I got.

The surface of the quarry went glassy and still, save for a fizz at my feet, where the barest edge of the water brushed the knife blade. I stepped back as the foam at my feet subsided, then started up again, this time further out in the water, creating four points of white.

The water rose up beneath those points in a column.

It wasn't like a fountain or jet; there was no force pushing up the surface of the quarry. Instead there was a continuous downward aspect to it, as if this were part of a waterfall, a stream falling from above, and all that was visible of the source was a bright spot in the air, a spot that slowly resolved itself into the skull of a deer, white bone and antlers bleached by the sun, endlessly pouring water.

Was there some trace of a human shape within it? A hint of shoulders, hands, something beyond the bone and water? One minute there seemed to be one, like a human wearing a mask, and the next it was only elemental shapes with no trace of humanity. I couldn't quite be sure, and the hollow bone eyes staring at me distracted me further. When it spoke, the sound came from the water by my feet rather than the manifestation. "*I . . . yes, I. I answer.*"

I edged back from the water, unwilling to get even the tips of my shoes wet. "Could you ease up on—" Damn, would this thing even understand idiomatic language? "—undo the attraction ward you've set up? It's very distracting."

The skull turned, and the water eddied around it. "*You don't want to stay?*"

"No," I said. "Thank you, no." Hell. What was I supposed to say after that? Sorry for waking you up?

The spirit—what could I call it? Naiad? Undine? Nixie? All of those presupposed some kind of sentience, and I couldn't yet believe that there was one behind those empty sockets. It couldn't have been as young as it seemed; anything coherent enough to unify something even as small as this quarry had to be old. All lakes, streams, springs and rivers had individual spirits—that was part of what made water so hard to magic. But sometimes one in a body of water was more distinct or more powerful than the others: there were lakes that had specific guardians, rivers that spoke with one voice. A unity, of sorts, deeper than the cobbled-together nature of the cemetery amalgam, and one that took time. Guardian spirits took centuries to develop, to find their own individual voice.

There shouldn't have been one for a quarry that wasn't more than a century old.

Its tone turned caressing, soothing, a clumsy attempt to recapture the seductive nature of the ward. *"This place is loved. You would be welcomed if you stayed."*

I shivered, but managed a gracious nod. "I don't doubt it. But don't put a glamour on me. I don't like it."

The skull finally nodded, then leaned forward on its column, as if trying to get a better look. *"You are hunting,"* it said, and something about the way it said *hunting* made it seem hungrier, like an alcoholic who's just seen a six-pack at a friend's house. *"I can tell you where it is."* It rippled, and the water across the quarry shivered once, as if in reply. *"The one you're looking for. I can bring him to you."*

"I don't think so." If I couldn't find Nate after all this, I didn't deserve to find him.

"It would be no great fee—only return here, swim in these waters and wait on this shore. This will be a haven for you and your children."

It was a superficially reasonable request. But something about it gave me the chills. This spirit maintained its strength not through worship, but through the love of place that it encouraged. In some ways it was the opposite of the genius loci of the Gardner; that drew its strength from the deep love that Mrs. Gardner had infused into it while she lived, while this drew on a constant supply of love for a place, for memories. "No," I said. "Thank you, no."

The surface of the water went steel colored, reflecting not the sky but the anger beneath it. *"I could ask for blood instead."*

"No!" I repeated. "There are some things you don't have the right to ask for." Did it not understand that? Most spirits had some idea of what could and couldn't be bartered, but this thing . . . It was as if it was only a juvenile, too young or too naive to understand the rules of the world it inhabited.

"*No reward?*" it whispered. "*Nothing, for all the good I do? All the watching, all the guarding . . . So long I protected this place, and no reward?*"

"Not from me." I yanked my knife out from between the stones, then held it edge forward. "Turn again, and follow no more," I said, hoping the simple courtesy of a goodbye would end this.

The spirit of the quarry accepted it. "*Ah,*" said the waves, and the column of falling water dwindled, the deer's skull fading into foam. "*Ah . . . but do come back, come back.*"

Not if I could help it. Grimacing, I turned back toward shore. Nate must have gotten ahead of me while I wasted time—but no, his scent was close, almost close enough to touch. If he hadn't heard me speaking, it wasn't because he was out of earshot. I climbed over a fallen birch log and struck out into the brush.

It hadn't been all that long since someone had hunted me, watched me as I watched others, and you never quite forget that feeling. So when I got that frisson up my neck and the prickle down my spine, I didn't turn around right away. Instead a trace of the hound's instincts in me made me stop and sniff the air.

When at last I turned to look, it was as if two separate signals were clamoring for my attention, canceling each other out. My nose told me that Nate was right there, in front of me, scent thick with adrenaline and dirt and sweat. My eyes saw nothing, only a pile of brush that no one would have been able to hide behind, a fallen tree, a gleam . . .

A gleam of eyes. Gray eyes, far too low. It wasn't a coyote, it wasn't a wolf, it was something in between and with a weird bunched aspect around the shoulders, as if its skin didn't quite fit—

I shifted in place, turning to face it fully, and the

wolf thing leaped up and fled. "*Nate,*" I breathed, and gave chase.

I couldn't think about what happened to him—there's no time for thought in a proper hunt. Thinking only gives your prey a chance to get further away. A hanging branch slapped me in the face, and I skidded down the side of a narrow ravine into a stream. The gray shape was out of sight, but Nate's scent was still strong, still present—

There—

I turned just as he leaped, my only sight of him a flash of mud-splattered hair. We went down together, his breath hot and rank in my face, and maybe it was because I was the Hound, maybe it was just that I knew Nate, but I could hear in the inarticulate snarls a note of panic and desperation.

"No you don't," I gasped. I thrust one hand against the wolf thing's teeth, prying them back from my face, while the other sought for purchase on its body. Goddamn him; even in the wrong form there wasn't enough flesh on his bones. I dug my fingers into its ribs and pushed.

Unfortunately, that left my throat wide open. The wolf tore away from me, and its jaws snapped together a millimeter from my gullet. I jerked my head back, staring down my nose at this mass of fury. Was there any trace of him still in there?

I didn't have time for soul-searching. "Goddammit, Nate!" I grabbed two handfuls of rank hair, curled up, and jammed my feet against the wolf's belly. "Wake the fuck up!" I yelled, and kicked out, using my entire body to fling it away from me.

The wolf slammed against a tree and dropped, shaking. I rolled to my feet, clawing for breath, then stopped and stared as its hide blurred and writhed like something was trying to burrow underneath.

For all the magic I'd seen, the earthfasting and pyromancy and creatures chained to serve the Fiana, I had never seen anything like this. It was magic, it had to be—the difference in body mass alone wasn't possible any other way—but if there was any trace of the fireworks-and-rain scent of magic in this, it was engulfed by the prickly stink of singed fur. I'd thought my own talent was blood-magic, the most embodied kind there was, but that was a pale copy of this painfully physical transformation. "Oh God," I breathed.

The grimy pelt peeled away like onionskin on fire, and Nate clutched his stomach, emitting something between a snarl and a sob. I took a hesitant step toward him.

"Stay away from me!" Nate scrambled back, lurching to his feet. He was naked, save for the streaks of mud that covered his arms and legs, and some completely unhelpful part of me noted that his body was just as I'd imagined it. Give or take a day's wear and tear. "Stay back, I'm . . . I'm not safe . . ."

"Nate, it's me." I spread my hands and held very still. "It's Evie. When have you known me to care about 'safe'?"

He stared at me, still panting, and for a fraction of a second I saw the Nate I knew. "Just stay back," he repeated.

"What happened to you?" He glanced over his shoulder, as if searching for a pursuer or for avenues of escape. "Katie tried to tell me, but she wasn't very clear."

Nate jerked away at the sound of her name, as if I'd struck him. "She's okay?"

I nodded. "She's okay."

He looked away for a moment, his jaw working, and briefly I remembered that terrifying ignorance that had caught me, kept me from remembering something as simple as how to use a lock. Now it was as if Nate had to struggle to remember how speech worked. "My f-father," he said, finally. "He kept calling, needling me, the same way he'd talked last night—and then it wasn't just him anymore that was the problem, it was the whole mess of it—"

Janssen had been purposefully trying to get him mad. Pass the curse on to his son. I hadn't known lycanthropy worked like that, but then again, there were at least as many kinds of werewolf as there were Wild Hunts.

"I lost my temper. I started yelling . . . and I thought it'd be okay, that I'd recover just like every time I've, I've felt myself starting to lose control, but I didn't." Nate drew a shaky breath. "It wasn't ever like this . . . I just, I could still taste that thing he hit me with. And then Katie—" He stopped, then stared at me, more humanity creeping back through his horror.

"You barricaded her in."

"For her own safety! I couldn't—She smelled like *prey*, Evie. Like food—alone and isolated, and I just, I—"

He shuddered all over, and for a moment that flicker of something else showed beneath his skin.

"Nate, it's okay," I said, just to forestall that shiver in him again. If he changed again, I'd lose him—not forever, not while I could hunt, but the difference was trivial enough at the moment.

"It's *not* okay!" His fists clenched, and he pressed them against his temples. "I ran. I thought—I couldn't think, and after a moment it was just easier not to think, it's all just running—"

Oh, I know something about that, I thought, but didn't say. Not just yet.

"I had just enough of my mind left to decide to put a spike in my father's plans. He said he'd wanted someone else to be the . . . the Ylfing in Boston, because he had no use for it anymore, and so I thought, fine, I'll get out of Boston. And I did—I nearly got run over, but I ran all the way here. But now . . ." He glanced over his shoulder again, and I didn't know who he was looking for this time.

I took a step closer, and he didn't bolt. That was something. "I . . . I think I know some of what you're going through. Not all—" *hell no*, "—but a little. Enough that you don't have to run. Not from me."

His eyes met mine, cool gray, not yet convinced. But he was still listening.

"Look, Nate, I know you're not the type to disembowel your sister. You don't do that."

"But I could have." This time he didn't look away from me. "I could hurt you too."

It wasn't a threat—it was almost a promise, and the strange longing in his words gave me a shiver. And I was close enough now that he wouldn't have to move too far to grab me.

But that meant I was close too. I snorted. "No, you couldn't. One, because you're Nate, and you don't do that shit. Two, because—"

I grabbed his arm and wrenched it around so that I stood behind him, one hand at his throat, the other twisting his arm up behind his back. Nate cried out, but more in surprise than pain. He had the reflexes to get away, but instead he stilled, not yet breaking my hold.

"Because I will not fucking *let* you," I said, my breath stirring the hairs at the base of his neck. "Got it?"

Nate tensed, and for a fraction of a second I could feel the shift in his muscles, preparation to change or flee or shake me off and tear my throat out. "My father was right," he murmured. "He said the wild part would always get out."

"You believe *him*? Nate, you can control this." I thought of his controlled anger, his need to let something out, the pressure building until it turned inward on him, and felt an answering shiver in my own skin. "Just because you have this, this side, doesn't mean you're not still human. It's not one or the other. You can do both. Do you understand?"

He didn't answer. His skin was cool—cool, on a day so hot my hair ached.

"Can I let you go now?"

The tension slowly drained out of him, and he gave a short, helpless gasp. "I don't know. Can you?"

"I'll risk it." I let go, first of his throat and then his arm, and stepped back. Nate turned to face me, and for the first time since I'd left him the night before, I knew him, whole and alive if not particularly happy about it. "If nothing else, I'm part canine too. Sort of," I added with a smile.

"It's not the same. You said—you can describe the things you track. It wasn't the same for me. I just saw Katie and it was all one impulse."

I eyed him. "And she smelled like prey."

"Yes."

That wasn't good, any way you looked at it. "So what do I smell like?" I asked, smiling, trying to make it a joke.

His breathing slowed, and his eyes met mine again, darker than before. "Mate," he growled, the word barely more than a groan.

I caught my breath. Nate looked away, a flush crimsoning the skin of his throat, and moved his hands to cover himself, but not before I saw the brief stirring at his groin. I swallowed, unable to hear anything over the thump of blood in my ears. "I bet you say that to all the girls."

"This isn't funny!" Nate snapped.

"Yes, it is," I said, and surprised myself by meaning it. "I mean, if you look at it the right way—it's got to be funny, Nate, it's too absurd to be anything else."

He stared at me for a moment. The corners of his mouth finally quirked, and he gave a snort of suppressed laughter. I started to giggle—it *was* ridiculous, when you thought about it, I mean, a math professor with fangs—and we both lost it, exhaustion giving way to hilarity. "Oh God," he said, finally, gasping for air. "What do I do, Evie? What do I do about all this?"

"I don't know." I put my hand on his shoulder, my palm grazing his collarbone. "For now, you rest."

Nate was silent a long moment, then brought his hands up to my face. I leaned in toward him, and the taste of his lips was nothing like what I'd imagined. "Evie," he whispered into my mouth. "I don't know if I—"

"I do." I took his hand and placed it against my chest, so that the tips of his fingers rested on my throat and the heat of his palm warmed the curve of my breast. "I'm in charge here, Nate. I won't let anything happen that you and I don't want."

His lips formed the last word, *want*, but without breath, and I slid my hand down his mud-splattered chest to clasp what he'd tried to hide from me.

If we didn't wake up the campers that night, it wasn't for lack of trying.

Nineteen

(M) oss is not nearly as nice a pillow as fairy tales
make it out to be. I woke with my head on
something cold and squashy. I sat up, or started to,
but Nate had curled up with his head on my chest
and one arm tight around my waist. I couldn't quite
see his face, so for a moment I thought he was still
asleep—after all, the man had been running a sleep
deficit for the last ten years, at least. But his arm
tightened around me. "I thought it might have been a
dream," he said without prologue. "What happened . . .
I woke up and I couldn't decide whether I wanted it
to have been a dream."

"Good morning to you too," I said. He laughed
against my skin. There's something wonderfully reso-
nant about someone speaking when you're lying next
to his chest. I was sore all over and very sore in some
places, I could feel the moss oozing all down my
back, and neither one of us smelled very good, but I
felt better than I had in ages. My conscience prickled
with a reminder of all the things waiting for us back
in Boston, but I pushed it to the back of my mind for
now. You took sanctuary where you could find it.

Nate reluctantly let go of me and sat up, rubbing at
the corners of his eyes. Even though it was only morn-

ing, the air was warm and sticky, so the chilly spot his absence left on my skin faded in a few heartbeats. "I'm glad you're still here," I said, propping myself on my elbows. More squish, this time from a drift of last autumn's leaves.

He stretched. "Well, it's a little hard to leave a note on the bedside table here."

"Terrible room service too. God, I'm starving." I sat up, winced as the rocks dug deeper into my butt, got to my knees, winced again, and finally pulled myself up hand over hand, using a nearby tree for support.

"Evie." Nate uncoiled to his feet, and though there was no trace of the animal in him now, the fluid grace of that movement was enough to tell me it was still there. "I still don't know if I should come back with you."

I took a moment uncovering the backpack from the heap of my clothes. "If I'd been smart, I would have used this for a pillow . . . Nate. Listen to me. You are more in control of this than you think."

"But—"

"If last night didn't prove that, then I don't know what would." I thought about what it meant to let go and not let go at the same time, and shivered happily.

Nate caught my meaning, and his smile blossomed into something goofy and only slightly embarrassed. "I don't know. I think we need more evidence."

"Oh, I agree." Even mud streaked and unshowered as he was, with moss sticking out of his hair—hell, even as sore and tired as I was, I still got a warm rush over me at the sight of him. "Can I suggest a more comfortable testing area, though?"

He made a vaguely affirmative sound. I laughed and opened the backpack. "Let's see what we've got . . . huh. Pop-Tarts. I'm not sure that qualifies as 'food,' but it'll do. And hey!" I pulled out a roll of faded blue material. "Pants! Just what we—well, you—need."

Nate shook his head. "You're so damn matter-of-fact about this." He took the jeans from me, turned his back, and began putting them on.

"Keeps me sane." I peered into the backpack, a little afraid of what else I'd find.

The final count was four packets of Pop-Tarts (Nate grumbled that Katie had gotten into his exam stash), one bottle of quarry water and one of tap water, one pair of sweatpants, sneakers but no socks, two T-shirts ("I'll take one, if you don't mind," I said, and Nate handed me the smaller of the two), one of Nate's ubiquitous first-aid kits, and his somewhat shredded wallet. Plus a battered paperback of *Harry Potter and the Something of Something*. "This is reassuring," I said, flourishing the book. "If she thought we'd need reading material, then she can't have had very clear Sight."

Nate took the book from me and turned it over in his hands. "I've been reading those to her," he said. "I guess she thought I might want to read ahead."

I slung the pack over my shoulders and glanced around the clearing. The quarry was off to my right—I could still smell the water laced with its trap of kindness—and the sun had risen to my left. "Okay, I think I've got my bearings. We can get to a highway if we go that way."

"You know where we are?"

I glanced at him. "You don't?" Nate shook his head. "Then why did you come out here?"

"First I was just trying to get out of Boston. After that, though . . ." He glanced over his shoulder, toward the quarry, and though there was still something of a hunted look to him, it was less that of prey in flight as of a recent escapee considering a new path. "It's . . . hard to think, when I'm like that. But I remember feeling that there was a safe place here."

"The quarry." Low-grade magic, over a wide area . . . I wondered how the vacation homes in this area were doing.

"Yes . . . No. I remember not wanting to go near the water, as soon as I'd gotten here. It was—" He paused, his lips drawing back from his teeth slightly. It was an expression I'd seen on him before, but now it carried a new set of connotations. "I can't quite explain it, but I knew I didn't like it."

Smart man. Wolf. Whatever. "Good for you. There's something in the water—I'm not sure whether you can call it a spirit, but it's not like any undine I've ever seen. And it's a lot hungrier than it ought to be."

He nodded slowly. "I didn't quite think of it that way, but yes, something about hunger. Only I had the sense that there was something else in the area as well. I think I was looking for it when I noticed you, and then . . ."

"And from that point it's all a mess." I grinned, but something still nagged at me. Judging from the spindly trees and low scrub around the quarry, it couldn't have been abandoned for more than fifty years, and there was no way a water spirit could manifest so quickly. It might have been a local spirit that made its home in the quarry—but then it'd have some knowledge of what could and couldn't be asked for, instead of its juvenile naivete . . .

I closed my eyes and tried to get my bearings. "Okay. The quarry's on that side, and I can scent exhaust off that way. If not a highway, it's at least a big road. And there's something else . . ." I frowned and opened my eyes. "This way, I think."

We climbed a gentle rise that led away from the quarry, and I tried to call Rena as we walked. It wasn't easy; I kept tripping over things as I dialed. This was part of why I preferred cities; why couldn't the ground be level? To top it off, the service was so spotty that the line cut out several times even if I held still. Guess that explained why no one had called me.

Rena still didn't pick up. Neither did Sarah, though, and after leaving a short message (I've found him, we might need a lift, give me a call), I tucked the phone away.

Nate paused at the crest of the hill, one hand on a birch sapling no thicker than his arm. "Is this where we're meant to go?"

I climbed up next to him. Below us a dirt road, so unused that saplings had begun to grow in it, wound through the woods. Through the trees came a faint gleam of light off metal: a car, or maybe a small house. "It's close enough. In the right direction anyway." I thumped him on the shoulder, then let my hand slide down to the hollow at the small of his back. Nate closed his eyes and made a sound deep in his throat, and I snatched my hand away. "Okay, no. Not here. Not right next to the road."

He glanced at me. "That wasn't quite what I was thinking."

"It's what *I* was thinking." I straightened my shoulders, exhaled, and started walking. That was the problem with having a libido; once it woke up, it wouldn't go back to sleep just because of inconvenient timing.

Maybe it was something about the gleam through the trees; maybe it was a full night's sleep or whatever other reason, but my nagging suspicion about the quarry began to take on a further resonance. Assawompset—I'd heard the name somewhere, and it wasn't the kind of name you forget easily. Something about a quarry too, and Yuen . . .

The shape through the trees resolved itself into a distressingly familiar outline. "Oh, no," I muttered, stopping in my tracks. "No. Not this again."

Nate glanced at me. "It's just an RV."

"It's—" a battered old RV, still trailing wires from its top from where the air conditioner had been knocked off somewhere along Storrow Drive. And here it was, settled into the woods as if it had never been anywhere else, with a little Mini Cooper parked next to it like a duckling by a dray horse. "I know the guy who owns it."

Nate stared at me a moment. "Of course you do."

I glanced at the clearing around the reverend's RV.

"Okay, you stay here—" Nate made a *hrumph* sound, like the beginning of a growl, and I stopped myself. "Okay. But keep on your guard."

Stealth was going to be difficult, considering that one of us was wearing a white shirt that had been bleached so many times it was practically glowing and the other a kelly green STEER ROAST '98 shirt. Not to mention this was the woods; twigs and things kept breaking underfoot. How did all those intrepid Leatherstocking types manage to walk on this crap? I finally gave up on any kind of discreet approach and just stomped through the next bush into the clearing.

The old sandwich board proclaiming *Woodfin Ministries*, the one that was responsible for most of the bruises along my ribs, had been set up in front of the door. On it, in removable plastic letters, was just one word: SANCTUARY.

"This is what you were looking for?" I murmured. "When you were circling the quarry?"

"Something like it. It wasn't what drew me here to begin with, but I had the sense that it was preferable to the water itself."

"Hm." I stretched, feeling all the muscles I'd strained unknot. Before I could get any closer, though, the RV's side door opened and Elizabeth Yuen stepped out. She looked straight at me, and her eyes narrowed. "Reverend," she called without taking her eyes off me. "We have company."

"From the tone of your voice, my dear, I expect they're not here for Sunday services." The blinds next to the door twitched, and I resisted the urge to straighten my shirt.

"Reverend?" Nate whispered.

"Traveling preacher," I whispered back.

"The same one you said practically kidnapped you?"

"Pretty much."

Nate exhaled slowly, and he edged forward so that he was just slightly ahead of me. "Well, let's hope he doesn't try it again."

Reverend Woodfin opened the door of the RV and put his hand on Elizabeth's shoulder. He gave me a long look. "Huh. Are you sure they're real?"

"For crying out loud!" I snapped. "What kind of question is that?"

"A valid one," Woodfin answered. "Particularly considering our surroundings."

"Well, we are real. What would you have us do to prove it? Recite the alphabet? Touch our toes? Hell, I can prove I bleed red—"

"No!" The reverend jumped sideways off the top step and hurried forward. "This is not a good place to bleed."

I had some idea of why. But Nate spoke up first. "Why not?"

"Unknown quantities. Very new inhabitants. It wouldn't have been a good place before, but now . . ." He walked up to Nate and offered his hand. "Reverend James Woodfin. Pleased to make your acquaintance. This is—" Elizabeth shook her head, and Woodfin nodded. "Very well, no names. This is an acquaintance of mine."

Nate glanced sidelong at me. "Nathan Hunter. Evie tells me she knows you."

Woodfin clasped his hand warmly. "Welcome to the sanctuary, young man. You look like you've had a rough night."

"It wasn't so bad," Nate said, and I very carefully avoided looking at him. "But it's been a bad couple of days."

"No disrespect meant," I said, and Woodfin's glance flickered toward me but didn't light on me, "but what in God's name are you doing out here?"

"We could ask the same thing about the two of you," Elizabeth said.

"It's a long story," Nate cut in. "And it's my fault."

"Hm. I'd guess it would be. A long story, that is." Woodfin looked him up and down, then turned to face me. "As for the young lady and myself, well, we're doing some clean-up work."

Clean-up? "Hang on." I finally put the last piece into place. "This is the place you were talking about," I said. "The man who killed Skelling is buried here. This is that quarry."

The reverend and Elizabeth exchanged glances. "Skelling and his wife killed each other," Woodfin said, a bit too gently.

I shrugged, remembering the dream I'd had. It wasn't important, not in the long run, but I had the feeling there was more to Skelling's version of events than the documentation Woodfin had found. "What was his name? The one who ran off with some of the loot that night, the one who was killed here. Prescott. Him."

Woodfin's eyes widened, but Elizabeth was the one who answered. "Yes," she said. "That's why we're doing clean-up work. Some of what you told the reverend, back when he brought you your ammunition, made us think that maybe the quarry should be checked."

Nate shook his head. "Do you mind translating for me?"

I glanced at him. "I've only just started figuring it out. Reverend, let me see if I've got this right. Close to a century ago, six men were paid to transport several packages across the country. One of them—" I glanced at Elizabeth, who shook her head. Okay, so I'd leave her out of it for now. But she wasn't the only one with family stories here. "One of them was Rory Skelling, who was like me." I tapped my nose, and Nate nodded. "They almost made it to Boston, despite losing a couple members of their party on the way. But just at the border of Massachusetts, one of them decided to claim some of the booty for his own, and . . . and either he used the double murder to cover his tracks, or he killed them both."

I stopped for breath, suddenly realizing that the long-coated silhouette, Skelling's palpable absence, was no longer there and hadn't been since I set foot on the path. Maybe Skelling had had the decency to go haunting somewhere else for a few hours. The other option was just creepy.

"In any case," I said, "it doesn't matter who killed Skelling. Prescott ran off with the loot, but the last two survivors caught up with him near here, killed him, and buried him in this quarry. They brought the packages to Boston, where they were distributed." And at least one of them made it to the Gardner. It was all coming together—except for Abigail. Why her? What did she have to do with all this?

"Very good," Woodfin said. "You must have spent some time putting that together." He gave me a hard look, as if trying to read where I'd figured it out.

"I had help." Most of my obeying-authority circuits were tied directly to my Catholic guilt, so I was a little better facing off against someone whose clerical collar didn't come with apostolic succession. But all that meant in practice was that I didn't have the urge to confess my sins as I explained myself. And I didn't have to mention Skelling's role in this.

Nate glanced back the way we'd come, toward the scent of the quarry. I wondered if he could smell it too, that cool, inviting scent. "This—Prescott person. He didn't stay here, did he?"

I looked over at Elizabeth, standing cold and untouched by the side of the RV. "No. I don't think he did." She bowed her head. "This is just conjecture, but some of the things they were transporting involved necromancy." Like Woodfin's Unbound Book. "So maybe what the men of the expedition did wasn't so much a burial as a . . . a sealing. Locking him away."

"Sort of," Elizabeth said. "They invoked a guardian and set it over this place to keep him imprisoned. I'd expected to find it still here—my father had talked with it, you see, when he was ten—but instead it's changed into that thing in the water."

Mana turning in on itself. The locus, the spirit, becoming sentient enough to ask for blood. If the spirit had been a guardian, set in place to contain something like what Yuen's father had tried to become, that would explain the obsession it had with keeping the nearby land safe.

"And that's why I was drawn here," Nate mused. His hand bumped against mine, then clasped and squeezed it. "And shedding blood here—"

"Would be bad," Woodfin declared. "It's too young—it doesn't know morality. It doesn't know what it can and can't claim."

"If Prescott were still imprisoned, it wouldn't be a problem," Elizabeth snapped, crossing her arms. "I thought I was done with all this," she added, almost to herself.

I could sympathize with that. "He's not still imprisoned," I said. "He's in Boston. I don't know how, but he's there, and I think someone must be working with him, because he's got the horn—"

"Horn?"

I stopped short. All three of them looked confused. "It's . . . I don't know what it is. It's called a Harlequin Horn, but that's not what it is." *Names*, I thought, *why can't anyone in the undercurrent name something what it is?* "I have to get back to town."

"So do I," Nate said. "Could I use your bathroom?"

"You're surrounded by *trees*," I pointed out, "and you ask for a bathroom?"

"Sign of civilization." Woodfin waved toward the screen door. "It's on the right."

"I'll give you a lift back," Elizabeth said as Nate disappeared into the RV. She glanced at Woodfin. "It's okay. One of us has to be here, but the other one can go."

When Nate returned, we piled into Elizabeth's

Mini, and the three of us got maybe two feet down the road before the reverend ran after us, carrying a clunky old suitcase. He handed it through the window to Elizabeth. "Not sure about this, but it can't hurt. Take a look and you decide, okay?" She took it without comment and stuffed it next to my feet.

We drove in silence for a while, leaving the dirt road for a sparsely paved one and that for a two-lane highway. "What's in the suitcase?" I asked finally.

"Don't know. Not checking till I drop you off."

Ah. I drummed my fingers on the armrest, then glanced into the backseat. Nate had curled up into a fetal ball, his chin pressed against his chest. It couldn't have been comfortable, but his chest rose and fell in the slow cadence of sleep.

There are some things, Yuen had said, *that you hold on to. Even when you know you shouldn't. Even when holding on costs you everything.* I'd thought I couldn't imagine holding on to anything that strongly, but I'd been wrong. If I hadn't known it then, I did now.

"The jar," I said. "The jar that held your grandfather—I think Prescott hired those goons to steal it from you. I can't prove it, but—"

Elizabeth didn't look at me. "I don't care about the jar, Hound. I wouldn't care about any of this if I hadn't promised my father I'd clean up after him." She took a turn a little too fast and honked at the motorcyclist who flipped her off. "I didn't think it'd be this much work."

It always is, I thought. *When we start cleaning up after the dead, it's always too much work. Or even those who aren't dead yet . . .*

"I have to care," I said slowly. "An old woman—she came to me asking for help, and I couldn't do a damn thing to help her." And when I'd tried, she'd screamed at me to keep away. It hadn't made sense—why keep me away, when I was the closest thing to help? Had she *wanted* to be the victim of those hounds? Couldn't be. Maybe it was just my own guilt at hesitating, at costing her those further wounds. "I have to find Prescott. I don't know why he hurt her, but I'll stop him."

"Says the hero." Elizabeth's tone had eased, though, and she looked a little less weary. "If you keep up like that, maybe I'll come back to Boston someday."

That was probably as much of an approval from her as I was going to get. A truck passed us on the right, smelling of hay and apples. I tried Rena's number again; still nothing. I thought of the shadow hounds and hoped to God she was all right. If she was, she was going to kill me for this; I'd left her a cryptic message and then run off: exactly the sort of thing she'd told me never to do. Still, I'd make it up to her.

Harlequin, Harlequin . . . that had been a stupid name for the horn; anyone could see that pattern had been added afterward . . . it was more like camouflage . . .

I hadn't thought I could doze, but the motion of the car had me blinking and drifting as much as Katie had been two nights ago. I didn't quite come back to myself until we'd pulled up a block from the Goddess Garden and Elizabeth was reaching across me to open the door. "Thanks, Hound," she said. "But don't look for me anytime soon, all right?"

"Thanks," I said, and let the rest lie.

Nate got out and gave the Goddess Garden's windows a worried glance. "You'll be all right?" I asked.

"I don't know." He rubbed at his chin. "I'm a little scared to talk to Katie just yet."

"She'll forgive you."

"I know. That's the problem."

I handed him the backpack. "If you see Janssen—"

"I won't. I don't ever want to see him again." He hesitated, then leaned forward and gave me a quick kiss, so light it was gone before I felt it. "I'll come find you later, all right?"

"Or I'll find you." I watched him go, then turned toward home.

There was a traffic jam on Park Drive. That wasn't

so unusual; college kids get confused by the whole concept of a one-way street more often than you'd think,
bollixing it up for everyone else. But as I got closer, the
snarl of cars looked less like a traffic jam and more
like something else. Police cars, several of them, lined
the road, but none had lights flashing, and while they'd
blocked off a lane of traffic, there weren't any ambu-
lances. *At least nobody's hurt,* I thought.

As if I'd invoked it with a thought, the first scent
of blood reached me. I stopped dead. The scent was
faint—I was still a ways away—but this wasn't an undercurrent scent, or even some trace of my talent going
haywire. This was a real, physical scent of blood, and
if I was catching it from this far away, there was a lot
of it.

I quickened my steps, barely aware I was doing so.
Not Katie, I thought, *not Sarah, not Rena, not Abigail, please not anyone I know—*

And then I stopped dead in my tracks, because the
scent entwined with the blood was one I did know,
the one that after last night I'd begun to associate with
Nate. The wild scent. Janssen. What had he done this
time?

I forced myself to move without any obvious hurry.
Cops don't like it when you come running up to a
crime scene; they tend to think that means you had
something to do with it.

The police had cordoned off a footbridge and a section of the park on this side of the stream, and a small
group of people had gathered at the edge of the yellow
tape. A tall policewoman was telling them that there
was nothing they could do, to please disperse. Her
counterpart was at the other end of the tape, arguing
with a man carrying a camera.

I didn't slow to look, but walked past and followed
the footpaths around to the far side of the bridge. The
cops had tied the tape to a forsythia bush, and while
that would provide me with a little cover, it also hid

most of the crime scene. I pushed a branch out of the way and peered past it.

The first thought that came to mind was *Where's the body?* I could smell blood and nastier things, bile and spilled bowels and a dreadful meaty reek that was going to put me off rare steak for some time. But while there were blue plastic tarps set up all over the grass, none of them had that distinctive lumpen shape of a body underneath, nor were they large enough to hide one.

Each one of the tarps covered something, though. I stared at them for a moment, counting—there were six at least, and probably more on the side of the bush that I couldn't see. *Christ,* I thought, *are those children? No—none of them are big enough even for that. If Janssen's done this—whatever this is—I swear I'll—*

A breeze—not a desultory, halfhearted thing like the ones that had tweaked at the hot weather up till now, but a stiff, cool breeze tasting of metal—blew across the fens. The tarps rippled, and two flipped open entirely.

I wouldn't have to go looking for Janssen after all.

There wasn't much of his face left, but the remnants were contorted in a scream that ended where the ragged edges of his lips pressed against the dirt. His shoulders were contorted, as if he'd been reaching for something, but his reaching arm ended in a hash of split bone and meat. Though the back of the tarp still stayed down, there wasn't enough space back there to allow for another arm, or even another shoulder blade.

One of the watchers at the tape screamed, almost delightedly, and the camera guy went nuts. It took them a moment to tack down the tarp furthest from me, and I took a step back into the forsythia before they could reach this one.

A hand grabbed the back of my shirt. "Where the *fuck* have you been?" Rena hissed.

Twenty

E very other time I'd been in a police station, it'd been in a much more friendly situation—picking Rena up at the front desk so we could go scare the DJ at Jillian's, arguing about parking tickets for a friend who'd gotten towed, waiting in the front room until my mom could come by and explain that it had all been a misunderstanding and I'd pay for the replacement sign. Hell, even the parts of the morgue I'd visited were the ones they kept visitor friendly. Not that I was eager to repeat that experience.

I'd still take it over this anonymous, concrete-block room. I didn't have claustrophobia—cramped towers in cemeteries aside—but this looked like the sort of room that would be perfect for triggering it. One table, one mirror set into the wall, four chairs, and a ceiling that hung over me like old guilt. Even the smell was anonymous: not the scrubbed and sterile cleanliness of the morgue, but the careful facelessness of a place that let no trace of events take hold. A thousand people might have been here before me, but I wasn't going to be finding out about any of them from this room.

The company didn't help matters. "Okay, Miss Scelan," said Cop Number One. I hadn't heard his name yet, and somehow I didn't feel comfortable asking for it. He was about my height, with thinning brown hair and a blotchy red birthmark along his jaw, and he gave the air of someone who had not only seen it all but dealt with idiots at every stage. "One more time. How did you know this man?" He tapped the picture of Janssen that lay on the table, a fuzzy telephoto blowup showing him in mid-laugh.

"I didn't know him," I said. Cop Number Two— Cop One had called him Dave when he came in, but every time I tried to assign that name to him, it slid right off—made a note. "Not personally or anything. I met him for the first time a few days ago. He wanted me to take on a job for him."

"And what kind of job would that be?"

I sighed and glanced at the last occupant of the room. Rena hadn't spoken since she'd brought me in. She stared at the table, refusing to look at me. "Am I under arrest?" I asked, speaking to her rather than the two before me.

"Arrest?" Cop One looked shocked. He did a good job of it. "No, not at all. We're just having a talk, aren't we? You're helping us with our inquiries, that's the phrase."

"Then I don't have to tell you anything about my job." That knocked the feigned shock off his face. "Besides," I said, "you know this stuff already. I mean, twenty minutes ago he—" Cop Two didn't even bother to look up, "—was threatening me with losing my license as a private investigator."

"You certainly could lose it," Cop One said. "If you've done anything to deserve it."

I sighed. "The point is, you know what I do for a living. So why do you have to ask what Janssen wanted me for?"

"Janssen," Cop One murmured, and Cop Two made another note. "So he wanted to hire you?"

I hesitated. "No. Not technically—he seemed to want *me* to hire *him*. I think he'd gotten the wrong idea about what I did, and he wouldn't believe me when I told him that I wasn't interested."

"And why would he think you wanted to hire him?"

Because six weeks ago I brought down the biggest undercurrent gang this side of the Atlantic. "I don't know. Maybe he was starting up a PR business."

That got a momentary tightening of lips from Cop One. Cop Two might have smiled, except that his face seemed to be stuck in permanent professional detachment. He had the same stocky build as his partner and even seemed to share the same flat-nosed face, or maybe that was just an effect of the official cop expression they were both so good at. "So you told him to buzz off. But you met him again."

"That wasn't for work, I told you." Jesus, this wasn't good. I didn't know how much I could hold back about Nate, especially since if they'd already called him in, he might be spinning a story that mine totally failed to corroborate. "Look, how do you know all this? Were you having me watched?"

Cop Two spoke up, still without taking his eyes from his screen. "The gentleman in question had been under our eye for a while." Rena shifted in place, but didn't say anything.

"Under your eye? What's that supposed to mean?"

"It means we know you met Janssen." Cop One leaned over the table. "And apparently got into a bar fight with him. Mind telling me the circumstances of that?"

"He started it. Any of the witnesses will tell you that."

Cop One grunted. He drummed his fingers on the table, skimming the edge of Janssen's photo. "Where were you between the hours of midnight and three A.M. last night?"

"A friend and I felt the need to get out of town for a bit," I said. "We were out by Assawompset." I tried to remember any of the road signs I'd seen on the way back. "Lakeville."

Cop One's lip curled. "And neither of you came back to Boston till this morning."

"No." *Could Nate have done it?* I wondered. As a wolf, he might have been able to tear Janssen apart, but not like that. Not like that. And I'd been with him all night, dammit. We must have been too far away to hear the hunt, or maybe the quarry's sanctuary wasn't in name only. "There's no way either of us could have gotten back here by then." As soon as I said it, I realized it was a lie. Nate couldn't have made it back, but I could—leaving him asleep by the quarry, running back along that gray path, though the thought nauseated me.

Cop One was watching me narrowly, and I pulled myself away from that line of thought. Looking guilty right now wouldn't help anyone. "Do you know the name Harold Westmark?"

What? "Who?"

"How about Erik Marsh?"

I shook my head. "I don't think so."

"Jonah," Cop Two said warningly, and for a moment I thought this was another name I ought to know, but he was looking at his partner. He nodded back toward Rena and shook his head.

Cop One—*Jonah? Really?*—exhaled a short, sharp burst, and got up from his seat. He tried to pace, but the room wasn't large enough for him to take more than a few steps. "You were at a crime scene two days ago," he said over his colleague's muttered protest. "Why?"

Crime scene? "You mean the dog attack?"

Cop One glanced at Rena, imitating his partner's action of a moment ago. "Yes. The dog attack."

"My statement's on record with the Newton cops. What does that have to do with this?"

"Were you aware that Mr. Janssen had met with Miss Huston several days ago?"

I shook my head. "No. No, I didn't know that." Although it seemed to make some sense—had she been involved with his contact, the one that "didn't like his kind"? Had whatever tore Janssen to pieces been

something like the hounds that had attacked Abigail?
It couldn't have been the exact same pack—if the
shadow hounds were capable of that kind of slaughter
in such little time, they'd have shredded Abigail in the
same way.

Unless something had changed between then and
now.

Cop Two rubbed his eyes. "Let's try this again," he
said. "Where did you first meet Karl Janssen?"

"I want to make a phone call."

"Answer the question, Miss Scelan."

"I want to make a phone call." What kind of lawyer
would deal with this crap? Who could I call? *Hell*.

Cop Two didn't say anything. The moment stretched
out, Cop One glowering at me, Rena still in the corner
like a ghost. Finally she looked up and met my eyes.

Crap. "I met him under the Seaport Avenue bridge,
near the Barking Crab."

And on. And on.

After another round or two and what felt like three
more hours, all three of the cops got up and left me
there. By then my lack of morning coffee had really
started to make itself known; I had a headache that felt
like Athena's soccer-playing sister was trying to kick
her way out of my skull. But there was nothing I could
do; I waited in that room, chasing my thoughts around
in a circle, until a uniformed woman brought me a cup
of water and walked me to the bathroom. I sponged
off yesterday's sweat and grime as best I could with
paper towels, then stuck my head under the faucet. It
wasn't much, but it'd do.

My escort also let me make a call on an unpleas-
antly sticky phone. I left a message with Sarah's assistant at the Goddess Garden, but I knew that girl; there
was a good chance Sarah wouldn't get the message
before the day was out.

And then it was back to the room for another hour
or so. I'd lost all track of time, and the mirror behind

me didn't help. The one-way glass had faded a little, so that my reflection was doubled by just a bit.

I stared at it for a moment, ignoring the knots in my hair and the caffeine-deprived zombie look, concentrating on that edge of the image. Something about that seemed significant, the doubled image . . .

Doubles. That was what was significant about the scent that had led me to the Gardner. It had been doubled, folded in on itself. It wasn't just a matter of scent, I knew; that was just how my brain interpreted the trail, but the mirror clarified what I'd sensed. You could hide someone's scent if you were able to superimpose it on yourself so that the two canceled out instead of building into something greater.

But the only way that would actually hide someone would be if one of the parties was dead. The dead had no scent—the rotted stink of Yuen's father aside—so that absence provided a perfect mask, hiding the living scent.

I put my hands to my head. Abigail had somehow gotten involved with Prescott. Prescott had stolen the horn. Janssen had gone first to Abigail for some reason and then to Prescott instead, to get a piece of this action. Only Prescott didn't like his kind.

The link was almost there, almost within my grasp. Abigail was the one part of this that didn't make sense, didn't seem to have some kind of connection . . . no, she wasn't the problem, but her great-great-grandmother was . . . buried at the feet of her patron, buried too deep for anyone to find . . .

The click of the door opening dragged me out of my thoughts, and I sat up to see Rena busying herself at the door. She muttered something that sounded like a prayer, then pulled one of the chairs over and sat down across from me. "The tape's off," she said. "No one's listening."

I licked my lips. My mouth tasted like the moss I'd been sleeping on that morning. "Are you sure?"

"You'll just have to trust me, won't you?"

She should have been smiling as she said it—that was how Rena was, right? I wished she were smiling. "Okay."

"Now." She turned over Janssen's photograph, pushed it to the side, and folded her hands in front of her. "Tell me what you're not telling them."

"I don't know if it'll —"

"Evie. Just tell me."

I sighed and ran my hands through my grimy hair. I smelled awful, and I wanted a shower and coffee and Nate . . . "Okay. I think Janssen was killed by a pack of unreal hounds, on the orders of a dead man. That's the gist of it."

Rena's expression didn't change. "And?"

"And the same person had Abigail attacked, only I got there too late to help her. I don't yet know why he's in Boston or what he wants, but he's here . . ." I paused. How had Prescott gotten out of the quarry anyway?

Rena was still waiting. "And I had to leave town in a hurry yesterday. A . . . a friend of mine had been cursed, and I had to follow him. That's why I didn't follow up with that message I left you, and I'm really sorry about that, but he was hurt—" My voice broke, and I caught myself. "I had to help him. I'm sorry."

She nodded. "That's your story."

Something in her voice made me look up at her. "Rena, you don't think—"

"I don't know what to think," Rena snapped. "You run out of town, this guy turns up strewn all over the Fens—yeah, the press are having a field day with that—and your goddamn message!" She glared at me, her fingers fidgeting the way she sometimes got when she needed a cigarette *now*. "What the hell was up with that, Evie? Why did you need to see Huston?"

"It's important," I mumbled.

"Important? Christ, Evie, I don't know what you've gotten yourself into but you have no idea how bad this is. And I'm not just saying this as your friend, I'm

saying this as a representative of the law. You understand?"

I waited a minute for her to calm down. "Not
really," I finally admitted.

"Oh . . . shit." Rena got up and stalked to the far
end of the room, kicking the chair in the corner, in
which she'd spent most of my interrogation. For a
moment she stood with her back to me, shoulders
heaving as she took several deep breaths. "Janssen was
our lead," she said. "He'd been involved in the Gardner thefts."

"You mean—"

"I mean the biggest fucking heist Boston has seen in
decades, Evie. The paintings from the Gardner, back
in 1990. You remember that?"

I thought of the empty frames, the green silk behind
them. *This is a loss.* And Janssen had said he'd "handled the first one." He'd as much as boasted about it,
and I hadn't even noticed.

"How did you find him?" I asked, trying to think.
Could I tell her about the second theft now? Did it
even matter in this context?

"*I* didn't find him. Foster did." She grimaced and
turned, glaring at the little window set into the door.
"He was the biggest lead any of us had, at least any of
us down here in the trenches. If they had something
bigger up among the *real* detectives," and the bitterness she put on that word was enough to make me
wince in involuntary sympathy, "they weren't sharing
it with us. But Janssen was *ours.*"

"This case was your big chance," I said.

Rena wheeled to face me. Her mouth worked a
moment, and I couldn't tell if she was holding back
tears or trying not to cuss me out. "It was," she said,
finally, clipping off her words as if it cost her not to
scream them. "Mine and Foster's. You know, sometimes I think they stuck him with me just so they
wouldn't have to listen to either of us. Stick the black
kid and the Latina together, let them waste their time

on the little stuff. If they've got any complaints, just forward them to the PC team up top without touching the levels where the real work gets done. Bring us out when there's something a beefy white guy can't do. Leave us with the shit jobs, unless we catch something real early, and I mean before-it-happens early."

She turned to face the opposite wall, blinking fast. "We wouldn't even have known Janssen was in the country if Foster hadn't caught it. The brass says hands off, hands off, let's see where he leads us. Well, this—" a savage gesture over her shoulder, maybe meaning me, maybe Janssen, maybe both of us, "—is where he leads us. One old woman in the hospital, and a heap of chunky salsa in the Fens."

I hadn't realized—but of course I hadn't realized, I'm a pasty Irishwoman, and the only time that means anything is when leprechauns get stuck on everything in March. And Rena never talked about the crap she got as a Latina on the force—but that didn't excuse me for being so goddamn ignorant about it.

I finally asked the question I should have asked straight off. "Where's Foster?"

"Hospital. Dog attack. Reilly's trying to make out he was involved in some kind of dogfighting thing, but we've got Huston in the hospital with the same kind of injuries, and Janssen had them too, just worse, so between the three I think they're going to have a hard time saying it's not connected." She took a shaking breath, and brightness gleamed at the corners of her eyes. "They say he'll probably be able to see out of that eye again."

"Shit."

"No, really?" She rubbed at her eyes and glared at the saltwater on her hand as if she wanted to arrest it. "He even had your goddamn down payment on him. The emeralds check out; Huston had the receipts for them and everything." She pulled out a chair and sank into it. "It's not just leather, you know that? The scrap that came with them—it's gilded, though the gold's worn off. Foster thought it was dogskin." She took a deep breath. "God, listen to me. I sound like him; concentrating on the little things in the middle of a crisis."

"When did it happen?"

"Night before last." She took a deep breath and let it out. "I'm telling you all this so you'll be honest with me, Evie. I'm not saying I don't believe you. But it's really a stretch."

"It's what happened," I protested.

"Doesn't make it plausible." She shook her head and sat down. "Why didn't you tell me about Janssen when we talked before? I could have done something. *You* could have done something."

"I didn't know he had anything to do—" I stopped. "I'm sorry. But there's a lot that I don't think I *can* tell you—I can't even explain it to myself." I looked down at my hands, thinking about Abigail, about the theft from the Gardner. How much would that throw everything into chaos? How bad would it make her look to have missed one theft when trying to solve another?

I thought of the empty box that had held the Harlequin Horn and shuddered. Something that could leave an echo like that shouldn't be let near Rena. Near anyone decent.

She held up a hand. "You know what? If you're telling the truth, I don't need to hear it, and if you're lying, I don't want to." She paused a moment. "If you're holding out on me, Evie, then I swear I won't just stop protecting you. I'll track you down. *Bruja* shit or no, friends or no, I will take you down."

I almost told her everything. The new theft, the suspicion I had about the thief's identity, a dead man wandering around Boston—but I knew how it would sound to her, and if what I'd already told her had strained credulity, what would she do with the full story? "I understand," I said, aware of how much I was leaving undone.

Rena's eyes narrowed, and she seemed about to say something more. The door creaked open, and the same officer who'd brought me a drink entered. "We're letting her go."

Rena stared at him. "*Go?*"

"Reilly says we got no reason to hold her." The officer nodded to me. "Miss Scelan?"

I got to my feet and stood, swaying, for a moment. All the aches from yesterday came back with a vengeance. "Rena—"

"Go on," she said, slumping back in her chair. "Reilly probably wants you out of here before the press can get hold of your name. It's not the first time I've had him go over my head."

She didn't get up as I left, only turned over the photo of Janssen and stared at it as if there were secrets written under his skin.

I was led out through the offices to the front, where my cell phone and wallet were returned to me, and then out onto the steps. The sunlight was bright—it wasn't too long past noon. I ran my fingers through my hair, grimaced at the feel of it, then paused as a figure across the street waved to me.

Sarah was in her full summer regalia, all gauze and fluttering skirts, and she'd even made a concession to the day by donning a pair of cat's-eye sunglasses and buying a lemonade from one of the street vendors. "You know, Evie," she said as I got closer, "it may have been a while since your last walk of shame, but that doesn't mean you have to ignore me completely."

"What?"

"You could have stopped by the Garden. I had cinnamon rolls out. And Nate certainly had an appetite."

"He's all right?"

"You'd know that better than I." She grinned and raised her lemonade in a salute. "Some things you learn to recognize quickly."

I shook my head. I had neither the time nor the temper to deal with Sarah in a good mood. "How's Katie?"

"Katie's fine, just scared." Sarah eyed me as if considering what else to ask—what Katie was scared of, for one—but eventually refrained from asking anything. "If Alison starts nagging me about having kids, I'm blaming you. She used Katie as an excuse to stay up watching *Sailor Moon* and eating Cocoa Krispies instead of working on her deposition."

"Oh. Good?"

"If you didn't have to watch with them, yes." She took another sip of her lemonade, then offered it to me. I drank it down eagerly. "I swear, I nearly found myself telling the guy at the coffee shop 'In the name of the moon, I will have a latte' this morning. Oh, and some woman dropped this off for you after they left." She held up a battered suitcase.

"Elizabeth Yuen?"

Sarah shrugged. "I dunno. Small, Asian, in kind of a snit. She took a cinnamon roll, though." She glanced over her shoulder and edged closer. "I can't believe you told Katie about the twinkle incident. Do you know how embarrassing that is?"

"Uh-huh." I took the suitcase, sat down, and set it on my lap.

"I mean, I'm still finding rhinestones in my underwear drawer." She glanced over my shoulder as I flipped the catches—then just as quickly slammed the suitcase shut again, my pulse thundering in my ears. "Holy mother of—Is that what I think it is?"

"I hate to say it, but I think so." The suitcase held an old-fashioned six-chambered pistol, resting in a worn leather holster dark with age. I'd only gotten a brief glimpse, but that plus the scent of it—old iron, and the tingle of both gunpowder and gold—told me that despite its cartoonish appearance, it was the real thing. "It's from a, a gunsmith I know."

"How many gunsmiths do you know?"

I ignored her and slid my hand into the suitcase again, trying to tell more about the gun without blowing a hole in my own leg. The barrel was slick and unnaturally smooth, chased with a fine pattern that my fingers couldn't quite make sense of, and the wooden grip was warm beneath my fingers.

Out of the corner of my eye, I caught a glimpse of a distortion, an emptiness in the air. *I never kept it in that good a condition*, Skelling murmured in my ear.

I didn't answer. I'd done enough talking to ghosts lately.

Something crinkled under my fingers, and I pulled a scrap of paper from under the holster. "What, operating instructions?" Sarah said as I unfolded it. "I thought those things were just point-and-click."

It was a handwritten note, printed on the back of a Silver Bullet Ministries flyer:

I hate to split up my collection, but if what young Elizabeth tells me is true, you and Skelling share more than just blood. Consider this an extended loan, until I come back in the spring. I've included ammunition, cast from the proper molds, but it is an antique, after all, and I expect you to treat it as one.

Which meant it was for show only, and not to be trusted in a firefight. Got it. And the "extended loan" probably meant I was breaking so many concealed-weapons laws right now that if Rena saw me, she'd drop my ass in jail before I could speak. I had a license for my own gun; I didn't think you could get a license for this sort of thing.

One thing about Prescott: I don't know his real name. None of the members of the expedition knew it; he refused to give it, on the basis that it was "that thieving whore's" name and he

*would not share it. I know that the kind of work
you do involves names, so don't attempt to use
"Prescott" in that work. Good luck.*

—*J. W.*

I closed the case again and laid a hand on it, thinking of Skelling, of how little this gun had helped him,
of the blind spot that persisted in hanging over my left
shoulder.

Well. If I had to be haunted, who better than
family?

Sarah took the note from my hand and scanned it.
"Sounds like someone had mommy issues."

"What makes you say that?" I got up and felt for
my wallet and cell phone, both in their usual place.

"A whore sharing his name? Might be a wife, but
he'd have recourse to strip her of his name. And that
doesn't seem quite right in context."

I shook my head. "That's assuming a lot. You've got
no way of knowing he didn't have a wife . . ." I paused.
No way of knowing about a wife, or children . . . or a
mother . . .

The box. The box at the Gardner. Mrs. Gardner
wouldn't have known how to build a seal like that.
Someone must have told her. And Abigail Huston was
buried deep at her patron's feet.

Why had Gardner supported the expedition
anyway? To own an item that she'd later fear so much
she kept it sealed, or to keep it away from someone
else?

"Evie." Sarah gave me a wary look. "You've got
that look again, Evie. Don't go running off on a whim
again."

"It's not a whim." I put my hands on her shoulders.
"Sarah, listen to me. If this goes wrong, things might
get very bad for a while."

"I've been through the 'very bad' part already, Evie.
I know how to handle myself."

"Not like this. If it gets dark, and you haven't heard from me . . . well. Stay inside, keep the door locked, and if you hear hounds, don't go looking."

She narrowed her eyes. "Evie . . ."

"Trust me." I gave her a quick hug, then picked up the suitcase and ran.

Twenty-one

I called Nate from the D branch of the Green Line of
the T, out where it turned into something between
a trolley and a commuter train, running through the
lush greenery that suburbs like Newton could afford. I
huddled in the back of the train; I'd had enough of the
great outdoors lately, thank you very much.

Nate's cell phone was presumably still in little bits on
the floor of his apartment, but his land line was working. "Nate, it's me," I said as soon as he picked up.

"Evie? Are you all right? I called your phone, but no
one picked up—"

"I was at the police station." I glanced over my
shoulder—no one but a pair of grandmothers talking
in Russian and one very tired woman in a wilting business suit. "Janssen's dead."

"Janssen?"

Shit. "Your father."

"Oh." Silence for a long moment, punctuated only
by the gentle rocking of the train. "I wish I could feel
something about that, Evie, but I can't. Not now. How
did it happen?"

"I think—It looks like it was the same thing that
happened to Abigail." Only much, much worse. "Nate,
I want you to meet me at Newton-Wellesley Hospital."

"Why?"

"Because you might be a target too. I didn't think
Janssen had anything to do with this, and now it turns
out he did. That means you're involved, even tangen-
tially, and I'm—" I swallowed. "I'm not risking you
again."

He was silent again. "I understand," he said, and
surely it was the air-conditioning in the T car that
made me shiver. "You be careful too."

"I will." I clicked the phone shut, then lay my head
against the window of the train and tried not to think
of the scent in the box at the Gardner.

I got off the T at the next-to-last stop, stepping out
into heavy, flat air. All the leaves were unnaturally
still against a hard, white sky; if there was a change
coming, the sunlight gave no sign.

I made it through the lobby of the hospital without more than a few stares (and one kind woman telling me that the emergency care center was that way,
and those were some nasty bruises), then did my best
to look as if I knew where I was going as I followed
Abigail's scent through the halls. She wasn't bothering
to hide herself, or more likely couldn't, now that she
was incapacitated. Her scent was very weak, though—
which didn't necessarily mean that she was as well, but
I didn't like the implications of it.

I turned a corner just behind another pair of visitors, then ducked back the way I'd come. A uniformed
officer stood a little way down the hall, and it didn't
take Sight to guess that he was in front of Abigail's
door. I didn't know if he'd seen me, but there was no
way that showing up here right now could look good
for me, for Abigail, or for Rena.

All right, I told myself. *Rena took me seriously
enough to post a guard. That should be enough for a
little while.*

I made it back out to the parking lot and scanned it
for Nate's mobile wreck of a car. Nothing. But there
was a familiar black Jeep Cherokee halfway down the
lot. It could have been anyone's—God knows enough

people in Boston drive them—but the three young men hanging out around it were also familiar.

I'd found the thugs from the Three Cranes.

They didn't notice me as I walked through the lot to them, taking me for one more visitor. As I got closer, I caught part of their argument: Thug Number Two, complaining again. "Shit, we are never gonna get paid for this."

"If you hadn't been a dumbass and believed that crap about 'getting my purse,' we might not be in this situation." The first, older, guy took a long drag on his cigarette and shook his head. "You're a total fucking moron." He turned to flick his cigarette into the lot and saw me. For a moment his eyes narrowed, as if he couldn't quite place where we'd met, and then he demonstrated his quicker thinking by taking off without a second look.

"Hey!" His friends jumped up from their places on the bumper, then turned to see what had spooked him.

Too late; I knocked the third guy aside and caught the complainer by the collar of his grimy shirt. "Long time no see, boys," I said, grinning with all of my teeth.

"Lady, I don't—" He stopped, eyes widening, and folded over a little in the ridiculous protect-the-junk position of scared guys everywhere. His friend, the one who'd opened every damn jar he could find in the Three Cranes, backed away but didn't go further than the next car, perhaps out of some misplaced sense of loyalty. "Shit," the guy I had by the shirt said. "Shit, you're not—"

"I'm pissed off, is what I am." I kicked his legs out from under him. "Do you know what kind of shit you pulled, breaking in like that?" I shook him, then switched my grip to the back of his neck. He hung like a stunned puppy. "You're not allowed to do that. Not in my city."

"Fucking crazy bitch—" he spat, and I swung his face into the door of the Jeep.

His friend choked. "Jesus, that's my car!"

It's also your friend's face, I thought, but just shook my head. "Want to tell me who hired you to break into the Three Cranes?"

The guy whose collar I held spat something garbled around the word "fuck," and I swung him into the door again. Somehow I could take the idea of spectral hounds, magical hunts, even a goddamn werewolf, but for two-bit assholes like this to even touch magic was more than I could take. They had no idea what kind of shit they were dealing with: if they'd had half an idea, maybe they'd show some respect—

Could you respect that? Any of those chattering idiots?

The blond man's words came back to me like a slap, and I let go of the guy. He dropped, and I stumbled back, into the next car. "Fuck," he mumbled, "fuck, I'm sorry—"

Sorry? His friend raised both hands. "We're sorry, lady. We didn't know it was . . . was protected or anything."

"It's Joey's fault," the guy on the ground mumbled, clutching the side of the car door to pull himself up. "He's the one who got us involved with that crazy old bitch. Bitch never even paid us—"

Bitch? I shook my head—hadn't Prescott hired these guys? Wasn't that how the jar ended up at the park where Abigail was attacked? "Hang on," I said. "It wasn't a man that hired you?"

He shook his head. "Little old lady. I was gonna go find her, but then she got put in the hospital, and so we thought we'd talk to her here—"

Jesus. Abigail. Abigail had hired them. Why the hell had she needed the jar? "Go away," I said, backing away from them as if their stupidity was catching.

The Jeep owner looked relieved. "Look, we can go get Joey if you want, since he's the one who managed it. We'll make sure he knows you're angry—"

"Get out of my face, you fucking sellout." My skin crawled, and I stalked away, shuddering. Janssen had been right about me, about the role waiting if I wanted it; those kinds of punks were ready to sell out to someone stronger, and they didn't even have the undercurrent reasons. I might want to protect the city, but where did protection end, and the protection racket begin? I turned and spat away the taste of bile.

At the thought of Janssen, I glanced across the lot. No sign of Nate's car, still. Maybe he'd come by T, the way I had? An itch struck the back of my mind, something about grade school . . . Why did grade school keep coming to mind?

The trouble with a talent like mine is that it's mostly subconscious. The result is that I have a very smart nose hooked up to a very dumb brain, and moments like this hammer that home.

I'd almost made it to the end of the parking lot when a hand caught me by the elbow. I jerked away from it reflexively, then stared.

Abigail's feet were bare, caked with grime, and bloodied from where she'd stepped carelessly, and they were the best-looking part of her. She still wore her hospital gown, with a flimsy cotton bathrobe tied in place over it, granting her a shred of dignity but no more. The cane she leaned on looked like part of an IV stand. Every inch of exposed skin was puffy and bruised, and the strips of gauze over her face couldn't hide the wounds beneath. "Hound," she whispered. "I've been trying to reach you."

"Jesus Christ." I took her hand; the bones that had felt frail before now seemed downright insubstantial. "What are you doing out here?"

"As I said, trying to reach you. Shall we go?"

"Go? You—" How was she even standing? "Why didn't someone stop you on your way out here? You're not fit to be out of bed."

She smiled, and even though her face was a mess, I could see a trace of her earlier composure. "I can keep security guards and cameras from noticing me; do you think a few pedestrians will be any trouble?"

And, indeed, the family that passed us (walking from one end of the parking lot to the other, with the oldest kid complaining about the heat) looked past us altogether. I shook my head.

Abigail switched her cane to the other hand and pointed. "You came on the train, yes? We'll go back along the tracks. Iron on both sides will be some protection against him."

Okay. That I didn't like, but it was more than I'd known before. "Abigail," I said, moving to catch up with her. For a wounded old woman, she sure moved fast. I skipped up a step and moved in front of her, blocking her path. "Who did this to you?"

"A pack of dogs," she said, avoiding my eyes.

"No. That's what he used. Who set them on you?"

She stepped around me and pushed the gauze out of her left eye. It was swollen almost shut. "I'll tell you on the tracks; there are some things that shouldn't be discussed without iron nearby—"

"Abigail." I touched her arm, and she stilled, staring past me. "His name is Prescott, isn't it?" She didn't answer me. "His name is Prescott, or that's one of the names he used, and he's a ghost. Or something close to it, something unnaturally preserved after death. He wanted the horn—" I stopped, unsure how much I could explain a dead man's reasons. But the memory of my dream, of Skelling's last story, came back as if Skelling himself had laid a cold hand on my head. "He wanted it because he didn't think anyone else deserved it. No one else was worth it."

"Respect," Abigail breathed. "No one else was worth his respect. Only him." She was silent a moment. "So that's the name he went by," she said at last and glanced up, blinking hard with the one good eye. "I suppose he changed it legally; he wouldn't have kept her name, of course, not with that kind of mother."

"I—what?"

"My great-grandfather, I think. Abigail Huston's son. He . . . the ghost of him, anyway."

And there it was. The blood link between the woman who'd first stolen the horn, the man who'd tried to steal it back, and the woman who'd stolen it again. Woodfin and I had both fallen into the same trap; we'd assumed that just because there was no recorded family for the members of the 1908 expedition, there was no family at all. Prescott could easily have had grown children before going on that expedition.

"But I've always called him Patrick," she went on.

That caught me off guard. "What?" I asked, but as I said it the last memory slid into place: a young man talking about respect, respect in magic, a young man named Patrick . . .

"My brother. Prescott's host." She took a deep breath. "He's dead, you know," she said, conversationally, as if she were telling me that her brother was gay or divorced or older. She tottered forward, then turned back and regarded me with cool, pained eyes. "I'll tell you about it. Just come to the tracks."

This is what she told me as we walked along the railroad tracks, the cool wind driving before us and promising rain:

She and her twin brother had been a pair of holy terrors. The two of them drove their parents to a sort of proud distraction, and though they fought every now and then, at the heart of the matter it was the two of them against the world. Back when they were ten (so, I guessed, fifty-some years ago) they'd gone with their grandparents to stay out by Lakeville. The twins had immediately found the highest trees to climb, the best hiding places, and the big quarry nearby, which had been abandoned years before and was now the local swimming hole. White marble cliffs streaked with rust and ivy, dozens of spots to dive from—even some that were safe—and countless places where a few well-chucked rocks would flush out angry teenage couples.

"We brought water balloons one day," she said with a faraway smile. "If I'd been in their place, I probably would have killed us . . . but it was so very worth it."

One day in high summer, Abigail stayed home—stomachache, plus she'd had a fight with Patrick the day before and didn't want to be around him. ("Something stupid, like who got to choose the radio station.") He went out to the quarry, and then it got to be dinnertime, and he hadn't come back. First her grandparents went out, and then it got dark, and then her grandmother returned, crying.

Abigail didn't even let herself think the word *dead* until her grandfather came home, looking twenty years older. They waited for word from the police, but by three in the morning both grandparents were asleep, and Abigail walked down to the quarry herself.

She'd stood on the high ledge, the one the boys dove off when they really wanted to impress a girl, and watched the lights of police cars across the water, the bobbing flashlights of search parties in the woods. And she'd spoken aloud, her words lost in the darkness above the flat, black water, swearing that she'd give anything, anything, if she could have her brother back. And she'd said more, words that she hadn't known but that came to her like someone whispering in her ear. She hadn't questioned them, believing that anything was worth it for her brother.

And the water stayed dark and unmoving, and she went home alone.

Just before dawn someone tapped on her window. It was Patrick, soaked to the skin and ghost-pale, but it was his smile and his voice, and so she let him in. She'd laughed from sheer joy, and hugged him, and almost went down to tell her grandparents, but he stopped her. *Let's not tell them yet,* he said. *It's kind of an adventure, everyone thinking I'm dead. We'll tell them eventually—it'll be like in* Tom Sawyer, *right?*

Abigail thought it was weird, but he was right—it was fun, having this secret. So she kept her mouth shut the next day, and the next, and the next . . .

And Patrick kept coming by, always when he

wouldn't be seen. Except he never came back to their grandparents, and whenever she asked when they could end the joke, he told her to trust him. And their parents arrived, and cried, and whispered to each other that their daughter seemed to be in shock, she didn't seem to quite realize what had happened, and the funeral was planned . . .

About halfway through the funeral, Abigail realized he wouldn't be joining them. She knew he was there—nearby, she was sure, just to watch—but as the eulogies droned on and her mother hiccupped and her father wept silently without a single change of expression, she knew. And along with that knowledge came the unwelcome realization that he was not entirely her brother. Not anymore. There wasn't just one person in that body anymore: the ghost-responses of an older, craftier man merged with the slow and muted reactions of a boy's personality. But the two of them together worked in concert, clinging to a form of life, and when she returned from the funeral they were there to meet her, laughing with her, sharing their old jokes, her brother but not her brother.

But still . . .

"I don't know if I can explain it to you," she said, twisting the cotton of her robe between her hands. "We were so close, and there was still some of him left . . . Even a shadow of my brother was enough. I knew it was a rotten trade, but I missed him so much."

If you have to be haunted, why not by family? My own thoughts came back like a spike of ice, and I shuddered, trying to ignore Skelling's empty presence just outside my vision. "I—" I stopped, remembering an old woman who was not my mother on a cot deep under Fenway Park. *Need deforms the undercurrent.* "I do understand," I said, fighting down revulsion. "It's hard to explain, but I do."

She gave me a hard look, then nodded. "I think you do. How strange. I'd love to learn more, but now . . ." She shrugged. "It doesn't matter."

They had gone on from then, Abigail and her secret brother. He'd disappear now and then, just for a day or two, but always returned to her side. In time she learned to recognize which of the two spirits inhabiting the body was speaking: Prescott's strong and unpredictable voice, Patrick's fading but beloved voice. And then, as the years went on more, she learned not to mind which one was which. The spirits in the body of her brother continued by her side, never quite aging, while she aged a little faster than she ought to.

He taught her the first few uses of magic, drawing on loci no bigger than a fingernail paring, and she followed in the footsteps of her great-great-grandmother, learning the tricks of theft both mundane and magical, and the sleight of hand that trod the boundary between. Because of his "empty aura," as she called it, they could easily hide behind each other, becoming something that didn't register on any record, whether video recording or ink spilled in a saucer. (I thought of the folded, hidden quality of Prescott's—Patrick's scent, and nodded.) Between the two of them they could steal the crown off a king. "We did steal the hat off a senator once. Just to prove we could do it. He didn't notice until he reached his plane."

It was about respect, Prescott insisted; they wouldn't steal from those worthy of respect. And at the beginning, that included a lot of people, those who'd earned Patrick's boyish idolatry as well as Abigail's growing esteem. But Prescott, though he was the one who held to this artificial code, seemed to hold no one as worthy of respect, especially no one who had anything to do with magic.

"He used to talk sometimes about what he would do if he had his inheritance. I thought—after a while I knew he didn't mean our parents. But he said he'd find a way to show the world what was so necessary, to force respect for magic and its power over the old chaos . . . That was his term for it, 'the old chaos.'" She looked at the bandages on her arms and shivered.

Chicago, Austin, New Orleans, Seattle . . . everywhere the twins traveled, they lived on the proceeds
of their thefts. New York was easy pickings but dull
after a while, and Florida was the surest way to make
a buck. San Francisco, as long as they stayed out of
the shadow of the Coit, was profitable, and they made
a score in Los Angeles that kept her in a high-class
apartment and Patrick in loci for close to two years.

"Your parents?" I asked.

"Dead. They wasted away." She caught my change
of expression and shook her head. "Look, there are
questions I haven't let myself ask, all right? If I don't
ask them, I won't have to answer them . . . This is hard
enough as it is, Hound."

Maybe. But I remembered that horrible dead smell
in Chinatown when Prescott came looking for me,
and the emptiness at the center of it, the hungriness
of it . . . Prescott might exempt Abigail from his devouring need for loci, but why should he care anything about the rest of her family?

Boston had been off-limits because of the Fiana, Abigail told me. But then came word that the Fiana had
gone down, gutted by a woman who went by the name
of Hound. And though there were times that Abigail
forgot that her brother was a ghost, his response was
not that of a living man. He hadn't shown rage or surprise, but a slow, grinding certainty, a grudge coming
to the surface like the rocks of a treacherous harbor.
"Your name, I think, was what triggered it . . ."

At the back of my neck I could feel Skelling shifting,
paying attention, and from the way Abigail's eyes narrowed, I thought she must have sensed the same.

He'd become obsessed with the Harlequin Horn.
"He spent days telling me about it, how he'd summoned it into existence—days, repeating himself because he couldn't remember what he'd told me." She
curled her free arm over her chest, as if protecting herself from the memory of endless, repetitive lectures.

Prescott—and it was only Prescott now, the fragments of Patrick coming and going like cloud shadows on a bright day—claimed that the horn was his by right, that it was only because of him that that "thieving whore" of a mother had even known what to do with it. Sometimes he mistook one Abigail Huston for the other, confusing mother with sister in terrifying displays of rage made worse by the connection they shared. His reactions to any occurrences outside his careful plans, never good to begin with despite the flicker of life he claimed, had become more erratic. And Abigail, after years of living with her secret, had decided that it was time for a rest.

"I have read enough of the *Liber Sine Termini*," she told me. *Unbound Book*, Skelling whispered in my ear. "I know that only the dead can kill the dead. So I thought that I could acquire some of the dead, use that to—to lay him to rest."

"You had the jar stolen," I said.

"You know about that? Yes. Only it didn't work. I thought that I could use the remnant of a ghost in that jar to act against my brother, to neutralize him at least for a little while. It should have worked."

"No," I said. "Yuen freed his father's ghost before you got the jar. It was empty when you had it."

"Empty. That figures." She paused a moment, looking at her mangled hands. They wouldn't be pickpocketing anything—not for months, perhaps not ever again. "I tried to bring my brother back, and it didn't work. I tried to kill him, and it didn't work. I think, maybe, the whole thing might have been a mistake."

If Sarah could have seen me right then, she'd have taken back everything she ever said about my lack of tact. *A mistake. A mistake? My God, that's not just an understatement, that's self-delusion on a grand scale.* I drew a deep breath and tried to think how to express this in a way that didn't involve the phrase *Are you completely insane?* "And you brought me into all this."

"To undo it! I thought that once my brother was

laid to rest, I could return the horn somehow, earn some fragment of absolution."

Something about her tone rang false, but when I glanced at her, there seemed to be no change in her demeanor. Maybe it was just that I had trouble imagining Abigail begging for absolution, or maybe it was Skelling's presence and his memories shading mine, reminding me of Skelling's desire for that horn and bringing into question how difficult it might be to let go of it.

The sound of a Green Line bell yanked me out of my thoughts "Train," I said. "Off the tracks."

The train passed by us with a rhythmic roar, and Abigail hopped back into the space between the rails. "If he's dead," I said, following her lead, "then he'll have the same approach to current events as he did to old ones."

Abigail exhaled, shook herself as if throwing off the memories of everything she'd just told me, and turned to face me. "Not quite. He's not fully dead, just . . . preserved. And that means most of the time he can think. But I can still get him out of Boston, and I can get the horn away from him." Her eyes narrowed. "Do you know what the horn is?" she asked.

"A Harlequin Horn," I hazarded. "It calls the Wild Hunt. But I don't know which Hunt, yet."

Abigail's expression went sour. "You don't know the half of it, do you? My great-great-grandmother wasn't just a thief, she was the best of thieves. She could steal something that didn't actually exist."

Her explanation included words like *catoptric* and *harmonic sub-frequency* and a lot of other terms that probably made sense if you had half of your brain marinated in magic, but the gist of it was this: if you have a thousand reflections that seem to be of one thing, you can focus those reflections and create a center— even if there is no center to begin with. A sub-myth. A Harlequin Horn.

"It can call any of them. The Gabble Retchets. The

Wild Hunt. The Host. All of them, and any of them. My namesake invoked and stole it, ages ago, and by the time she knew what she'd done, it was well out of her hands and on the other side of the country." She caught a glimpse of my expression. "But I've fixed it now, crippled the horn, and without the missing piece he can't do anything with it."

"Well, that makes it all better then, doesn't it?" I snapped. "And you're wrong; he's already killed Janssen. For crying out loud, the man was torn to pieces."

"Janssen?"

I glanced at her, but she seemed genuinely confused. "Big blond guy? Kind of oily? Worked on 'facilitating' things?"

"Oh . . . him."

I stopped and turned to face her. "What is wrong with you? He was slaughtered—even if he was a rotten piece of shit, the same thing almost happened to you. How can you just shrug it off?"

Abigail tilted her head to the side. "I told him not to set up anything with Patrick. Not while he had that little problem."

"Little problem?"

"Patrick doesn't like skinshifters. I think it's because the wound that killed him was a skinshifter bite—from the woman traveling with the expedition, someone's wife."

"Good for her," I muttered, then stopped. "Skinshifter?" Janssen's little problem, the one he'd tried to pass on to Nate . . .

Only it hadn't worked. Patrick knew enough to recognize a . . . a skinshifter when he saw one, former or not, and he'd torn the man to shreds—

Jesus. Why hadn't I heard from Nate yet? I knelt and unclasped the suitcase, unstrapping Skelling's gun from the webbing that held it in place. Wind gusted past me, suddenly cold after the day's heat, carrying the sound of another train. I cursed again and dragged the empty suitcase off the tracks, turning my back in a half-assed effort to hide what I was doing.

"You know a skinshifter?" Abigail asked, following me off the tracks.

"What—" I hesitated, then shook my head and loaded the gun, sliding one bullet after another into the chambers. "How do you know Skelling's wife was a skinshifter?"

"I don't know. Patrick knew. And he was there, after all . . ." The train rocketed past me, drowning out her words briefly. " . . . and a hound, again. Perhaps you're drawn to each other, the same way you're drawn to the horn."

I got to my feet, a little unsteadily. The holster hung awkwardly on my hips, and I didn't have a good way of hiding it. The gun was in much better condition than the holster, but neither one was top of the line, and I really didn't want this thing falling off me at a bad moment. (Then again, the gun didn't have a safety catch, so there was no way I was going to stick it into my waistband the way I sometimes did with my other gun.) Still, it might work to distract Prescott for just a moment.

Abigail leaned on her cane, regarding me with that same detached curiosity. Here was someone who'd drawn her deciding line, and it encompassed her and her brother, no more. Let the rest of the world go hang, so long as she had her twin. She smiled at me, completely oblivious. "History repeats itself, I'd say, only it's a bit tactless—"

"Oh, you think?" I drew a deep breath, then glanced back the way we'd come.

She shrugged. "I just thought it was an interesting coincidence."

God save me from this brand of adept. I caught Abigail by the wrist; she flinched but didn't protest. "Where is your brother?"

"I don't know. About, I assume; I don't keep track

of him all the time." She patted my hand. "But I can assure you—"

Not good enough. I raised her hand to my face as if I were going to kiss it. There was barely enough of her own scent to follow, and it still had that odd, attenuated sense to it, as if I were sensing her at a great distance. But that didn't matter, now I knew what I was looking for. There: the link with her brother was still active, a line of mirror-scent threaded through her own like a vein of precious metal through stone. Maybe it couldn't be broken anymore, not after the years they'd spent using that link to hide their tracks. (And at the back of my mind, I recognized why I'd thought of grade school around her: not because of her age or her demeanor, but because somewhere in there she was still the ten-year-old who'd gone searching for her brother, who'd never been able to admit that she was wrong to hold on to him.) With an effort of will I wrenched my senses onto that alignment, seizing that link.

It was like kissing a corpse. I gagged and reeled away, spitting into the brush. Abigail rubbed her wrist and sniffed at my ill manners. But I had the scent, and like a tendril of poison flowing through a river, it led on. "He's close by. Maybe he was coming to see you . . ." Even as I said it, I knew it wasn't true. Patrick—Prescott wasn't looking for Abigail; he had a new prey, and he'd follow the same pattern he had once before.

That's how he isolated us, Skelling whispered. *Lured us out away from the rest, made his offer . . . Don't let it happen again.*

Another Green Line train rumbled by, this one traveling inbound, and Skelling pointed after it, the gesture less visible than tangible. I let go of Abigail's hand, and for a moment she held it out there, as if unsure what to do with it. "Get someplace safe," I told her. "The hospital—or no. There's a lake down that way. The dead don't like water, and I think Prescott won't be an exception, given his posthumous history."

"I refuse to hide myself in a kiddie pool," Abigail snapped.

"Then find another place to hide," I said, and took off running.

The train that had just passed us was stopped at the station just up ahead. I didn't slow down—transit police might not pay attention to a running woman near the tracks, but a running woman with a gun was probably high on their list of things to watch out for.

In the back of my mind, I heard Skelling's voice murmuring. *This is how we did it out West; you'd match your speed to them just for a moment—*

Shit. He wasn't asking me to do what I thought he was, was he?

The train in front of me blurred, doubling into an old-fashioned caboose, clacking down the tracks, and for a second I felt a cool emptiness surround me, mimicking my motions, coat flapping in the wind. *Like so,* Skelling murmured, *and then you catch on like this— DeWitt and I did this once, that was back before I met my wife, God rest her—*

The idiot repetition of a lived moment, the hallmark of a ghost—but right now it was moving with me, adapting one to the other. *Bad idea,* I thought as I neared the end of the train and the bell sounded to signal the doors' closing. *This is such a bad idea . . .*

But hell. I was going to do it anyway.

The train began to pull away, and I jumped for it. My left foot landed on the little spur of metal that normally connected the cars, and I scrabbled for purchase on the smooth green-painted hull.

Like so. Skelling's hands guided mine, finding the crevices that should not have been there, and as if following a careful dance, my right foot twisted behind me, balancing on the connector. I clung to the end of the T car, the holster at my hip banging against it, too scared even to cuss. This was so going to get me arrested or hurt, and that was the *least* of my worries right now—

"Hound, I can assure you that my brother's not currently a danger to anyone."

I risked a glance up, pressing my cheek against the car as if an extra square inch of contact would keep me from falling off. Perched on top of the car, cane propped across her lap, sat Abigail. She still looked sick and worn down, but her posture carried a patrician calm that didn't belong on top of a speeding T car. "What the fuck?" I managed.

"My brother isn't going to hurt anyone. If you go looking for him, then yes, he may very well react badly to your presence, but if you'll be good enough to stay out of his way for a little while, I can promise—"

"How in God's name are you sitting up there?"

She sniffed at me. Sylvia at the Gardner could have taken lessons in disdainful sniffs from her. "My point is, even if your shifter friend does run into him, my brother is not in any position to do him harm."

"The hell you say!"

Abigail waved one hand dismissively, ducking out of the way of a dangling electrical cable without even a backward glance. "At the very least, he cannot use the horn. That was my point, Hound; he's powerless without the horn in its entirety. He might use it as he did on me, but the hounds can't kill anyone in that capacity. It's a matter of degree. Do you understand?"

I started to shake my head, thought better of it as the train lurched around a curve, and held on tighter. *This isn't happening*, I thought. *I am not discussing magical theory while clinging to the back of a speeding Green Line train*—

"One would think you understood nothing of catroptic theory. You see, the horn isn't entirely real *qua* real, and so it's not subject to the same laws as a reified object. It's not even the same as a locus, which can be split and split again and still function. Remove any part of it, even a part that wouldn't be important to an actual hunting horn, and you fragment the essential state of its being."

—I am not being lectured on magical theory while clinging to the back of a speeding Green Line train—

"Thus by removing the baldric, I crippled the horn. Now, if you'll be good enough to return it to me, I should be able to calm things down long enough for you to return the horn. I know my brother; I can get him out of your city with a minimum of fuss, and we should be able to take care of our own affairs from there. The baldric, please." She held out her hand.

I stared up at her. My fingers were starting to ache with the strain of hanging on like this. "What are you talking about?"

"The baldric for the horn. I gave it to you with the emeralds. Remember?"

"What the hell is a baldric?"

"It's a—" Abigail sighed. "The leather strap I wrapped the emeralds in. It's part of the horn."

I shook my head. "I handed all of that over to the police, after you were attacked." Abigail's face went dead white, paler than the clothes she wore. "Well, if you hadn't been so goddamn cryptic—"

The train screeched and slowed to a crawl, and that was enough to disrupt my precarious balance, ghostly assistance or not. I lost my grip on the train, banging my forehead against one of the window ridges, and fell off just as the train slowed to a stop. One of my ankles hit the rail with a dull clang.

Abigail glanced over her shoulder. "It looks like there's a signal ahead. Are you absolutely sure you handed it over?"

"Yes!" I climbed to my feet, made sure Skelling's gun was still in its holster, and limped away. Someone shouted inside the train, but I didn't turn back just yet.

We were in the midst of the Hammond Pond Reservation, the spot of greenery that Newton uses to prove it's a suburb, and though the trains ran through it, the scent of deer and semi-wild creatures was strong. As pretty as it was, I didn't like this place. I'd been here once before on a missing persons case—nothing of the

undercurrent, just generalized nastiness all around—
and that hadn't ended well. "Either the cops still have
it," I called over my shoulder, "or Prescott took it
when he sicced the dogs on Foster."

"Who?"

I snarled and quickened my pace, moving away
from the tracks. Prescott was nearby. I could feel his
scent on my skin—I'd become attuned somehow, the
same way that Skelling had become attuned to me, and
that first moment of disgust I'd felt when I'd seized the
connection between the siblings was nothing to how it
felt to carry that connection with me. I kept wanting
to shake myself clean, to bare my teeth and snap at the
air till it went away. Not good, Evie, I told myself. *If
Nate can keep hold of himself, so can you.*

And speaking of Nate—here he was, too close to
Prescott. Nate's scent didn't have the same wildness
as I remembered, but not the iron control either. He'd
come into himself, just in time for Prescott to kill him
for what someone else had been.

"Could I possibly convince you to retreat?" Abigail,
just behind me again. The train lurched and moved on.
"If what you're telling me is true—"

"It's true," I said, and headed for a break in the
chain-link fence. The holster got caught, but a second
tug got me through.

Over the hills—what idiot put so many little hills
in this part of Newton?—and through the swampy
bits, past thickets that smelled of deer and stones that
smelled of coyote. A wind followed me, heavy with the
scent of oncoming rain, tossing the trees into disar-
ray. I scrambled up an outcropping of lichen-encrusted
rock and stopped dead, panting through my teeth.

In a hummock not far away stood a man in a gray
peacoat, his yellow-bright hair gleaming in this overripe sunlight. At the sight of him, the glamour of his
living and dead body broke whatever link I'd been following, and his scent resolved into the blank, folded-

together scent that I'd first sensed on Patrick, back on Summit Hill. Nate stood in front of him, hands out to his sides, tensed in a posture that I would not have recognized had I not seen it in a different shape.

" . . . simple matter," Prescott said, the thrum of trucks downshifting on a nearby road drowning out some of his words. I tried to move closer without drawing his attention. "You've wanted to walk off with it too. I've been watching." In his right hand, he held a black-and-white horn, the curve of it like a slash in the world, and from that horn came the scent of rotted flesh. It seemed to writhe in his hand, like a trapped snake.

"I don't care what you've been watching," Nate said. He still wore the faded clothes Katie had packed for him. "But you can stuff it."

Katie, where was Katie? I glanced around—neither Prescott nor Nate had seen me yet, too devoted were they to their personal face-off, but a squeak from overhead caught my attention. Katie was up a tree, a little way behind Nate. He must have told her to hide as soon as Prescott showed, and she could wriggle up a tree faster than a squirrel. She stared at me, trembling, then back down at her brother.

Prescott—Patrick smiled and turned his head, as if listening to someone else. "That's really too bad." A little tic shivered over his face, like a roach scuttling across the floor. "Listen to me: This is the kind of thing that magicians these days lack, and that thieves should fear. You hate that sort of thing as much as I do. So why should it matter if I try to stop it in my way?" His hand tightened on the horn. "It's about respect. How can you respect something that won't hurt you? If we remind people how much it can hurt, how horrible the night can be, won't they value the day more—"

"I don't—" Nate drew a ragged breath. "Look. I don't really care about any of this. But you have three options right now. You can leave me and Evie alone. You can go to the reverend, and he'll find some way to put you to rest."

It was a noble thought, and one that would be right on target with most ghosts. But Prescott wasn't quite having the same conversation. He was sliding in and out of the past, responding to a remembered conversation as much as to the current one. Erratic, Abigail had called him.

That meant I could surprise him. I slid my hand down to Skelling's gun. Would he recognize it, having carried one like it for so long?

Patrick began to reply, but Nate stepped forward, hands held up. "Or you've got a third choice." He swallowed. "You can say no, and I'll . . . I will make you regret it."

I glanced at Nate and all of a sudden realized what he was planning. "Son of a bitch," I hissed, and tried to quicken my pace without tipping off Patrick. "Don't you dare do this to me, Nate."

Patrick shook his head, as if ridding it of a fly. "That's really too . . . really . . ." He stopped, blinking hard, and his eyes seemed to go out of focus. "No," he breathed. "No, didn't I . . . I killed you already, didn't I?"

Nate took another step, and I could see him steeling himself for what would happen. He wasn't a killer—he didn't have a killer's instinct—but he'd try, just to keep this man out of our city.

Patrick raised the horn, and I jerked Skelling's gun from its holster.

Abigail grabbed me by the wrist. "Stop," she hissed. "Just wait, wait—"

I shook her off, but too late: Patrick had the horn at his lips, and though there was barely enough breath in him to speak, there was enough to blow the horn.

The sound that followed was so soft it was background to the rustle of wind against leaves, but it cut through me as if the horn had been placed against my head. My teeth rattled with the sound, and for just a moment I had the urge to answer, to run where that horn bade me and hunt where it sent me.

I wasn't the only hound to respond, though. The shadows flickered, and instead of keeping the hounds within their dark boundaries they bulged and spat, birthing emptiness into the world. Patrick raised his other hand and pointed at Nate, and I didn't need to see the hounds to know that they had turned toward him, grinning.

"Nate!" I screamed. He turned, and for a fraction of a second his eyes met mine—

—and the world went gray around him, gray with hounds' fur and wolves' pelts and the colorless space in which the Wild Hunt chased its prey—

The bright sun recoiled from the air around them, and I could almost hear the rip as the path of the Gabriel Hounds opened up around them, the world parting to give them free rein in their chase. I sprang off the rock outcropping and after them, sobbing with rage and terror, but a colorless hand caught at my hair, dragging me down, yanking me back to the world —

—to the rock—

—to darkness, and a red-edged whirlpool of pain.

 Twenty-two

The first sense to come back wasn't scent, or even the analog that matched it, but simple pain, pulling me back to myself. I tasted sour dirt, and an ammonia stink curled around me: skunks and scat and unclean things. It was just my good luck that the puddle I lay in smelled of nothing but mud.

I opened my eyes and immediately regretted it: my vision swam in and out of focus so drastically that it even hurt to blink, and my stomach heaved with each heartbeat. With the nausea came a memory that hurt more than the concussion: Nate, glancing back at me before the Gabriel Hounds chased him into nowhere. "Nate," I whispered, and tried to sit up.

"He's not here." A shape passed in front of me, a colorless, bloodless scent distorting the world like a lens. Abigail, still barefoot and in her hospital gown. "I *trusted* you, Miss Scelan. I can't believe you've repaid me this way."

I flopped onto my stomach, then pulled myself into a kneeling position, bit by painful bit. "Where's Nate?"

"It's no good. He's long gone." The words started out sharp and angry, but dwindled off into unexpected softness. "And you would be too, if I hadn't acted. Have the decency to thank me for that at least."

I risked the nausea to lift my head. Sallow afternoon light shone through the branches of the trees, leaving Abigail and me in shadow. The rumble of traffic nearby made my head throb even worse, but it told me where we were: a culvert near the road, where the runoff drained down to Hammond Pond. *A whack on the back of the head,* I thought, *and then she dragged me here. How? She's barely strong enough to walk . . . or she should be.*

"It's no good," she said again, almost to herself. "Not now that the horn is whole."

I put both hands to my head and drew a great, hiccupping breath.

"I can't believe you didn't hold on to the baldric. Do you know how much I trusted you? Do you have any idea?"

For about two seconds her tone did exactly what it was supposed to do: reduce me to a shivering, penitent wreck. I huddled closer to the ground. "If you had bothered to tell me—" I stopped as the rest of my brain began to wake up.

"Don't you blame this on me," she snapped. "I'll acknowledge you had good intentions, but there's only so much I can do to rectify the situation now that you've blundered into it."

"No," I said. "I am not going to sit around here arguing over who's to blame. Not while Nate is out there." I pulled myself to my feet, swayed a moment, and decided I could stand. "Now. Where is he?"

Abigail opened her mouth, then closed it again. "Dead."

The word, short and blunt as a blackjack, hit me harder than Abigail's rock had. I put my hands to my head, and while my body didn't react—it had too much to deal with already—inside I felt as if I'd been knocked to the ground again.

"Or as good as," she went on, and the part of me that had been curled up and screaming paused, waiting to hear more. "The Gabriel Hounds don't give up their prey. What we need to do now is make up for your error." She paced back and forth, her bloody feet leaving no trace in the culvert. "I can rein in my brother, convince him to leave the horn in my keeping and then disable it again in the same way. What I need you to do is stay out of sight for a day or two. Probably it'd be best if you went to ground in a hotel; I can cover your bills. The one thing we don't want is for him to notice you again."

I closed my eyes. Not dead yet. Okay. I could work with that. I started to climb to the road, clutching the closest sapling to steady myself.

Abigail's voice broke into my thoughts like a buzz saw through a cello. "This is *important*, Hound. I can work with him only so long as he's mostly my brother. If you confront him directly, Prescott will come to the fore; he's already obsessed with you and Skelling both. Wait a couple of days, and I'll get Patrick out of town. Do you understand?"

"I understand," I echoed. I understood all right. I'd been thinking with my head, juggling responsibilities like they were weighted pins, treating them all the same. I'd thought I could draw a line around my city, around my loved ones, and keep them safe so long as the line remained. But those lines meant nothing, not outside my own head. It was time to think with my blood. "I'm going."

Abigail shook her finger in my face. "I owe you a debt, Miss Scelan, regardless of what failings you've had, and I don't intend to lose the chance to pay you back through your folly."

"*My*—" There were limits. I grabbed her by the shoulders, ignoring the screech of pain in my head. "My folly? What about yours, Huston? How many people have died because your brother is walking around half dead?" She flinched, and I knew I'd guessed right. "How many of your own family have faded away and died, bit by bit, drained for loci, just because you brought him back?"

She lifted her chin and met my glare with a cool and weary defiance. "He's my brother," she said, but at the back of her eyes I saw a flicker, and knew. "You don't understand."

"Oh, I do. They didn't die because you brought him back." My skin started to crawl, and I wanted nothing more than to shove her away and scrub the feel of that family from my hands. "They died because you *kept* him alive. If you had stopped, if you'd cut him off and kept him from stealing more life, you'd have to admit you'd done something wrong in bringing him back. And you just couldn't do that."

Abigail's eyes blazed white with fury, but the line of her mouth crinkled and wavered, and I knew I'd struck home. "I said as much to you—"

"You said you might have made a mistake. Might! Lady, that's like saying this place might smell a little bad." I shook her so hard her head rattled back and forth. "You kept your monster alive all these years— you even helped him get the goddamned horn, even when you knew what kind of man he was. Even after he went on about 'respect' and 'the old chaos'—how could you imagine that he'd use the horn for anything good? And now, now he's gone after Nate!"

She jerked out of my grip. "How dare you—"

Something rustled on the far side of the culvert, something larger than a chipmunk finding its way through the brush, and Abigail turned to look, puzzlement eclipsing her guilty rage. I took my chance. I knocked her cane away and kicked her feet out from under her so that she fell full-length in the mud, then caught a handful of her hair when she tried to rise. "Now," I said, crouching down to whisper in her ear, "you are going to tell me how to get him back from the Hunt, and you are going to get the hell out of my way so I can put down that horror you call a brother. Do you hear me?"

She gave a shaky, sobbing gasp, and abruptly I realized that I was beating up an old woman in a hospital gown. I relaxed my grip, and she slumped to the ground, panting in great wheezing rasps, the kind that no one with whole lungs makes.

"I knew you'd be here," said a treble voice.

I turned. Katie stood at the side of the road, looking down at us. "Katie," I said, and let go of Abigail entirely. "Are you all right?" God, I'd completely forgotten about her. How long had she been there, looking for me, alone and vulnerable?

"I'm fine," she said with the carelessness of a kid describing a day at school. She skidded down the side of the culvert until she reached my side. "Evie—"

Abigail pointed a shaking finger at her. "How did you get here? How did you find us?"

Katie blinked—not abashed or shocked by the question, but genuinely surprised by it, as one would be surprised by one's cat talking. She looked at me, as if asking permission to answer. "You got down from the tree okay?" I asked, getting to my feet.

She nodded, and when she answered, spoke only to me, turning a little away from Abigail. "When the . . . the dogs came out, I stayed up the tree and didn't look. But when they were gone, you were too, and so I found a clear puddle and looked into it, the way Sarah showed me. And I saw you." She stopped, huge gray eyes searching my face, but whatever she sought, she couldn't find. Abigail made an impatient "go on" gesture, and Katie glanced at her again with that same puzzlement. "And I saw you, so I could figure out where you were from that."

"Good work," I said, mentally filing away *the way Sarah showed me* for later.

"Followed you," Abigail said in a tone I knew well. Adepts always have the bad habit of stopping to process the implications of new magic even if they're in danger. I suppose it could be fascinating to know how the demon devouring you got to this plane, but I'd never had the presence or absence of mind to care about such things. For Abigail, it was a way to keep from dealing with the immediate consequences of her actions. "That makes some sense. I'd aligned myself with you, so maybe we'd be entangled—"

"'Aligned'? What do you mean, 'aligned'?" And how long had that been going on, for that matter? I didn't like the idea of having an undercurrent chaperone when it was Skelling, and even less if it was Abigail.

She brushed off my question. "But there's a binding on me, Hound. No one should have been able to find either one of us."

I glanced over my shoulder at her. "You don't know the half of it," I said. "I'm the Hound, descendant of Sceolang the hound of Finn Mac Cool. No binding could hold him, and none can hold me, not unless I wish it."

Abigail snorted. "Oh, yes, the great Hound. Which is why you have to have little girls coming to rescue you."

It was a petty, useless retort, and I think she knew it. I turned to face her—the landscape wobbled, but not badly, and while the pain hadn't lessened, I seemed to have gotten used to it. "She's not rescuing me," I said, and put a protective hand on Katie's shoulder. "She's just worried about her brother."

Abigail actually flinched, and for a moment her scent flickered, as if her hold on existence had faltered. She took a few steps forward, reaching for Katie. "I'm so sorry—"

I stepped between them. "Don't you touch her."

"Evie, it's okay." Katie took my hand from her shoulder and walked up to Abigail. "She can't hurt me. See?"

Before I could do anything, she stuck her hand out—right through Abigail's stomach. Abigail winced but didn't seem to be in pain, not even when Katie waved her hand back and forth, apparently encountering no resistance.

"She's not really here." Katie withdrew her hand. "I didn't see her in the puddle either."

Puddle or no, I knew what I'd felt when I hit her. I caught Abigail's hand. It was bony and frail, but still solid under my touch. I could even feel a faint pulse under my fingers. "But—how did you drag me here, how can I touch you?"

"I'm aligned with you, idiot," she snapped, though there was now a weariness in her voice, and her gaze kept returning to Katie. "I had to find an anchor to make it out here, and I knew I'd have to take the baldric back from you. So I'm present for you, if no one else."

I shook my head. I'd heard of projection—hell, I'd read my share of woo-woo theory back when I first encountered the undercurrent. In some branches you couldn't swing a dead cat without hitting someone who claimed to have mastered the art of astral projection (usually with an offer to demonstrate, for a fee). But I'd never had a reliable report of it. Even the Fiana, when they were powerful, hadn't been said to do that.

How many loci had this woman absorbed over the years in order to pass them on to the thing in her brother's shape? How much of those loci had stayed behind? Or—and the thought made the back of my neck go clammy—was it just a sign of how the link with her brother had unmoored her spirit? Had her link to a dead man made it easier for her to slip the bonds of the physical world?

I took Katie by the shoulder and pulled her back to my side. "Where's the rest of you?" I asked, not sure I wanted to hear the answer.

Abigail plucked at the hospital gown. "Still in my bed, getting prodded with needles. I'm not *dead*, Hound."

"Not yet," Katie said.

The silence that followed her innocent declaration might have been funny under other circumstances. "Let's go, Katie," I said.

Abigail looked up, her eyes wide and bloodshot. "No. No, you have to stay under cover—if Patrick finds you, if you go searching for him, he'll have the advantage—"

"Goodbye." I turned my back on her, and Katie and I began climbing up towards the road.

"You'll only find his corpse!" she screamed after us. "He's dead, they've killed him, and now you're going to get yourself killed too!"

Katie closed her eyes and shuddered as Abigail's shrieks faded behind us. "I don't know if Nate's alive," she said in a small voice. "I couldn't see."

"Neither do I," I said. "We can hope."

I took her as far as the hospital lot, and Katie insisted on staying there. "Nate's car is here," she said. "I can wait in his car. Or . . . or I can just go and call Sarah from the desk. I'll be *fine*, Evie."

I knew that tone of voice; it was the same note that she'd had when explaining why she'd called me over several nights ago, the scary self-sufficiency that she'd developed, whether to deal with her Sight or her home life, I didn't know. "Promise me you'll call Sarah," I said. "I don't want you to be here in the car on your own."

"Go get him. I'll be fine." She glared at me, her lip trembling. "I can be just as stubborn as he is, Evie."

I agreed, but some things you made an eight-year-old promise, if you were human. If you wanted to stay human. I glanced at the sun. It was low in the sky, too low. I'd been unconscious too long, and Nate could easily have tired, the Gabriel Hounds could have caught him, the Hunt could have ended.

Or it might not have. I had to hang on to that. I knelt and put my hands on Katie's shoulders. "I can't waste any more time, Katie. Promise me."

She nodded. "I promise. Good hunting."

That won a smile from me, and I kissed her forehead. "I'll see you soon."

I stood and let my mind slide away from this place, from the scents that made it alive: Katie's electric blue and the gritty gold of the parking lot and the ozone of the oncoming thunderstorm, and even the hopeless, watered-down scent of Abigail's projection. I sharpened my focus until only two scents remained: Nate's trail, smooth like polished stone, and the far too familiar pack-scent of the Gabriel Hounds.

And with them, the alignment they followed, the path that Skelling had told me was not mine. But I was the Hound of hounds. There was no road closed to me. And on this path nothing—nothing—could ever catch me.

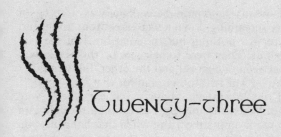

Twenty-three

There is no world outside the hunt. You can leap fences, trample fields, mow down everything in your path, but none of that will matter, because none of that is part of the hunt. Maybe after, you'll have regrets, perhaps even make resolutions that next time it'll be different. But no matter how binding those decisions are in the world outside, within the hunt there is only the quarry and the hunters, the pursued and the pursuer.

I knew this space now. This world out of the world, the space in which the Wild Hunt ran, only barely congruent to reality. You could be damned into this place, forever so at odds with the world of flesh and wood and stone that to even brush against it once more would reduce you to dust.

This wasn't my world. This was only a pathway, a shortcut any cur could follow if she knew the way. My place was the world of real scent, of sunlight so bright it made you sneeze, of the baked smell of asphalt before a storm. But I could use this world, perhaps in the way that Skelling had longed to, and the part of me that wasn't quite human reveled in it. With me, Skelling—finally letting go, allowing himself to run on the path he had so long shunned—bared his teeth in a feral grin.

There wasn't any pain here. Pain was a thing of electricity screaming down a web of neurons and meat; here there was nothing but the long howl of the Gabriel Hounds. They were somewhere on this track, wavering between one world and the other, but I couldn't tell where—I was still too human for that.

I had one advantage, though. I knew where Nate would go. When the impulses of rational thought run out, you work on instinct, and when that happens, you don't care whether the instinct is true or implanted. Both of us had lingered near the quarry, and the guardian spirit there would have put the same imprint on his subconscious that it had on mine: here was a safe place.

Even monsters sometimes knew the right thing to do.

Just ahead of me was the scent of water and bone; I slid out of the half-world—

—and caught a handful of cold rain right in the face. I gasped, choked, and stumbled backward, into ankle-deep water. I'd run right into the storm.

I turned in a circle, trying to see through the first fringes of rain. This wasn't the part of the quarry I'd seen last time; this was a narrow strip of gravel that could have been either a beach or a driveway. On either side of me, green-stained outcroppings of stone rose up, to ragged edges from which kids probably risked their necks diving. Black skies roiled above me, and the birch trees on the shore shrilled in the wind. There weren't even any friendly Girl Scouts to tell me where I'd landed this time. I tried to catch my breath and got a mouthful of rain instead.

I hesitated, the sentence *You dumbass, Evie*, expanding to fill all available thought. I'd miscalculated; Nate had run somewhere else, or worse, he hadn't had the strength to run far and I'd overshot him, the Gabble Retchets were pulling the flesh off his bones even now while I stood waiting for them to show up—

Lightning cracked from one side of the sky to the other, and below the following thunder I caught a sound I shouldn't have been able to hear: the crackle of branches ahead of me.

A gray shape burst through the trees. "Nate!" I yelled, and though his eyes were wide and white all around, he saw me and knew me. "Get in the water and stay there!" I ran to the shore, away from him. Whether he followed my advice was his call now; I just had to invent a distraction.

I yanked out my pocketknife and fumbled with the catch. If the Gabble Retchets really were hounds, if the kinship I had with them went both ways, then I could risk one thing: I knew what distracted me in the middle of a hunt.

For the barest fraction of a second, the trees at the edge of the water stilled as if drawing breath, independent of the tempest around us—and in that moment the rain paused, like a strongman before his last lift. Then the storm broke in full, and the Wild Hunt came hallooing through the trees.

They were blinding white, with ears so red they might have been dipped in blood; they were soot black with golden eyes, they were hounds of shadow; they were none of these, but holes torn in the world, ravenous and howling with the force of the first chaos. Regardless of what form the first Abigail Huston had forced onto the Harlequin Horn, the creatures it summoned were hounds only by default. The thought came to me that if humans had created dogs, if we had shaped them out of wolves and made them part of our lives, we had only been imitating this shape and taming it into something understandable. These creatures went beyond hounds as much as my talent went beyond scent; this old chaos had only the palest reflection in reality.

And the part of me that was hound dragged me forward a step, closer to the pack. "No!" I shouted, and dragged the knife across my forearm so that blood followed it in a brain-numbing rush. "Here!"

It wasn't a virgin sacrifice, but it was red blood,

heavy with iron scent. The pack checked as one and paused, sniffing the rain-lashed air. I held out my hand as if offering it to a puppy, and so aligned were we on that road I'd used to follow them that I scented my own blood, and salivated for it.

The Gabble Retchet closest to me bayed, a cry that should have come with its own pack of demons, and charged me. I turned and ran, leading them up into the trees, away from Nate. Great. I'd successfully distracted them, now what?

I got nothing, responded the part of my brain that had come up with the brilliant plan in the first place.

I swung myself up onto the closest outcropping and risked a glance backward. Not all of the Gabriel Hounds had followed me; two lingered at the shore, either less easily distracted or—no, one was hungrily lapping at the puddle where I'd stood, blood and rainwater smearing its half-present muzzle. I cursed, slipped on the rocks, and dragged myself upright just ahead of the closest hound. Vaulting over a fallen birch, I skirted a marshy spot where a stream flowed into the quarry, grabbing branch after branch to pull myself up the slope. My arm shrilled with pain every time a branch glanced against it, and the rainwater on it seemed to fizz like peroxide. But the bright ribbon of blood kept flowing, and the scent filled my nose and mouth, sickeningly powerful.

At the top of the hill, a final thicket of blueberry bushes dragged at my shirt, then gave way to slick stone and empty air. I stumbled and pinwheeled backward, landing on my ass against the bare stone, right where hill turned to ledge. In the storm's dimness, I could barely distinguish the mottled gray of stone from the rain-swept gray of the water fifteen feet below. I hadn't gotten away from the quarry; I'd circled it like a dog on a leash.

The howl of wind behind me died, and that was enough to tell me that the Wild Hunt had caught me, and now there was nowhere to run.

But another sound split that emptiness, a scream like a demonic chain saw. I lurched back to my feet, staring down at the beach I'd left.

No sign of Nate—but of the two hounds that had lingered, one rolled on the sand, clawing at its muzzle and making a noise that for any canine other than one of the Gabriel Hounds would have been a whimper. The timbre of its cry altered, shifting into something new the way that Nate's skin shifted, the way that loyalties shift, and the howl it ended on turned my bones to ice.

That was the cry of the Wild Hunt. Not the half-assed, leashed thing that Patrick and his imperfect mastery of the horn could command. This was chaos itself, and it screamed for blood.

But not my blood. The hound turned and caught its companion by the throat, snarling like a thing possessed—no, more like a monster let free. I caught my breath, then ducked as a Gabriel Hound behind me leaped.

Blood, it had to be the blood, I thought, as I rolled out of the way. I'd thought to use it as a distraction, but something about it had broken Patrick's hold on that hound—was it because I was a hound too, and more, one whom no bindings could hold? Or was it just the trick of blood given freely, of a gift with no bargain behind it? I came up into a crouch, my sneakers sliding over the stone. Did it even matter which, so long as it worked?

All this took no more than a few seconds: the howl and the leap and the fierce, fragile hope that formed in its wake. The next hound charged me, but I didn't get out of the way. Instead I rocked back as if to catch it, jamming my bleeding forearm against its muzzle. "Here!" I yelled for the second time. "Have it! Take it!"

Teeth like vicious thorns sank into my flesh. I screamed, the sound blending with the cries of the hounds. Muscle tore under its fangs; for a moment I knew that this thing could just as easily rip my arm off at the shoulder as it could rip out a mouthful of flesh. The hound's eye, so close to mine I could have spat in it, burned with baleful hunger—and then, like a lens opening, shifted into something that looked back out at me and understood, understood my role and its role and the sham of a Hunt into which it had been called.

It was no less horrible for that. Sentience, wisdom, knowledge—none of these things matter when it comes to the fundamentally *other* nature of the Wild Hunt. I knew it, and it recognized me in turn, and it was no less horrible for that knowledge.

It let go, red streaming from its jaws, and howled. Its brothers regarded it uncertainly, and it took the opportunity to seize one by the muzzle and throw it down into the bloody smear on the rocks. I couldn't stop to watch; the first hound to attack me had recovered, and now advanced on me, slavering and ignoring its fellows as if they no longer existed.

Instinct, or something older, still had a hand on my soul, and I dragged myself to my feet, hissing as my mauled arm banged against my side. The hound charged, and I danced aside like a clumsy bullfighter, catching the thing around what passed for its neck. Then I wrenched the hound's head up, using my weight rather than any strength in my hands. The resulting *snap* vibrated down the length of my spine.

The hound shuddered and went still, and the change in it wasn't from living thing to corpse—I'd learned how that feels, and it's not a memory that leaves you— but rather from one kind of object to another. These were monsters for gods and heroes to kill, the definition of implacability. There was no life in it, there never had been, at least not the sort of life I should have been able to take. But in spite of everything, in spite of the wholeness of the Harlequin Horn, these hounds were not the full embodiment of the Wild Hunt, not so long as they were compelled rather than called. The veneer of purpose Patrick Huston had imposed on them was cracking, and those cracks were enough for mortality to catch hold.

Six hounds remained—two that had tasted my blood, a third writhing on the bloody stone, and another crawling up from the beach, licking red and sand from its jaws. The last two, still under Patrick's compulsion, bared their teeth and charged. Their brothers were on them in a heartbeat, grabbing them by the throat and tossing them down, growling in a way that could almost be words. *Sharing*, I thought as I got to my feet, *like prisoners passing around the keys to their cells.* None of the freed hounds wanted to leave its pack-mates; even the one that now forced its brother's nose into churned red mud did so in order to free it. I staggered to the second knot of hounds, to the last one that hadn't been freed, then pressed my lacerated forearm against the hound's muzzle in a vile sacrament.

I really, really hoped that the old saw about dogs' mouths being cleaner than humans' still held in this case.

Lightning flared above us, too far away to illuminate more than the clouds, and I just had time to draw breath before the thunder followed. "Well," I said, and laid my unbloodied hand on the head of the hound closest to me. "Truce, then?"

It rolled one eye toward me. "*With us*?" The words were poorly spoken, and not even properly words at all. But they were understandable, and just that was enough to make me shiver. "*Never. We are no more yours than we were his.*"

"Yeah, well, you're no longer his. I'll take that." I got to my feet, looking down at the beach, trying to see where Nate had gone, whether he'd had the sense to stay out of the way.

At the back of my mind, I caught the blind-spot sense of Skelling's presence, the cool buzz of emptiness. I turned to face the quarry and saw the rain open up like curtains pulled away from a stage.

He walked through smelling of rain, not violent thunderstorm rain but the chill icy rain of a March morning, of November spiting winter with its nails. And with him came the trace of fireworks and the lingering sweet stink of a corpse, noticeable only in his passing and never his presence. The white cliffs cracked under his feet, as if they couldn't stand his step. And though the rain continued to lash down, obscuring everything but this space on bare stone, he still retained that immaculate composure, so similar to his sister's.

He's dead, I hoped. *He won't react as quickly—he'll see only what he expects.* But Patrick's eyes as he glanced around—his frown as he took in the blood even now washing away—were as alert as any living man's. "Not what I expected, certainly," he murmured as he turned those colorless eyes on me. "Why should your blood be special, Scelan?"

"I'm the Hound," I told him, as I'd told his sister, but inside, my stomach turned over. This wasn't just a ghost wrapped in meat; this was an adversary entirely cognizant of his surroundings. And one who not only held the Harlequin Horn, but had enough magical skill to keep himself in this undeath for years. "I thought you knew that."

"And hounds do tend to form packs. Hm." He nudged the fallen Gabble Retchet with his foot, and even though I'd been the one to kill it, I went scarlet with rage. A hound's body should be covered in oak leaves and crowned, carried by its fellows to the next world, where it would wait for the Hunt to be called again, not poked at by some jumped-up corpse.

The Gabriel Hounds milled on either side of me, their growls so deep they were almost subsonic. I shifted in place, the same growl making its way through my teeth. I reached out and stroked the hound nearest me at the base of its skull. The fur there was thick and spiky, like pine needles bunched together. "If I ask you to kill him," I said, "will you?"

The timbre of its growl shifted, and a shiver or ripple passed through it. "*No*," it said in that voice like frost. "*You fed us, you freed us, but you do not have us. And he still has the horn.*"

The one beside it turned to look at me, jaw dropping open in a hungry and devious grin. "*If we were fully free, if we ran, we could make him the first of our kill.*"

I didn't like the eager, longing look in the hound's eye, or its use of the word *first*. Swiping rain out of my eyes, I withdrew my hand from the hound nearest me. It sighed, almost languorously. Time to hope I'd kept my powder dry.

Patrick pulled at his collar, clawing at it, and the high line of cloth showed a dark stain. "It's a novel way of breaking the Hunt," he said, still casually, as if all of this mattered not at all. "And I suspect you could do it again, and again. But you only have so much blood in you."

"At least I'm better off than you," I snapped, and yanked Skelling's gun from its holster. It felt natural in my hand, as if Skelling were guiding me, and I pulled the trigger.

Click. Nothing. A misfire, an antique called on to do too much. Patrick smiled—absently, as if I'd made a weak pun—and his questing fingers found what they sought. His hand clenched, not on his collar but on the skin beneath, and surely it was my imagination that provided that horrible wet ripping sound as he pulled something free from the hollow of his throat.

For a moment it looked like a scrap of damp paper, flapping in his hand. Then lightning shivered from one end of the sky to the other, and Patrick held the Harlequin Horn.

No wonder the hounds were mortal. Patrick had hidden the horn in his own dead flesh, in that prison of preserved mortality, and the death that he could not stave off fully had seeped into them. The sight of that shredded, flapping skin at the base of his throat turned my stomach as much as the sacrilege of it did.

The Gabriel Hounds tensed, and on that connection we shared, the tenuous taste of blood in our mouths, I could feel how they both longed for this and loathed it, craved the hunt and despised the man who'd called them to it. But they were the Wild Hunt, and they'd go where the horn sent them. And I no longer had any space to run, or the breath to do so anymore.

Patrick shook rain off the horn, then drew breath, a strangely deliberate motion for someone who didn't usually breathe—then lurched forward, falling to his knees. A grimy, rain-slick hand closed around his ankle and pulled. The Harlequin Horn flew from his hands, into the bushes.

Naked and streaming with blood and rain, Nate dragged himself over the edge of the outcropping. Patrick scrambled away, but not fast enough, and Nate caught him by his ruined throat.

I raised Skelling's gun for a second shot, but couldn't see enough to aim—or perhaps . . . perhaps that was a cool, ghostly hand on mine, staying it, saying, *Wait*.

"Not this time!" I yelled, and Nate answered me with a cry that only just clung to humanity. Patrick's head rocked back on his neck with a sickening crunch, but even more sickening was the crackle as he swung upright again, glaring at Nate with the fury of the dead.

I stumbled closer and aimed again, just as lightning struck so close that there was no space between the blinding light and shock of thunder. Scent returned before vision, thick with fireworks, and I raised the gun blindly.

Patrick's hands glowed red—the remnant of locus after locus, absorbed into his flesh and used to fuel his unnatural death—and I had just enough time to catch a glimpse of Nate's face, lit from below like a kid using a flashlight to tell a scary story. No resignation or farewell in his expression now; this was plain fury—and it did not change, even as the light in Patrick's hands exploded.

There had to be sound, I knew that there had to have been some sound, but all I remember is the pale smudge of Nate's body flying back off the cliff, over the steel-gray water. I screamed—I couldn't hear it, but I felt it in the pain in my throat—and scrambled to the edge. Nothing. Not even the splash of a body striking water.

It's not that far a drop, I told myself, *not that far a drop, and into water—he's all right, he's got to be all right*—I switched the gun to my other hand and dropped to a crouch, trying to find a way down.

"Your shifter's dead, Skelling." Patrick straightened up behind me, vertebrae crackling as they slid into their proper place.

I turned, raising my gun. "I'll kill you for this."

He laughed—he'd edged closer to where the horn had fallen, and the wound between throat and chest where he'd pried it free still flapped like the edges of a torn shirt. "You can't. No one can, Skelling, something your little shifter forgot. Just give me the horn and I'll let you be."

Give him the Horn? Skelling? It was as if liquid nitrogen ran down my back, turning my entire body into something hard and brittle. He'd called me Skelling—not the name he knew was mine. Patrick had broken in the midst of the fight, lost with the horn and whatever strength Nate had knocked from him; this was Prescott, the ghost in the midst of him, and he had a ghost's memory and reactions.

This was how he'd responded after Skelling's wife had attacked, after she'd lost her patience with this man and inflicted the bite that would kill him in time. For a moment I remembered her face, wished her ghost well in whatever world it had gone to.

To either side of me, the Gabriel Hounds waited, uninterested. This had nothing to do with them, not until the horn was winded again. They could wait.

Just behind Patrick, standing where Nate had been thrown from the cliff, a shape blurred through the rain. I caught my breath, but the shape became clearer: a figure in a long duster and broad-brimmed hat, a shape close to my own in posture and form and even face, if you ignored the whole ghost part and the mustache. It spoke, and I matched its words with my own. "I didn't think you were an idiot, Prescott."

Patrick—Prescott—turned as if pulled by an invisible string, facing the ghost of the man he'd killed. "What are you talking about?" He turned back to face me, directing the question to both of us.

I spoke in unison with Skelling's ghost. "Only an idiot would think I'd let you go now." Skelling raised his gun, turning to the side a little, and I did the same, mirroring him. Had Patrick not been there, we might have resembled a pair of duelists.

"Let me go? You don't have a choice in it, Skelling!" Prescott shouted. "I'll still give you a chance—don't pretend you can't be bought!"

"You killed her," Skelling said, and "You hurt him," I said, praying inwardly that history had not repeated, that Nate was all right, even now swimming to shore. "Five months across the country, and you killed her for one little horn."

"It's mine! I made that thieving whore invoke it, I taught her how—it'd have been mine long since if she hadn't fled!"

"Do you really think I give a shit?" For this, at least, I didn't have to imitate Skelling; we shared the same exhausted contempt.

Patrick snarled, a sound almost pitiful after the howls I'd heard this night, and that same light began to build between his fingers. He spun, half a turn, half a turn again, staring first at me and then at Skelling, unable to decide which of us was the real one.

Thunder rumbled on the far side of the quarry, the last vestiges of the storm. The rain opened around me as it had around Patrick, peeling back like a curtain, and like an image from a broken mirror, Abigail Huston walked through me and to her brother.

Maybe that decided him. Maybe not. For whatever reason, he chose the wrong hound—the dead one, Skelling's ghost—to attack. Both guns—real and unreal—went off at once, and though I couldn't see which one hit him, I'll go to my grave believing it was both.

Patrick staggered back, his shoulders bowing inward around the ruined mess of his chest. Abigail caught her brother in her arms as he fell, and for a moment they were two children, together against the world. Then the rain swept over them both, and she was gone, and his body slumped to the ground, inanimate at last.

Skelling looked at me—directly in the eye, the first time he'd done that—and touched the brim of his hat in either thanks or the acceptance of thanks. The last of the rain trembled, and he was gone.

I stuffed Skelling's revolver into its holster and scrambled toward the edge of the cliff. Behind me the Gabriel Hounds slid over the ground like shadows, congregating. They did not even acknowledge Patrick's body as meat; it had been too long dead for that.

The horn of the Wild Hunt hung from a wild rose-bush a foot away from me, twisting slightly, beaded with rain. I stared at it for a moment, then dragged it from the thorns. It didn't tingle in my hand so much as subside, as if it had been resonating up till then and my touch stilled it.

I slung its baldric over my shoulder, then scrambled down the bank, rocks and mud following in my path. The rain had stopped, but the sky was as dark as before, clouds giving way to late evening. And the damned water didn't reflect a thing.

"Nate!" I clambered over the rocks at the foot of the cliff, trying to guess where he'd hit the water. His scent—bloodied and thick with adrenaline—was around here somewhere, but the water and the remnants of the Hunt had muddled it, and I couldn't spare the time to stop and sort out trail from trail. "Nate! Goddammit, Nate, answer me!"

He didn't answer. But something else did. The water

at my feet rippled away from me, snaking toward the center of the quarry.

A low growl emerged from the Gabriel Hounds, and I turned just as the tines of a stag's skull broke the water's surface, rising up like a bad memory. The empty sockets of the skull shouldn't have been visible, not in the lack of light, but somehow the shadows of bone on bone were clear, as if they'd been etched into the sky.

Cradled against the pillar of water, like a child's toy or a broken piece of driftwood, was Nate. I cried out and stumbled into the water, trudging through the weeds that grabbed at my feet.

"*I caught him,*" the spirit of the quarry said. "*I caught him. I wanted . . . I thought—*"

Nate's face was turned away from me, but his arms and legs hung limp as any discarded doll's. I couldn't see if he was moving. I couldn't tell if he was breathing.

"*I caught him,*" it repeated, and I remembered what it had said, how it had grown from a guardian into something that didn't quite understand what it was, how its power and innocence made it unaware that there were things it should not take. The quarry had grown in power from the gifts of loyalty and love given it by those who came to this place, but the sacrifice of a life was much, much more powerful than that slow accretion of magic. It'd be a temptation to older and stronger spirits than this one.

"*Don't.*" The words came not from the water but from the hounds behind me, their fire-pit eyes staring out at me. "*Don't.*"

"Hell with you!" I yelled, slogging forward till I was waist deep, the rocks underfoot threatening to drop away into hidden depths. "Give him back! He's not yours!"

The stag's skull turned to one side. "*What will you give me in return for him?*"

I howled and thumped at the water with my fists, doing nothing but splashing myself. Even if Nate had only fallen in, if the blast hadn't hurt him, how long had he been in the water? Was it already too late? "You son of a bitch," I gasped. "Just give him back to me."

The quarry spirit paused, its waters as motionless as Nate's body, then bowed, curling over him like a wave. "*I accept.*"

It dropped back into the water as if a string had been cut, taking Nate with it. I shouted and splashed forward, then stopped as the water suddenly receded.

A wave rose up, higher than my head, high as the cliffs around us. I backed away, but too late: the wave struck me in the face, then passed through me as if I were no more than a net. For a moment icy water surrounded me, invading all the way down to the bottom of my lungs, and then it was gone, leaving me with only the lingering taste of ferns and stone.

I floundered backward, blinking water out of my eyes. Something silvery flickered under the surface, like the gleam of fish scales, darting away toward the murky shape of the stag's skull, deep under the water. Then there was only the reflection of the moon, wan and mottled through the clouds.

Nate lay on the shore in a gray heap. I half ran, half swam toward him and dropped to my knees beside him. Turning him over, I pressed my fingers to his throat.

"*That was a bad bargain you made.*" One of the hounds circled me and snorted at Nate's body.

Bargain? "Shut up," I said. He still had a pulse, unless I was mistaking my own heartbeat for his. But he wasn't breathing, even if he no longer had the frightening bonelessness of before.

Another hound nosed at Nate's hair. "*He's the only one of our given prey to survive our chase,*" it murmured, in a tone that might have been thoughtful coming from a human throat.

"*Unusual,*" said the first. "*Yes. But you still should not have bartered that.*"

"Bartered what? Get out of my way." I tilted Nate's head back, praying that I still remembered how to do this, and put my mouth to his.

It seemed forever, but it could only have been a few breaths before Nate twitched against me—then shoved me away from him. I fell back, landing on my mauled arm, and Nate rolled over and vomited a long stream of black water. Panting, he turned to look at me over his shoulder.

"You utter idiot—" I started, the words cracking and failing me.

"You damned irresponsible—" he said at the same time.

"—ever put yourself in danger like that—"

"—never do that to me again."

I don't remember which of us moved first, but then we were clinging together, pressed so tight there was almost no room to breathe. " . . . couldn't take it," I heard myself saying, and turned so that I spoke against his skin. "I couldn't stand losing you, not like that, not at all."

"I would have done anything—I was your damned decoy, I wanted to draw them away from you." He laughed, soft and broken, and his hands moved over my neck and back. "You weren't supposed to be my decoy."

"Supposed to, my ass." I took a long breath, slowly coming back into myself again and remembering that yes, I still hurt quite a lot. "One of these days, you and I have got to work out who's saving whom and when."

He laughed again, a real laugh this time, and though it hurt I held on tighter. "We'll have to work out a schedule. I get Mondays and Fridays." He sat back, still holding on to my shoulders, and his eyes widened as he finally noticed our entourage. "What—"

"They're with me." I unslung the horn and stared at it.

The Gabriel Hounds regarded it hungrily. *"Will you then command us, cousin?"* one asked, its jaws dropping open into a grin.

"Don't particularly want to."

"*Then we run* free," it said, and something about the way it said *free* made me want to find cover and stay there for a week. "*Our hunt does not end till we are called home.*"

Unbidden, an image of what this meant flowed into my head: a Hunt like no other, under no control, tearing anything it found to pieces, driving anyone unfortunate enough to see it insane. I shook my head.

"Evie—" Nate said. I looked at him, reached for his face, then grimaced as the motion pulled at the gnawed parts of my arm. He took my wrist and turned it over, wincing at the sight of it. "We can't waste time here; we need to get you to a doctor."

"And you. Didn't you—did you hit your head, when you went off the cliff?" My voice broke at the end of the sentence, as I remembered that last crimson flare.

He reached back and touched the back of his head, as if to confirm it, then frowned. "I hit the water pretty hard, and I remember starting to panic, but after that—I don't think so. I'd hurt more, if I had."

Nothing? The quarry spirit must have done more for him than I'd thought; it had caught him, held him in an instant that had stretched out for the rest of us. I searched Nate's eyes, trying to see any trace of bone, of water remaining in them. But it was dark, and he was hurt, and I was hurt.

Another hound—possibly the one who'd first lapped my blood from the sand, though it was getting impossible to tell them apart—joined the first. "*Wind the horn, even to call us off, and the Hunter will never forgive you.*"

"The Hunter?" Nate asked, startled. I shook my head at him—they didn't mean him, last names notwithstanding.

"*He whose Hunt we are.*"

Odin or Gwyn or even Hecate . . . Sarah's academic recitation came back to me, and my fingers flexed on the Horn, almost dropping it. Hell of an enemy to

make, and given that this wasn't any one Wild Hunt,
but all of them . . .

I didn't have time for this.

"The only Hunter I care about," I said, raising the
Harlequin Horn, "is here." And I put my lips to the
horn.

It was a muted sound, not the cry Patrick had
loosed from it, but a soft, questing call that wound
about the trees and cushioned the lessening raindrops,
a subtle leash, a web that gathered everything up—
olly olly oxen free, everyone home now. The Gabriel
Hounds murmured, a quiet doggy sound that could
have come from, say, twenty Dobermans, and were
gone like a shadow at nightfall. The horn flared in my
grasp, its false diamond pattern blurring to a natural
bone white, and was gone. I closed my hand on where
it had been, then gasped at the sudden pain in my
throat, wrenching and painful, as if one of the hounds
had bitten me.

And the Wild Hunt came to its end.

Twenty-four

It was early September before I finally got to try the coffee at the police station. One taste made me understand why Rena thought I was nuts for having this particular addiction, but it didn't stop me from having two cups while I waited for her to see me.

I shivered, tugging at the ragged cuffs of my shirt, as I watched a parking-ticket victim argue with the officer on duty. I'd worn a long-sleeved shirt because I wanted to avoid questions about the bandages on my arm, but the air-conditioning in here was strong enough that I needed the extra layer. It just figured that during the hot spell it'd been pretty weak, but now that the summer had revolved on toward autumn the blowers were on full blast.

Rena emerged after about forty minutes, pausing at the door to talk to someone in the office behind her. I got to my feet as she approached. "How's Foster?"

"Back at work," she said. "Come on."

I followed her outside and down the block to a scrap of greenway that passed for a park. "Here's good," Rena said, and settled down on a bench.

"You're sure?" I glanced at the station, so close it seemed to be listening in.

"I'm sure." She took a pack of toothpicks from her

hip pocket and uncapped it. Tea tree oil; I grimaced at the scent, but she didn't notice. "So."

"So."

Rena took a microcassette recorder, the kind reporters used to use for interviews before everyone went digital, from another pocket and carefully set it on the bench between us. The tape in it had been marked over several times. She hit the *record* button. "You know Huston confessed."

"I'd heard." I'd had it from Katie, of all people, who apparently didn't have the sense I'd thought she had. For whatever reason, she hadn't stayed in Nate's car or called Sarah. Instead she'd gone to the hospital, talked her way past the guard Rena had set, and met Abigail in the flesh. I didn't know for certain what had happened then, but I remembered the way Abigail's face had changed when she'd realized that Katie too was looking out for her brother. Maybe Abigail had asked her to scry one last time; maybe Katie had wanted to learn more about what her brother was up against. Or maybe she'd been able to convince Abigail what needed to be done, one scared little girl to another. She hadn't told me, and I knew better than to ask. "Do you happen to know when that was?"

"Evening of the day we brought you in, soon as she woke up." Rena flipped the toothpick case over in her fingers, watching it with a look of abstract concentration, as if the conversation were incidental to her sleight of hand. "Dictated it to a nurse, signed it, and practically slapped it into the officer's hand." She sucked on the pick a moment. "By the time Reilly and his partner showed up to question her, she was gone. Clot in her brain, or something. Reilly pressed for an autopsy, but he's not going to get one."

I nodded, thinking back to the quarry and to that last ghost, the image of Abigail sweeping in to catch her brother. Regardless of what the time on that confession said, I knew she'd been dead from that moment on. The Hustons were good at lingering after death, and she'd certainly been one for family traditions.

I regretted now how I'd spoken to her, the accusations I'd made.

"I went to her funeral," I said. Twenty minutes in the crematorium at Mount Auburn with a few people I knew from the undercurrent, most of whom were there out of curiosity. Her ashes had been interred in a little pit on a hill, overlooking a long, skinny lake, close to her great-great-grandmother's ashes. Buried too deep for someone like me to ever dig up.

"I should think so," Rena said.

I didn't know what to say to that. A bus stopped at the corner to pick up an old man with a walker, then drove on, leaving a haze of exhaust in its wake.

"She claimed she'd set up Janssen's murder—set it up days before it happened, mind you. Said she'd had someone come in to handle it, in case something happened to her, as revenge. And she confessed to a string of petty thefts as well. Enough to satisfy a few people." Rena shifted the pick from one side of her mouth to the other. "She even gave us two of Janssen's other aliases."

I risked a sidelong glance at her. "That's . . . good, right?"

Rena nodded. "Foster's working on them now. Says he might find something." She shook her hand once, listening to the rattle of the picks within the box, and gazed across the street. "My boss is saying it's perfect. It's not, no one's quite buying the Janssen angle, but . . . yes, it does fill in the gaps."

It did. Everything Abigail had said matched, every bit of evidence supported her confession . . . and every bit exonerated me, never quite by name, but always close enough that the lack of a name was damning on its own.

There's such a thing as too perfect. Rena knew it. I've known it a long time.

"Michaels says he saw you at the hospital," Rena added. "Maybe an hour after we talked."

I pressed my fingers against the lumpy bandage under my sleeve. It still hurt, but it was healing, to the point where I could even manage on the beat-up loaner bike I was using these days. "I went to see her," I admitted. "I wanted to make sure she was safe, so when I saw you had a guard on her I turned back."

Rena nodded, but didn't say anything.

I cleared my throat. "I don't suppose I could convince you to turn that off?"

Rena glanced down at the recorder. She must have dug the creaky little thing out of storage; it was hardly the kind of modern police equipment I'd thought she had access to. Or maybe this was the sort of equipment you got when you and your partner got stuck with the rotten cases, the ones that had big DEAD END signs written all over them. "No," she said after a moment. "No, I don't think so."

"Okay." A kid on a scooter whizzed past, yelling at someone behind him; a woman pushing a stroller walked the other way. "Okay. Here's what happened."

I told her everything—Yuen and his daughter, and his father; Reverend Woodfin and his strange ministry out there by the quarry; how Abigail had come to see me, walking out of the hospital on her own strange alignment; how Patrick had been the one using the Harlequin Horn to kill Janssen and assault Foster and the Gardner staff and his own sister; how his dead man's vendetta against Skelling and his plans for the horn had put the city in danger and threatened the release of something wholly unfathomable. Some of it Rena might have guessed already—Nate had gone in to give a statement about my whereabouts when Janssen was killed, and that had done a lot to paper over any official reasons to bring me in again for questioning. The only things I left out were the nature of Nate's curse, because that secret wasn't mine to tell, and the spirit of the quarry itself. At the thought of the latter, a cold knot formed in my stomach, and my mouth was full of the taste of icy water.

"I haven't brought the horn back to the Gardner," I added, finally. "I just . . . I can't. If you want, I'll swear to it, but I can't bring it back to them." I didn't want to explain why; the small, horn-shaped scar at my throat, just barely hidden by the collar of my shirt, was an unwelcome reminder already, and Rena's credulity had been strained enough today.

Rena didn't answer. The tape reached the end and clicked off, and she turned it over without speaking, setting it again in its spot between us. She spat the mangled toothpick out and scuffed it into the dirt.

"Rena?"

She drew a deep breath and let it out slowly, as if blowing smoke, then dragged another toothpick from its case. "I can't do this, Evie."

"Can't do what?" It was the worst thing to say, but I couldn't help myself.

"Can't keep buying into all this *bruja* shit on your account. Not when it's covering your tracks like this. Not when it's always so convenient." She shuddered and turned to face me. "How much of this could you have told me back when you were at the station?"

I made myself lay my hands flat on my thighs. "Most of it. Probably."

"And how much could you have told me before then? Just by picking up the goddamn phone—" The toothpick she held snapped, and she stared at it as if it had bitten her. "No, Evie. I'm drawing the line and I'm drawing it here. I won't cover for you anymore, and you won't bring this *bruja* shit into my work. I don't care how good a story you can spin; if it gets people torn to bits, I don't want it."

Her lips pressed tight into a thin, pale line. "It won't go away," I said finally. "It'll still be there, whether I talk about it or not."

"Yeah, maybe. But I won't have to cover for it."
She stood up. "You can handle that shit. Keep it away
from me."

"I will," I said. Rena glanced sharply at me, as if I'd
said it as a challenge, but I'd meant it as a promise: if I
could keep the undercurrent away from Rena, I would.
She was too good to get tangled up in it.

You draw your lines. You protect what you can. But
by drawing those lines, you automatically place people
outside them. And now I was outside Rena's lines, but
she wasn't outside mine. I'd protect her, if I could, even
if only by keeping her ignorant.

"Okay," she said, and swept up the recorder. "*Vaya
con diablos*, Evie."

"I expect I will."

I watched her walk back to the station. She didn't
look back once.

September had moved in slowly, the last few hot spells
spending themselves out in daylong rushes followed by
slow, gentle storms. I headed for Nate's through the
start of one of these, ignoring the rain.

I locked up my bike—the new one, though "new"
couldn't really apply to such a beater—on the front
porch of Nate's building. The apartment was dark; tonight Katie was at Sarah's, either learning more shreds
of hedge-magic or, more likely, staying up watching movies with Alison. I locked the door behind me,
turned on the light in the kitchen, and waited up on
the couch for a while, reading.

"Reading" was a misnomer; I couldn't concentrate on more than one sentence at a time, and so
long minutes went by as I stared out the window, one
hand running over the scar at my throat, trying to see
a reflection. On the radio, the Sox creaked their way
toward another postseason fumble, but I couldn't
bring myself to care enough to even turn it off.

Something clattered outside the kitchen window,
followed by a faint scratch, and I got up from the

couch. "You could just change out there," I said as I opened the window, careful not to look directly at him. "Opposable thumbs are useful for things like opening windows."

A gray shadow slid past me. I waited a moment, trying not to hear the gristly sound of sinews rearranging, then turned to look. Nate was still fumbling with the ties on his robe. The robe was designed to look elegant, but for the first few minutes after his change, any clothes he wore always looked more like a bonnet on a panther: flimsy civilization over something uglier. The rest of the time it just looked like a bathrobe; Nate didn't do elegant. "I'd have to leave it unlocked," he said. "Besides, a naked guy on the fire escape would draw attention."

"More attention than a wolf?" I shook my head. "Besides, this is Allston. You could claim it was a college prank."

His smile turned to a grimace. "I'm going to brush my teeth."

I went back to my book. Nate emerged from the bathroom, then leaned over my shoulder and stroked the back of my head. "From Sarah?"

I shook my head. "Woodfin. I asked him to send what he knew of the Harlequin Horn, and he contacted some friends. They might know something more about getting rid of this." I tapped the scar, uncomfortably aware of how it tried to resonate when I did so.

"What happens if you do? I mean—those things had said he wouldn't forgive you. The Hunter. Whoever he is." I'd told him a little of what Abigail had said about the horn, that it wasn't just one Hunt but all of them, and that as a result I'd probably ticked off a whole host of otherworldly figures. He hadn't found it funny. But he hadn't offered to help—which was good. What I knew of math and magic was pretty polarized; either they were incompatible (as in Sarah's woo-woo work), or you got into serious brain-melting territory fast. And despite evidence to the contrary, Nate did know better than to get himself into too much trouble. "Are you sure you want to give it back?"

"I signed a contract with Abigail." To return it to its original owner. Whoever that was. "Even if she's gone, that still holds. And besides, I want this thing off me. It's . . . I keep wanting to use it, Nate." Though I wouldn't admit it to Nate—or to anyone—I kept hearing the Hunt, the call of the horn, the pack singing to me. And I wanted to listen.

"You won't," he said, and his hand closed on my shoulder, solid, centered, assured.

I wasn't so sure. *I'm not up to it,* I thought of saying. *It might be too much.* I didn't say anything, though. It was too late at night, and there were some things that, if brought up, precluded sleep.

For now, right here, I was all right. I turned a page, and Nate's hand slid from my shoulder to my back, turning touch into caress. "Come to bed."

"Soon."

Nate was silent a moment, then circled the sofa and crouched to face me. "What's up?"

Hell. "I talked to Rena today."

"Your friend with the police."

Not anymore, not really. "Her partner's recovering, and she's all right, but . . . I kept secrets from her," I said, finally. "She didn't like that. And she's not going to forgive me for it."

Nate touched the back of my hand. "Either she'll come around or she won't. If you want to try to make up with her, I'll help."

"Not sure how you could," I said, managing a smile. "But thanks."

He stood, waited a moment, then sighed and headed toward his room. I folded the pages and looked out over them blankly, into the reflection above the street. It didn't show my face, or even my shadow; the whole couch was one dark blot through which the first turning leaves of the tree across the way gleamed.

I'd lied to Nate. It wasn't Rena that I was worried about. Well, I was, but I could live with what we'd worked out. I'd just keep an eye out for her, and try to keep the undercurrent away from her.

The thing was, ever since we'd gotten back from the quarry, bandaged and rattled and insanely glad to be alive, I'd had a feeling that something was missing. And not just Skelling's ghost, which I'd been happy to lay to rest.

Bargains mean a lot in the undercurrent. If you make a trade, you damn well better carry through on it. And the quarry had taken something in exchange for Nate.

I kept telling myself that it was nothing to worry about, that I'd have noticed if I'd actually given up anything, and that anything I'd given up without noticing wasn't something to freak out over anyway. I was alive, Nate was alive, all our pieces were in place and functional, and that was what counted.

I kept telling myself all that, and yet I couldn't help wondering. That water, rushing through me as if I weren't even there . . . and that glimmer, real or imagined, fading under the surface.

I don't know. I don't know anything for certain.

I got up from the couch, turned off the light, and stared out the window a moment longer, trying to see any reflection, any glimmer. Nothing. The room might have been empty, for all the reflection told me.

Save for Nate. He stood in the doorway to his room, watching me in the glass, seeing the reflection that eluded me. I turned to face him, and he smiled, reaching out without speech.

I don't know what to tell him, I thought.

It didn't matter just yet. I'd figure something out in time, and for now . . . for now this was enough. I went to him, and he opened his arms to me.

Acknowledgments

Although I spent several years writing *Spiral Hunt*, *Wild Hunt* took only a little over a year to complete. I'd like to say that this was because I'd achieved some great authorial enlightenment, but the truth is that I'm still as clueless as before. Instead, the pace of this novel was a result of caffeine addiction, sheer terror at what I'd gotten myself into, and the loss of any kind of social life. I don't know that I'd recommend that method in future.

The spark that started this story came from Yoon Ha Lee, who sent me a package with a note on scrap paper. The back of the paper included a tantalizing reference to the Gabriel Hounds, and in tracking them down, I discovered the next path for Evie to run.

I owe a lot to the staff of the Isabella Stewart Gardner Museum, who were patient with my questions and who do not deserve the crass purposes to which I've put their work, nor the characters I've put in their place. Thanks, also, to Mrs. Gardner herself, who I hope would have regarded this story with amused tolerance.

With this book as with *Spiral Hunt*, I owe much to the members of BRAWL, who took an early draft apart and got it pointed in the right direction. Allegra Martin read another draft, and her enthusiasm made sure that I kept on with the revision even when I wanted to tear it into little pieces, fling it against the wall, and declare myself Empress of Confetti. And again, the staff, students, and faculty of Viable Paradise were extraordinarily helpful. Shana Cohen listened to me babble about the plot, and Kate Nintzel took the draft I gave her and hammered it into shape. What is good in this book can be attributed to them; I claim credit for the flaws. (And for the Storrow Drive scene, because that was too much fun to give up.)

And again, many, many thanks to Joshua Lawton, who listened to my ideas, doubts, and frustrations, and gave in return support and love (and, in one case, a well-timed suggestion that I take a walk down to Mount Auburn Cemetery). This book wouldn't be here at all if not for him.